MAIL ROYAL

'A Gray – aye, a right Gray! Fine I see it all. Do you take me for a fool, man? Your sovereign lord! Andrew Gray wants his sheriffdom back, and thinks to barter these letters for it! Seeks to play the pedlar wi' *me*, his king! Is that no' the truth o' it?'

David swallowed again. 'Not, not that, Sire. My lord but seeks to know your royal will in the matter . . .'

'He kens fine my royal will maun be to hae those letters. But he doesna bring them, nor sends them. Only sends his brother's by-blow to make a trade! His sheriff's office for thae letters.'

There was silence in the royal bedchamber for a space.

It was the King who broke it. 'I could have Andrew Gray's neck, for this,' he said grimly. 'And yours, my bonnie lad! And yours! If it's what I believe it is, it is treason!'

Also by the same author, and available from Coronet Books:

Mail Royal

Nigel Tranter

CORONET BOOKS
Hodder and Stoughton

First published in Great Britain in 1989 by Hodder and Stoughton Ltd.

Coronet edition 1991

British Library C.I.P.

Tranter, Nigel, 1909–
   Mail royal.
   I. Title
   823'.912[F]
   ISBN 0-340-53539-3

Printed and bound in Great Britain for Hodder and Stoughton Paperbacks, a division of Hodder and Stoughton Ltd., Mill Road, Dunton Green, Sevenoaks, Kent TN13 2YA (Editorial Office: 47 Bedford Square, London WC1B 3DP) by Clays Ltd., St Ives plc.

PRINCIPAL CHARACTERS *In order of appearance*

Andrew, Seventh Lord Gray: Sheriff of Angus
David Gray: Land-steward: illegitimate nephew of Lord Gray
Patrick, Master of Gray: Son and heir to Lord Gray
Anne Gray, Lady Kilspindie: Great-aunt of Lord Gray
Patrick Douglas of Kilspindie: Lothian laird
Barbara Home: Daughter and heiress of the Laird of Bilsdean
Janet Home: Illegitimate daughter of the Laird of Bilsdean
Mary Gray: Illegitimate daughter of the famous late Master of Gray
Sir John Stewart of Methven: Illegitimate son of the Duke of Lennox
Ludovick Stewart, Duke of Lennox: Cousin of the King
King James the Sixth and First
George Villiers, Marquis of Buckingham (Steenie): Favourite of the
    King
Sir Lionel Cranfield, Earl of Middlesex: High Treasurer
James Hay, Lord Doncaster: Friend of the King, later Earl of Carlisle
Elizabeth, Countess of Buckingham: Mother of Buckingham
John Villiers, Viscount Purbeck: Brother of Buckingham
Charles, Prince of Wales: Son and heir of the King
Sir William Alexander of Menstrie: Courtier, Master of Requests
Alexander Home of Bilsdean: Merse laird
Henry Rich, Lord Kensington: Courtier and ambassador
Bishop William Laud of St Davids: Court cleric
Sir George Goring: Courtier and envoy
King Louis the Thirteenth of France
Queen Marie of Medici: Mother of King Louis
Jeanetta, Comtesse de Charville: Lady of the French court
Duchesse de Chevreuse: Lady of the French court
Anne of Austria, Queen of France
Princess Henrietta Maria: Sister of King Louis
Cardinal Richelieu: French statesman
Sir Thomas Home of Primroknowe: Illegitimate son of the late Earl
    of Dunbar

5

1

The three Grays eyed each other doubtfully, more than doubtfully, suspiciously. At least the two younger looked suspicious, whilst their elder's handsome features reflected an unusual admixture of aggression and pleading.

"This is a great matter, something vital for me and for our house," Andrew, seventh Lord Gray repeated. "If it is not put to rights it could mean near ruin. For us all." It was at the youngest that he looked hopefully.

"Why me?" David Gray wondered. "I am nobody. I do not know the King. Nor London. If you will not, cannot, do it yourself, my lord, Patrick would make a deal better envoy than would I."

"Not for me." Patrick, Master of Gray shook his good-looking head definitely. "This whole matter stinks in the nostrils! I want no part in it."

"More fool you, then!" his father jerked. "For it could mean riches for you, or penury. Do not forget it."

Patrick shrugged. He and his sire did not get on.

Lord Gray, frowning, looked at David again. "You, at least, are in no position to be so nice, Davie," he said significantly.

That young man schooled his attractive features, finely wrought but notably far from effeminate, to show little of the resentment he felt. He was used to doing that. They were a well-made, well-favoured lot, these Grays – as they ought to have been, since they were the son and two grandsons of the famous or notorious Master of Gray, who had been, amongst his other claims to renown, reputed the handsomest man in Europe.

"King James must be made to change his mind," Lord Gray went on. "Down in that London he knows and cares little for what goes on in his ancient kingdom, I think. He

7

must be taught that Scotland's sheriffdoms are not for disposal to his London favourites!"

"How can *I* teach His Grace anything? Or even get sufficiently close to him to speak? I, the bastard grandson of a man he hated!" David demanded. "I am but a land-agent, a steward. I have never been to court, know not how to behave at court, know none there. This is not for me, my lord."

"Not for yourself, Davie, no. But armed with what I hope to give you – that will be different. These letters, I am convinced, are the key. The weakness in James's armour, King or none. With them, or the threat of them, you can open the doors."

"Then why not yourself, Uncle? You, a Scots lord, could appear at court in London, as of right, seek audience with King James, speak with him as I can not."

"It is not suitable, Davie. Cannot you see it? Appearances must be maintained. *I* cannot enter the King's presence and threaten him with these letters, a lord of parliament and royal representative for Angus. Forby, I am the son of the man who, as Master of Gray, was his great enemy. It cannot be me."

"This of threatening the King. Is it not treason, in itself? Could I not find myself in the Tower of London?"

"Not with what you will have to hold over him. These letters. If we can but lay hold of them."

The two younger men exchanged glances.

"These letters," Patrick said. "You say that you have never seen them. How can you know that they are so . . . potent?"

"I know that my father used them until his very death. To gain advantage, aye and moneys, from the King. However much he was hated. They are sufficiently important for that."

"What are they? Whose letters?" David asked. "How can mere letters be of such import? May it not be but some old tale?"

"No tale, no. We would not be sitting here in Broughty Castle now, I think, but for these letters."

"The King's own?"

"No, not as I have heard it. My father never told me. He was entirely close on this matter – as on others. He but said

8

that they meant much to James Stewart. Enough to provide himself with royal sustenance all his days – or leastways, after he fell out with the King in 1603 when James went to London, to succeed English Elizabeth Tudor."

"But you, my lord, do not have those letters now?"

"No, but I know where they are."

"Then why this mystery?" Patrick demanded. "Why this need for us? Or for one of us. Why not get them, read them, so that we know what we are at?"

"Because, Pate, although I know where they are, I might find it difficult to lay hands on them. I have known for many years, but wanted nothing to do with them, well content to let them be. As with so much of my father's affairs. But now, it is different. The King gives my sheriffdom to another, and for no good reason. I have done him no hurt. No doubt in memory of that George Home he doted on, whom he made Earl of Dunbar. For it is another Home, one of Dunbar's bastards, who is to be the new Sheriff of Angus – or so I have heard. Some Border kin of his, some cut-throat moss-trooper, not even an Angus man! So now I must defend myself as best I can against a prince who misgoverns and surrounds himself with rogues. Aye, and who hates this house."

Although David Gray questioned much about this entire affair, he did not question the seriousness of his uncle's complaint, the extent of his loss, even if treason seemed over-much as a remedy and reprisal; and admittedly a treason committed against a monarch who now lived and ruled over England, the Auld Enemy, was hardly to be equated with *real* treason committed by Scots in and against the Scots throne. To be Sheriff of Angus meant a great deal more than being merely the King's chief justice and enforcer of the law in that great shire. It meant responsibility for all taxation – and a percentage of commission on all moneys collected; the holding, protection and dues from markets held in the city of Dundee and other towns, and the harbour-fees of its port; the authority to levy fines and tribute and to requisition armed support from lords and lairds; and much else. So there was a great deal at stake here: money, influence, power. Safe to say that all the revenues of the large estates of the lordship of

Gray did not produce half the wealth that was derived from the sheriffdom, hereditary in the Gray family until now.

"You wish to obtain these letters, my lord. To whom do they belong? And where are they?"

"They belong, I must believe, to myself, as heir to my father. In that they were his – or at least in his possession when he died, and for long before. And they are at Fast Castle."

"Fast! Fast, on the Merse coast? That cliff-side hold of the Homes?" David looked incredulous.

"This same. An ill place, of bad repute. But there, yes."

"But why? Why there? In a Home house. If they belonged to my late Lord Patrick?" David never liked to call his grandfather that in front of his legitimate descendants.

"My father, I must believe, considered them to be safest there. It is one of the most secure holds in all Scotland. Logan of Restalrig had it – his father had married the Home heiress. Now, with Logan dead and his estates forfeited, it has reverted to the Homes, although it is part ruinous, I hear, and they do not use it. See you, these letters, so potent as they must be, would be much sought after. If my father could all but hold the King to ransom over them, then you may be sure that James would make every endeavour to lay hands on them, over the years. Therefore they would have to be hidden most securely, where the King's men could never get at them. I know of no house where they would be safer. None can gain entry to Fast, by land or sea, if they are not wanted."

"And yet you expect Davie to go there and get them?" Patrick said. He made no pretence now of considering himself as a possible retriever of the said letters. "How do you know that they are at Fast?"

"My father revealed it once, two or three years before he died. In my presence – indeed here in this room. That would be some ten years ago. One of his minions had come to him from London, bringing news of the court. He ever wished to know all that went on there. This man told him that George Home, then one of the King's favourites, had been given the English Order of the Garter and created Earl of Dunbar, and was being sent back to Scotland to be Commissioner of the Border; that was when he hanged the one hundred and forty

10

Border thieves and rievers. Although few of his fellow-Home thieves, I warrant, the worst of the lot! My father, hearing it, slapped his knee and laughed aloud. He declared that if Geordie Home knew that he was safely hiding the Casket Letters in his castle of Fast, he would die a well-deserved death – if the King did not hang him first! I well remember his unholy glee."

David shook his head helplessly, no glee evident. "You want me to go to this Fast and get these letters? How do I gain entry, if it is so secure? And how to obtain the letters?"

"You will have to use your wits. I am told that there is only one old man and his wife roosting there these days. Somehow you must persuade him to let you in. Use some excuse. Pay him, if need be. I will give you some siller. Once inside, it may not be so difficult to find the letters. They will be hidden, yes. But it is not a large house. The keeper will not know of them. None would know of them, where they are, save my father and Logan – and they are both dead. They will be in their silver casket . . ."

"And you think, my lord, that even if I win into this hold, and find them, that this keeper will let me take away a casket of silver full of papers? Me, a complete stranger!"

"You will say that they belong to you. Or to me, the Lord Gray. The old man will have known my father, or leastways heard of him, for he was often at Fast."

"And if he does not let me take them – as it seems to me likely?"

"Then, if the siller does not serve, try steel! Threaten him with your dirk, man! He is old and should not be beyond your powers to convince, Davie!"

Patrick hooted a laugh, the first amusement of that interview. "I can see our Davie brandishing naked steel in Fast Castle!"

"That I shall *not* do! I, I mislike this matter, from start to finish, my lord."

"Nevertheless, you will do as I say, Davie," his uncle said thinly. "Or you will suffer my displeasure. And require to seek other employment! You are my land-steward, employed to see to my interests. This is very much my interest. Refuse to do it and I must seek another steward." Lord Gray changed

11

his tone somewhat. "See you, Davie, you do not lack wits. You have more than most in our family, I think; more than Pate here, I swear! Use them in this matter – for the benefit of us all, yourself included."

David made a last effort. "My lord, must you *have* these letters? Hold them? If Lord Patrick could use them in his hold over the King all those years, without the King ever seeing them, then could not you? If you but *refer* to them, in a letter of your own to King James, then he will know sufficiently well what you are about, this threat that you can hold over him. Do you need the letters themselves, in this?"

"I do, yes. I am not my father, see you. I must know what is in those letters before I can use them as he did: to effect. He knew all the King's weakness and business. He had been close to him all his days. I do not. Without knowing, I could not say what was needed to James Stewart, by letter or by your speaking. He is no fool, mind – although the French have called him the Wisest Fool in Christendom – he would soon know. Recognise that I was assailing him out of ignorance. No, I need those letters."

David sighed. "I cannot think that laying hands on them will be easy."

"Easy or not you must get them, Davie. I rely on you. And when you do, you will not go unrewarded, I promise you. So, you will go. And at once."

"At once . . .?"

"To be sure. There is no time to be lost. This new Home interloper – Sir Thomas Home of Primroknowe he is styled – is nominated by King James to be Heritable Sheriff of Angus. But he is not yet installed. He must not be. Once installed and sworn before the Scots Privy Council, he will be much the harder to unseat, if at all. I want those letters quickly. So be you off tomorrow."

Patrick rose. "I wish you well, Cousin!" he grinned.

Lord Gray had the final word. "On your way to Fast, Davie, go you and see my great-aunt, Anne. At Aberlady on the Lothian coast. She is married to Patrick Douglas of Kilspindie there. She is none so old, although my father's aunt – younger than he was. She lives some thirty miles from Fast. She it was told me of the situation there now. She knows

12

the Homes, although does not love them; the Douglases and the Homes have always fought. Anne Douglas might well give you good guidance."

Scarcely grateful even for that crumb of comfort, David took his leave.

Broughty Castle, a massive and tall gaunt fortalice, stood on a projecting rocky promontory at the narrowest point of the Firth of Tay, where it was only one mile across to the Fife shore, yet only three more miles to the mouth, and the same distance east of the city of Dundee – a highly convenient situation, given the requirements and interests of the Lords Gray. Soaring to five storeys and a garret within its high courtyard walling, it frowned down on the humble converted stabling which comprised the offices and home, such as it was, of David Gray, illegitimate son of Lord Gray's younger and disreputable brother, another Patrick, who had died young and unmarried. His mother, a dairy-maid on the Broughty farm-demesne, had died at the child's birth; so David had had but a doubtful start in life, much looked down upon, despite the fact that he had royal blood in his veins. For his grandmother had been the Lady Mary Stewart, called after her aunt the hapless Queen, daughter of Robert Stewart, Earl of Orkney, one of James the Fifth's many bastards. So, in fact, David Gray was in cousinship to the present monarch in London, James the Sixth and First, whatever illegitimacy intervening, since the King's uncle had been his great-grandfather. Not that this was apt to preoccupy him in any degree.

Oddly enough, that next morning, David set out from Broughty, not exactly in holiday mood and anything but hopeful as to the outcome of his mission, but appreciative of a fine June morning, the fair scene around him, the distant high hills of Strathmore on one side and the sparkling firth on the other, with the lightsome feeling of freedom from daily tasks upon him, a change in the dullish routine of duty. He did not dislike nor resent being a land-steward, and indeed found certain satisfactions in the farming aspects of his duties in particular; but it was not the life he would have chosen had there been any choice in the matter. To be riding free for a few days would make a pleasant change, whatever awaited him in this strange quest.

Leaving Dod Carnegie, his farm-grieve and deputy, with his instructions, David led his horse out of the high-walled, gun-loop-pierced courtyard, without mounting. There was no point in mounting, for the fortified gateway opened directly on to the stone jetty which jutted out from Broughty Craig, where the ferry-boats were tied up, an unusual site for a powerful lord's castle. But a very useful and profitable site. For none could use the ferry over to Fife, or back, without paying toll to Lord Gray; and since he owned the ferry-boats also, and there was no other crossing of the firth for a dozen miles and more, there was very considerable advantage in it, especially with the city of Dundee so close at hand. Not only that, but judiciously placed cannon on Broughty Castle and on a suitably placed small fort opposite at the Fife terminal, at Ferry-Port-on-Craig, could all but close the entire firth to shipping, a notable convenience at times, ensuring that all Dundee's harbour-dues were always paid. Supervising this ferry service was one of David's many responsibilities.

He led his mount down on to the first ferry-scow, where already sundry other passengers waited. He was respectfully greeted as he gave orders at once to cast off.

David chatted companionably to the crew and fellow-travellers as the eight oarsmen put out their long sweeps and started to pull, for he was of a friendly nature – too friendly, according to his uncle and lord; in his position sterner attitudes were allegedly required.

It did not take long to cross the seven furlongs of water to the green shores of Fife, where a small crowd was waiting, for this the first ferry of the day, to visit the market at Dundee. Waving to all, David mounted his roan, to head due southwards. By taking that route he was going to save scores of miles of riding, by the Howe of Fife, Kinross, Queen Margaret's Ferry and Edinburgh.

His way lay through the pleasant rolling north Fife countryside, by Scotscraig, Leuchars and Bishop Wardlaw's Bridge over the Eden. Thereafter, skirting to the west of St Andrews, up till sixty years before the religious metropolis of Scotland, he rode on by Strathkinness, climbing somewhat

14

now, and over the moorland plateau of this eastern end of the great peninsula, by Lathockar and the heights of Kellie Law, Arncroach and Kilconquhar. Now, with twenty-odd miles behind him, he was confronted with the mouth of the wide estuary of Forth, so much broader than that of Tay, all aglitter in the midday sunlight.

He was making for another ferry, the Earl's Ferry at Elie, a very different undertaking from that at Broughty, less of a commercial venture. It had been instituted, as its name implied, by the ancient Celtic Earls of Fife as a convenient short-cut for themselves and their servants between their Fife territories and their lands in Lothian, to save them the seventy-five miles detour round the Forth. Later it had been much used and indeed maintained by the ecclesiastics of St Andrews, who required to visit the great Church lands and abbeys in the south of Scotland. Since the Reformation, it was much less used, reduced to only the one vessel, but still functioning, one double voyage daily.

Unfortunately, David arrived at Elie less than an hour after the day's service had departed; he could see the ferry-boat a mile or two out in the firth, still with eight or nine miles to cover to its destination at North Berwick on the Lothian shore, near the majestic towering Craig of Bass, which even from here dominated the scene. He had been told that the boat sailed at noon each day, and he had timed his arrival to catch it; presumably he had been misinformed. There was nothing for it but to wait, to kick his heels until the next day, for although he might have hired a fishing-coble and crew to put him across the ten or eleven miles, such craft could not have taken his horse.

He filled in time by taking a swim from the golden sands which fringed all this coast, finding the water chilly but refreshing after his riding; and then searching for rubies, or garnets, along the shore of the bay famed for these gem-stones. He did find one or two tiny, gleaming fragments, producing a satisfaction out of all proportion to their worth. Then, on a warm sand-dune, gazing out to the Isle of May, where an enterprising Cunningham laird at Crail was main-taining – at a fee paid by the merchant guilds of the many Fife ports – the beacon lit each night on that dangerous island to

15

warn shipping entering the firth, a safety measure hitherto provided free of charge by Holy Church, the first such in all Scotland, he considered the weighty implications of this, and fell asleep.

That night, he put up in the former hospice, established by the Church for travellers, but now run for profit as an inn – which led to further meditation on the alleged reforms of the Reformation.

Next noon he duly caught the daily ferry, and had to pay sweetly for his passage across those miles of the estuary. He was a good Protestant, but . . .

At the North Berwick haven he learned the reason for the different timings of the ferry-crossings. The harbour on this side was tidal, and dried out at low water, so access by larger vessels had to be adjusted accordingly.

Although Fast Castle lay south-by-east of North Berwick by at least twenty-five miles, David turned his horse's head westwards. Aberlady, where he was advised to call upon the Lady Kilspindie, was some six miles distant in that direction, on the shores of its great bay. David had never visited here.

This coastline, with its offshore islets, sandy beaches, dunes and small cliffs, he found much to his taste. At the village of Gullane he found more echoes of the reforming zeal of sixty years before, in the fine Priory of St Andrew abandoned and ruinous, even the parish church which had succeeded it removed, at King James's personal orders, to the neighbouring village of Dirleton, leaving the Gullane villagers with a two-mile walk to worship. Yet this had been an important religious centre since Knights Templar times, with its Provost, eight collegiate priests and many subsidiary chapels around, all swept away in the name of reform.

Beyond Gullane, the bay of Aberlady opened vastly, fifteen hundred acres of tidal sands and mud-flats, all covered at high tide, with far behind the crouching-lion-like outline of Edinburgh's lofty Arthur's Craig beginning to hold the eye. On the far side of the bay, quite close to the tide's edge, rose the Douglas castle of Kilspindie. Behind it, oddly enough on higher ground and almost more prominent, was the ancient red-stone tower of the parish church of Aberlady, battle-mented and loop-holed, looking quite as fortified as the castle itself. This one at least had escaped the reformers' efforts.

Rounding the head of the bay and having to splash across the ford at the mouth of the Peffer Burn, David came to Kilspindie – and saw that it occupied a stronger site than its level sea-shore position might have indicated. This because a canal had been cut from the beach, so that the tide could flow further inland for about two hundred yards, in the style of a great mill-lade, to surround the castle with a protective belt of bog and marsh, the level of which could be controlled by a kind of lock-gate, raised or lowered. A drawbridge across the moat formed gave access.

To say that David was warmly welcomed by his great-great-aunt and her husband would be an exaggeration. He meant nothing to them, the Gray connection unimportant now anyway. In her brother's time it had been different, when the Master of Gray had all but ruled Scotland, indeed had been acting Chancellor or chief minister for a while. But they accepted the young man and offered refreshment.

In the circumstances David came quickly to the reason for his visit. He desired to go to Fast Castle and gain entry, and Lord Gray had suggested that the Lady Kilspindie might advise him on this.

Extraordinary was the effect of that name, Fast, on both of his hosts. The Douglases were suddenly guarded but interested, more than interested.

David sought to be careful as to what he said. He had to mention the letters, for he knew of no other excuse for Grays to wish to enter Fast; but he did not say that it was to enable his uncle to blackmail King James. However, Patrick Douglas said it for him, a grey-haired, stooping, hawk-like character, apt grandson of the notorious Greysteel Douglas of Kilspindie, who had helped to terrorise young James the Fifth.

"So Gray wants the Casket Letters? No doubt to use them as did his father to coerce King Jamie! It will be over this new Home appointment to his sheriffdom?" The Douglas was seemingly as well-informed as he was shrewd.

"What my lord requires these letters for is no concern of mine," David averred. "But it is the letters, yes, that I go to seek."

17

"And think to lay hands on, laddie? I would not wager on your success!"

"I must try. That is why I am here. My lord believes that you might advise me."

"My advice to you is to go back to Broughty Castle and tell Gray to forget it," the other said grimly. "Fast is not for breaking into! Others have tried that, with troops and cannon and ships, and have failed. Have you ever seen the place?"

"No, sir. But I must make the attempt."

The lady, handsome still, like all the Grays, was somewhat more helpful. "Let him try, Pate. Or my nephew will not look kindly on him. Nor on us."

"My lord says that there is but one old man and his wife in charge there now?"

"So we hear, yes. But if he denies you entry, as is likely, you will nowise get in."

"Then I must seek to sweeten him. Or threaten him!"

"Threaten him with what?" Douglas demanded. "*He* is not King Jamie, with secrets to hide! He will but piss at you, laddie!"

Lady Kilspindie frowned at such vulgarity.

"This old man, the keeper – he does not *own* the castle?" David asked. "Who does? The laird might be more helpful."

"A Home?" Douglas all but spat. "Whom have the Homes ever helped but themselves!"

"My older sister married Robert Logan of Restalrig, whose father had won the place by marrying the Home heiress. But when Logan died, and his estates were forfeited for his crimes, Agnes married the fifth Lord Home, and so the Homes got Fast back. Now a grandson of that lord, Alexander Home, Laird of Bilsdean, owns Fast. So he is in fact near kin to me, but . . ." She glanced at her husband. "We have no dealings with him."

"Nor shall we!" Douglas barked. "I want naught to do with that false house. No wonder that they named their robbers' hold Fast, or False!"

David had been warned that the Douglases and the Homes were ever enemies. "False . . .?" he wondered. "Another Home hold?"

18

"No – the same. Have you never heard, man? Fast is but a Scots rendering of the French *faux*, false. They named it that, in their coarse arrogance, because it was used as a wreckers' hold. For the deliberate wrecking of ships. It is halfway down cliffs, on a savage, rock-bound coast. They used it to hang lanterns down the cliff, on chains, two of them apart, to seem like the entrance lights to a haven, in the darkness. False lamps. And they had horses led along the cliff-tops, with lanterns tied to them, to lure ships on and in. So that the ships struck on the rocks of the shore, and they could rob the wrecks. And slay the survivors, if any! I told you – Homes! Barbarians!"

David stared.

"Not all of them, Pate," his wife protested. "Sandy Home, my good-brother, was no wrecker."

"He was little better. He was in Elizabeth Tudor's pay, and sold his Queen, Mary, to the English."

David recollected that the Douglas Earl of Morton, another of the Protestant Lords of the Congregation, had done the same; but he discreetly did not say so. "Laird of Bilsdean, you say, sir? Home of Bilsdean? He now owns Fast. Is it near?"

Lady Kilspindie answered him. "Bilsdean lies this side of the Fast, seven or eight miles. Near Dunglass. You will pass it on your way there, after Dunbar. But I cannot think that Alexander Home will give you any joy."

"More like take a whip to you!" her husband jerked.

Scarcely heartened by all this, David changed the subject somewhat. "These letters in this casket – do you know what they are? What is in them that makes them so . . . valuable?"

"None knows for sure, I think," Douglas said. "I may know more than most, probably – which is why Gray sent you here, I jalouse. For my kinsman, Morton, held them for a while when he was Regent of this realm. On his death, Robert, Earl of Orkney got them, the Queen's half-brother. When *he* died, his son Patrick of Orkney inherited them, and used them against the King – this was partly why he was taken and executed for treason. Since your rascally grandsire, the Master of Gray, had a hand in bringing that about, as so much else, he

19

acquired the Casket Letters, but kept them secure at Fast, then his cousin Logan's house. They are believed to be there still."

"And their importance, sir?"

"They are Mary the Queen's letters. Written by her to Bothwell, before she wed him. Indiscreet letters, love-letters. And poems, Morton said, which she composed for Bothwell. Likewise less than . . . modest. Or so he told me."

"And is that so grievous? To so alarm her son, King James?"

"Some of them are said to show that she knew of the plan to slay her husband, Darnley, the present King's father, at Kirk o' Field, in Edinburgh. And connived at it. Copies to that effect were made, and used at her trial in England, by Elizabeth, to condemn her. Accusing her of being art and part in murder."

"Copies – or forgeries!" his wife put in.

Douglas shrugged. "Who knows! Whatever, they served their turn! And the letters served your nephew to coerce the King thereafter."

"I still do not see why," David insisted. "That was all nothing to do with James. He was born before Darnley's death. Crowned king before Mary fled to England, after she abdicated in his favour. What is so damning for him? They say that he never loved his mother, never really knew her, reared apart from her, of set purpose. Why should he pay anyone to keep these letters secret now?"

Again Patrick Douglas shrugged, offering no explanation.

Recognising that he had probably got all that he was going to get out of these two, David thanked them and soon thereafter sought his couch, little the wiser.

In the morning, taking his leave and accorded little in the way of well-wishing, he rode back eastwards along that coast, almost wishing that he was indeed going home to Broughty, whatever his reception there. At North Berwick, however, he turned southwards, as did the coast, which now faced not into the Firth of Forth but to the Norse Sea itself, with that mighty Craig of Bass standing two miles offshore, like the Forth's sentinel. Soon he was passing the great and frowning Douglas castle of Tantallon, seat of the Earls of Angus, one of the most powerful in the kingdom, impregnable on its cliff; even James the Fifth, besieging it with his entire armed strength, had been unable to take that one. Onwards past the White Kirk of Hamer, place of pilgrimage which a Pope had cursed for giving him rheumatism in his feet after a barefoot visit, and over the Tyninghame ford of Tyne, he came to the red-stone town of Dunbar, where another great castle, that of the former Earls of Dunbar and March, whence sprang the Homes, now ruinous and abandoned, thrust out on seven rock stacks into the sea, these linked by covered bridges of masonry. This Lothian was a land of extraordinary and formidable fortalices, most apparently.

David had now come some eighteen miles from Kilspindie and reckoned that he had another fifteen to go. This Bilsdean, near Dunglass, which the Douglases had mentioned, where the owner of Fast was the laird, seemingly lay about halfway. He debated with himself whether to call in and see this Home first, but decided, since it was now early afternoon, to press on. After all, he might not need this laird's so doubtful help anyway; and any call there might well only lead to complications.

So, presently negotiating a deep wooded dean, really a steep ravine which the road had to dip into and out of, he found himself directly under the walls of a hitherto hidden rock-top castle, where a massive gate, huge timber beams reinforced with iron, was placed to bar all passage. Fortunately at present this stood open, and David kicked his tired horse into a canter, to hurry through before these Homes changed their minds and closed it, to demand toll – obviously the reason for the gate. He had heard of such arrangements on the King's highways, even on this the main road south from Edinburgh to England.

Beyond Dunglass there was another dean, even steeper and wilder, a notable hazard for travellers, although this with no guardian castle in evidence. Beyond this he came suddenly to more open country, green swelling folds rolling down to a cliff-girt shoreline.

But not these open grassy slopes, nor the endless blue plain of the sea eastwards, were what held David's eye now. It was what reared two or three miles ahead, to the south: tremendous precipices of naked rock thrusting upwards and outwards, like a clenched fist shaken at heaven and ocean both, where the Lammermuir Hills came abruptly dropping to the sea. And on a spur of one of these towering cliffs, halfway down, could just be discerned, at that range, a seemingly tiny projection, different from the rest, square of line, which could only be Fast Castle.

By no means encouraged by the sight, David moved on.

He passed an isolated small red-stone church and nearby hamlet, which a field-worker told him was Aldcambus. He had heard of this place, where Robert the Bruce had won a victory against the English occupiers. Thereafter he started to climb, swinging away from the coast now, up and up and on to the bleak wastes of Coldingham Muir, heather and gorse, sheep-strewn. The Douglases had told him that it was soon after reaching this plateau-land that he should turn off seawards again, by a track which wound for a couple of miles over the moor before reaching the remote farmery of Dowlaw, that which supplied Fast with its meat, milk, poultry and grain and where its horses could be kept, for there was apparently no room for such at the castle.

David, when he reached this lonely place, was prepared to be challenged; but although he was eyed strangely by cottagers, none spoke nor indeed acknowledged his greeting.

After Dowlaw, suddenly it was a different world again, a cliff-edge world dominated by sea and sky, screaming fowl and the noise of breakers crashing on the rocks far below. How far below David was not prepared for, although he had seen those fierce precipices from a distance. The track, such as it was, led through short heather, strange to find growing so close to the sea, right to the dizzy brink of nothingness; the most astonishing and off-putting approach to a castle, or any haunt of man, he reckoned, edging a sheer drop of perhaps four hundred feet to the foaming rollers dashing themselves in spray on the reefs and skerries. Yet still no castle in sight, only the empty, wrinkled plain of the ocean.

That cliff-top track was no place to ride a horse unused to

22

such, so close to the rim it clung, for one false step or sidle and beast and rider could be over. So David dismounted, to lead the animal, already showing its alarm.

The track led eastwards, and he had gone nearly half a mile when there was a major, steep drop downhill into a sort of hollow of the cliffs, although still its foot high above the sea. David was so preoccupied in the careful coaxing of his mount down this difficult descent that he had no eyes for the further prospect. Surely this could not be the only or true approach to any fortalice, however strangely placed? Then at the bottom, stroking his trembling horse's sweating neck soothingly, he looked onwards, and saw his destination.

Still a long way below him, three tall slender towers rose on top of a lofty projecting buttress of the cliff-face, not exactly a stack, since it was joined to the main massif at the base, but dividing from it as it rose to form a high, fang-like pinnacle, a yawning gap separating its uneven top from the rest. Jostling each other on this restricted, broken platform rose the walls and battlements of the fortalice, much of its stonework actually overhanging the supporting rock below, a builder's and stonemason's nightmare. How many men had died erecting those walls? And how this sea-eagle's nest of a place was to be reached remained unclear.

The final approach did nothing to allay doubts and alarm. The track had to circumnavigate two perpendicular rifts in the cliff-face, which it achieved with only inches to spare, and then coiled down round a thrusting bluff before dropping to the level of the castle itself, this still some hundreds of feet above the waves. The gap between cliff and stack-top was now all too apparent, perhaps a dozen yards across. It was to be spanned by a drawbridge, but that bridge was upraised.

David, gazing, shook his head at it all, almost in disbelief. No sign of life showed anywhere, save for the wheeling, wailing sea-birds. Leaving his horse on a narrow grassy shelf, knowing that at least it would not bolt here, he moved down to the level of the drawbridge.

There, on the edge of that dizzy drop to the swirling tides, he scanned the iron portcullis which could be seen behind the uphoisted bridge-timbers, the heavy wooden door under the gatehouse, and all the blank walling of the castle. It might have been a place of the dead, save that he could smell woodsmoke, although from this viewpoint no chimneys were visible.

How to draw attention to himself, since presumably his approach had not been noted? Fast would have few visitors, he imagined. He could shout – but the noise of the waves far below and the screaming of the gulls would blanket that. There was no bell to toll, and he carried no pistol to fire. For want of alternative summons, he picked up stones, of which there was no lack lying around, to hurl over the chasm at the gateway. Those which hit the bridge-timbers made only a dull thud, but where the iron of the portcullis was struck there was a satisfactory ringing sound. He kept up his bombardment.

The small gatehouse-tower over the arched entrance had a window, thick glass above and wooden shutters below. Presently these shutters opened and a grey-bearded face peered out.

David raised a hand. "Greetings!" he called. "I am David Gray. I come as messenger of Andrew, Lord Gray of Fowlis. Son to the Master of Gray whom you would know. From Broughty in Angus."

The face continued to peer, but no words came.

With all the noise going on, the old man might not have heard. So David raised his voice to its loudest and repeated his announcement.

This met with equal non-reaction.

"I have come . . . for the property of Lord Gray!" he bellowed. "Papers held here, at Fast. Let down this draw-bridge for me. I will tell you more."

The face at the window being some distance off and in shadow, it was difficult to perceive any expression or change thereof. But at least there was no doubt about a non-facial gesture. A hand came up, and out, with a pointing finger. And that finger jabbed three times in a westerly direction, back whence David had come, and almost viciously. Then the hand was withdrawn and the shutters slammed tight. Nothing could have been more eloquent. As far as David could see, the face did not remain behind the glass of the window.

At a loss, he threw a few more stones, to emphasise his determination, but totally without effect. After a while, having to accept the realities of the situation, David turned and climbed back to his horse, to take that daunting track back to Dowlaw.

2

It was early of a golden evening when David Gray got back
to Aldcambus and the Dunglass area, the entire seaboard
looking lovely in the north-easterly aspect, the frowning cliffs
left behind. There was a low-browed inn for travellers at
Aldcambus village, for this was the main road to the south;
but he reckoned that it was not too late in the day to make a
call at Bilsdean Castle, to see if he could make any impression
on its Home laird. He could always come back to the inn
thereafter, if there was any point in doing so.

Where the road dipped down into the more southerly and
larger of the two deep, wooded deans, at the foot it skirted
the sand and rock shore of a sheltered bay. As he rode by
this, David suddenly reined up in astonishment. Out there,
towards mid-bay, was what seemed to be a projecting reef,
only a few feet above the waves, perhaps stretching fifty or
sixty yards out from the eastern shore. And at its seaward
end, separated from its tip by another score of yards, was an
extension, a skerry, somewhat higher. On this, a horse and a
dismounted rider were isolated, presumably stranded. And,
by the long hair and skirts, the rider was a woman. She was
tugging at the horse's reins and belabouring it with her hand,
but seemingly to no effect. The creature was backing away
from her in very evident rejection of her commands and
efforts.

Staring, David felt bound to do something. He shouted.
What was to do? Did she need help? Could he aid her?

Evidently she was too busy struggling with her horse to see
or hear him, and again the noise of the seas would cover his
voice. She paid no attention at any rate.

He chewed his lip. He could not just ride on and leave the
woman there. But what, in fact, could he do? There was at
least a couple of hundred yards of sea between him and her.

Hastily scanning the shoreline, he decided that if he rode round that eastern horn of the bay to the root of the projecting reef, he could at least get himself along it to within the score of yards of the skerry, and so find out what it was all about. Reining his beast about, he trotted round the mixed sand and stones of the beach.

The reef, when he reached its base, proved to be wider than he had anticipated, with even sea-pinks growing on it. Dismounting, he left his horse there, to hurry out along the ridge of it, some four feet above the water.

Before he gained the end of the reef he was able better to see both the situation and the woman. She was young and well-made, that was very evident as she pulled and beat at her horse; and they were on something larger than just a skerry-like extension of this reef: a small islet, grass-grown sand and rock. There was plenty of room there for the animal to back away from its mistress, which it was determinedly doing.

He shouted again. "Can I help you?"

This time, so much nearer, she heard him and looked up and over. At first she did not answer, looking flushed, uncertain and, yes, angry.

He repeated his question.

"This fool . . . of a horse!" she exclaimed, breathlessly. "Young. Scared . . . of the water."

"Yes. You need some aid, lady?"

"Well . . ." She neither admitted nor denied that. "It is crazed, the creature. The water is not deep. Not up to its belly. But . . ."

"If I came over . . . ?"

"Well . . ." she answered again.

David looked at the score of yards of sea between reef and islet. The water was clear and there was sand below. But it looked to be at least three feet deep, perhaps more in the centre. Should he just plunge into that? Get soaked? This was a ridiculous situation if ever there was one. He did not want to turn up at Bilsdean Castle looking like a drowned rat. On the other hand, he could hardly leave this young woman out there now . . .

Then, as his downward glance left the water, he perceived

27

something relevant – horse-droppings there on the rock at his feet, and fresh-looking. So that horse had come this way, out along the reef to the islet. If it could do so, his could also. And he had had no trouble with his mount in fording innumerable streams since leaving Ferry-Port-on-Craig, however little the animal had liked that approach to Fast.

"I will get my horse," he called. He turned to hurry back to the shore proper. As he went, he judged the reef-top quite practical for riding.

At his beast, he mounted and nudged it into a traverse of the projecting rock, it showing no reluctance.

At the end, he was prepared to do some coaxing to get the roan to enter the water; but this proved unnecessary, the animal plunging in without hesitation.

So they splashed across. The water did reach up to the horse's belly, and the wavelets slapped up to David's riding-boots; but that was as wet as he got.

The girl, for she was little more than that, had stopped struggling with her recalcitrant steed, a handsome grey mare, to watch his approach, although she still held on to the reins as the beast sidled and fancy-danced in sweating, white-eyed alarm.

"There was no need . . ." she announced in greeting, not exactly crossly but scarcely gratefully.

He shrugged. "Perhaps not. But . . . I mean well!"

That produced a faint smile, cut quickly short by another sudden backing and heaving by the grey, which instead drew something like a curse from attractive red lips. David, who had a reasonably quick eye for such matters, perceived that more than her lips were attractive, her dark eyes large, spirited, her features fine-cut, her colour warm – although that could be all the exertion and choler – and her dark-brown hair touched with a tinge of red, plentiful, however untidy at the moment. He also saw that this last was wet, not just sweaty-wet but hanging in soaking coils over the shoulders of her shortish olive-green gown and silken shift beneath. He was an observant young man, and further noted that her person swelled very satisfactorily a little further down, and with all the tugging and struggling, itself heaved not unpleasingly. He dismounted.

28

"This fool young mare . . . will not enter the water," she panted. "Affrighted . . . for no reason. I am training her . . . but she will not . . . go."

"Yet she got here!"

"Before the tide came in. When the water was shallow."

"So. Think you that she will follow my beast? If I take her reins and ford it back as I have come."

"We could try it, yes. She might do it." She went to mount, but her grey kept backing away and tossing its head, making it almost impossible for her. David went to her aid, took the grey's reins from her and forcefully, almost savagely, jerked the brute's head round and down. As it swung over, the young woman saw her chance and took it, hoisting herself up into the saddle nimbly and with no nonsense about a large display of white legs. Nodding approval, David, still holding on to the grey's reins, moved to his own animal and mounted.

"Now, we try it," he called. "Kick her into it."

"I do not need instruction in riding horses!" she declared shortly, and he turned in his saddle and grinned at her.

He nudged the roan into the water, aiming towards the reef-tip again, and after a momentary reluctance the grey followed. But when the older horse began to splash deeper, the mare abruptly jerked backwards. Heaving on the reins, David was all but pulled out of his saddle. It was his turn to curse.

The girl behind began to beat at her mount's head and neck with her fists, but to no effect. The grey would not budge.

David turned the roan back. "*That* will not serve," he asserted unnecessarily. "What now?"

She shook her head in exasperation.

He looked at the water's edge. "The tide is still making. If you do not wish to spend the night here, lady, you will leave that animal. Mount up behind me, and come. She will be safe enough here. With grass to graze. Come and get her tomorrow, at low water."

She stared from him to the shore and back. "Devil-damned fool horse!" she burst out. Then she spread her hands. "Nothing else that I can do," she admitted. "Perhaps she will

29

follow when she sees us leaving without her." Agilely, even gracefully, she executed the difficult manoeuvre of swinging skirted legs over saddle and dismounting, and came over to him.

David was extending a hand down to help her up behind him when she turned away. "One moment," she said. "I have forgot the lobsters."

He gazed as the young woman strode over to an out-cropping rock, where she stooped to pick up a net in which he saw two large lobsters, claws still moving rhythmically, and came back with these, clearly a female of unusual interests.

"Can you take those? At my back?" he wondered, doubtfully.

"To be sure. Would you have me leave them?" She held out her free hand. Lobsters or none, she lifted herself up to behind his saddle with a minimum of fuss.

"Your hair is wet," he remarked, as coils of it dragged over his wrist.

"I was swimming," she declared briefly.

"For lobsters?" he asked incredulously.

"I like swimming. And I like lobsters," she told him, as she settled behind him. "I have pots out there. And elsewhere. Sometimes I can ride out to them, when the tide is out. Sometimes use a boat. Sometimes swim." She appeared to consider that sufficient explanation.

Wondering whether those lobster-claws would nip his back through the netting, he wondered more than that. David urged his roan back into the water.

They splashed over without incident. The shore reached, they looked back. The grey had turned away, and was actually seeking to graze the islet's vegetation. The girl shook her damp head.

"She will have to bide the night there. Teach her a lesson," she observed. "She is wise-like enough in other ways. I am training her."

"Perhaps she does not share your taste for lobsters! Or swimming? I must admit, I have never come across a lady lobster-fisher before!" Unsuitably, it crossed his mind that had he arrived just a little earlier he might have been rewarded by the delectable vision of the girl swimming out to her lobster-pots and back with the catch, presumably in a state of nature.

"This is a notable coast for lobsters," was her only comment. "If you set me down here, sir, I can walk home."

"If you can walk, it cannot be far, and I can take you. Whither?"

She pointed. "A mile or so that way. Out of this Pease Dean and into Bilsdean. Above that."

"That must be somewhere near Bilsdean Castle?"

"Yes. I am Barbara Home."

"Lord!" He turned round to gaze at her face, so near his own. "I was on my way there. To Bilsdean Castle."

"Indeed. Then I am not taking you out of your way, sir. The road lies forward yonder."

As they rode on, he pondered. Was this strange encounter fortunate or otherwise? This very forthright young woman might be helpful. Or again she might not. For clearly she was one who would go her own way. How much should he tell her?

She spoke first. "What is your business at Bilsdean, may I ask?"

"I seek the laird. Home of Bilsdean. Seek . . . guidance. My name is Gray – David Gray, from Broughty in Angus."

"Gray? That is a weel-kent name, sir. And from that airt, Angus. But I fear that you will not see my father, for guidance or other. He is gone to London."

"Save us – London! Then, then . . ." Shrugging, he left the rest unsaid.

"I have far-out kin of the Grays," she went on. "My father's great-aunt. She is married to Douglas of Kilspindie. But . . . we have no dealings. I have never seen her. She was aunt to the famous Master of Gray."

"I am glad that you name him famous, at least! Some can say otherwise! For I am his grandson. In bastardy. So we two will be far-out kin also. Is that not strange? I was at Kilspindie last night."

"You say so? Here's an odd chance. Cousins thrice removed – or more than that! How does it feel to have the great Master of Gray your grandsire?"

"I scarce knew him. Only *of* him. I was but fourteen years when he died, in 1612."

"That makes you twenty-six years now, then. Five years older than myself."

They had climbed out of Pease Dean and crossed high ground above a small harbour sheltered below grassy headlands, and then dropped again into the woods of the second dean. David made no comment as they reached that massive open gate which could bar all passage.

His pillion-passenger pointed to a track branching off seawards, round a thrusting rocky bluff. Past this, the track doubled back on itself and began to climb, quite steeply. A little way up and the red-stone walls of a not very large castle came into view, a square tower of five storeys overhanging the dean but out of sight of it, with a courtyard reaching landwards. It was no great fortress like Tantallon or Dunbar or Broughty, nor a dramatic stronghold like Fast, but a stout fortalice nevertheless, effectively sited.

Round the west side of the walling David was directed, past an orchard and pleasance, to an arched courtyard entrance with small gatehouse over, decorated with the arms of Home. In the cobbled yard, its walling lined with stabling and other domestic lean-to building, the young woman slid to the ground and immediately raised her voice.

"Jock!" she called. "Jock Lumsden! Come, you."

"Coming, Mistress Barbara. I'm no' deaf!" An elderly man emerged from one of the outbuildings, rubbing hands on his backside. "Och, lass, what's this? What hae you been at, noo? Whaur's the grey?"

"Out on the Partan Craig still, the wretched brute! She would nowise leave it, with the tide come in. This gentleman came and lifted me off. Take his horse, Jock, and see to it. And give these lobsters to Janet." She turned to David. "Welcome to Bilsdean, David Gray!"

It was a better reception than he had looked for. He dismounted and handed over his roan to the old man and followed the young woman into the keep, by a doorway guarded with an iron yett or grille, and two shot-holes, and surmounted by more heraldry, painted in the green and white Home colours.

He was led past a vaulted porter's lodge, to the foot of the winding turnpike stairway. Here the girl paused, to call again, across the vaulted passage to where a door stood open and the flickering of a fire was reflected on the walling of further vaulting.

"Janet, you there? Hot water. For two. Two, I say."

Another young woman appeared in the doorway of what was evidently the kitchen, a smiling, sonsy creature, bold-eyed and buxom, not much older than the other.

"Ho ho!" she exclaimed. "Who have we here? A finer catch than a wheen lobsters, I'm thinking!"

"Hold your tongue, Janet!" that was said without rancour. "Jock has the lobsters. This gentleman needs hot water to wash. As do I. See you to it." Barbara Home set off up the spiral stair.

On the first floor she ushered him into the hall of the castle, a noble apartment with a great fireplace, portraits, walls hung with somewhat tattered tapestries, window-seats in the thick masonry, the ceiling decorated with a number of heraldic devices and painted figures, not all of the utmost decency, the floor strewn with sheep- and deer-skins.

"Wait you here while Janet brings the water," she instructed. "I will go up and prepare a chamber for you."

"But . . ." he began. "I did not mean to put myself upon you like this. Only to bring you home. And . . ."

"And to seek guidance! Where else would you go? It will be night soon. Have you other plans?"

"No-o-o. I could go to the inn at Aldcambus . . ."

"That fox's earth! You would get no hot water to wash, there! No, you will bide here. It may not be what the Grays are used to, but you will sleep clean and nowise starve!"

"See you, Mistress Barbara, I am a Gray, yes – but only a bastard one! I told you. Patrick, the old Master, was my grandsire. And the Lord Andrew my uncle. But I am only his land-steward. I manage his affairs, but do not live in his house. I am no lordling, for you to put yourself about for me."

"I would not put myself about for any lordling in Scotland, sir! But you came to my aid, unbidden. I could have won ashore, mind you, without you! But you showed me a

33

kindness. And you were coming to this house, you said. Forby, we are kin, are we not?"

"You are kind . . ."

There was a clanking on the stair behind them and the woman Janet made an appearance with two steaming pails. Presumably she kept a cauldron of water boiling on the kitchen fire.

"Where do I take this?" she enquired, eyeing David up and down assessingly. "To mak bonny folk bonnier!"

"Up to the topmost chamber, Janet," she was directed. "He will be best there."

"The roomie next to your ain would be mair convenient, would it no'? And spare me mounting mair steps with this watter!"

"Off with you . . ."

"I'll carry the water," David volunteered.

"Och, awa' with you! I'm no weakly wabbit female, sirrah – any mair than *she* is!" She laughed. "Na, na – nae weak women here, mind!"

"I will remember it!" he nodded.

"You must forgive our Janet," his hostess said. "She has never known her place, I fear. You see, she is my elder sister. In bastardy!"

"Ah!" He blinked and cleared his throat. "I . . . understand." Then he smiled. "So we have something in common, Janet. For I also am born out of wedlock. No fault of ours, but with its problems."

"This gentleman is David Gray. A grandson of the Master of Gray, whom you knew, Janet."

"Sakes! Him! That accounts for it. The guid looks o' him! The Maister was the bonniest man ever I did set my e'en on. And now this one!"

"Yes. Well, upstairs with us." That was authoritative.

The two women led. On the next floor there were three doors off, all closed, but these they passed, no doubt the laird's own rooms. On the floor above, Janet deposited one of her pails at the first of two doors, in the process looking at David, sniffing and jerking her head at her half-sister. They all went higher with the second pail, Janet panting dramatically now.

34

The stairway ended in a little conical-roofed caphouse, the door of which stood open and led on to the parapet-walk of the wallhead. Another door beside this gave access to a garret-chamber within the roof, lit by dormer-windows; a bright room, with the sunset glowing in at the one side and the spread of the boundless sea vast at the other. A four-poster canopied bed stood in mid-floor, and there were more skin rugs and sundry furnishings.

Barbara Home went over to the bed and threw back the covers, to stoop and actually lay her cheek on the mattress. "Warming-pans here, later," she directed. "No one has slept in this for some time."

"I could think on beds that wouldna need a warming-pan, this night!" Janet observed judiciously.

She was ignored. "There is a bell yonder," the guest was told. "Ring it if you require aught. Janet will come – if you ring sufficiently loud and long!"

"Och, he'll no' have to ring that long! Mind, I could just bide here while I am up. He could maybe do wi' a hand at the washing!"

"Enough of that. Come down to the hall when you are ready," the other said to David. And to her half-sister, "Come, you."

Janet swept a deep mock curtsy, bending forward sufficiently low for a notable bosom to all but spring out of its covering. Then they were gone.

David, somewhat bemused by all that had transpired in the last hour or so, went to gaze out of those lofty windows at the wide panorama of the Merse and Lothian coasts, while he collected his thoughts, before stripping to wash himself in the bath-tub provided. He would not have been at all surprised if that Janet had suddenly entered to assist, with the excuse of bringing up the warming-pans.

When, refreshed, he went down to the hall, it was to find Janet there, setting out platters and beakers for a meal at one end of the great table.

"You'll be hungersome, I wager," she asserted. "You'll no' hae to wait that long, never fear. Mistress Barbara will be prattyfying hersel' up for you."

"No need for that. She was handsome enough as she was."

35

"Ooh, aye. She's nane sae ill-seeming. So you rescued her, on yon craig in Pease Bay! Right galland, as they say! Was she at the swimming when you saw her?"

"Er . . . no. Unfortunately not!"

She skirled a laugh. "A pity, that! She's great at the swimming, is Barbara. I'm no' bad at it mysel', mind."

"I can believe that . . ."

Just then her half-sister came into the hall, and David could see what the other had meant by her word prattyfying. However Barbara had appeared previously, she now looked most strikingly lovely, all trace of stress and untidiness gone, hair carefully combed and arranged, features glowing, shoulders gleaming white above a gown simple but sufficiently well-cut to show them off to advantage, a single gold chain around her throat.

"I told you!" Janet said, and flounced out, chuckling.

"I hope that Janet has not been . . . incommoding you?" he was asked. "She has an unruly tongue. But no ill to her."

"No, no. I like her. The, the relationship. It must be difficult for you both, at times, Mistress Barbara?"

"Not often. There are times. We are fond of each other. And no need to mistress me. We are kin of a sort, after all."

He sketched a bow. "You are kind."

"My father begot her on a servant-lass here, before he married. My mother insisted that Janet should be cared for, reared in this house. So we have been close all my life."

"Not all wives would have so chosen, I think. Your mother, the Lady Bilsdean, is she gone to London with your father?"

"No. She died some years back. Having borne only myself. My father would have preferred a son, I expect, but he has to make do with me!"

"He requires no sympathy in that, I swear!" Was that the reason behind it all, the lobster-potting, the swimming, the horse-training? Was this girl trying to be as near to a son for her father as was possible?

"Shall I light this fire?" she asked him. "It is a warm night, but a fire is cheerful . . ."

"Let me do that, at least." He went over to where steel, flint and tinder sat in a salt-box alcove at the side of the wide fireplace, struck sparks into the tinder, blew it into a flame and applied this to the already laid kindling and wood.

She watched him. "You are a man of some . . . sensibility, I think, David Gray. Unlike some I know! You say that you are a land-steward. But do not live in the Lord Gray's house, although he is your uncle. Where do you live, then?"

"I have two rooms beside the stables in the Broughty Castle courtyard. Humble quarters – unlike this! But I roost there comfortably enough."

"Alone? Or are you wed?"

"Alone, yes. I manage none so ill. But . . ."

"But . . .?" she repeated.

"I sometimes wish for . . . better things. A fuller life than stewarding and living alone." Looking down at the fire, which seemed to be burning up satisfactorily, he asked himself why he had told her that?

"I believe you," she said. "You do not look, nor sound, like a land-steward. We do not have one here – my father manages his own lands – but our kin have one over at Dunglass yonder. And he is very different from you. The Home Castle one, also. Rough, hard men."

He smiled. "My uncle says that I am not hard enough. So perhaps I was not born to be a steward!"

"Your father was a son of the Master of Gray?"

"The second son. He died young. But not before producing me! On a dairy-maid. The like happens, not infrequently."

"Yes. Yet you have grown up a gentleman, it seems! This interests me. Why?"

He shrugged. "I do not know. Leastways, I suppose that I have to thank my grandsire. He had me educated, even though I saw little of him. Along with his other grandson, the present Master of Gray, my cousin. We are quite close, like yourself and Janet. That is it, I suppose . . ."

"Perhaps any offspring of the celebrated Master of Gray would be a, a man of parts? He was a strange character, was he not? I was too young to know him. I saw him only twice, when he was staying at Fast Castle. But I remember him as a man most kind to a small girl. And to Janet. As well as so handsome. And I have heard so many stories about him."

"Not all to his credit, I vow?"

37

"Perhaps not. But tongues are apt to wag unkindly about prominent folk. Other men jealous of their achievements, women envious. He all but ruled for the young King James, did he not? None had so much influence, until . . ."

"Aye, until!" This was where he could bring in Fast Castle and those letters. But somehow it did not seem the best moment, with echoes of coercion and extortion. Later. "King James had no use for him when he went to London. Said that he would find rogues aplenty there to do his bidding, without the Master of Gray! Turned him back when they were at Berwick Bridge, going south. I believe that was an ungrateful act. But I may be wrong, prejudiced."

"So say I – ungrateful. But our monarch is a strange man also, is he not?"

"The Homes have done well out of him!" David could not prevent that from coming out.

"Oh, yes. And my father gone to London to see what *he* can gain! But . . ."

Janet arrived back with a great silver tray, laden. "Lobster soup," she announced. "Cold roast duck thereafter. And then honey and cakes. Will that serve your excellencies?"

"It sounds excellent!" he said. "I have never tasted lobster soup."

"No? We eat sae many lobsters here that they're near coming oot o' our ears! But the soup's no' bad, mind . . ."

David noted that there were only the two places set at the table-end, so evidently Janet was not going to eat with them. As she departed with the empty tray, he mentioned the fact to Barbara.

"No, she never eats here," he was told. "Father makes such rules. When we are alone, we often eat with her in the kitchen. It will be different with you?"

"I do not often eat in Broughty Castle. But when I do it is at my uncle's table, yes."

"I guessed as much. This soup, do you like it? Leave it if you do not. Lobster soup is not usual, I think."

"I like it, yes. I like much in this house – as I scarcely looked to do."

"No? Why, may I ask?"

This was it, then. "Because I was coming here fearing a,

38

a rebuff. Patrick Douglas of Kilspindie said that your father might take a whip to me! Not that I expected that, but . . ."

Astonished, she eyed him. "You said that you were coming for guidance? But expecting rebuff? I cannot think what this means."

He spoke carefully now. "It is to do with Fast Castle."

"So? I conceived that it might be, since your grandsire was much there. In the Logans' time, and later."

"Yes. Well . . . have you ever heard of what are called the Casket Letters?"

"Oh, yes. There is indeed a tale that they were once kept at Fast. By the Master. But that is an old story. I have not heard them mentioned for many a year. They were letters of Queen Mary, were they not? Private letters. Indiscreet, it is said."

"So I understand. You say *were* at Fast. Not now?"

"I would think not. Why should they be there? They were the Master's, or at least in his care. Once Robert Logan was dead and his property forfeited, the Master was not so often at Fast. Why leave the letters there? It was never *his* house."

"Why there in the first place, then? Because it was the most secure hold in the kingdom, I think."

"The Master, or Lord Gray as he became, had his own castles, had he not? Broughty, Fowlis, Castle Huntly, more perhaps."

"These letters are not there; leastways I assume not. Or my uncle would have found them. He it is who wants them, has sent me to try to obtain them for him. They are his property now, he says."

"I suppose that they will be, yes. And he wants them, after all these years?"

David hesitated, picking his words. "It is something to do with the King. In London."

"King James? Does *he* want these letters?"

"I . . . think that he might, yes."

"Ah. I see it now. My father told me that one of our kinsmen, Sir Thomas Home, has been appointed Sheriff of Angus – which was the Lord Gray's sheriffdom, was it not? Could this be that your uncle wishes to gain favour with King

James? Hand him back his mother's letters, in the hope of retaining his goodwill, and his sheriffdom?"

She was shrewd, he perceived. But he also perceived that this her proposed explanation sounded a lot better than that Lord Gray might be using the letters to bring pressure on his sovereign, to extort, as his father had done.

"Something of the sort, yes, I believe. I am but a messenger in this matter, see you. Lord Gray only sends me to try to find these letters. But, what you say makes sense, Barbara."

"And he, your uncle, thinks that they are still at Fast . . .?" She paused as Janet came back with the cold roast duck, and wine-flagons.

"Fast, is it? Yon ill place!" the half-sister asked, with no pretence of not entering into the conversation unbidden. "Better if it fell into the sea, I say! Who's still at Fast? Only auld Rob Calder and his wifie."

"But making a sufficient guard!" David said. "I was there this afternoon, and he would nowise let me in. Nor even speak with me."

"Aye, he's a sour auld deevil! But what would you want at Fast? A place to keep awa' frae, I'd jalouse."

"Perhaps. But I am . . . interested."

Barbara changed the subject. "The soup was good, Janet. But it could have done with more salt, I think."

"You can put in your ain salt, can you no'?"

When she was gone, David resumed. "Yes, Lord Gray believes the letters are still at Fast, somewhere. Hidden, no doubt. He thinks that his father always kept them there, for security. What is in them I do not know – but they must be precious, for some reason."

"His mother's letters would have value for the King, I suppose. Why, think you, your grandsire kept them all those years? Did not give them over to James? As your uncle seems like to do?"

"James treated the Master badly, from 1603. He may well have harboured a grudge." That was the best that he could do.

She nodded. "That will be it. And now Lord Gray thinks to put it all right. And regain the King's favour. That would be

40

fair. The poor Queen's sad letters. When were they written? Fifty years ago, and more?"

He said about that.

"I cannot think that they are still in Fast," she went on. "My father has never mentioned them, as surely he would have done had he known that they were there. But we can go look."

David swallowed, more than his cold duck. "You, you would take me there?"

"To be sure. *I* like Fast. Not its reputation. But the sight of it there on its rock, between sea and sky. I go there often, just to look at it. And to talk with old Rob Calder and his wife Beth. Janet will not go near the place."

"This is excellent, Barbara. You are kind."

"Well, the letters, if they *are* there, are yours. Or your uncle's. We can look for them. Will we ride? Or go by boat?"

"Boat? Could we get there by boat? It is halfway up a great cliff. How could we reach it from the sea?"

"Ah, but Fast has its own secret! Partly why I favour it. How think you it could have held out against siege so often? Because it can be supplied by and from the sea. There is a great cave underneath it, at sea-level. And a shaft has been hewn from the roof of this right up through the rock, to open into the castle's basement."

"A mercy – you say so! A secret entry. From below. On that savage coast!"

"It is a wonder, yes. Hewing that shaft must have taken as much toil and labour almost as building the walls and carrying the stone of the castle itself. It is not only for supply from the sea, to be sure, and for the fishing. But for fresh water. Every castle must have its well within the walls, I need not tell you. But Fast is built on the top of a pinnacle of rock. No spring to be tapped below. So water had to be led in from outside, and stored. There is water draining down the cliffs around it. One spring has been tapped and the water led underground by a kind of gutter, well down beneath the drawbridge, where it cannot be seen, led through the pinnacle's rock into a cistern near the top of this shaft from the cave. So there is always good water there. Another cistern has been cut, for rain-water. Fast is never short."

41

"So! Whoever built that hold did not lack for wits! And determination."

"He did not. But I am scarcely proud of him, that Home ancestor. For it was built partly for wrecking. The shameful destruction of ships, for gain. And the cavern and shaft were useful for that also, for reaching the wrecks on the reefs, and for hoisting up the plunder. A wicked trade!" She shook her head. "Shall we go by boat?"

"My horse, at least, would so wish! It misliked that cliff-top track. Nor did I blame it. I shall find the approach by sea of much interest, I think." It occurred to him, also, that this would involve coming back here to Bilsdean afterwards, for his beast at least, something to which he thought he would not be averse. "Is it no trouble for you to get a boat? And crew?"

"None. We have three cobles here for the fishing. In that Cove Haven which we passed, coming here. And my own small boat for the lobsters. Four rowers. The men will be well pleased enough, for the change."

When Janet came back to clear away the remains of the meal, she was obviously reluctant to depart. Moving over to the fireside, David asked, as she left the hall, whether it was only eating there which was not allowed to her, or could she sit with them on occasion – for he felt somehow guilty that this other illegitimately-born should be excluded on his account. Barbara seemed pleased, and said that often her half-sister sat with them, of an evening, and if he did not mind she would suggest it now. Meantime, she herself would go down and have Jock Lumsden tell the fishermen to have a coble ready for them in the morning.

So presently David found himself comfortably ensconced beside a fire of aromatic birch-logs, a beaker of wine in his hand and two comely females for company – a situation he could by no means have foreseen earlier in the day. Moreover, with access to Fast Castle evidently no longer a problem, whatever the chances of finding those Casket Letters. Meantime, he was enjoying himself. He found reason to thank that young grey mare.

They talked, companionably, of great matters and small, of the Homes and the Grays and lesser folk, of lobsters and horses, of hawking – of which Barbara seemed fond – of stewarding and stalking roe-deer with bow and arrow, which was David's favoured sport. And sometimes they just sat and stared into the fire.

Presently that young man sought his couch in a notably different state of mind from that of the night before.

3

Wakened in the morning by Janet with more hot water, and wondering whether he wanted his back scrubbed, David shooed her out of the room, to much hilarity for so early an hour. He was still shaving when he heard a clatter of hooves from the courtyard below, and going to open the shutters of one of his dormer-windows, he peered out and down. Barbara was dismounting from her young grey mare. He noted that her hair looked wet again. So he had overslept, it appeared. What delights had he missed?

They ate in the vaulted kitchen this time, a substantial breakfast of porridge and cream, grilled mackerel and oatcakes with honey. Barbara said that she had found the filly grazing quietly on the lowermost slopes of Pease Dean; so it had come ashore on its own, at low water. Deliberately she had mounted and ridden it back out to the islet again, in the making tide, collected another lobster or two and so returned. She hoped that the foolish creature had learned its lesson. David said that she ought to have wakened him, to Janet's knowing looks.

Thereafter, with Jock Lumsden the groom and handyman, they rode eastwards from Bilsdean the mile or so to Cove Haven, where they found a coble, broad-beamed, high-prowed and tar-coated, with four fishermen awaiting them. They embarked, Jock taking the horses back to the castle.

Barbara was clearly very much at ease with the fishermen, calling them by their Christian names. She was wearing today the same homespun green gown, short in the skirt, and silken shift, as when he had first met her, all serviceable and suitable for boating, she managing to look entirely feminine and attractive for all that. She said that they had a row of about five miles, which would take them an hour with this westerly breeze following; coming back somewhat longer.

The coble had four long oars, and with its up-thrusting bows rode the seas well. David offered to take his spell at the rowing but had his suggestion smilingly rejected.

Once out from the shelter of the cove, they were into a long swell which lifted their craft in a slow seesawing motion as they turned right-handed along the cliff-girt coast, rock-ribbed save for the sandy crescent of Pease Bay. Seen from the sea, it offered David a very different impression, the cliffs here rose-red, throwing out buttresses and slashed with crevices and caves, water gleaming where burns drained the land. It made a pleasant little voyage, with Barbara pointing out features, the stepped headlands of Siccar Point and Meikle Poo Craig, the Partan Stells, notable for crabs, the dangerous Hirst skerries thrusting seawards, and inland where Bruce had won his victory near Aldcambus, on which the girl waxed enthusiastic.

But soon she had him looking ahead, to where the cliffs rose ever higher, blacker, fiercer, to identify Fast Castle perched upon its stack. At first David could not see it, so well did it blend into its savage, rocky background from this angle, built of the same coloured stone, its contours adapted to those of the precipices. When at length he did discern it, he realised that it was the comparative regularity of its window-embrasures which gave it away.

He saw now that there were not a few caves below these cliffs, where the seas had hammered out weaknesses in the rock. But, oddly, there was no sign of one below the castle – that is, until they went further on a little and then turned towards the shore, the coble pitching now in the backwash of the waves, and it could be seen that the stack topped by the castle sent out a buttress, bent eastwards at its foot, which had hidden the dark yawning mouth of the cavern.

The rowers had to work their long oars very carefully now as their craft tossed and dipped in the swirls and turbulence of the water seething and breaking amongst the projecting reefs and skerries, no place to approach carelessly or in rough weather. Barbara, however, stood up in the stern to call and wave directly upwards. Whether she was heard, seen or their arrival observed, there was no means of knowing.

The oarsmen aimed their boat, heaving and lurching, right

for the mouth of the cave which, it now could be seen, the tide entered. As they also entered, suddenly it was chill, dark and eerie, with the susurration of waves running along the walls and breaking in muted booming far within.

When his eyes had accustomed themselves to the gloom after the sunlight, David perceived that there was a sort of shelf along the left side of the cavern, weed-hung and perhaps four feet in width. Barbara, directing the rowers, halted them about forty yards along this, and as they brought the coble close, nimbly leapt out on to the slippery weed, with a rope, to tie this to a rock projection which served as bollard. The young man felt almost offended as she offered a hand to help him ashore.

On the shelf, the girl looked upwards, cupped hands to mouth and produced a hallooing call, thrice repeated, David wondering whether anyone could possibly hear it above the noise of the waters. He said as much.

"They will have seen our coble's approach," she asserted. "They will be expecting this, never fear, and will send it down."

She was proved right, and the it she referred to turned out to be a long thick knotted rope, which presently came down out of the darkness above to land on the seaweed almost at their feet. Barbara took hold of this.

"You can climb a rope?" she asked casually.

"Surely. We have cliffs in Angus." He hoped that sounded equally casual.

"Good. Then follow me up."

Without more ado she grasped the rope as high above her head as she could reach, at one of the series of knots, and hoisted herself up, feet groping to grip a lower knot. These were tied about eighteen inches apart. Using hands, knees and feet, up she went, the rope swaying and jerking. It occurred to the man below that it was perhaps as well that the cave was so dark; not, he imagined, that this one would care greatly.

"Come on," he was directed, from above.

One of the fishermen came to steady the rope for him, and he started to climb. It was not really difficult, using the hands and arms to draw and the feet and legs to push himself up. It was the darkness of it all which was off-putting, for quite quickly such light as had percolated in from the cave-mouth faded away entirely and here was only blackness. Bumping elbows and knees soon informed him that he was in a fairly narrow shaft. The thought came to him that if Barbara Home above by some mischance lost her grip and slid down this rope on top of him, it would be the end of both of them.

It seemed a long climb – as indeed it had to be, with the castle at least two hundred feet above the waves. Every score of feet or so the young woman called down pantingly to ask if he was all right – to which his answers were gruff. If she was just a little less energetic about her climbing, and did not jerk the rope so much, his knees and elbows would be spared some bumping. He did not say so, however.

After a while, arms aching, he thought that he detected a lightening of the mirk, fitful but persisting. Looking up presently he realised that the fitfulness was caused by Barbara's bodily movements against pale light above her, yellow light, so it must be from a lamp.

Then he heard a man's voice and the girl's answering. Thereafter, in a moment or two, the rope stopped jerking and there was more light. Then hands were grasping his quivering arms and he was being aided out through a trap-door and into a lighted vaulted chamber. He was inside Fast Castle.

"You climbed well," Barbara commended. "Some just will not attempt it. This is Rob Calder, who keeps this hold for my father. Rob, here is David Gray, from Broughty Castle, grandson to the Master we all knew."

The older man looked at the younger expressionlessly. "Aye," he said.

"He has come here to try to find some property which belongs to his uncle, the Lord Gray," she went on. "A package of letters, said to be in a casket. Do you know aught of this, Rob?"

The other scratched his chin. "Letters?" he said carefully.

"Yes. *I* have heard of them. So I would think that you would have done."

"I'ph'mm."

"Well – do you know where they are?"

47

"I do not, Mistress Barbara." That at least sounded definite enough.

"Lord Gray believes that they are at Fast. They were the Master's, his father. And he is thought to have left them here. Did you ever hear that?"

A shake of the grey head.

Barbara eyed him directly. "You are sure, Rob? This is important, see you."

"I ken o' nae letters," the keeper insisted.

"Then we must search for them."

Calder shrugged.

"Come, David," she said, and led the way out of the chamber.

They entered a narrow vaulted passage, at the end of which a doorway opened on to daylight. Out through this they emerged into a breathtaking-seeming immensity, after the constriction of the shaft and dark enclosing masonry, only the sky and the wheeling sea-birds before and above them, as on a dizzy ledge of the cliff-face, only a low parapet separating them from the abyss. Almost involuntarily David pressed back against the comfort of solid masonry, which was in fact the basement of one of the three towers of the place, four if one counted the gatehouse. These rose all at differing levels of the stack-top, linked by galleries and steps cut in the naked rock. The total length might have been something over one hundred feet, the width half that. All around was a sheer drop.

"We will try the main keep first," Barbara said, pointing to the most highly placed tower, oblong on plan and three storeys and a garret in height, surmounted by a parapet and wall-walk.

"I do not think that your keeper likes me well," David observed when he could find words.

"Heed him not. Rob is none so ill. His manner is the worst of him. Perhaps being shut up in this place all his days would make any man so!"

"It may be so. How do you think to search all this hold for the letters? It will be a lengthy task, no?"

"We shall see. It might not be so difficult. There are not so many plenishings and chambers."

48

They moved along to that main tower. The basement chamber was, as usual, a vaulted kitchen with arched fireplace, at which an elderly plump body was stirring a pot which hung on a chain. She rose, beaming, to greet her young mistress and the visitor with a deal more civility than had her husband. Barbara explained what they were about, but Beth Calder clearly knew nothing of any hidden letters.

The young woman led the way upstairs, for obviously it was highly unlikely that anything could be hidden in the kitchen without the wife knowing of it. The hall on the first floor was not large and was sparsely furnished, looking little used indeed. Apart from the normal long table, benches and a few chairs, there were two chests. These they opened and examined. One contained beakers, flagons and platters, mainly of pewter, with some oddments of cutlery; the other only one old and dusty sheepskin. There were however two aumbries, or wall-cupboards, with wooden doors. These likewise produced nothing of interest. There was a salt-box cavity at the ingoing of the large fireplace, but this was plainly empty. David crept under the fireplace arch itself, to grope and peer up into the sooty flue, in case there might be a hiding-place there, however unsuitable for papers, but found nothing.

They went further upstairs, not omitting to inspect the narrow window-embrasures and lamp-rests of the stairway. The two main bedchambers above, with their garderobes, aumbries and chests, they searched closely, even examining the tops of the canopied beds, dust-covered, also the fire-places and flues again, but to no purpose. In the garret chamber, still higher, a single large space under the roof, they spent longer, for here were more apt hiding-places, along the wall-head, amongst the rafters and in crevices of the masonry and under stone slates. But probe and seek as they would, they found nothing but cobwebs and a dead bat or two. They went out through the caphouse on to the parapet-walk, although open to the elements as this was, it was hardly the place to seek letters.

The second tower provided in its basement the sleeping quarters of the Calders; the searchers could hardly examine all here; but Barbara declared that she could trust Beth's assertion that she knew of no letters or casket, as she surely would have done had they been hidden here. Above, the rooms were clearly never now used. Their careful scrutiny was again unproductive.

The third and most seaward tower, on what amounted to an overhang above the waves, was a place to induce vertigo. Barbara thought that it might well be the most likely for their quest, in that exposed as it was and cramped as to dimensions, it would never have been much used. But pry and rummage every corner of this as they would, nothing of interest was uncovered.

There remained only the gatehouse-tower, the least probable hiding-place, surely. Here Rob Calder followed them, looking discouraging, and announcing that if there had been anything hidden here he would have discovered it long ago. They searched it, nevertheless, even to the splayed ingoings of the gun-loops.

Frustrated, they went all round the perimeter walling of the castle, investigating crenellations, shot-holes and gaps in the stonework.

"I fear that the Lord Gray is mistaken," the young woman said. "No letters have been left here."

David nodded. "It looks so. I am sorry. Sorry to have put you to all this trouble for nothing, Barbara. You have been very good. And patient. But, I thank you."

"No need for thanks. But you must look elsewhere, it seems. Or your uncle must."

Their searching had taken some considerable time inevitably and Barbara was becoming concerned for the fishermen waiting below – although she expected that they would have whiled away the time by seekings of their own, for crabs and shellfish amongst the reefs and skerries. So she said goodbye to Beth Calder and they made for the chamber above the shaft to the cave.

It was here that it struck David that the shaft itself might possibly have provided a hiding-place. The girl doubted it, saying that she had climbed up and down that narrow chimney-like gullet times without number, and would surely have discovered if there had been any opening or ledge where anything could be deposited? But they could take a lantern down, to look, if he wished. She would do it.

David would not hear of such a thing. Any such awkward searching, *he* would do.

Awkward was indeed the word for it. While Rob Calder was sent for another lamp, David took his lantern and climbed through the hatch to grasp the knotted rope. It was difficult enough to descend this, without having to hold the lantern and keep it approximately upright. He burned his hands, even his chin, with the heat of it, swaying and birling and groping with his feet for the lower knots. All Barbara's excellent advice from above did not greatly help. He did more cursing beneath his breath than examining the walling. More than once he all but fell.

Halfway down he decided that there were no hiding-places in this wretched shaft, and began to ascend again. It was a little easier, if that was the word, going up.

When Barbara took the lantern and helped him out, she told him that it had just occurred to her, in this of shafts and passages, that there was another possibility, however faint. He would remember that she had said that water was led into the castle, from the hillside, by a gutter or duct cut in the rock below the drawbridge-level. This came into a cistern situated below the gatehouse arch. It was just a possibility . . .

David was reaching surrender-point, but he agreed that this last suggestion was worth investigating. So it was out and back to the gatehouse again, Calder humphing and head-shaking.

The drawbridge, of course, was up and the iron portcullis down. But under the gateway pend there was a trap-door in the entry passage. When the keeper raised this, it was to reveal a ladder leading down into darkness. A lantern was needed again, and this time Barbara insisted on making the descent. This was not long, she pointed out, only a dozen feet or so to the cistern. She said that she had never been down this, and Calder admitted the same. All he had to do here was lower buckets on a chain for the water, which he had never known to dry up.

The young woman went down with her accustomed agility, and thereafter only the glow of her lamp was evident. David shouted down to ask if he should come too? The answer was scarcely clear, but he took it as affirmative and descended the ladder in turn.

Thereafter he found himself in a sort of chilly artificial cave the size of a modest room. This was not entirely filled with water, for round either side of the central pool was a ledge or shelf about one yard wide, horseshoe shaped. Barbara had left the lantern near the ladder-foot and was crawling round the left side, above the black-seeming water, feeling her way in the dim light. David got down on hands and knees to do the same on the other side, feeling the rock-walling on his right as he went – and tending to bark his knuckles on the damp stone.

He had not gone more than three or four creeping steps when his hand encountered nothingness. Fumbling around, he realised that he had found a small cavity, no more than a foot high. Leaning closer, he thrust in hand and arm – to touch cloth and something hard inside the cloth. "Barbara!" he cried. "I have found it! Or . . . found something."

She came crawling round.

He drew out his find, feeling the weight of it, and an oblong shape within the stiff, rough, damp cloth.

In the faint light of the lamp this proved to be sail-cloth, canvas. Excited, exclaiming, they edged their way back to the lantern at the ladder-foot with their trophy.

They did not wait to climb out before untying a cord round the neck of what was obviously a bag. David thrust his hand inside, his fingers closing on metal, shaped. He drew this out, weighty.

It was indeed a casket, about twelve inches long and half that in width and height, and even in that poor light, corroded as it was, they could see that it was of silver, finely wrought, chased and decorative. It was provided with a curved lid engraved with scrollwork and with a lock-plate. The lid did not open.

"So-o-o! Your grandsire knew how to hide his property!" Barbara got out.

"If it *was* his! This is locked." David groped back into the canvas bag. "No key."

"Welladay! So the Master has us guessing still!"

Up the ladder, they showed Rob Calder their find, to his complete lack of comment. Then it was back to the cave-shaft and a careful descent to sea-level. At least the casket and bag did not burn David's hands, however awkward again to take down. At the foot, they found they had to shout for the fishermen who were, as anticipated, out in their coble seeking crabs.

In daylight the two searchers proved to look distinctly untidy and dishevelled as to clothing, with smudges of dirt and soot on hands and faces, to the amusement of all.

The row back to Bilsdean, in the face of quite a stiff breeze, took some time – but at least it delayed the leave-taking for David. At the castle, however, Barbara would not hear of her guest's departure that day. It was now mid-afternoon and by no means could David get to North Berwick in time for that day's ferry over to Fife. The young man was far from loth to accept another night's hospitality in present company, needless to say.

In Janet's kitchen they examined the casket more closely, that young woman as interested as the finders, insisting on cleaning and polishing the silver until it gleamed satisfactorily. It was a handsome thing, solid but ornate, quite apt receptacle for a queen's letters – if indeed that was what it contained. The lock, however, was as substantial as the rest and no amount of poking and testing offered any hope of the lid opening. Where would the key be, they wondered? Presumably somewhere amongst the late Master's possessions. Lord Gray might have inherited it without knowing what it was for. That would be *his* concern.

The three of them passed another pleasant evening at the hall fireside. The day's searchings together had had the effect of bringing David and Barbara into an easy and frank relationship – and Janet had been easy and all too frank from the first. So there was no constraint, no awkward pauses, as they discussed the day's doings, what might be in those letters, King James's treatment of the Master, and more personal matters. By bedtime David felt as though he had known these two for long.

When it came to yawns and retiral, both young women escorted their guest upstairs to his attic-room door. There, thanking them and using his wits, he turned first to Janet, to plant a kiss, intended for her cheek but which somehow landed on her lips, and was returned with interest, accompanied by a hug of generous character. Thus, having paved the

53

way, as it were, he could do no less than offer a like salute to Barbara, tentatively hovering for a moment between cheek and lips. It was the latter which contacted, however, and in that most pleasing couple of seconds he could have almost sworn that the lips under his own did move and open just a little.

Janet skirled a laugh and remarked that her half-sister's room was directly below this of his, and that if David should have ill dreams of Fast Castle or otherwise, or suffer discomforts of the night, a thumping on the floor *might* produce solace. Her own bedchamber was further away, off the kitchen, in the former door-porter's lodge, but not uncomfortable. If he failed to gain any satisfaction from Barbara, he could always come down and seek easement there. She was not a heavy sleeper.

Barbara, turning for the stairway, told her to hold her tongue, but without rancour, called goodnight over her shoulder and went down.

It was some time before David slept.

In the morning it was not quite possible to recapture the atmosphere of closeness of that evening, even though Barbara did ask him if he might not stay for another day. He was tempted, but recognised that he would have difficulty in explaining the delay to his uncle. He declared, however, that if they would have him – and their father when he returned – he would come back, and before very long, and perhaps go lobster-fishing. This produced a satisfactory reaction.

His departure kisses were perhaps a little less successful than those of the previous night, but still sufficiently encouraging. Janet presented him with a bag of provender, which balanced the bag with the casket on the other side of his saddle-bow, for sustenance on his journey; and to cries of haste-ye-back, he rode off westwards.

4

Andrew, Lord Gray, needless to say, was well pleased to have that silver-gilt casket in his hands, and not too concerned that it was locked. If locksmiths could make locks, they could also unmake them. He knew of no key having been amongst his late father's possessions to come to him. Let David fetch Will Lyle the blacksmith and they would soon see what was inside this box.

The Broughty smith had little difficulty in opening the casket, without seriously damaging it. He was dismissed, however, before his betters looked inside the red velvet-lined container. There were indeed letters, or at least papers, discoloured with the years. Lifted out, there proved to be no fewer than twenty-two sheets, all but two apparently written in the same hand, but none signed nor dated. Eight appeared to be letters, twelve sonnets or parts of a poem, and two marriage contracts – all written in French. Examining these eagerly, Lord Gray had to admit that his French was not of the best. Could David do better?

David could, in some degree. For, situated as he had been, he had paid rather more attention to his studies at St Andrews University, paid for by his grandfather, than had his lordly legitimate relatives. He did not claim that he had any expert command of the French language, but given time he could probably make out the sense of these papers. Rather reluctantly his uncle put them back in their box and handed it over. David was to do his best with them, and quickly – and none other was to learn of it all.

So the younger man returned to his house in the courtyard, with a distinctly unusual task to perform.

Intrigued himself by this mystery, he laid out the papers on his table in some sort of order. Despite the same writing, some appeared to be more hurriedly and carelessly set down than others. The two in a different hand were the marriage contracts, or probably copies thereof, one with the Dauphin Francis of France, the other with Henry Stewart, Lord Darnley, son of the Earl of Lennox. Of the letters, none of which bore the name to whom they were addressed, one was very long, of three closely written pages, the others considerably less so. The twelve pages of verses seemed to him, after a preliminary scrutiny, to be components of a single poem, presumably written over a period.

Where to start in all this? It was always the letters which were being referred to, the Casket Letters; so presumably they were what was most important. He would commence with them.

Settling down in a chair at his table, with quill, ink and paper, David set to.

There were no dates on any of the letters, so he just began with that on top of the pile. Going over it, first, to seek to get the sense of it, he recognised that it was a fairly straightforward communication, headed "From Glasgow, this Saturday morning." Since David had been told that the letters had been written by Queen Mary to the Earl of Bothwell, her third husband-to-be, before King Henry Darnley's death, he knew enough of the romantic Mary's story to realise that this heading must refer to the time when Darnley, that weak and foppish individual, had fallen ill in Glasgow, allegedly of some venereal disease, and the Queen had gone there from Craigmillar Castle at Edinburgh, not exactly to nurse him, for by this time she had quite fallen out of love with her petulant and effeminate second husband, but at least to be with him for a little while, leaving her infant son James, by him, at Edinburgh.

This first letter very quickly indicated Mary's disdain for Darnley. But thereafter there arose a problem, for the writer went on to speak of "that man who was merriest that ever you saw and doth remember unto me all that he can to make me believe that he loves me". Then added, "You would say that he indicated love to me wherein I take so much pleasure that I never come in there but the pain of my side doth take me. This man to be brought to Craigmillar on Wednesday."

That, or David's translation of the French to that effect,

56

puzzled him considerably. Was it some sort of code, with a secret meaning? The man referred to could not possibly be Darnley, whom the writer no longer loved – and who anyway was in no condition to be taken to Craigmillar. And the letter was allegedly written to Bothwell, in whose possession this casket had been found, on his flight and exile. Who then was the man so affectionately commended to the Earl Mary was going to marry? To David, the only possible explanation was that it referred to her young son James, by then about six months old. If the writer had added the one word, *petit* before *homme*, all would have been clear. He could think of no other interpretation.

There was certainly nothing in this first letter to worry King James.

The second on the pile, the long three-page one, was very different. It was much more vehement, graphic and evidently hastily written, starting with the words, "Being departed from the place where I had left my heart, it may be easily judged what my countenance was. Seeing that I was like a body without a heart; which was the reason that until dinner-time I talked to nobody. Nor yet any dared present themselves to me." There followed an account of what was presumably the Queen's journey from Edinburgh to Glasgow, of her meeting with a gentleman of the Earl of Lennox, Darnley's father, and with Sir James Hamilton and the Colquhoun Laird of Luss, with about forty horsemen, adding that none of the townspeople of Glasgow came to acknowledge her.

Then this letter took on a more intimate note, declaring that the King – that is Darnley who was claiming the crown matrimonial – wanted her to come to his bed. When she went to him he seemed as in a daze, but said that he was happy to see her, and that people here were being cruel to him, blaming her for being withdrawn and pensive, even accusing her of being the cause of his illness through her neglect of him. He confessed that he had done wrong, but averred that she ought to have forgiven him; for was he not young and of an age to make one or two mistakes?

There was more in this self-pitying vein. Then Mary had asked him why he had planned to leave Scotland in an English

57

ship – this a circumstance of which David knew nothing – Darnley denying this but admitting that he had spoken with English sailors as to the possibility. She had then charged him with being involved in a plot to seize herself and have young James crowned King, with himself to rule for the child; and this he had likewise denied. She had refused to lodge with him until he was purged of his disease, but offered to convey him to Craigmillar in due course, where she could be with her son. She promised to resume physical relations when he was cured.

After this, the letter added, "Fear not, for the place shall hold unto death. Remember also, in recompense thereof not to suffer yours to be won by that false race that would do no less to us both. We are tied to two false races, the goodyeare untie us from them. God forgive me, and God knit us together for ever for the most faithful couple that ever he did knit together. This is my faith. I will die for it."

The writer then went on in some jealousy against another woman in Bothwell's life, no doubt his wife, the Lady Jean Gordon, sister of the Earl of Huntly, and referred to his false brother-in-law, calling herself "a most faithful lover you ever had or shall have".

It went on, "I am ill at ease, since I cannot sleep as I would desire, that is in your arms, my dear life, whom I pray God to preserve from all ill and lend you repose. Cursed by this poxy fellow that causes me all this trouble. He is not too much disfigured yet he has had a bad attack. He has almost slain me with his breath – it is worse than your uncle's . . ."

There was a sort of postscript, evidently written the next day, for she mentions that she had had no more paper yesterday. "You make me dissemble so far that I have a horror of it and you cause me almost to play the part of a traitress. Remember that were it not that I am obeying you I had rather be dead than doing it. My heart bleeds for it. He fears the thing that you know of, and for his life. Burn this letter for it is too dangerous. Love me as I shall love you."

David stared down at those sheets of paper with a strange mixture of emotions. Here was tragedy, at various levels: a disastrous marriage, a young woman torn – for Mary would have been not twenty-five years at this time – passion, fear, guilt. And this last, the guiltiness, struck him most forcefully in that revealing postscript, "He fears the thing that you know of, and for his life." For only a few days later Darnley had been murdered, in Edinburgh at Kirk o' Field, a carefully contrived assassination involving the blowing up of his sick-bed with gunpowder. Did the Queen know of this beforehand, then?

Long he pored over that dire letter, before moving on to the others.

The six remaining were all comparatively short and of a very different character, written in an affected style, complaining of neglect and unfaithfulness but asserting her own constancy. One evidently had enclosed a lock of her hair, sent by Paris her servant. Another warned Bothwell against the wiles of some other woman, with an astonishingly humble plea for the thing she most desired, his good grace. One declared her obedience, faithfulness, constancy and voluntary subjection, extraordinary to have been written by a queen-regnant. One said that Huntly insisted that they could never marry, seeing that he was already wed, and that the lords would never tolerate it. The last of all spoke of her pretended rape by Bothwell, saying that the Earl of Sutherland was reluctant to be a party to the charade, adding that Huntly and Livingstone had three hundred horse gathered, and begging Bothwell to ensure that he had a larger force.

There was nothing in these, however, to match the long second one he had read.

David turned his attention to the poetry, all one hundred and fifty-eight lines of it, he counted. Even to an untutored eye, and in French, he could not believe that it was any very excellent composition, however heartfelt, merely a love-sick young woman's outpourings in verse. Three of all those lines said it all:

> Into his hands and into his full power
> I place my son, my honour and my life,
> My country, my subjects, my subjected soul.

Strangely moved, David took up his pen to write his translations, wondering, wondering . . .

It was late before he took the results of his labour round to

Lord Gray. That man scanned all the transcripts carefully, his perplexed frowns deepening as he read. At length he threw the papers aside.

"Are you sure that this is all, man?" he demanded. "You have not missed anything? Is your French sufficiently good? For there is nothing here worthy, that I can see, to cause King James to lose a wink of his sleep. Nothing."

"I think that I have the full sense of it all, my lord. Have another to go over it, if you doubt it."

"I want no others prying into this."

"I do not believe that I have missed anything to the point. Are these letters not sufficiently guilt-laden?"

"Oh, to be sure. But there is nothing in them which has not been known, or guessed and talked about by many, for years. At the Queen's shameful trial in England, most of this came out. Indeed copies of these letters were produced – or some of them. There is nothing new here."

"But this of the Queen's seeming foreknowledge of Darnley's slaying – as in that ending to the second letter? If that is true and no forgery. Is it not sufficiently damning?"

"Damning for Mary, perhaps, but not for James. He was only a baby at this time. Why should his mother's concurrence in his father's murder concern him greatly thirty or forty years after? Yet it did. *My* father used these letters to wring concessions out of the King. Why? His mother's guilt need not have troubled him greatly. He was reared to hate her, by Morton, Moray, Huntly and Gowrie. His tutor, Master George Buchanan, was one of her fiercest enemies. I cannot see anything in this casket to cause him anxiety. There was nothing else in it, no other paper?"

"Nothing." David shrugged. "I know not what it can be. But these all make sad reading."

"That may be – but it is of no matter. There must be something more . . ." His uncle crammed the papers back into their box but gathered up the translations. "Leave these with me. I will consider them further. Sleep on it . . ."

David left, to retire to his own couch.

In the morning, and remarkably early for that man, Lord Gray paid an unaccustomed visit to David's humble quarters, bringing with him casket and transcripts.

"I want you to take these to Methven," he announced. "To my half-sister, Mary Gray. There is something we are missing, here – that I am sure. Your aunt, if anyone knows, she will. She is a clever woman. She was closer to my father than was anyone else. She understood him, as I never did. Go to Methven and show her these letters, in secrecy. She is to be trusted. Mary may know the answer. Go at once. Today."

The Broughty land-steward was to become a travelling-man, it seemed.

5

David's new journey was a very different one from the last, no
ferrying involved, only riding due westwards, past the city of
Dundee and into the fertile Carse of Gowrie. He went by
Castle Huntly, nothing to do with the northern Gordons of
Huntly, but which had been the principal seat of the old
Master of Gray, sold some years earlier to the Lyon first Earl
of Kinghorn. Twenty-two miles of the level Carse, by the
north shores of the Firth of Tay, brought him to St John's
Town of Perth and the crossing of that great river. Then on,
still due westwards, by Tippermuir, into the wide strath of the
Earn where, after a few more miles, he came to the handsome
Methven Castle on the brow of its hill above a hidden loch,
looking out southwards over the far-flung prospect which
included the vales of Earn, Teith, Allan to that of Forth.

Methven was no rude fortified strength but an almost
palatial pile in rose-red stone, strange domicile for the
illegitimate daughter of the former Master of Gray and her
own illegitimate son. But thereby hung a tale indeed. For this
was the Scottish seat of Ludovick Stewart, Duke of Lennox,
closest male kin to the King after Prince Charles, and closer in
association to that strange monarch than anyone else alive.
Lennox, although married three times to suitable high-born
ladies, had always been in love with Mary Gray. He could not
wed her, although he had wanted to do so, for James would
have had the marriage annulled straight away, nothing more
certain, it being inconceivable that the Duke, for long the
nearest heir to the throne, could have a bastard as wife. But
he had remained faithful to Mary, after his own fashion, and
when she bore him a son, illegitimate again necessarily, he
had made over Methven and its great estate into the little
John Stewart's name, in order to provide for him but also to
ensure a permanent home for the mother. The Duke, a man

of modest tastes and no political ambitions, came to Scotland as often as he might from court at London, and always stayed at Methven.

David had been here before, of course, and did not doubt his reception, for Mary Gray was as kind as she was good-looking, a very talented and able lady.

She was aiding two workers in the kitchen-garden when David rode up, and greeted him to a warm welcome, a woman now in her forty-fifth year but still lovely, indeed the loveliest that young man had ever set eyes on – although Barbara Home now, to be sure, came into a special category. She was slenderly built, with the figure and carriage of one twenty years younger, delicate of feature, with grey humorsome eyes and a ready smile. The celebrated Gray good looks showed here at their warmest, kindest – but that there was spirit behind them none could doubt.

She conducted her nephew into her private sitting-room, with his burden in its bag, and ordered wine and refreshment for him after his thirty-odd-mile ride, before she allowed him to broach the object of his visit. A room would be prepared for him for the night, and they would eat supper in an hour or so. She asked after her half-brother and other nephew at Broughty, with neither of whom she was in fact particularly close, David knew. He was glad that she clearly approved of himself.

By way of introducing the subject of this unheralded call, difficult subject as it was, David took the casket out of its canvas bag and laid it on a table before his aunt without immediate comment. Her eyes widened and she looked from it to him quickly.

"So-o-o!" she said, quietly but significantly.

"You know what this is? You have seen it before?" he asked.

"I think that I have, David. But not . . . for long. An old story – and not a pleasing one, if I am right. It is the Earl of Bothwell's casket, is it not?"

"Yes. With its letters – the Casket Letters, Queen Mary's."

"That poor Queen! And how did this come into your hands, David? Many, I know, have looked for these."

"I found them. Hidden at Fast Castle. Three days ago."

"Fast, yes. I thought that they were there. But . . . I am surprised that you were able to find them, even to win inside that grim place. And you have brought them to me! I cannot say that I am joyful to see them!"

"No. The Lord Gray sent me there. And sent me with them, here."

"I guessed as much. How did you lay hands on this casket, David? For I would think that it would be hidden most securely, and in that most secure hold."

He told her of his mission, of his early non-entry to Fast, of his good fortune in being able to offer help to Barbara Home and of her assistance thereafter, their reaching the castle, their diligent search and their ultimate finding of the casket in the cistern.

Mary Gray listened heedfully. When he had done, she nodded. "You have succeeded where many another, I think, has failed. But, why? Why do you – or at least, my brother – want these papers?"

"Lord Gray believes that they can perhaps help him. You have heard? The King in London has appointed a new Sheriff of Angus in his place. A Home. He, my uncle, hopes that these letters may provide him with something to offer the King, some . . . some gift which might cause James to change his mind. To give back the sheriffdom. It is his belief that the King would wish to have these letters." That was the best that he could do to make the entire project sound respectable.

Mary Gray eyed him, and those fine grey eyes could be shrewd as well as kindly and humorous.

"Offer? A gift? Is that the truth of it, David? I *know* the story of these letters. I know that my father used them shamefully. To bring pressure upon King James. As others had done before him. It was nothing to Patrick's credit. I had hoped that with his death, and the casket hidden, all would be finished, forgotten. And now – here you bring them! Tell me, my brother Andrew does not think to do what his father did, *constrain* the King? Use these to seek to force him? Not a gift but a threat?"

David bit his lip. What did loyalty demand of him? "My lord does not confide all in me. I am but his land-steward, to do his bidding. I can but repeat what he said to tell you."

"I see." That sounded as though his aunt saw rather more than she was meant to see. "The King is to be pressed to change his attitude towards Andrew's sheriffdom, on account of these letters? I do not greatly like it, David. It smacks of coercion."

"Yet James has behaved unkindly to him, to my uncle. The sheriffdom has long been held by the Lords Gray. It is all but hereditary. Do you not agree? He has done nothing to offend the King, indeed he has had no dealings with him, in London."

"I am sorry for Andrew in this, yes. I only wish that there was some other way to seek to make James think more kindly of him than using these letters. But, that is not *your* concern, David, I give you that . . ."

A maid-servant came with the refreshments, and they waited until she was gone.

"Why do you bring this casket to me, David?" Mary Gray went on. "What can I do in the matter?"

"Do you know what is in these letters?" he asked. "Have you ever read them?"

"Not read them, no. I have never even seen them – although I have seen their casket. But I think that I know the sense of them. Or some of it. My father told me, one time."

"They are, of course, in French, the Queen's language. I have sought to translate them, to my best ability. I may have erred here and there – but I believe I also know the sense of them. A sorry story!" He put his hand into the bag and drew out the sheets of his own writing. "Here they are – my translations. But . . . there does not appear to be anything in them which my lord thinks would greatly concern King James today." That was carefully said. "He, he wonders whether *you* think differently?"

"So that is it!"

"Yes. He believes that you knew your father better than he did, better than anybody else. That you might know what it is that the King might so value in these old letters of his mother today, so long after her death. They scarcely show her in an honourable light. But Lord Gray says that James never cared for her or honoured his mother anyway."

"Very well. I shall read them. For I have the French also. I

65

will take you up to your chamber, David, and will read them while you wash and settle yourself . . ."

When David came downstairs to the private hall of Methven, to the ringing of the supper-bell, it was to find his aunt changed in dress and looking more beautiful than ever. She did not refer to the letters at table, with servants coming and going with viands, but asked after all at Broughty, and went on to tell of her own son John who, it seemed, was not presently living at Methven, although it was in his name, but dwelling further up Strathearn some four miles at a lesser property of the estate, Keilour. There he lived with Janet Drummond, daughter to Lord Madderty, as good as his wife. As good as, since they were not in fact married – and that was another strange story, of love and hatred and royal interference. Sir John Stewart, knighted by King James for services rendered during the monarch's one and only return to Scotland four years before, after succeeding to Elizabeth of England's throne, had, like the Duke his father, been forced to wed without love, at the King's command, a court lady of uncertain morals. She had a hold over the monarch's reigning favourite, Buckingham, and James would by no means allow a divorce since she could set the cat amongst pigeons best left undisturbed. So Lady Stewart remained in London whilst her husband stayed resolutely in Scotland with his true love Janet Drummond, managing his and the Duke's great estates, and well content to have nothing more to do with the royal court. He had now a two-year-old son, a grandson for Mary – although it seemed impossible with her so youthful looks – and a joy to all, apparently. Sir John, to keep *him* quiet, had been rewarded with the keepership of the royal castle of Dumbarton, a major responsibility, so that he cut quite an influential figure in Scotland, young as he was.

The meal over, and back in Mary Gray's own comfortable room, she took the casket and papers out of a locked aumbry.

"I have read all, and your translations, David – which are, I judge, sufficiently accurate. Tell me, are these all that were in the box?"

"All, yes." He eyed her questioningly. "That is what Lord Gray asked me also. You expected more?"

She nodded. "Yes. I would have thought so."

66

"You agree then that there appears to be nothing in these letters which could gravely concern the King? This of his mother's apparent complicity in Darnley's death – that would not be sufficient to, to distress him?"

"No. Probably not. Not James Stewart. He is a strange man." She paused. "As I told you, David, I had not *read* those papers before, only heard my father speak of them. But . . . there is something missing here, which he spoke of. Something of much greater import. To King James."

He waited. His aunt seemed almost reluctant to go on.

"I can tell you only what he told me, all those years ago. I misliked it then, as I mislike it now. I cannot be sure that it was in one of these letters, or one that is now amissing. It may not have been. But . . . he told me of it when he was speaking of this casket and these papers. It had to do with James's parentage."

"Not that old story of a changeling? In Edinburgh Castle, when James was born? That the Queen's child died at birth and a substitute was found?"

"No. That was a story which was put about by Mary's ill-wishers, who sought to cast doubt on the child's right to be heir to the throne. That was disproved long ago. No, this is something other, something grievous. It is that James was not Darnley's son."

"Sakes! Not, not . . .! Whose, then?"

"David Rizzio's. Mary's secretary."

"Lord! The Italian! The Queen's child – but not her husband's?"

"Yes. Or so my father claimed. Said that he had now proof. I assumed that it was in one of these letters. Mary's own confession to Bothwell. But, no, it is not there. Was there another letter, then? Destroyed? Or removed elsewhere? Or was there never one? Did my father learn of it somehow other? Or, or . . . did he but invent it, pretend it? To hold the King to ransom?"

"But . . ." David wagged his head, incredulously. "James would never have believed that, surely? Her Italian secretary! Is it not inconceivable? A low-born foreign servant and the Queen of Scots! No one would ever credit it."

"Oh, but some did, indeed many did, at one time. Mary

67

was fond of Rizzio, allowed him many intimacies. She was not always discreet. And he was a fascinating man, they said. That is why he was murdered, and before her eyes, at Holyroodhouse, by Darnley and the other nobles. Not, I think, because they believed that she was with child by him, but because he had over-much influence with her, at court, that she showed him too much attention."

"You do not believe this?"

"I do not know. Cannot say yea or nay. But it matters not what *I* believe, David. Many thought that there was truth in it, as I said. The townsfolk of St John's Town of Perth did. You have heard of the Gowrie Conspiracy? In 1600, when the King invented some strange story about a man with a pot of gold enticing him to Gowrie House, in Perth – the Earl of Gowrie was Provost of Perth – and there had the Earl and his brother slain, a dreadful deed. Believed to be really because the Earl's father had loaned James £85,000, a vast sum, when he was Treasurer of the realm, and James had never paid it back, nor wished to. So young Gowrie and his brother were killed and their estates forfeited, and the King never had to repay that loan. When James was surrounded in Gowrie House afterwards by the Perth mob, when they heard of the slaying, he only escaped by a secret door to the riverside. The townsfolk were chanting up at his room 'Come down, thou son of Signor Davie, come down!' Signor Davie – not Henry, Lord Darnley! So it was believed there."

"I knew naught of this . . ."

"Most have forgotten it, I would say. But my father had not. And when James treated him so ill, refused to have him go to London in 1603, he used this, I think."

"You believe that he had another letter? With the Queen's confession that James was the Italian's son. Used this to coerce James?"

"That was my understanding of it."

"Then where is that letter?"

"I know no more than you do. He could have taken it out of the casket. Kept it elsewhere, for additional secrecy. Or . . . it may never have existed. He may have invented it all. Patrick, my father, was an extraordinary man – as extraordinary as is

68

James Stewart! He could be a delight, could do great good. But also could do great wickedness. And he was clever, clever. More than anyone, he ensured that Queen Elizabeth Tudor decided that James was to be her heir, Margaret Tudor's great-grandson. He worked hard and long for this uniting of the two kingdoms. Then, after it all, James rejected him, thrust him off. It was ungratefully done. And my father never forgave him."

"And you think that he might have invented it all, the proof of this of Rizzio? Possibly no letter, no writing?"

"I had never thought of that until now. I always believed that it *was* in one of these letters. But now . . ."

"And would the King have believed it?"

"He might well. He would know of the existence of the Casket Letters all too well, after all. There might have been such a confession. And he has tried to get these letters into his possession, there is no doubt as to that. But none knew where they were – save one or two of our family. Why they were safe hidden at Fast."

"It all sounds past crediting, to me. And this of Rizzio . . ."

"Not so unbelievable, David. I do not say that it is true. But . . . think on James Stewart. He is quite unlike all of his line and blood. Always the Stewarts have been good-looking men and women, tall, handsome, with presence and the grand manner. But not this James. They have never been renowned for their wits, however, and this James is. He is of a sallow complexion, not fair and of reddish hair as most, somewhat uncouth, his tongue too large for his mouth. He is short and knock-kneed, this unlikeliest Stewart ever. And fears much, especially cold steel, whereas all his forebears had courage, at least. Admittedly he has fine Stewart eyes, but *something* he could have heired from his mother. See you, all this does not mean that I accept the Rizzio story, only that it could have been possible."

"And the King does, also?"

"It has looked that way. Since he was prepared to pay my father to keep it all secret. And others before him."

"Would it be so important, if truc? Now, so long after-wards."

"To be sure it would. Think of it, David – the King a

bastard! *I* am a bastard, as is my son. As are you! But the monarch of two realms . . .! What would the English lords and parliament make of this, if they knew? The illegitimate son of an Italian secretary on their throne! Kings must not be illegitimate, like lesser folk. I am not sure whether he could be dethroned, since he has had a coronation ceremony – two, for he had one here also, as a child. But it could make his rule in England all but impossible. He is not popular there, as it is. The English lords mislike him, for he is more clever than them all. And the English parliament seeks always to counter him. But with this in their hands . . .!"

"I see, yes." David both sighed and shrugged. "What, then, am I to tell my uncle?"

"Tell him what I have told you. That there may be such a letter. Or may not. Tell him that King James may be sufficiently glad to be given this casket and its contents and to learn that there is no such confession in it, to be suitably grateful. It may well serve its turn, without the Rizzio connection. Tell him so."

David sought his bed that night his mind in a whirl.

Back at Broughty by early evening, he found Cousin Patrick with his father Lord Gray all impatience for David's report.

He sought to tell them the long complicated story in the best order and sequence possible – he had been turning it all over in his mind on his long ride from Methven. But his account, however ordered and coherent, was constantly interrupted by exclamations, questions and objections. In consequence, it all took a considerable time.

When he was approximately finished, his uncle picked up and shook that casket and its contents, and looked as though he could shake David also, in his frustration.

"That letter! The important one – missing!" he cried. "God's mercy, of all things, that! The one, the key to all, not there! A plague on it – so nearly mine! Damn him. Where did he put it? Look, it may be at Fast, also. Apart from the rest. You must go and seek it again . . ."

"I told you, my lord, we searched every corner before we found this box in the cistern. If another paper had been there, we would have discovered it."

70

"Where else could it have been hidden? At Castle Huntly . . .?"

"There may not have *been* another letter, she said. Your father may have invented it. Hoodwinked the King . . ."

"I believe that! I believe anything of my grandsire!" his namesake said, grinning.

"I do not," his father declared. "There must be proof somewhere. For he was not the first to threaten James with these letters. Others did it before him – Morton, old Gowrie, Patrick of Orkney. And they were not all so clever as he."

"But . . . is it so important?" David asked. "As your sister said, and I told you, that very gift of the casket and letters, which have caused James so much trouble, could well be all that is necessary. He would be bound to be grateful, and probably restore the sheriffdom to you. No need for this of Rizzio."

Lord Gray eyed him assessingly. "I do not think that would be enough," he said.

His son laughed. "It looks to be all that you will get! Worth the trying, at any rate."

"I will consider this further," they were told.

The next morning saw a repetition of two days before, Lord Gray appearing at David's lodging again.

"You are to go back to Methven, David," he was told abruptly. "I want my sister's further help. And possibly her son's. As to how to approach James in London to best effect. The Duke, her lover, could help you there. And John Stewart knows the King and his ways, and the court, passing well. They will be able to guide you."

"But . . ." David shook his head. "Must it be me who takes the letters? Surely yourself, or Patrick, would be better. More telling. To offer so important a gift to the King. I am insufficiently notable . . ."

"You will not be offering any gifts!" That was said almost grimly. "You will be bearing only a message. The same message that my father kept sending James. My sheriffdom back, or I will let the English lords and parliament know of David Rizzio's son!"

"No! How, how can you do that? Without any proof?"

"My father did, without showing the proof. If he could, so can I. James fears it – that is enough."

David almost pleaded. "Why go to such lengths? When a gift of the casket and papers would probably serve? To threaten the King. Almost treason!"

"James, I swear, will not risk all the trouble of arraigning me for treason, or anything else, with that Rizzio secret assuredly then becoming known to all, when he can stop it by merely restoring what is mine, the sheriffdom."

"And if the King refuses?"

"Then we may have to reconsider. And *then* make him a present of the letters, in the hope of gratitude. But I think that he will yield, indeed I do."

David grimaced. "I say that this is foolish, my lord. And wrong."

"I am not asking your advice – but giving you your orders! You will do as I say." Gray paused. "But . . . I think that you should not tell Mary Gray, nor her son, of the threat to publish the letters in seeking their help for London. Let them believe it is to offer the gift. Meantime. Later, we shall see."

"I do not like it . . ."

"Need *you* like it, man? Remember your place, Davie Gray!"

6

David felt embarrassed, almost ashamed, to present himself at Methven Castle again, however kindly and understandingly he was received by Mary Gray, who well recognised that he was no free agent but acting under orders. Most of all, he did not like to deceive her as he had been instructed to do over the matter of threat as distinct from gift to the King; not that he was entirely convinced that she *was* deceived in the circumstances – for she would know her half-brother well enough and would perceive that her nephew was choosing his words carefully.

At any rate, she was helpful as to matters of approach to King James, telling David what she knew of that odd monarch's habits, interests and behaviour. She would write a letter for him to present to the Duke of Lennox whom, she was sure, would help if he could. But her son John would be the best one to see, for he had had much negotiating and waiting upon James to do fairly recently and would know how best to go about it.

David said that his uncle had advised him to go and see Sir John, and he proposed to go on to Keilour forthwith. He was told that it was only four miles further. After he had seen John, he should come back to Methven where his bed would be ready for him again, and the letter for the Duke written.

So on the four miles to Keilour in its wooded side-glen, with the mountains drawing ever closer to north and west and the strath narrowing. There, at an old fortified laird's house, less than any castle or fortalice, David found a happy and friendly couple and their child, living the simple and essential life, scarcely what might have been expected of a knight who was Keeper of Dumbarton Castle and the daughter of a lord, but this by determined choice. David did not really know John

Stewart well, although they were, of course, cousins by blood, and had met him only a few times and never of recent years; and Janet Drummond was attractive, quietly eye-catching, tall, slender, dark-eyed. It was time for the evening meal, and David sat down with them, after the child had been put to bed, feeling at ease despite the reasons behind his visit. He found that he had a considerable fellow-feeling for this cousin of his, with shared interests, for they were both managing landed estates, farming, stock-raising, timber planting and harvesting, and both fond of stalking deer. They had no lack of things to discuss before they reached King James.

Sir John it was who introduced that subject, by saying that his mother, whom he had seen the day before, had told him something of Lord Gray's problems and proposals. So it was less difficult for David to go on from there than he had feared. He was able to declare that he was being sent to London to see the monarch, if possible, and to tell him that the famous Casket Letters had been found and were available for His Grace if he wanted them. He thought that was the best way of putting it.

"Available?" John asked. "You are not taking them, then, to give to the King?"

"No. Lord Gray thinks that . . . unwise. At this stage. He feels that, being so, so celebrated, they might perhaps be stolen." This *was* difficult.

Strangely, his cousin did not seem to see it so. "Ah, yes. Perhaps he is right. James is a law unto himself. It may be that all kings are. But, I agree that he might well arrange to have your precious letters, shall we say, abstracted from your baggage, once he knew of their existence therein! He has his own ways of looking after his royal interests!"

That was not quite what David had meant, but it served well enough. And it was a warning, too, that all might not be as straightforward an exercise as Lord Gray envisaged.

"Have you any guidance, then, for me? In seeking to approach the King?"

"I do not see why a letter sent by Lord Gray to James would not do as well as having you to make the long journey, David. He would send it to my father, who would hand it to the King.

74

Tell him of the finding of the casket. And end by hoping that His Grace might reconsider this of the sheriffdom."

"I thought of that," David admitted. "But my lord feels that it should be more . . . personal. In case the King merely orders him to deliver up the casket and letters, and he could not refuse a royal command. Why he will not go himself but sends me without the letters in my possession."

"I see, yes. There is some point in that. Well, James, as I say, is as strange a monarch as he is a man. He is not difficult to speak to – if you can win into his presence, past his henchmen. And my father can ensure that, I think. James cares nothing for kingly dignity. He is as like to grant you audience from his bed as anywhere else! He demands little of bowing and flourish. But he is clever, shrewd. Do not think, because he treats men easily, that he is readily cozened or deceived. And if he thinks that you do try to deceive him, he can be quite ruthless. He is called the Wisest Fool in Christendom – but he is no fool, I assure you."

That sounded an ominous note for David, in view of his errand. "How, then, do you advise me to put my message to him? To ensure, if I can, that he heeds me. Lest he mistakes my meaning . . ."

"Be quite frank. Tell him the truth. That you found the casket at Fast Castle, and took it to Lord Gray. That Gray recognised its importance and felt that it probably should be in the royal hands. You could say that your uncle was afraid that the King might somehow have doubted his, Gray's, goodwill and loyalty, in that he had thought to give the sheriffdom of Angus to another. Whereas he was entirely loyal. And thinks to prove it by handing over these famous letters of the King's mother's – if His Grace wants them. But, because they are so precious, keeps them under lock and key at Broughty meantime, and sends you to enquire His Grace's will in the matter. James will understand very well."

"Ye-e-es. You think that he will do it? Restore the sheriffdom? As it were, in exchange?"

"I do not think that you should put that into words. Just stress Lord Gray's loyalty. He will recognise what is desired."

"There is nothing else that you can tell me? That would aid me?"

"Only that if you could intrigue him in some way, it might help. He is like a child in some ways, however acute in others. He can be interested in strange stories, unlikely happenings, secrets and the like. Why not tell him of your search at Fast, and how you found the casket. Hidden all these years. That would interest him, I feel sure. And James interested would be part-way towards your success."

David had to be content with that, since he could not divulge the essence of his mission and the threat involved. He thanked his host and hostess, and presently took his leave, saying that he must not keep his aunt late from her bed.

Back at Methven, however, he found Mary Gray in no hurry to retire, and they sat up late in pleasant converse. She gave him the letter for the Duke of Lennox and suggested that he would be wise not to speak of his errand to any other whatsoever, for the court was a hotbed of intrigue and scheming factions all seeking advantage and unscrupulous as to how they obtained it. Confide only in the Duke.

David retired, with a sufficiency on his mind.

When he returned to Broughty next day he made a last effort to persuade his uncle to change his priorities, to do what John Stewart had suggested and stress loyalty and the gift of the letters first, and only to resort to the threat and the Rizzio connection if the King proved unyielding. But Lord Gray was not to be moved. That sequence of events would take time, he averred, bringing back the word to Scotland and then going down again with the threat. And time was important. Already it might be almost too late. Once this Sir Thomas Home was actually installed as High Sheriff of Angus, before the Scots Privy Council, it might be all but impossible to have him unseated. They could not wait. And by the same token, the sooner Davie was off to London, the better. He must leave no later than the morn's morn . . .

Only one gleam of satisfaction and compensation could David Gray descry in this unwanted and unpalatable mission, and that was that he could surely contrive that he spend the nights, going and coming, at Bilsdean Castle. To that end he ordered a notably early start for the Broughty ferry-boat two mornings later, with his uncle's approval, which enabled him to reach the Earl's Ferry at Elie on Forth in plenty of time for the daily crossing, so that, riding southwards from North Berwick thereafter he was able to reach Bilsdean by mid-afternoon.

There was no doubt about his welcome, however surprised Barbara and Janet were to see their visitor back so soon, the latter remarking frankly that if she had known of this she would not have troubled to wash his bed-linen. David was quite glad to learn that their father had not yet got back from London, for he was uncertain whether the laird would receive him as kindly as did the daughters; also whether he would have been prepared to hand over the Casket Letters.

So they spent another enjoyable evening together by the hall fire. He gave the girls some account of the contents of the letters, to their interest and exclamations; but he made no mention of the Rizzio connection. Also he offered them the respectable version of his mission to James's court, and received their well-wishes. That night the bedtime kisses were even more satisfactory. When he left Bilsdean in the morning he was surprised and pleased when Barbara announced that she would ride some way with him on his road southwards. Taking leave of Janet, he was bold enough to suggest that she might spare herself the bed-linen washing as they might well have him back again on his return journey, if they could put up with him. That was not discouragingly received.

They rode companionably, by Aldcambus and up on to the Coldingham Muir. Where the track forked off seawards for Dowlaw farmery and Fast, some five miles, David expected Barbara to rein up and say farewell. But she waved him on.

"A favourite place of mine is St Ebba's Head," she told him. "Another six or seven miles. I have not been there for some time. So I will go with you as far as Coldingham and turn off there."

They trotted on over the rolling heather moorland, which was really just a plateau-like extension of the Lammermuir Hills which walled off East Lothian, all Home country as far as eye could see. David mentioned this, asking how it felt to belong to such a far-flung yet close-knit family, almost like a Highland clan, which dominated, through more than a score of ancient lairdships, this knuckle-end of Lowland Scotland, the Merse?

"I do not often think of it," she admitted. "Although perhaps I ought to. For my father speaks now and then of marrying me off to one of them, one of the young Homes. There is a tradition of Homes wedding Homes – how they have managed to keep their lands so firmly in the family, I suppose."

David found himself not liking the sound of that at all, without asking himself just why. He made no comment.

She laughed. "I do not think, however, that I am in great demand! I have the name for being difficult, I understand, not sufficiently docile and decorous! Forby, Bilsdean is not a large and rich inheritance, and Fast scarcely a catch. Most Home lairds could do a deal better."

Feeling better himself, David was able to say, "More fools them, then! If they had any judgment . . . .!" He left the rest unsaid.

"Ah, but that depends on what you marry for. Lands or wealth, or power or prestige. Aye, or a breeding strain as in horses! Or for love." She smiled. "What would be your standards in the matter, David?"

"The last," he answered simply.

"So! We think alike in this, then. Well said."

"I am not in any position to elect otherwise, anyway," he told her, almost roughly. "I am a mere land-steward, owning no property. Illegitimate. I may have royal blood in my veins, far enough back. But I am nobody. Whoever weds me will have to do so for love, for she will get nothing else!"

"She could be none so unfortunate, despite that!" Barbara observed.

All too soon, it seemed to David, they came to Coldingham township with its handsome priory, as large as many an abbey, the Commendator-Prior thereof a Home naturally, still sitting in the Scots parliament as of right, Reformation or none. As they drew rein, David further regretted that their parting here, in such public place, must be very undemonstrative. The girl asked him if he had ever been to St Ebba's Head, for it was one of the most exciting places on the Lowland seaboard – and it was only a mile or two distant.

He succumbed. After all, in a journey of almost four hundred miles, what did such short diversion and brief delay matter? Nodding, he turned his horse's head north-eastwards, with hers.

After a mile or so down the valley of a stream they came in sight of the sea and a harbour and fishing community, St Ebba's Haven, Barbara said. They did not proceed down to this, however, but swung off northwards into low, green, cattle-dotted hills, soon dipping down to a long and narrow loch where wildfowl squattered and heron stalked. Beyond rose a steeper and lengthy ridge of hill, up which a rough track wound. This they proceeded to climb.

At the top, emerging from something like a little pass, Barbara pulled up. She did not have to speak. Abruptly before them the land fell away in enormous cliffs to the limitless sea, breathtaking, awe-inspiring. These precipices were half as high again as the Fast ones, towering, majestic – and noisy, with the screaming of thousands of seafowl and the roar of the breaking waves far below.

"I see . . . why you come here," David said inadequately.

She dismounted and led her mount to tether it to a bent and twisted hawthorn tree, for this was no place for horses. He did likewise. Then she moved on, down a short and quite steep apron of grass, whereon sheep grazed precariously, to the very cliff-edge.

Even after that first prospect he was unprepared for what now plunged before him. For this was no simple cliff-face, however impressive, but a jagged series of mighty rock-buttresses soaring many hundreds of feet out of the foaming seas in savage majesty, with between them huge chasms, sheer, frightening in their yawning depths. Down in these the birds wheeled and swooped, far below the watchers, and on every crack and ledge of the cliff-sides they nested and squabbled, while in the surging tide at the cliff-foots the divers swam and fished amongst the seals.

"I thought that Fast was beyond all," David told her, staring. "But this is past all telling."

"Come," she said briefly, and held out her hand.

Surprised, he by no means rejected that hand, however unsuitable for a man to be helped downwards by any woman.

For she led him down a dizzy-making drop, no track or pathway, part naked rock, part clinging sea-pinks, some two score more feet of it, and their long riding-boots scarcely the ideal footwear for the descent. This brought them to an extraordinary little formation in the rock, not a cavity but a ledge on a thrusting spur, hollowed, within a sort of natural parapet, this seeming to hang suspended between sea and sky.

"I call this my pulpit," she confided. "Here I can sit and preach to myself better sermons than I have ever heard in the kirk!"

She sat, and by the pressure of her hand indicated that he did likewise. There was not much room in that pulpit for two, which meant that they had to sit very close together indeed, for which the man made no complaint. Despite any misinterpretation as to fearfulness, he clung to that other hand.

"This . . . I have never seen the like. Or thought to see," he got out. "I would not have believed it. And for a woman . . .!" He wagged his head. "What sort of sermons do you preach yourself here?"

"That is *my* secret!" she answered, smiling. "Am I not allowed that? Even a woman!"

"Oh, I do not pry. But wonder . . ."

"Wonder, yes. Is that not sufficient? To wonder. I have heard it said that wonder and worship are much the same. So I come here, on occasion, and wonder."

"And alone?"

"Oh, yes, alone. I sought to bring Janet once, but she would not come down here. She mislikes heights. You, indeed, are the first person I have ever brought to my pulpit."

He looked from all that breathtaking prospect to the loveliness so close to him. "And why?" he asked thickly. "Why me?"

"I thought that you would find it . . . to your taste," she said. "You might feel here something of what I feel."

"I feel enough to, to quite tie my tongue," he admitted. He released her hand now and raised his arm to encircle her shoulders and hold her still closer, if that was possible. "How can I put my thanks into poor words, Barbara?"

"No need for words, David, in this place. And women have

come here always. Ebba herself, who was daughter of King Ethelfrid of Northumbria, who founded her nunnery here. Etheldreda, who founded the great abbey of Ely, in England, received the veil here, from St Wilfrid. And when the Danes sacked the nunnery, the nuns cut off their lips and noses, it is said, to preserve their honour! How think you of that?"

He shook his head, not venturing an opinion.

For how long they sat there, gazing out, and wordless, he neither knew nor cared, despite the length of the journey he had ahead of him. Only occasionally they spoke, or pointed something out – such as a fulmar sitting on a ledge only a few feet away and regarding them with an unwinking stare of yellow eyes, or a pair of inquisitive puffins that found them of consuming interest. David had never before sat thus quietly and holding a woman. He was not wholly inexperienced as to the other sex, but his associations had been either with country girls in brief physical explorations, or else, infrequently, with more formal ladies in castle halls, these usually considerably older than himself.

"I shall not forget this," he told her, after a while.

"Even in London, amongst the court ladies? Who, I am told, can be very . . . captivating!"

"There in especial. As I think that you know, I have no wish to be going there, and the sooner that I am back, the happier I will be. This entire matter of the letters pleases me nothing – save that it has brought me to know you. For that only, I bless the Casket Letters! That they led me to you. And us both here, to this good place. I shall not forget St Ebba's Head in London. Or anywhere else."

"That is why I brought you," she said simply.

He gripped her still more tightly, temptation to go further strong upon him. "I wish . . ." he began, and stopped.

She said nothing now, did not ask him of what he wished.

Biting his lip, he sought to take himself in hand. He must face realities. This young woman moved him as none other had ever done. And she must have some fondness for him to have brought him here, trusting him. But . . . what had he to offer her, if he sought to go further with her? Nothing but himself. And that was not enough, not for a laird's daughter – aye and an heiress, since there was no son to heir Bilsdean and

Fast. He had no lands, no wealth, no position, nothing that could commend him to her or her father, other than a pleasant enough friendship. He would have to be content with that . . .

Deliberately David loosened his hold on the girl's shoulders, indeed lowered his hand and arm. Not that there was any room to return it to his own side without seeming to insinuate it lower against her person.

"You sigh?" she said.

"Did I?" He shrugged. "I suppose . . . because time presses. And I have a long way to go." And that was true in more ways than one.

"Ah, yes. I have delayed you, bringing you here. No time for sermons today!"

"I would not be so sure," he told her. "Perhaps I just heard one!"

She rose. "Come, then, you must be on your long road."

They extricated themselves from that pulpit and climbed the steep slope up to the horses, this time without holding hands, the man leading. At the top, he turned to gaze back.

"I want to remember everything of this, every yard and corner and scene, to take with me," he said.

"It will still be here. When you come back," she observed.

He switched his gaze to the young woman. That was an invitation, undoubtedly. "That I shall not forget, either."

As they were about to unhitch the horses, he turned to her. "Barbara, may we say our farewells here, in this place, rather than amongst the folk of Coldingham?"

"Assuredly." She came to him without hesitation.

He took her in his arms and held her against him, all the well-made, shapely delight of her. He kissed her hair, her brow, her eyes and then her lips, and found them parted for him. For long moments they stood thus, scarcely still since their persons made their own appreciative movements and stirrings. But when David realised that his hands had begun to stray, he raised his head and put her from him, gently but firmly.

"I am a weak man, I fear, my dear," he asserted thickly.

She patted his arm, wordless.

Mounting, they left St Ebba's Head.

Practically in silence now they rode back to Coldingham. In the village street where the roads parted, they reined up and sat eyeing each other, still unspeaking. Then David drew a great breath, raised his hand in salute, jerked his beast's head round and kicked urgent heels to its sides. He did not look back as it quickly broke into a canter, southwards.

David Gray had never been south of the borderline before, but he was in no mood for sightseeing now. The walled town of Berwick-on-Tweed was picturesque and interesting, and as he rode across the new stone bridge which the King had ordered to be built as the first charge on his English Treasury, to replace the rickety timber one which had alarmed that easily-alarmed monarch on *his* journey south, David could not fail, however, to recollect that this was where it all started, the sorry later story of the Casket Letters. For here James had deliberately turned on the Master of Gray and sent him back to Scotland, with his famous remark that he would find sufficient rogues in London without having to import Patrick Gray; and from that public rejection had come the Master's revenge, the years of coercion and payment. And now a new chapter in that reprehensible tale.

On over the bare Northumberland moorland country David rode, not forcing the pace but maintaining a fast but steady trot. Since he could not afford to change horses at change-houses and inns, this animal must take him all the way, so it must not be over-ridden. But it was a fine and spirited creature, one of Lord Gray's best, and ought to be good for a regular fifty miles a day. Seven days, then . . .

He made the town of Alnwick that first night, under its huge Percy castle, larger than any David had ever seen in Scotland although less strongly sited than most nearer home, making even Methven look small. He put up in a modest hostelry, amongst farmers attending a two-day cattle-sale. A noisy lot, it was late before he slept – but he had a sufficiency to occupy his mind from that day's doings.

The day following he covered more ground than he had anticipated, reaching Durham, huddled beneath the whale-back ridge in the River Wear on which rose the notable cathedral and bishop's castle, having earlier passed through

83

Morpeth, where he felt that he left the borderland, and the city of Newcastle-on-Tyne, larger than any town he had visited in Scotland. At Durham he asked where was Neville's Cross, scene of a great defeat for David the Second of Scots, but none there knew of what he talked.

His third day, with the horse bearing up well, took him by Spennymoor and Darlington and York to Doncaster, David now marvelling at the richness of the land, its so numerous large towns and cities, its great population. He had always known that England was wealthier and more populous than his own country, but he had never quite visualised the scale of it all. The further he rode southwards the more impressed by it all he grew. Although he saw the countryside, however fertile and fair, as so much tamer and less challenging than his own, missing the high hills, the lochs and firths, the crags and deans and outcropping rock. Scotland seemed somehow so much closer to God's basic creation than did this man-moulded England. He was, to be sure, prejudiced.

This impression was further enhanced the next day as he travelled through ever softer landscapes, by Retford, Tux-ford and Newark to Grantham, level lands and far vistas, slow-running reedy streams, meres and meadows and the towers and steeples of innumerable parish churches dotting the scene, many extraordinarily close together, manor-houses of timber and clay, not stone, almost as plentiful. As a land-steward he was particularly struck by the number of mills on all those slow-flowing rivers, requiring quite lengthy lades frequently to give them sufficient fall for the water to drive their great paddle-wheels – sign, he recognised, of the great yields of grain produced and the needs of a large population for bread and forage.

The fifth night he spent at Huntingdon, interesting to him in that from this rich English earldom, with its lands and manors in no fewer than eleven counties, came the wealth which had built so many of Scotland's splendid abbeys – Jedburgh, Kelso, Melrose, Dryburgh and the rest; for this had been the heritage of the Countess Matilda whom David the First had married, the richest heiress in England, to that pious and able monarch's satisfaction.

Only two more days, David reckoned, to London.

Now the villages and towns seemed almost to run into each other on this principal highway, too numerous to remember as he neared the famous Thames valley. His horse was now showing signs of weariness, inevitably, and he was not pressing the beast. It had served him well and would have earned its rest in another score or so of miles. Then, at Hatfield that sixth night, David learned from talk at the inn that his beast might gain respite rather sooner. For it seemed that King James was at present at his favourite hunting-park of Theobalds, only some eight miles to the south-east. No need to go to London and Whitehall Palace.

Then it occurred to him to wonder whether this, in fact, was wise? Mary Gray and her son had stressed the advisability of approaching the monarch only through Duke Ludovick. He might not be at this Theobalds Park. He asked the innkeeper if he had any idea whether the Duke of Lennox was likely to be with the King at his hunting, and, after a strange look, was told that he would be, to be sure – the Scotch Monkey never went anywhere without his Scotch Poodle! This curious announcement was revealing in more ways than one, some indication that James and his Scottish courtiers were less than popular with his English subjects.

So next morning David turned his mount's head south-eastwards, leaving the main highway. Now that he was nearing his destination, which indeed might even represent his destiny, he knew a growing trepidation.

He was quickly into wooded country now, down the valley of the River Lea – although it was scarcely a recognisable valley by Scots standards. Theobalds itself, it seemed, was these eight miles off, near Waltham Cross, but he soon came to the great wall of its park, ten miles of it he was told, enclosing the best hunting territory near London. James, coveting it, apparently, had forced Robert Cecil, Earl of Salisbury, to exchange it for Hatfield House.

At length David reached a gate in the wall and was immediately challenged by armed guards. He declared that he sought the Duke of Lennox. The gatekeepers seemed doubtful about letting him in. Admittedly he would not look an impressive figure, young, very modestly dressed and travel-stained; but when he announced that he was in fact kin to the Duke – not quite accurate but near enough in that Ludovick's son was his own cousin – they allowed him entrance but insisted that two of their number escorted him to the house. So he had to dismount and walk with this pair of surly guards.

The mansion was the best part of half a mile within, an enormous pile of evidently fairly recent construction, with nothing fortified about it, having more great mullioned windows in the one building than David had ever seen in total, legions of tall, decorative chimneys, and having wings spreading out from a huge three-storeyed central block. He was conducted round the back to an equally extensive stableyard, where a groom took his horse, paying the fine beast more respect than its rider, and he was handed over to a supercilious major-domo who looked him up and down and likewise seemed to question his right to admittance, and only grudgingly passed him on to a junior servitor to take to the Lennox quarters.

It appeared that the Duke had rooms of his own in one of the wings of the establishment. On the way thither, David saw various over-dressed men and under-dressed women hanging about corridors and ante-rooms, all of whom ignored him.

But at the ducal quarters, which were by no means grand, he fared better, being received by a young man of about his own age, having a broad Scots accent, who proved to be the Duke Ludovick's personal body-servant, hailing from Methven no less, and named Dand Graham. When he heard who David was, he could not have been more helpful, offering refreshment and plying him with questions as to what went on at Methven and Strathearn these days, clearly homesick. He explained that the Duke was out at the hunt with the King, but he jaloused that he would be back long before King Jamie himself was, for the Duke was not nearly so enamoured of the chase as was the monarch, who, despite complaints as to his health, could and did hunt all day and every day.

Dand Graham was accurate in his guess, no doubt from experience, for David had barely washed and eaten before Lennox came stamping in, calling for hot water and a beaker of wine and declaring that he would be glad never to see another deer in his life. Presented with his visitor, however, he swallowed his complaints and greeted David kindly.

Ludovick Stewart, now in middle years, was a stocky, open-faced man, neither handsome nor aristocratic-looking despite his royal ancestry and being third in succession to the throne, with quite rugged features which all the years of court life had failed to smooth away. He was the only son of the first Duke, Esmé Stewart of Aubigny, first cousin of Lord Darnley and descended from the Princess Margaret, daughter of James the Fourth. It had not failed to occur to David that, if this of Rizzio was true, then Ludovick was not quite so close-related to the King as was supposed.

"So, Davie Gray!" he exclaimed. "I have heard of you from Mary – and of course knew your father. Although not as well as I knew *his* father, Patrick, Master of Gray. Here is a pleasant surprise. Is it one more Scot come to London to seek fortune?"

"No, my lord Duke, scarcely that. I come only as a messenger of the Lord Gray of Fowlis."

"From Andrew Gray – to me? What can I do for your uncle?"

"It is a long story, my lord Duke . . ."

Ludovick laughed. "I see. Then let me wash the sweat and grime of the hunt off me and I will come join you in some refreshment. Hunting is cursedly thirsty work, as our liege lord does it! You would think, at his age and the shape of him, that he would have got past it! I shall not be long . . ."

David used the interval to turn over in his mind just how he could put his mission to the Duke, and how far to go in explanation. There was Mary Gray's letter, of course.

7

"So you want to see the King, tell him of the finding of these letters?" the Duke of Lennox said, and he was no longer smiling. "You realise, I hope, Davie, that that will be no simple and genial occasion!"

"I do, yes." That was not genially said, either.

"These letters, I know well, have been a source of misery and pain ever since my unfortunate kinswoman, Mary the Queen, wrote them. I had hoped that they were gone, lost for ever – and so, I swear, does James. He will scarcely love you for telling him otherwise."

"No."

"Why did not Lord Gray bring them to court himself?"

"He feared, my lord Duke, that the King might . . . misuse him. Even put him in your Tower of London! And take the letters."

"So he sent you instead! To take that risk."

"He believes that the King will not imprison *me*. I am nobody. That would serve no purpose. I am only the messenger."

"I see. Andrew Gray, I think, is a very careful man! Unlike his late sire! And have you brought these letters with you?"

"No. He, my lord, thought that they would be safer with him, at Broughty, meantime. Until the King's wishes be made known."

"The King's wishes? Is there likely to be any doubt about his wishes in this matter? I would say, to obtain the letters and destroy them."

"Yes. But . . . my lord keeps them secure. Until His Grace declares . . . what is best."

Ludovick looked at the younger man levelly. "You do not think to *bargain* with James, Davie Gray! Over this of the sheriffdom?"

"Scarcely that, no. But to, to ascertain the King's will." David looked no happier than he sounded. "My lord Duke, if I had brought the letters, His Grace could just have taken them from me, by his royal command."

"He could, yes. I think that you play a dangerous game, Davie – or Andrew Gray does! And do not call James Grace. He now prefers the English style of Majesty. And, for myself, you can dispense with the lord Duke. Have you any notion of what you are attempting here? The risks you run?"

"I have not chosen to do it. My lord ordered it. I am but his land-steward . . ."

"Yes, no doubt. But . . . better, I think, that those letters had never been found!" Ludovick shook his head. "What do you want of me, then?"

"Your aid to win me audience of the King, my lord – private audience. My aunt and Sir John both urged me to come to you."

The Duke rose from the table, to pace the floor. "I think that I can gain you audience, and secretly, yes. But ought I to do so? For your sake, or any other's. It might be as good as sending you to the Tower, as you said. If not worse! James, angered, can be vengeful, harsh – even though that is not his normal nature. And he has power to do as he will, with none to question him."

"I understand that. And wish that it did not have to be so. But . . ."

"Very well. I will seek to bring you to him. But you may not thank me for it hereafter. Nor may James!"

They eyed each other doubtfully.

The Duke left David, to have dinner in the King's company, and it was quite late in the evening before he returned, by which time the younger man, tired after his long riding, was thinking of bed. However, that was not to be, yet. James would see him, right away.

Surprised and less than confident, David sought to spruce himself up, but Ludovick told him not to trouble. The King was seldom concerned with appearances, his own or others' – and in fact would himself be in bed, to which he habitually retired after dinner if he could. He added that he had explained to James that David Gray had come in connection with the lost Casket Letters. He could not promise that his reception would be cordial, for the King had scowled darkly at the mention of those wretched papers; but at least he was prepared to see him, and forthwith.

So the apprehensive visitor was conducted along to the main block of the enormous mansion and up a wide stairway to the principal royal suite of rooms on the first floor. Passing through a large and ornate chamber where courtiers played at cards or dice, and into a smaller apartment where Yeomen of the Guard lounged, they came to a closed door, with two standing sentries in scarlet uniforms. Signing to David to wait, the Duke knocked and called loudly, "It is Vicky, Sire," and opened the door, to enter, closing it again behind him.

There was quite a wait thereafter. Then a dandified young man came out, all scent and powder, more like a woman indeed, who looked at David strangely, disparagingly, then, without a word, gestured to him to enter, and minced off, head in the air.

The first impression that David received, as the guard closed the door behind him, was that of smell. The exquisite youth had left a scented trail, but this was quite overlaid by a very different aroma, off-putting in the extreme – unwashed humanity, an odd, acrid odour and a general stuffiness. However, suddenly aware of this as he was, other matters had priority. The room was dominated by a great canopied bed on which, amongst an untidy heap of bed-clothes, an extraordinary figure sat up. James Stewart was extraordinary by any standards, but what struck David first was that the King was actually wearing a hat, not any bed-cap but a tall, outdoor green hat, sporting a green feather. That was as much as he took in at this stage, save that the Duke Ludovick was standing at the far side of the bed, and that there was nobody else present.

David bowed deeply. "Sire," he got out, "your most humble servant."

"David Gray, James, from Broughty in Angus," the Duke presented.

The odd-looking occupant of the bed regarded David assessingly – and whatever else was unlovely about him, he had fine large eyes, almost feminine in character. For long moments he said nothing into an uncomfortable silence.

"Ooh, aye," the monarch observed at length. "So you're Davie Gray. An ill breed, the Grays!"

It was not a reception calculated to put a nervous visitor at his ease. David swallowed and said nothing.

James nodded that large hatted head portentously. He was of a sallow complexion, far from handsome, with wispy and uncombed hair and beard. His speech, in a broad Scots accent, was indistinct, because his tongue was too big for his mouth so that he tended to dribble.

"You'll be yon Patrick's grandson, then?" he went on. "Unless you're a right improve on him, I'd be better to clap you in the Tower here right away!"

Again there was nothing David could usefully reply to that. He inclined his head, silent.

"And what's this about letters, eh?" James raised a hand to point a jabbing finger. He was clad in a bed-robe of sorts over what presumably was a nightshirt. "You've come about letters, I'm told. I dinna like the sound o' that, I do not!"

David moistened his lips. "Your Grace . . ." He corrected himself hurriedly. "Your Majesty, I come from the Lord Gray of Fowlis. I am his land-steward, no more. It is about the letters Your Majesty's royal mother wrote. To the Earl of Bothwell. They call them the Casket Letters. They, they have been found."

It was the King's turn to say nothing. He stared at his visitor less than kindly.

"Sire, my lord heard that they might be hidden in Fast Castle. That is on the coast of the Berwickshire Merse. On a cliff . . ."

"Fine I ken Fast, my mannie. A rogue's hold if ever I saw one! Where yon spawn o' Satan, Logan, roosted! Aye, and Patrick, Maister o' Gray with him."

"Yes, Sire, the same. My Lord Gray, knowing that his father had had the letters in his possession, believed that they might be at Fast. He sent me there to search for them . . ."

"He did? For why? Why now? After all these years, man?"

David hesitated. "He, he thought that your Majesty might be glad to have them."

"If he kent that they were there, he could have done that years syne. His ill faither didna die yesterday!"

91

"No, Sire. But he thought that Your Majesty might have come to think ill of him, for some reason. Of late. And that this might assure you of his love and loyalty."

"I'm no' like to think other than ill o' the Grays!" James declared, nodding that hat so that its feather waved.

"What of *Mary* Gray, Sire?" Ludovick put in. "You find *her* to your taste, I think."

"Yon quean o' yours, Vicky. Och well, she's the best o' them, maybe."

"I saw her before I set out for London, Sire," David said, eager to profit by this kinder note. "She thought that Your Majesty might heed me. And sent her loyal duty and regard."

"Aye, aye. But this o' the letters? You have them?"

"Not here, Sire. We found them, after long searching. Hidden in an underground water-cistern at Fast, in a silver casket . . ."

"And you've no' brought them, man?"

"My lord thought that they were too precious to send by me. He holds them safe, at Broughty Castle. Until he knows your royal will . . ."

"He could have brought them his own sel', could he no'? Safe enough. Instead o' sending a laddie like yoursel'."

David glanced uncomfortably over at the Duke. "My lord felt that Your Majesty must be displeased with him for some reason. Since you have taken the sheriffdom of Angus from him, to give to another. And so he did not presume to come before you. Sent me as his messenger . . ."

"Aye, and kept those devil-damned letters! A Gray – aye, a right Gray! Fine I see it all. Do you take me for a fool, man? Your sovereign lord! Andrew Gray wants his sheriffdom back, and thinks to barter these letters for it! Seeks to play the pedlar wi' *me*, his king! Is that no' the truth o' it?"

David swallowed again. "Not, not that, Sire. My lord but seeks to know your royal will in the matter . . ."

"He kens fine my royal will maun be to hae those letters. But he doesna bring them, nor sends them. Only sends his brother's by-blow to make a trade! His sheriff's office for thae letters. Vicky, have you ever heard the like?"

"Not quite like this, Sire. But there have been similar . . . arrangements, have there not? In the past. I do not commend

92

it. But if these letters mean so much to you, then perhaps the price is not too high?"

"You are taking Gray's part?"

"No, no, James, not so. If what you make of it is true, then it is a sorry, ill-judged and unsuitable business. But Andrew Gray may mean no ill, no insult. It could well be as Davie here says. His uncle but wishes to know if your mother's letters, which he now has in his possession, mean any great deal to you. After all, they might not. They were written nearly sixty years ago. All concerned in them are long dead. So you might not want them. But if you do, he could send them, or bring them. And hope that, in return, you might show him some little . . . appreciation."

"Yes, that is it, Sire!" David confirmed earnestly.

"But the man only thinks to find these letters when he loses this sheriffdom!" James declared. "You're no' telling me that he's no' bargaining!"

Neither of his hearers could counter that.

There was silence in the royal bedchamber for a space.

It was the King who broke it. "I could have Andrew Gray's neck, for this," he said grimly. "And yours, my bonnie lad! And yours! If it's what I believe it is, it is treason!"

"Surely not, James, not treason!" Ludovick protested. "Even at the worst it could be only a misbehaviour, malfeasance. On Lord Gray's part. Ill judgment, yes. But no fault of this young man, who is merely a messenger."

"He it was who went and found the letters, was it no'? For use against me. As his grandsire did, years syne. And his uncle does now. He's a Gray! One o' an ill breed. Why should he be so innocent, eh?" James's finger jabbed again. "You, Davie Gray, have you *read* these letters?"

David blinked. "I . . . I . . . yes, Sire. I had to. They are in the French, you see. The Lord Gray has little French. So I had to translate them for him . . ."

"Ho, ho, so you are a learned young rogue, are you! You have the French. Do you ken any other tongues?"

"I have a little of the Latin, Sire."

"You do? See you, *Caveat emptor, cum grano salis*. What means that, would you say?"

"I think, Sire, he who purchases should take the seller's word with a pinch of salt."

"No' bad, no' bad. Aye, and you think on that! Where did you learn the like, my mannie?"

"At St Andrews, Your Majesty – the university."

"You? A land-steward and a by-blow!"

"My grandsire sent me there. Paid for me . . ."

"He did? Guid sakes – Patrick did that? And wi' my siller, like as not! Think on that!" James astonishingly produced a chuckle. "You hear that, Vicky? Patrick Gray held thae letters against me for years. And used my siller to train this bonnie lad in the French, to translate them for his son to use against me in turn! Is that no' beyond all?"

"Hardly all that, James! Patrick had his good points. He no doubt saw this Davie as having wits, and so provided for him when his father died young . . ."

"Saw him as having something o' his ain wits, aye! For Patrick aye was clever, clever, whatever else." James turned back to David. "So you read the letters. You ken what's in them." There was no chuckling now, but a penetrating stare.

"Yes, Sire." David felt almost as though he was sealing his own fate with that admission.

"So-o-o!" The King continued to gaze at him from those strange, luminous eyes. "I think that you might be better . . . silenced, then!" he said.

Out of the hush which followed that, the Duke spoke. "Sire, David is but a messenger, the courier. You cannot blame him . . ."

"But he *kens*, Vicky, he kens! What those letters say. And yon's knowledge nae land-steward, nor other, should have." The monarch tapped his high hat and tipped it further over his brow, in an oddly final gesture. "Tak him awa', Vicky, the noo. And haud him close, aye close. I'll hae to think on this, so I will – aye, think on it." He waved a dismissive hand. "Begone."

Duke and land-steward bowed themselves out.

Unspeaking, the pair found their way back to the ducal quarters. It was late now, but David no longer felt like bed and sleep. Apparently nor did Ludovick, for he called for

94

wine for both of them, and sat down at table, gesturing for his visitor to do likewise. Long he gazed at David, or past him.

"This is a bad business," he said at length, inadequately.

The younger man moistened his lips and nodded, wordless.

"I did the best for you I could. I guessed that it would be difficult, unpleasant. But scarcely so bad as this. James, threatened, is dangerous."

"I made no threat, my lord. I was careful not to do so."

"Yes, but you admit that the threat was implicit?"

"No-o-o. Not in anything that I said to the King."

"But there *is* a threat? And James well perceived it."

There was no denying that.

"What *is* in those letters, Davie?"

"Should, should I tell you, my lord? Since the King says that it is knowledge no man should have. Might it not just endanger you to know also?" That was the best that David could think of at short notice.

"Do not play with me!" the Duke said. "If I am to help you, I must know what it is that makes James so concerned. He has never told me what is in them – if he knows himself, since he has never seen them, I presume. You have. Tell me."

David recounted the gist of those letters, the sonnets and the two marriage contracts, to the best of his memory, a lengthy catalogue.

When he had finished, the other shook his head. "Indiscreet, sad writings," he said at length. "They seem to prove Mary's foreknowledge of Darnley's murder. But that has been guessed at for long. I cannot see anything here that could hurt James now. Was there nothing else?"

That was what everyone had asked. "Nothing that I read, no."

"Something else that Andrew Gray took out before he gave the writings to you to translate?"

"I was there when the casket was opened. It was locked and had to be forced. There were no other papers."

"Then I do not understand this, why James is so troubled. Patrick Gray made him pay, for years, to keep silent over something in that casket. What?"

"I can tell you only what was there, my lord. What I saw."

95

"There is mystery here – *you* must see that, Davie. James dreads something, something even for a king to dread."

Eyeing the Duke, David held his tongue, and hated himself for doing it; for he liked and respected this man. But he was torn, trapped in a tangle of loyalties.

Belatedly they sought their couches.

David seemed to have been asleep for only a brief spell when the man Dand Graham was shaking his shoulder to wake him. He was to arise, and quickly. The King commanded his presence at the day's hunt. They would move off within the hour. So, haste . . .

Bewildered at this summons and still half-asleep, David sought to make himself presentable at the same time as snatching at the food he was brought. What could this mean? There was no sign of the Duke.

He found his horse saddled and waiting for him in the stableyard, grooms in attendance, and mounted amongst others. Following these round to the front of the mansion, he joined a party of about a score, all very lordly-seeming and dressed in hunting green, but none looking particularly happy nor anticipatory. It was barely seven on the clock.

The silent company, none of whom acknowledged David's presence, had not long to wait. The King came out, at a sort of shambling run, all in green and wearing the same hat, seemingly, that he had worn in bed. He stared round at them all, as though checking up on who was there and who was not, his gaze lingering for a moment on David. He greeted none nor acknowledged the muttered good-mornings of the party. Then helped on to his horse by one of a group of huntsmen who waited apart from the others, he set off, to the blare of hunting-horns.

David took his place at the tail-end of the company.

They rode out of the parkland and into the fairly open forest of old trees, beeches, oaks and elms, which the Duke had declared was part of the ancient hunting-grounds of Enfield Chase, going by grassy rides, the huntsmen on ahead. David noted that the King's riding was as extraordinary as the rest of him, sitting his horse like a sack of meal, slouched and ungainly, strange indeed for a man who loved hunting more than anything else, and boasted that he could rule two kingdoms from his saddle. Jolting along with no bodily spring, and frequently tapping down that high hat, so unsuitable for hunting, he presented a figure of fun – only nobody thought to laugh.

They covered perhaps a couple of miles before one of the huntsmen halted them in a leafy glade, and went into consultation with the King, his fellows no longer in evidence. Presently James turned in the saddle, clearly master of it all, and directed the company to split into three groups, pointing at only three who were to accompany himself. David was surprised to find himself included in this select quartet.

They now trotted down different rides in the wood, the King's four straight ahead, with the chief huntsman.

Another quarter-mile and they paused, where various woodland trails met in a sylvan cartwheel, and another huntsman was waiting. James began to question him.

Hardly had the man answered when there sounded the distant baying of hounds and, high above them, the blare of a hunting-horn. The King nodded and led the way, still mounted, into the thickness of some surrounding bushes, to wait.

Quickly the baying drew nearer, while the horses fidgeted. Then suddenly four fallow deer broke out from cover, two does, a young buck and an older male with a good head of antlers, to race across the open space and disappear down one of the rides. With a shout, James dug in his spurs and was after them, the others following.

David had never hunted like this, on horseback. In the Angus glens there were many deer, not these dappled fallow creatures but larger red stags and hinds, as well as the dainty roe-deer which were his favourite quarry. There he stalked them on foot, or more often on his stomach, with bow and arrow, until he could get within range, if at all, a strenuous and difficult sport, with all the advantages with the deer; or else attended great deer-drives, with little of sport about them but to garner large quantities of venison for the table, where the animals were rounded up over considerable areas of open hillsides by beaters, and driven and coaxed towards narrow funnel-like lanes between turf-banks where marksmen waited to shoot them down as they ran past, or tried to. So this chasing them on horses was new to him, and he wondered at it, for surely the deer were likely to be more fleet of foot than the horses?

At least the chase was exhilarating as the riders pounded along the rides in the greenwood, presently to be overtaken by the racing, baying deerhounds, perhaps a dozen of them, grey, shaggy but long-legged and slender. James jounced and swayed in his saddle, having difficulty with his hat, but keeping up a spanking pace despite that, his companions careful not to get in front of him. There were no signs of the deer now, but presumably they were on the right track since the hounds would be following the scent.

The woodland was criss-crossed by many rides and aisles and, turning down this one and another, David quickly was lost. However, he was merely an onlooker here and followed the others.

The baying of the hounds had grown fainter for a while, but it began to sound nearer again. And then David perceived the point of it all – the wall. It was the same lengthy park enclosure which he had ridden round the day before on his way from Hatfield. Now he saw that its purpose was not only to keep the King's deer from straying and from the attentions of poachers, but to act as the necessary barrier for them to be driven against in the hunt. The wall was too high for the animals to leap, so on reaching it they had to turn left or right. And here the other huntsmen had stationed themselves, in advance, at points along the wall, to turn back the fleeing quarry. So the creatures were trapped within a stretch of the walling, with the hounds there to prevent them breaking back into the wide woodland.

Now, as the animals ran up and down, back and forward, it was the hunters' turn. At their saddle-horns each carried a cross-bow, compact and easily managed weapons firing a foot-long bolt called a quarrel, effective up to about one hundred yards. These were now brought into play and the shooting began – all there heedfully leaving the old buck with the fine head to the King.

Despite all this being so carefully arranged for the marksmen, it still represented a test of skill. The panic-stricken deer racing to and fro along that wall presented no easy target, especially with hounds leaping up at them; and the marksmen themselves, after all their riding, were inevitably somewhat breathless and sitting mounts that stirred and sidled and tossed heads. Not all the quarrels shot found their marks, and those that did did not necessarily kill, although the hounds usually were able to bring down wounded beasts.

James was more effective than some there, his second bolt hitting the old buck in the shoulder and bringing it down. It managed to rise, but two hounds jumped on it and bore it to the ground again. The King let out a whoop of triumph.

One of the does was also down and the other staggering off obviously sore hurt. The hounds would deal with her. But the young buck seemed to be going to get away, with only one hound chasing it. James pointed and yelled at the unedifying sight.

"Jamie Hay, shame on you! Shame! Get it, man, get it! You're failing, Jamie, failing!"

A large bulky man of late middle years muttered something and spurred off after the buck, one of the others joining him. David and one more were left with the King.

James urged his horse forward to where the old buck lay struggling on the grass with the hounds worrying at it. "Davie Gray," he called. "Come, kill me this beast."

Less than eagerly David rode up and dismounted, looking from the animal to his liege lord. "What with, Sire?" he asked. "I have no dirk."

"Nae dirk! You come on the hunt wi' nae dirk?"

"The Duke told me that I must not carry a weapon in Your Majesty's presence . . ."

"Ooh, aye. Well, that's right. But the hunt's different, mind. Here." James drew a dagger from his own belt and handed it down. "Cut its thrapple, man."

David had killed many a deer in his day, but found this task especially distasteful, with those hounds leaping and snarling over the victim. He had to kick them aside to get at the buck, which then struggled to rise, and he had actually to sit on its head, finding the antlers much in the way, before he could bend over to cut its throat, the King giving vehement

99

instructions the while from above. Thankfully he rose, as the creature expired.

James dismounted now. "Gie's that knife," he ordered. Taking the dirk, he bent over the still twitching carcase and, poking into the fur of the pale belly, dug the sharp point in and quite expertly drew the knife down, ripping open the skin. The steaming entrails came heaving, almost bubbling out, smelling strongly.

"Fine! Fine!" the monarch commented. He handed the dagger back to David and stooped further to plunge both hands into the coiling mass of gut, to lift it all out of its gaping cavity into his own arms, drawing the last trailing tubes clear, to dump the unsavoury armful on to the grass nearby, with every appearance of satisfaction.

As David stared, astonished, he was given a further order.

"Here, gie's a hand wi' these boots, man." And James held out one foot. "Off wi' them."

Mystified, David did as he was told, helping to pull off the royal riding-boots. There were no stockings within, and the feet were less than clean.

The King thereupon stepped barefoot into the warm heap of entrails, to tread up and down in it, holding out a hand for David to steady him.

"Guid for the gout, Davie," he informed. "Naething better. Guid for ither ills forby, mind, but best for the gout. Mind it. One day you'll need it yoursel', belike – if you live that long!"

David, pondering that remark in the midst of his surprise at the entire situation, was consoling himself that it sounded as though he was not to be silenced by losing his head immediately, at least, when James, still at the gut-treading, turned his attention to the remaining member of their quartet, who had dismounted to watch – for none might remain up in the saddle when the monarch was down on his feet.

"You, Lionel man, awa' wi' you and gie Jamie Hay a hand wi' his bit buckie that got awa'. He's getting auld, is Jamie, and no' up to it. Forby, he's younger than mysel', the man."

"Yes, Sire," the other, a slender, handsome man of early

middle years, said. "As you say." He turned to mount and ride on.

"Yon's Lionel Cranfield – or Middlesex, as I've made him. A decent-like body."

David had heard that Sir Lionel Cranfield, recently created Earl of Middlesex, was Lord Treasurer of England.

"Aye, well, I want a word wi' you, Davie Gray, a privy word, see you." James stepped out of the guts. "Here, gie's a hand wi' the boots again."

David knelt to assist in the inserting of those distinctly unprepossessing blood-smeared feet back into the boots, seeking not to breathe in the odours. "Yes, Sire."

"Aye." James looked about him. There were only the huntsmen present now, keeping their respectful distance after having driven the hounds away from the deer carcases. "This o' thae letters. You read them. What did you read, man? Gie's the meat o' it. No' a' the words, but the meat, see you."

Straightening up, David sought to condense the contents of those fateful papers, as he had done for the Duke the night before, only still more concisely, all too well aware of the picture he was painting, to a son, of his mother's guilt and folly, and seeking to be not only brief but to sound factual, level-voiced – and dreading the consequences.

James heard him out without many interjections or signs of emotion. When it was finished, came the inevitable, "And yon was all?"

"In the papers that I saw, yes, Highness."

The King was pulling at his wispy beard. "There was naething aboot yon Italian?"

David swallowed. "Which Italian was that, Sire?"

"I think that you ken! The Queen's secretary, the man Rizzio."

So the monarch knew very well what the threat was. For himself, there was no pulling the wool over those so expressive royal eyes. "Not, not in the letters that I read, Your Majesty," David said.

"You say no? Is that the truth, man? I hae means o' winning the truth out o' you, mind! Ooh, aye – plenty means. I got right guid at justifying witches, putting thae ill critturs to

101

the question. I aye got the truth oot o' them, in time. D'you ken how I did it? I had a bit rope tied roond their brows, see you, Davie Gray. Put a dirk through the loop o' the rope, and twisted. Aye, twisted. Done wi' skill, it lifted the scalp off maist effectively, hair and a'. Effective, aye. Sae, speak truth, Davie man.''

"I do, Sire. In nothing that I read was the name Rizzio mentioned.''

"Then . . . was there another letter that you didna see?''

"That I do not know, Sire. I can speak only of what my lord showed me, as he took them out of the casket.''

"But does he *hae* another letter, man?''

"If he has, Sire, he has not shown it to me. Nor told me.'' That was picking words carefully.

For long James stared at him. "I think that *Patrick* had some such. The Maister. And if he had, his son could hae it now.''

David felt that he had to take a chance. "Is it so important, Highness? Are not these letters in the casket sufficient?''

"Sufficient for what, eh? For what, Davie Gray?'' That was quick.

"To, to be important. To Your Majesty. Your royal mother's words . . .''

"My royal mother was a fool!'' James said thickly. "But I'm no'! I am not! As your fine uncle Andrew will discover, laddie! I ken what he's at, if you dinna. But maybe you do? Eh?''

"All I know, Sire, is that my lord sends me to ask if Your Highness desires him to send you these letters? And hopes that you may recognise his leal goodwill in the matter, his faithful duty . . . and perhaps reconsider the matter of the sheriffdom.'' God forgive him that lie – but his head might depend on it.

"So you say, laddie, so you say! Weel, we'll see.'' James turned and waved the waiting huntsman over, leaving David at a loss to know where he stood in the matter, whether the King believed him or not, what was likely to be the outcome.

After a brief conference with the chief huntsman, the King mounted and rode off, without a word to David, who followed on doubtfully, whilst the remaining huntsmen dealt with the carcases.

They returned approximately in the direction they had come until they reached a great clearing in the woodland, which was evidently a recognised meeting-place, for there were already a number of riders waiting here, amongst whom was the Duke of Lennox. These the monarch greeted with mocking salutations, congratulating them on belatedly managing to get out of their beds in time for noonday, and observing that they would have to watch and not fall asleep in the saddle. Then ordering the chief huntsman to blow his horn loud and long in the repetitious rallying-call, he announced that they would proceed to Hensingham Holt for the next hunt – there were reported to be a packet of deer there these days.

Leaving a groom to direct onward other hunters summoned by that horn-blowing, James led off westwards.

David reined over beside Ludovick, to ask whether he should continue with the hunt or return to Theobalds, to be told that since the King had specifically commanded him to attend, he could nowise leave without the royal permission. Moreover he, Ludovick, had been ordered to keep close watch on him meantime, so he had better stay in sight. He had not been thinking of bolting, had he?

David assured him that no such thought had entered his head. He was, he feared, becoming something of a liar.

There was no opportunity for further talk, and the Duke rode forward to be near James.

The hunt proceeded. And continued to proceed for much too long for David Gray, who found this less than enthralling sport. And never once did his peculiar sovereign lord seem to even glance in his direction. It seemed astonishing that anyone so obviously physically inert and unfit as James Stewart should wish, and be able, to keep up this activity hour after hour, day after day.

When he could wean his thoughts away from anxiety over his own mission and future, David found himself being sorry for Ludovick of Lennox, who had to live with this.

8

That evening, when the Duke returned to his quarters from the King's table, he was not long in settling into conference with his visitor. Relaxing, with a beaker of wine, he sighed thankfully.

"No hunting tomorrow," he announced, "Sunday. James observes the Sabbath – thank God! Church is less hard on the bottom and thighs than is the chase, at least!"

David had lost track of the days and did not realise that this was Saturday.

"What happened then, Davie? Between James and yourself today."

"He made me ride with him. And spoke with me, alone, when he had killed his first buck."

"Yes, yes, but to what end? What did he say?"

"He asked what was in the letters. I told him, as I told you last night, my lord."

"And . . .?"

"He did not seem surprised at what I said. Nor greatly interested, even. In the matter of Lord Darnley's death, or other. But asked, as did you, was there nothing else."

"Aye, he would. And when you told him no, what then?"

David hesitated. "He asked after the Italian. Rizzio."

"So-o-o! It came to that, then. I feared so." Ludovick shook his head. "That thrice-damned name!"

David did not speak.

"What did you say to that?"

"I could not tell him anything. Only that David Rizzio's name did not appear in any of the letters I had read."

"And that is the truth?"

"Yes."

"Did it satisfy him?"

"I, I think not. He told me that he was not a fool, again –

although his mother had been! I asked him if Rizzio's name was so important . . ."

"You did! You asked that, man?"

"Why not, my lord? Was he not only the Queen's Italian secretary?"

"Are you so innocent, Davie? I think not. You must know the stories that were put about at the time? That James was not Darnley's son, but Rizzio's."

"That was long years ago. And long forgotten, surely?"

"Not forgotten – by some! All these years it has been a shadow on James's life. The dread of the possible truth of it. And of any proof to confirm it. Such as his mother's admission in writing. These letters."

"Would it be so serious? Now, after all this time? After all, he is still Queen Mary's son."

"Man, Davie, do you not realise? Illegitimacy! For the monarch, it is all but impossible to contemplate. In Scotland, we might just thole it. But here, in England, it would be disaster. Think what the English parliament would make of it! They do not love James, as it is. Ever keep him short of moneys. He is all but at war with them. If they learned that he was illegitimate, it could be the end of all."

"They could not unseat him, surely? Dethrone the King!"

"I do not know as to that. Not in Scotland, no, once crowned. But here? The English succession laws are different, I think. And there are others who could succeed. My cousin Arabella. Even myself, come to that – which God forbid! But, this of Rizzio, if it could be proved, could lead to untold trouble, all but revolution. Can you wonder that James fears it, above all?"

"Then, then . . .?"

"This is what, I believe, your grandsire the Master held over James all those years. And why James paid. Now – again!"

"He believes it true?"

"I do not know. He has never admitted as much, to me or to any, I think. But that is not the point. Even the suggestion that it could be proved, by the Queen's written admission, would be enough to set all ablaze. James would declare that any such admission was a forgery, no doubt – as has been

105

suggested of other of these Casket Letters. But that would not still the uproar. There was the Gunpowder Plot in 1605, two years after James came to Elizabeth's throne. This could be almost as bad."

"*You* believe that there is truth in it, my lord?"

"Heaven knows what to believe! It could be, I suppose. My cousin Darnley was no great lover – some said that he was incapable of fathering a child anyway! The Queen quickly lost all fondness for him. And she was indiscreet and passionate – aye, and beautiful. Forby, Rizzio was much in her confidence, close – and he was stabbed to death in her presence when she was heavy with child, James, with Darnley looking on. It could have been jealousy. Certainly the Perth townsfolk, at the Gowrie affair, believed him Rizzio's son. I was there, and heard them shouting at him as Signor Davie's son. But . . . there were other tales put about by the Queen's enemies. It was the Reformation time, remember, and she was a determined Catholic. So she had no lack of ill-wishers, did poor Mary, the triumphant Protestant clergy in especial. Some suggested that James was a changeling, that Mary's child had died at birth and this was a low-born substitute. Others that he was Bothwell's own brat and that was why Mary had to marry him. There were other stories. Her father James the Fifth's reputation for producing bastards did not help her. So you see the problems. Half her courtiers were in love with her – and the other half hated her for her religion."

David drew a long breath but said nothing.

"Did James say what he intended?" Ludovick went on.

"No. Nothing. He said only that he would see. Nothing else. Do you think, my lord, that he meant me ill when he said, before, that I might have to be silenced? Was he speaking . . . seriously? Did he mean . . .?"

"Who can tell what James means, in much that he says? I know him probably better than any other does, but I am frequently at a loss. He could mean anything by that, or nothing. But, he did, in fact, speak not unkindly of you, Davie, as we rode back from the hunt. He was in a good mood – he had killed another two bucks. He said that you had some wits in your head, and that is praise, for him. And he called you a bonnie lad!"

106

David was taking what comfort he could from that, when he realised that the Duke was looking at him rather oddly. "You mean . . .?" he asked.

"James has, shall we say, a partiality for good-looking young men!"

"Oh. And that is . . . hopeful?"

"It depends on what you would mean by hopeful! Some would say otherwise – but not all, I suppose, not all. He can invite handsome young men into his bed, you see!"

"Lord!" David stared, appalled.

"I do not say that this may be your fate! But – you are warned."

"Save us – you mean that? He is . . . that way?"

"Not always. And not so much now as he used to be. He grows older, like the rest of us. And now, of course, he has Steenie – George Villiers, whom he has made Marquis of Buckingham, no less! And Steenie is of a, a jealous disposition, see you!"

"Lord!" David said again. "This is beyond all. What am I to do, then, if, if he . . .?"

"In the circumstances, I do not say that is likely, Davie. But I would advise that you do not give him, shall we say, encouragement! If he shows signs of approval of you."

"But, how am I to behave, then? On the one hand, I might be sent to the Tower! And on the other, this . . .! Would it not be better if I just fled? Secretly. Back to Scotland. Right away . . ."

"And get *me* into trouble! James placed you in my hands and keeping. Forby, he is King of Scots, still, as well as monarch here. So he could send after you, have his people in Scotland apprehend you there. No, that would not serve. We will have to play it differently. Mind, he may not fancy you that way at all. And once Buckingham returns, there may be less danger. James dotes on his Steenie. But then, of course, there could be a different danger – if *he*, Buckingham, thought that James was becoming too interested in you." Ludovick shook his head. "Probably I am making too much of this. Do not look so alarmed, man. Belike James did not mean anything of special significance when he told me that you were a bonnie lad – but passing a remark. However, now you are on your guard . . ."

David gulped down his wine, although scarcely aware of it. Was ever anyone in such a pickle? In danger of his life, for knowing a dire royal secret. Of possible conviction of treason for seeking to coerce the King. In danger of the monarch's unwelcome and unnatural attentions and possible advances, yet entirely in his hands. And also, it seemed, of the possible jealous hostility of the reigning favourite! Why, oh why, had he ever left Scotland?

"This Buckingham?" he got out. "I have heard of him. Is he not here, at court?"

"Not at the moment. He is down at Greenwich Palace, with the Prince of Wales. Charles. But he is expected to return at any time. Both of them. James has never greatly loved nor trusted his remaining son. It was different with Henry, who died. So he ordered Steenie to take Charles in hand, to keep an eye on him, guide him. And this policy has been almost over-successful. Steenie, who did not like Charles either, at first, is now his greatest, almost his only, friend. They are very close – not to James's entire approval. Charles is a strange, moody young man, stiff, very unlike his father. And as James grows older, Steenie, I swear, sees that he will be able to dominate the next monarch, and so hold the power in this realm."

"You do not like this man Buckingham, my lord?"

"Not greatly. I mislike his undue influence with James. He is clever, to be sure, and mighty good-looking. But over-ambitious and lacking scruple. I, for one, cannot trust him."

"And he is not going to like *me* – if the King shows me any favour? So he could advise that I be . . . silenced, perhaps!"

Ludovick did not answer.

"I am beset, then, every way. The King gave you no hint as to his intentions towards me, my lord? In the matter of the letters."

"None. He keeps his own counsel."

"Would it serve anything if I approached him again? Said that I should return to Scotland with his message for Lord Gray? Seek permission to leave. Even if he gave me no

108

decision on it all, at least I would escape from this coil. And, and my lord still has the letters!"

"You could attempt it. Whether James would permit it, I do not know."

"Can you gain me audience again, my lord?"

"Probably, yes. I can always approach him, and can take you with me – although he may dismiss you. I will do what I can, Davie, I assure you. At least it will give me something other than lobsters to think on!"

"Lobsters? *Lobsters*, my lord?"

"Aye, lobsters and salmon-fish. That is my concern, these days, believe it or not! The lobster and salmon-fish monopoly."

"But . . . why you? A duke . . .!"

"It is Steenie Villiers again – or at least his brother. You will know of these monopolies? They do not have them in Scotland. But here, yes. There are monopolies in commodities of all sorts, in the power of the Crown. Paper, wines, cloths, gunpowder, coals even, and the rest. None may trade in these, nor bring them into the country, without paying dues to the Crown, or to those to whom the Crown grants the monopoly. They are a great source of wealth, so much sought after. Especially by the Villiers family! Steenie works on James to grant any available to his own relatives and friends. And that for lobsters and salmon he has granted to John Villiers, Steenie's half-witted brother, whom James has made the Viscount Purbeck."

"A mercy – lobsters! I was dealing with lobsters but a day or two back! Or at least with one lobster and a horse!"

"A horse? I would not have thought . . .? Never heed. It is not horses which are my trouble, but Homes rather. And others. Folk who catch and supply the lobsters and salmon, from Scotland in especial. There is a great traffic in them southwards. There are objections to the high charges that Steenie's brother is imposing on them, those coming into England from Scotland particularly. For some coastal lairds lobsters and salmon represent much of their revenues, it seems. They are protesting to the King, since it is a royal monopoly. Nor do I blame them . . ."

"Homes, you say? Can it possibly be . . .?"

'Homes, yes, from the Merse coast – great lobster-grounds, I believe. And from the Tweed valley, for the salmon. Others, to be sure, many others. From the Fife shores and the Tay. Are you not affected in Angus, at Broughty?"

"We do not catch many lobsters, no. Some salmon – but these we sell in Dundee town. We send none to England. But, this is astonishing, scarcely to be believed. I have just come from Merse, from Bilsdean, near to Fast, a Home house. Where they do fish for lobster and salmon. I knew that the laird had come to London. They said to seek the King's favour, in some respect. But I had no notion of this. They did not say what."

"Home of Bilsdean, yes – he is one of the protesters. Also Aytoun and Linthill and Gunsgreen. Aye, and Paxton and Whiteadder and Blackadder."

"I know of all these Home lairds. But why you, my lord? Why are you concerned?"

"James turns to me to deal with his problems, frequently. He cannot ask Buckingham to smooth it over, since he it was who got the monopoly for his brother. And James does not himself wish to seem to counter his favourite. So *I* am expected to put all to rights – and I have no notion as to how to do it! I tell you, it is not all joy and gladness to be cousin to a king – especially such a one as James!"

"I can see that." But David had his own problems to consider. "What am I to do now, then?" he wondered.

"You can only wait to see what James decides. I would advise you not to try to press your case with him – he does not like being importuned. But keep yourself before him, so that he is aware of you. I can see to that, I think. Tomorrow, come to church with me – James approves of church-going."

David retired to bed, once again to ponder deeply before he slept. Just where did his prime loyalty lie? He had come here as representing his uncle, employer and head of his family. But the King was his liege lord. And now the Duke was becoming involved, his cousin's father. Was it *right* that his sovereign should be threatened with this of Rizzio? And apparently dire upheaval in the kingdom if the secret came to be published abroad. But in fact there was *no* written proof, only the assumption and fear of such. His uncle held no such letter. So all this was in effect a fraud, and he the reluctant minion of it.

He was to go to church tomorrow, go to worship God. What would be God's will in this matter? His uncle had certainly suffered injury by the King's act; but was he justified in seeking to right it by such methods? And this of the King's unnatural fondness for young men. To escape the possibility of that made nonsense of any loyalty, surely . . .?

Church-going next forenoon was a new experience for David, his regular attendance at the parish kirk of Broughty nowise preparing him for the procedure at Theobalds, which had its own royal chapel in another wing of the huge mansion. It was a Church of England service, of course, with everything more elaborate and formal, as laid down by the Book of Common Prayer – save for some surprising innovations here – and the clergy robed in colourful and varied vestments, not in the plain black with white bands of the Scots presbyterian ministers. But it was not so much these aspects as the attitudes and behaviour of the presumed worshippers which surprised him and made him wonder about the impact of the Reformation here in England.

The chapel was packed, for the King insisted that all servants not on duty, all guards likewise, and all officials attended, as well as expecting courtiers, visiting notables and guests to put in an appearance. So Dand Graham the manservant followed the Duke and David. In the crowded church, which was as noisy with talk and laughter as any fair, Ludovick apologised for having to leave David with Graham, for he himself had to share the royal gallery, and of course he could not instal David there without express command of James. So they went to sit amongst a group of fairly senior officials in a side aisle – and were eyed somewhat askance by these, all of whom were considerably better dressed than David was, who had to wear only what he had ridden south in. The Duke went on, to mount steps to a raised enclosure decorated with the royal arms, actually at the right side of the chancel and near the altar, where there were about a dozen handsomely upholstered seats, some already occupied. David noted that here everyone sat, where in Scots churches

111

most still stood, although stools were frequently brought in by women and the elderly.

Dand Graham helpfully pointed out and named various celebrities, including some in the royal gallery, most, in the visitor's opinion, grossly over-dressed, these including Don Diego, Count of Gondomar, the Spanish Ambassador, an especial crony of the King's; the Earl of Pembroke, the Lord Chamberlain; the big man, Jamie Hay of the hunting-party – who it seemed was Lord Doncaster; Sir George Calvert, the Secretary of State; and Cranfield, Earl of Middlesex, the Treasurer, whom David had already met. There were not many women present, except amongst the servants, and the only one in the royal gallery was a hard-faced and much-painted female of uncertain age, whom Graham named as Elizabeth, Countess of Buckingham, the mother of the favourite, to whom the King had given that title when her eldest son was raised to the rank of marquis. Beside her sat a seedy-looking, simpering young exquisite with a very receding chin, identified as her second son, John Villiers, Viscount Purbeck, of the lobster connection. All this information had to be shouted at David to be heard above the general unseemly hubbub.

An alternative and more suitable sound presently had the effect of lessening the clatter of tongues in the chapel: singing; and in at a side doorway filed a choir of singing boys behind a cross-bearer, followed by acolytes and clergy, all robed, and finally by a magnificent figure attired in alb, chasuble, cope and mitre and bearing a golden crozier, whom Graham declared was Dr John King, Bishop of London. These took their places in the chancel, the Bishop and senior clergy before the altar, the choir and acolytes at the other side from the royal gallery. All remained standing, and the congregation accepted this as the signal to get to their feet also.

Two trumpeters came in and blew a resounding fanfare, which effectively stilled any remaining chatter. Before it was finished, the lone and ungainly figure of James himself came in, almost at a shambling trot, untidily dressed and still wearing his favourite high hat with the nodding feather. Everyone, clergy included, bowed deeply.

In his odd progress across the transept, the monarch halted

where worshippers normally turned and bowed towards the altar. But he turned the other way, to stare for long moments at the congregation, as though checking on who was there and who was not. "Aye!" he said eventually, and that sounded critical rather than approving. Then looking towards the altar, he waved a hand and nodded, scarcely any genuflection but rather an order to let the service commence, and trotted on and up the steps to the gallery, to his throne-like chair and sat down, tapping his hat more firmly in place.

All save the celebrants sat down, with a corporate sigh.

"He keeps his hat on. Even in church!" David whispered to Dand.

"Och, aye. He's feart o' bats. They say a bat made droppings on his head, one time. So he aye keeps a hat on."

The Bishop made an introductory pronouncement, apparently as much to the monarch as to the Almighty, to which James waved another acknowledgment. Then that dignitary retired to his own high chair at the side of the altar and two other priests moved up, glancing towards the gallery. James flicked a hand. Clearly the King was very much in charge.

The service of hymns, prayers, chants, responses and Bible-readings proceeded, per James's own prayer-book, with himself sometimes standing when others did, sometimes not. Once, during a reading, he turned round and had a chat with the Countess of Buckingham. At the psalm, number 21, he rose, to gaze all round the church, peering, as though to ensure that everyone was singing and paying due heed, before, apparently satisfied, himself sitting down again.

"It's aye the same psalm," Dand muttered.

David quickly perceived why. It was all about the King's might and glory and wisdom, presumably King David's. *The King shall joy in Thy strength, O Lord . . . For Thou preventest him with the blessings of goodness: Thou settest a crown of pure gold on his head . . . His glory is great in Thy salvation: Honour and Majesty hast Thou laid upon him.* None sang it more heartily than James Stewart.

It was at the sermon, however, that the monarch really demonstrated his very individual ideas about public worship. The Bishop of London, in the pulpit now, took as his text the story of Lazarus and the link with leprosy, pointing out that this dread disease was still by no means eradicated in England, indeed was on the increase in certain areas, London not least. It was not enough to say that this was the divine judgment upon the sufferers, the finger of God upon them for their sins, as all too often had been the attitude in the past; and the driving of the lepers out from the company of men, not to come within a mile of any community, as was still the usage. This was, the Bishop proclaimed, inhuman behaviour unworthy of a Christian nation . . .

At this point the King applauded vigorously by beating his hand on the arm of his throne, and called out, "Aye! Aye!"

Presumably encouraged, the preacher went on to say that he had sought, in the House of Lords, to have reform in this matter initiated, and to have lazar-houses set up throughout the kingdom for the care of such unfortunates, so far, sadly, without result . . .

"Shame! Shame!" James cried, and turned round to glare at such members of the Upper House as he could readily identify, including the Lords Pembroke, Middlesex, Doncaster, Purbeck and even the Duke of Lennox.

The Bishop bowed. At present, he resumed, the only authority to concern itself with the care of lepers was that ancient Order of Chivalry, the Knights of St Lazarus of Jerusalem, to which Order he had the honour to belong. These knights had hospices and refuges in various parts of His Majesty's realm, with their centre at Burton St Lazars. But these places were greatly insufficient for the task, owing to the Order's lack of moneys, and it was his strong conviction that the Order should be assisted in this excellent Christian work by moneys from the Treasury . . .

"Hech, hech, Johnny King! Bide a wee! Bide a wee!" the King interrupted. "My Treasury's gey near empty. Is it no', Lionel man?" He turned to Middlesex, the Treasurer. "Yon parliament o' yours will no' provide me wi' siller, as is their duty, aye their duty. It's no' just leper-folk they should be finding siller for, it's their sovereign's Treasury. It's a right scandal!"

This declaration occasioned a pause in the sermon, the preacher looking uncertain.

James wagged a finger at him. "Forby, if it's siller for the lepers you're after, Johnny, what about the Church, eh? The Church has got plenties, aye plenties, I'm told. Thae Church Commissioners could spare a pickle siller for the leper-bodies, I'm thinking. Aye, for was it no' the Church which made a' thae laws and rules about lepers being God's outcasts and civilly deid, aye deid, man! Their wives widows! So your Church has a right responsibility in the maitter. In Scotland, we got a' that put to rights at the Reformation, mind. The Scots parliament now kens what's what."

The Bishop, presumably stung, was a brave man. "But in Scotland, Sire, I am told that there is, or was, only the one leper hospice set up by the Order of St Lazarus. That at a town called Lithgow, I think . . ."

"Na, na, Johnny King, that's whaur you're wrang! Your English ignorance, just! There were plenties o' lazar-houses – still are. Only they're no' named after St Lazarus. See you, in Scotland we dinna pronounce the letter Z as you do. We dinna say the name Menzies as that, but as Meengis. Aye, and Dalziel is Dee-ell. So, what d'you mak o' Lazarus, eh? Laarus – St Laarus. Aye, and that's become St Lawrence, or whiles, St Leonards. If you look for a place called St Lawrence or St Leonards or the like a mile ootside a town or village, yon's been a St Lazarus hospice just. And there's plenties o' them. We didna treat oor lepers sae ill as you did, and dae, here – na, na. Mind, King Robert the Bruce had the notion he had the leprosy and encouraged the knights of St Lazarus."

James beamed around on all, obviously pleased at being able to educate all present.

The Bishop coughed, and resumed. His teaching was to the effect that sickness, pains, incapacities and other afflictions of mankind were not, as so often assumed, God's specific judgment on individuals, but could even be a means of grace, in the patient bearing of which the afflicted person could come closer to his or her Creator, and serve as an example to others. It was not only lepers. Think of the blind, the deaf and dumb, the malformed, the lame, even the witless and the poor. In Heaven, no doubt, there were none of these afflictions; but here they were sent to try us – but to try, that is to test, not only the sufferers but all who came in touch with them. For the judgment of God hereafter would be not upon

115

the victims but upon those who showed them no love, no pity, no help, no understanding. On these would the finger of God be placed, hereafter not on the victims . . .

At this James nodded sagely, tipped his hat down over his brow, and leaned back, apparently to sleep.

The preacher was able to proceed uninterrupted.

But not for long. For presently there was something of a disturbance at the main door of the chapel, which was opened less than quietly and two men came in. Both were dressed in the height of fashion, both carrying wide-brimmed, ostrich-feathered hats, both fairly tall and slender. But there the similarity ended. One was not so much handsome as beautiful, fair-haired, elegant, walking with a confident swagger and smiling upon all; the other dark, good-looking in a long-featured way save for some weakness about the mouth and chin, large expressive eyes looking distinctly mournful, and walking stiffly just half a pace behind his companion.

The King sat up and pushed back his hat, staring. Then he jumped to his feet. "Steenie!" he cried. "Steenie, my ain comfort and joy! Aye, my cosset Steenie! You're back! Och, it's guid to see you. I've missed you, I have so. Aye, and you too, Charlie, to be sure. Aye, you too. Here's a right relish! Come you, come up and let's tak a hand o' you!" And James pushed along to the gallery steps.

The Marquis of Buckingham flourished a multiple bow, laughing, hat describing circles, while Charles, Prince of Wales, jerked his head briefly.

With the monarch standing, all others must rise also, while the Bishop halted in his discourse, lips pursed, episcopal features carefully stilled.

Buckingham came forward to mount the steps and be embraced by his liege lord, hats somewhat in the way. Taking him by the hand, James led him to the chair nearest his own – which happened to have been occupied by Duke Ludovick who, grinning, moved aside. As an afterthought, the King turned back to his son, patted his shoulder and, still holding on to Buckingham, sat down. Thankfully everyone else sat again, although there was some stumbling about in the royal gallery where Prince Charles had to be found a seat.

The preacher waited patiently.

116

James promptly engaged in animated conversation with his Steenie, with no attempt to lower his voice, to the effect that he had been suffering with the gout, bad, bad, that the physicians were ignorant mountebanks, that he had been sleeping badly – but all would be well now that his beloved Dog Steenie was back. He stroked Buckingham's cheek fondly, and then, turning towards the pulpit, signed for the service to proceed.

Probably wisely, Bishop John wound up his sermon expeditiously and announced the final hymn.

"Yon's saved us a hauf-hour!" Dand Graham confided appreciatively.

"I've never seen the like!" he was informed.

Outside they were soon joined by the Duke, for James had no eyes nor time for any other than his Steenie. Ludovick smiled at David.

"I hope divine service did your soul good, Davie," he said. "We are all in need of mercy, I think! Except James, of course."

"I would not have believed it," the younger man admitted. "To behave so in church! It was so, so undignified as well as shameless."

"Ah, but James is the Lord's Anointed, you see. He requires no dignity, he says – that is for lesser folk! He sees himself as on the closer terms with the Almighty than such as bishops and the like." They were walking back to the ducal quarters. "I think that I will not be required for Sunday dinner with His Majesty today – it will be a private feast of love with Buckingham! What do you think of him, now that you have seen our Steenie?"

"I see that he will be a difficult man to cross, in the circumstances."

"Aye, that is the problem. Why I am in this trouble with the lobsters and salmon-fish! And other matters. James wants the trouble smoothed out, over this, with the Homes and others – but will not have his Steenie offended. It is a sorry sight to see a man of his years and wits – for our liege lord does not lack wits – so doting on such as George Villiers."

"He, the King, treats Prince Charles as though he is of little import beside the other. It seems very strange."

"James has never been very fond of Charles, unlike Henry Frederick, the son who died – he was devoted to him. Charles is a strange character, moody, seldom smiling, suspicious, silent; indeed he did not speak a word until his fifth year, and it was feared that he was dumb. A more different man from his father would be hard to find. But he has his virtues – in fact, he is very virtuous! Which makes it strange that he has taken to Buckingham as he has done. What Charles thinks of his father's court, only God knows! That church service today must have troubled him, such of it as he saw, for he is very religious. And he has the dignity which his sire lacks so notably."

It was over the simple meal which Graham improvised for them that Ludovick came out with his suggestion.

"I have been thinking about your problem, Davie, and to some extent, my own. And wondered whether there might be some answer that we could contrive. James will now be so taken up with Steenie's presence that, for a day or two at least, he is not likely so much as to look in your direction, nor decide what to do about your uncle's mission. Mind, he will still be holding me responsible for you. I know James. But it occurs to me that you might use a couple of days or so possibly to some good effect. I could not go with you, but if you went to London, something might be achieved."

"London? Alone?"

"Yes. To Whitehall Palace. You tell me that you are friendly with Home of Bilsdean. He and the other complainers about this monopoly are there, hopefully awaiting the King's pleasure. He did not invite *them* on this hunting-party!"

"I cannot say that I am friendly with Bilsdean, my lord – indeed I have never met him. It is his daughters that I know . . ."

"Ha, is that the way the wind blows!"

"No, no, nothing like that! She, or they, have been kind to me, that is all. Barbara Home helped me to find the letters at Fast. Fast belongs to her father now."

"Well, at least you are acquainted with his family and house, know his circumstances – as I do not. If you would go speak with him, and the others, act as *my* emissary, try to discover what terms they might agree to, how far they would go to meet John Villiers's demands, then possibly we might get nearer to some arrangement, some dealing, which would not upset the Villiers clan too greatly – and therefore James. And, Davie, if you could achieve that, not only I would be grateful, but the King. And that could help with the other matter."

"Ye-e-es. Although I do not see what *I* can do . . ."

"Use your wits, man. That is all. You have shown plainly enough that you *have* wits – even James conceded that. Something must be attempted. And I cannot be seen to be directly involved; there are some disadvantages in being the only duke in the realm, and the King's cousin."

"Very well. But I do not see why it is all so important? I understand the lairds' anxiety, with much of their living at stake. But why the King, and therefore yourself?"

"Parliament, lad, parliament, that is why these complainers are threatening to protest to parliament . . . not only on this of the lobsters and salmon but on the entire monopoly system – and two of them, I am told, are members of the *Scottish* parliament. And that is the last thing that James wants, particularly at this present. He has long been at war with his English parliament, although not with the Scots one, and as you know, they deny him the funds he needs to rule, one reason for his setting up of these monopolies, and why he sells knighthoods and even peerages, and other unsuitable ploys. James is ever short of money. He is extravagant, of course – but the monarch of two great kingdoms should not be reduced to such straits."

"And could the parliament here cancel these monopolies?"

"Middlesex, the Treasurer, thinks that they could, if sufficiently determined to do so. But it is not only that. James is seeking to woo parliament over to this of a French match for Charles . . ."

"French? I thought that it was to be a Spanish match?"

"No, no, that is over and done with. Have you not heard? The Spanish negotiations broke down. Buckingham and Charles himself went secretly to Spain, to try to arrange it all – a winter-time folly! Parliament was against it, but James was eager – for Spain is the wealthiest nation in Christendom, with all the treasure of the Americas flowing in, and the Infanta was to bring him a huge dowry. Also, if England and Spain were in alliance, it could be the saving of James's son-in-law, Frederick, Elector of the Palatinate and King of Bohemia, whom the Spaniards have unseated. That is James's daughter Elizabeth's husband. But all foundered on the King of Spain's insistence that it must be a Catholic wedding and that any offspring of the marriage must be reared as Catholics. England's Protestant parliament would not hear of that. So Buckingham and Charles came home empty-handed."

"I had not heard of this."

"Yet Scotland ought to be concerned in the matter, for one day Charles will be King of Scots also. Anyway, now James, who sees himself as the arbiter and peace-maker of Christendom, has this new ploy – a French match instead of a Spanish. King Henry of France has a daughter, Henrietta Maria, and James now wants her as Princess of Wales. She would not bring so great a dowry as the Infanta of Spain, but it would be something large – and James has personal debts of £900,000! It would be a good match enough. And France could act as a buffer between Spain and the Palatinate and Bohemia, for Spain would not want to go to war with France *and* England both. So if they were allied, Elizabeth and her husband would be given a breathing-space . . ."

"But France is a Catholic nation also. Would the same not apply? About a Catholic marriage."

"James believes otherwise. He says that the French Ambassador has assured him that there would be no pressure to rear any children of such a marriage as Catholics. France is by no means so fervidly Catholic as is Spain. So James is seeking to gain his parliament's approval of this proposed match – and it is touch-and-go, for they do not really want a Catholic marriage at all. To fall out with the parliamentarians over this of monopolies now would be fatal. So you see the problems? There must be no clash between King and legislature meantime, if at all possible."

"Can the King not tell Buckingham that, then?"

"Well may you ask. But Steenie is James's weakest point. You saw how he dotes on him. So, if you can do anything to help in this broil, James will be grateful, nothing more sure."

David shrugged. "Very well, my lord. I will go to London, do what I can. Although I cannot believe that I can achieve much. Someone as lowly as I am, and uninformed. These lairds and other complainers – are they likely to listen to me?"

"As you come from me, they will, I think. Make the most of our relationship. We are not truly kin, but my son is your cousin by blood."

"Both bastards! When, then, shall I go?"

"Now, I would say. If you ride this afternoon, you can be at Whitehall this night. It is but a score of miles. I will lend you Dand Graham. I will make shift to do without him for a couple of days; he will guide you in London, take you to my quarters in Whitehall. But – do not stay away longer than two days, Davie, or James will notice your absence. And we will still require to deal with John Villiers when you get back. Before we can put anything before the King."

"If there is anything to put . . .!"

9

David rode southwards again that afternoon, with mixed feelings. It was good to get away from the strange and strained atmosphere at Theobalds, and fears as to the decisions of his unpredictable monarch. But the sense of inadequacy regarding what he was about to attempt was strong upon him – and if he had to come back to Theobalds empty-handed, he would be the worse off.

However it was good to be riding free meantime, and he was interested to see how the countryside grew still more populous as they neared London. They went by Hatfield and Barnet and Finchley, to reach Hampstead and its heath. Far ahead now the towers and spires and smoke of the city loomed, a barrier left and right as far as eye could see. David knew a tremor of excitement, despite his apprehensions. After all, this was the greatest city he was ever likely to see.

But when, after Euston Park, they actually entered the confines of London town, it was not its size and fame which preoccupied him so much as its smells and suffocating airlessness this summer evening. Never had he experienced such prevailing stench, of excrement, animal and human, of drainage or the lack of it, of unwashed bodies, of decaying matter, and every sort of stink that man and beast could make, all worsened by the towering, close-set wooden housing, each storey projecting above that below so that those on either sides of the narrow streets and lanes all but met, denying light and air to all beneath. Edinburgh and Dundee had their smells and garbage, but the Scots cities were not flat, and cleansing winds off hills and sea swept through them; but here no winds penetrated. David all but choked, to Dand Graham's amusement. He would get used to it, he was assured.

Sheer numbers of people he would have to get used to also, and lively, noisy people, for the streets were thronged this Sunday evening, and folk leaned out of windows everywhere, gossiping and calling, children playing and shouting, dogs barking, poultry clucking in the streets, even pigs snorting and grunting amongst the rubbish. The two horsemen had difficulty in threading their way through it all, and David's mount, unused to such congestion, grew very nervous, especially when jeering children threw sticks and filth, to the amusement of their elders.

David was thankful that he was escorted by Dand, for he feared that he would never have found his way alone through this maze of streets to Whitehall, and, from the attitude of the inhabitants, doubted whether he would have received acceptable direction. When at length they reached the Thames, a noble river used apparently as a sewer and depository for the great city's refuse, they turned off left-handed up a wider avenue, with finer buildings, mainly now of stone. At least there was no difficulty in identifying the palace, once they reached its vicinity, for it was almost like a small town of its own, a vast rambling establishment, built obviously at various periods, surrounded by fine gardens and approached through an extensive tilting-yard. An extraordinary feature of this last was the collection of no fewer than thirty-four tall stone pillars, each topped by a heraldic beast, the significance of which eluded the visitor.

It was as well here, also, that Dand Graham was present, for David doubted whether a lone and undistinguished-looking young man such as himself would ever have got past the host of guards, haughty servitors and officials who thronged the place and held every entrance and doorway. But Dand went straight to one of the many wings of the palace, with its own stabling, domestic quarters and even private garden, where he was well known and accepted without question. David noted that the stable-lads who attended to their horses, and some of the guards here, had Scots voices.

Compared with the almost humble quarters Duke Ludovick occupied at Theobalds Park, his suite of rooms here was handsome and commodious. Dand said that his master shared this wing with two other important Scots, the King's

123

Master of Requests, Sir William Alexander of Menstrie, and the Lord Doncaster, who David had met at the hunting. Hence the Scots servants.

Installed in the finest bedroom it had ever been his lot to occupy, David was thereafter conducted down to the kitchen premises to partake of an excellent meal, better than any he had had at Theobalds. Clearly the servants here knew how to look after themselves. He asked Dand about where he was to find the objects of this visit, the monopolies complainers, since, with only two days to go, the sooner that he set about his awkward task the better. For once that useful man could not guide him; but he suggested that, if anyone knew, Sir Will Alexander would, as Master of Requests, for apparently it was through this official that all approaches to the monarch for concessions, privileges, indulgences and the like must be channelled, as the title implied. And he had his chambers in this wing. Dand would go and discover whether Sir Will was in, and if he would see the Duke's emissary.

David was surprised, presently, when Dand brought back into these scullions' premises a notably well-dressed and courtly elegant, but who seemed genially at ease with the servants, addressing them by name. He came over to the visitor, and held out his hand.

"I am Alexander of Menstrie," he said pleasantly. "Dand here tells me that you are kin to the Duke of Lennox – and therefore ought to be a friend of my own! Welcome to Whitehall!"

Sir William was a youngish man of good looks and graceful bearing, with a noticeable and almost musical lilt to his voice which had David wondering. He sat down at the table, and Dand brought him a glass of wine.

"I am no true kin to the Duke," David hastened to tell him. "But Mary Gray is my aunt, so that her son by the Duke is my cousin, Sir John Stewart of Methven."

"Better and better!" the other exclaimed. "Sir John was, and is, my very good friend. We had many a ploy together when he was here at court. Would that he was still here – although no doubt he has chosen the better course. Perhaps I too should return to Scotland and till my acres in the Ochil foothills?"

124

"The Ochils? I would have thought that your hills were higher than the Ochils, Sir William," David said. "By your voice I would have said that you were from the Highlands."

"You have a keen ear, friend. Yes, I am of Highland blood. My grandsire was MacAlister of the Loup, in Argyll. He came to the Lowlands with the Earl of Argyll when that one became Chancellor, and married the heiress of Menstrie, near to Stirling. And there I was born. But we spoke the Gaelic much at Menstrie and I was reared amongst Highland folk. Alexander is but the English form of Alister. So there you have my confession! Now, how can I serve you?"

"It is this of the complainers against the monopolies, Sir William. The King has put the matter in the hands of the Duke, and wishes the least possible trouble in it all, you understand. Because of the Marquis of Buckingham's brother. The Duke has sent me to speak with these complainers, for I know Bilsdean and the Merse coast. I do not know Home of Bilsdean himself, but I know his, his family."

"I see." Alexander looked at him thoughtfully. "And what do you hope to achieve in this, my friend? These Merse lairds have been here for all but a month, and nothing to effect has been accomplished, so far as I know. Has the King sent new proposals? Or the Duke, shall we say?"

"No-o-o. But he thinks that if I was to talk it all over with them, we might come to some . . . arrangement."

"M'mm. But – why you? Since this is an issue between these complainers and the new Lord Purbeck. With all respect, my friend, what can *you* do if John Villiers will not relent on the monopoly charges he has set out? These salmon lairds are determined, and threaten to appeal to parliament here if the charges are not amended."

"So the Duke said. I do not know what I can suggest," David admitted helplessly. "But there must be some way out."

"I think Duke Ludovick should be seeking an answer at *his* end, not this! Working on Villiers himself. He it is who is being difficult. Making his charges far too high for the trade in salmon. But he holds the monopoly, and it is an offence under the law for the fishermen to sell their fish to traders without paying the tax. In England, that is, of course, not in Scotland."

"Then why is it that it is the Scots lairds who are here protesting? There must be many more English proprietors of fishings who resent it equally?"

"Not equally, no. For the charge on each stone of fish is not so very large – one penny, as I understand it. That sounds little enough for Villiers, but in the many thousands of stones caught and sold each season all over the country that adds up to a goodly sum. Even after the collectors have had their share. So the English fishers are not too greatly concerned, although they do not like it. But the Scots, now – they have to pay much more. Import duty. Because *their* fish come across the Border, from another realm, Villiers charges four times as much. And these Merse and Tweedside lairds apparently have always sent much of their very great catch across into England. The North of England eats largely Tweed salmon. As to lobsters, I do not know. And Scotland has many other salmon rivers to supply its cities and people. My own Menstrie land sits on the upper Forth and I sell my salmon in Stirling and Alloa. So these southern lairds have to send their trade to England, there being little for them northwards."

"But does not the King make much of there being now but one United Kingdom of Britain? So this of an import duty from Scotland is surely against his wishes? Keeping his kingdoms separate."

"No doubt. But James, in his present state, will do nothing to offend the Villiers family – there's the folly of it! And so long as there are the two parliaments, two different codes of law and so on, they in fact do remain two nations – for which I for one thank God!" Alexander smiled. "I have no wish to become an Englishman, even though I do eat their bread here!"

David sighed. "What I can do in this coil, I do not know. But the Duke sent me to try, and I must make the attempt. Can you tell me, sir, where I can find these Merse lairds?"

"That at least is not difficult. They are here, in Whitehall Palace. There is a part of it set aside for the King's guests. James, whatever else, is not mean, especially to visiting Scots, for he still has a fondness for his old countrymen. Indeed

126

this guests' wing is known as Scotch Corner! You will, I think, find your quarry there. See you, I will take you there myself."

"You are kind . . ."

David was led, then, by endless corridors, up and down stairs, through galleries, rooms and salons, some empty, some thronged with finely-clad folk, many of whom Alexander greeted or waved to, a most evidently friendly man. David quickly lost all sense of direction. It occurred to him that if the King had to pay for all this, keep these crowds of courtiers fed and housed, he would be better keeping his monopolies to himself, not handing them out to favourites. Small wonder if the Treasury was apt to be empty.

At length they came, across a stretch of garden, to a large chamber, almost a hall, where music was being played by a group of instrumentalists to many men and a few women who sat at tables, drinking, dicing or playing cards, some just talking, some asleep. It did not take long for David to recognise that many of the voices were Scots.

Sir William paused to survey that scene, and then, pointing, started to weave his way between the tables and benches, nodding right and left, David following. He approached a group of perhaps a dozen men who sat around a large table at the far side of the salon, and there took David's arm, to introduce him.

"A good evening to you, gentlemen," he said amiably. "I hope that you are comfortable? While you await His Majesty's pleasure. Here is a fellow-Scot come seeking you – David Gray, from Broughty in Angus. He comes, at this present, from the Duke of Lennox. I commend him to your company." He smiled to David, and sauntered off.

That young man eyed the group doubtfully, and was eyed equally so by the seated men. None of them were younger than early middle-age, all were well dressed in good, sober broadcloth, although none in the elaborate and colourful garb favoured by most of the palace denizens. No hearty welcome was evident.

"Am I right in believing that you, or some of you, are lairds from the Merse lands, here to seek some, some betterment in the lobster and salmon monopoly, sirs?" he got out thickly,

127

all too well aware of his comparative youth and undistinguished attire. "Amongst other things, no doubt."

There were curt nods around that table.

"I am sent by the Duke of Lennox to speak with you on this matter of the monopoly, gentlemen. To ascertain your, your attitudes. Bearing in mind that this is a delicate and difficult business. If any good is to come of it, there must be some . . . arrangement."

"Tell that to King Jamie's catamite!" one of them jerked.

"Has the Duke anything new to offer?" another asked. "And who are you that he sends? A beardless lad – and a Gray, from Angus! Not one of the *Lord* Gray's house?"

"In bastardy, yes, sir. I am kin to the Duke – also in bastardy! But that is not important, is it?"

There were some faint smiles at that. One of the company, a heavily-built man of rugged good looks, moved aside a little on his bench.

"Come, sit, and have a beaker of wine with us, at least," he said.

"Thank you, sir." David sat down. "The Duke is scarcely in a position to *offer* anything," he said carefully. "Save his good offices. For he has some sympathy with your complaints, gentlemen."

"We require more than sympathy!" an elderly man declared flatly. "This monopoly is an iniquity. They all are. But we are here concerned with salmon and lobsters. We have petitioned the King, but got no satisfaction. We have sought to discuss it with this Lord Purbeck, but he will not see us. Has the Duke of Lennox anything better for us? I am Home of Paxton, with much fishery in the Tweed."

"At least *he* is prepared to discuss the issue, sir," David pointed out. "And he is close to the King."

"Close he may be," a dark, saturnine-featured man put in, probably the youngest there. "And sympathetic he may be. But we have been here for three weeks and more and neither he, nor any other, has gained us anything. I am Rutherford of that Ilk, and I sit in the Scots parliament. I think that we will have to take our rightful complaints there – if not to the parliament closer at hand!"

There were murmurs of agreement from around the table.

128

"I suggest that we hear what this young man has come to say to us, before we speak further," the individual who had invited David to sit said. He turned. "I am Home of Bilsdean."

"Then, sir, I am proud to meet the father of the two ladies who entertained me at Bilsdean on my way south – Mistress Barbara and Janet."

"Ha! So you called in there, did you? For why, may I ask?"

The last thing David wanted was to have to explain about Fast Castle here and now. He coughed. "The Lady Kilspindie, who is my great-aunt, recommended it," he said, less than confidently.

"She did? I warrant that her husband did not, unless he wished you ill! Patrick Douglas of Kilspindie hates all Homes! But, yes, I know Anne Gray. You are at least well-connected, young man."

David was somewhat relieved.

"What has the Duke of Lennox sent you to say to us?" another demanded. "I am Home of Aytoun, and my interests are much hurt by this folly."

David picked his words. "He feels, gentlemen, that to win any easement in the matter, you would be advised yourselves to make some gesture, some offer. So that there might be some, some excuse for negotiation. A possible arrangement. The monopoly-holder is in a strong position. He has the law on his side . . ."

"Laws can be changed, lad. Parliaments can change laws."

"No doubt, sir. But parliaments have to be strongly persuaded, have they not? And are not always interested. That takes time . . ."

"What sort of offer does the Duke suggest that we make?" Bilsdean asked. "We cannot afford to offer anything much, if anything at all, or our profit has gone. We have our fishermen to pay, nets, boats and gear to keep up and tranters to hire to carry the lobsters and fish to the English markets."

"I realise that, sir. But without some offer there is no room for discussion, for negotiation. Some small token would serve for that. Perhaps a penny on the stone? Instead of four pence . . .?"

"Too much," Paxton declared. "For there is the English

129

penny to pay, after that. There is much siller involved in all this, young man."

"I understand that, sir. But is it not better to forego some small proportion than to lose all . . .?"

He got no further at this moment because of a sudden outbreak of noise, above both the music and the prevailing chatter in that salon, loud laughter and guffaws, with a woman's skirling high over all. The men around David, as those at the other tables, all looked up. A party of gallants had entered, escorting one young woman, striking in more than her uninhibited laughter, good-looking, bold-eyed, auburn hair piled high on her head and tied in place with strings of pearls, dressed in the height of contemporary fashion, or depth perhaps, for the neck of her satin gown was so low-cut that her already prominent breasts seemed in danger of bursting right out of all constraint. This eye-catching female and her attendants pushed their clamorous way through the throng to a table nearby, over which but the one man lay sprawled asleep, presumably in drink. Him they unceremoniously pushed to the floor and took over the table, amidst much hilarity. As all watched and some commented varied reactions, it was to be seen that Sir William Alexander, the Master of Requests, came strolling over, smiling, to speak to the lady, who patted the bench beside her for him to sit.

"Aye, well," Home of Aytoun said, "Meg Hamilton ploughs a wide furrow! You were saying, young man, that we should make some offer of sorts. I agree that one penny on the stone is too much. A half that might be just possible?" He looked round at the others.

There were some nods, some shrugs, a frown or two. But at least the notion of some form of negotiation seemed to be generally accepted.

"Does the same value apply to lobsters as to salmon?" David asked.

"Scarcely that, no," Bilsdean told him. "But for this purpose, it would serve. There is more waste in the lobster, shell against meat. But the meat itself fetches more. So, yes, half a penny in the stone would serve for lobsters also."

"Can I tell the Duke, then, that you would be prepared to go some small way to meet Lord Purbeck's demands? I cannot think that so little will be acceptable, gentlemen, but . . ."

Again the loud and prolonged laughter from the nearby table drowned his speech. He waited as patiently as he might, the others less so. The woman who had been named Meg Hamilton, he noticed, was actually looking at him assessingly.

When he could, he resumed. "At least it could possibly be sufficient to talk over with him. Would you meet him, the Lord Purbeck, to discuss it?"

"He has refused to see us hitherto, the arrogant puppy!" Paxton said.

"If the Duke could persuade him . . .?"

"Why should he change his tune now?"

"This of the parliament might reach him. He will now be a member of the House of Lords, yes? And might not relish having to defend his monopoly there, where others have been less . . . fortunate. Is it not worth the attempt, gentlemen?"

There seemed to be grudging assent.

David did not see that there was anything else that he could say at this stage, and was prepared to leave them. But there was something else which he thought he might learn from these Homes, and which had puzzled him. He waited for a lull in the racket from the Hamilton party.

"Why, may I ask, sirs, is King James so kindly disposed to Sir Thomas Home of Primroknowe, also in the Merse, when he heeds not *your* complaint? Sir Thomas has recently been given the sheriffdom of Angus, in place of my uncle, the Lord Gray." He had to shout. "Why such different treatment? Of Homes?"

"Well may you ask!" Bilsdean said. Others were answering him also, but he could not hear them. "Presumably Primroknowe is prepared to do what we are not! To cater for the King's peculiar tastes! Forby, he was bastard of George Home, Earl of Dunbar, who was the King's right hand in Scotland, and Chancellor of the Exchequer here. He . . ." The rest was lost in the din.

David recognised that he was going to get little further this night, in the circumstances. He finished his wine and stood up.

"Thank you, gentleman. I will tell the Duke that you are

131

prepared to go some way towards Lord Purbeck, however small. And urge him to try to arrange a meeting . . ." He stooped, to seek to hear what the Rutherford chief was saying – but unsuccessfully. Then he realised that Sir William Alexander was back, standing beside him.

"You are finished here?" that man asked. "Then I will conduct you back to the Duke's quarters, lest you lose yourself in this place. But first, the Lady Stewart would speak with you."

"Lady Stewart . . .?" David wondered. The only lady at the table from which Alexander had just come was this Meg Hamilton.

"Yes. Come, you."

Nodding to Bilsdean and the others, David followed Alexander over to the noisy group.

"Here is the Lady Stewart of Methven. You have a mutual . . . friend, I think. David Gray, from Broughty."

David blinked. So this bold and handsome piece was the estranged wife of Sir John Stewart, Duke Ludovick's son. He recollected now that he had heard that his cousin had married a Hamilton, more or less at the King's command. He bowed, not too deeply.

"Save us, sir – so you are kin to my deserting husband!" she exclaimed. "You are better-looking than he, at least!"

He bowed again, still less deeply, but said nothing.

"How is John? It is near two years since I saw him. Is he still living with that Drummond woman, somewhere in Strathearn?"

"Yes, lady, and very happily."

"Happily! How pleasant for him!"

"Yes. I saw them both but two weeks past."

"How pleasant for *you*! I do not expect that he asked to be kindly remembered to me?"

"I do not recollect your name being mentioned, lady."

"Ah, do I detect some lack of ardour towards my poor self, sir?" She touched his wrist. "We must seek to amend that. Eh, Will?"

"I am sure that you wrong our friend, Meg," Alexander returned easily. "How could any man with eyes and ears and senses fail to appreciate your ladyship's excellences?"

132

"You are mocking me, Will Alexander? I warn you, that is dangerous!"

"I would not dare."

"As well!" She turned back to David. "And what brings you to court, sir, from . . . Broughty, was it?"

"Interests of the Duke of Lennox, lady," he told her briefly.

"Ah! In other words, no business of mine! No?" She touched his arm again, almost stroked it. "You have scarcely a courtly way with you, David Gray from Broughty! I think that if you are to be at court for any time, you would be the better of some lessons! And who better to instruct than Margaret Stewart! Will, you must bring our friend along to my chambers one day. And soon. A pity that one so handsome should fail in his . . education!"

"I fear that I shall be gone tomorrow, lady," David announced stiffly.

"Indeed? What a loss!" She turned a notably bare shoulder on him.

He bowed to her back and turned to Sir William who, grinning, led him off. The loud laughter recommenced behind them almost immediately.

Out of that salon and in the garden, Alexander mentioned that he did not think that David had been very friendly towards the lady, who meant only kindly.

"Did she? Then I must be sorry, sir. I had not realised that it was all kindness."

"Tush – be not so prickly, man! That is just her way. Meg is none so ill. And she has her parts – not only those we all see so evidently! Forby, she might even be of use to you, in the matter of the monopolies. For she has influence, that one. She is Buckingham's mistress, you see."

"Sakes! Buckingham! Does he . . .? I thought that he was, was otherwise!"

"Ah, no. Like James himself he enjoys the ladies also. Indeed, I would think that it is only because the King is the King that Steenie . . . indulges him! He prefers women, I would say. But not, it seems, his little mouse of a wife!"

"He is married? I did not know that."

"Oh, yes. And to one of the richest heiresses in England.

Kate Manners, daughter to the Earl of Rutland. James arranged that for him. But he can see little of his Marchioness Kate, for he keeps her hidden away in the country. Meg Hamilton is much more to his taste."

"And yet she behaves . . . as she does! Tonight, there. With those men. Her manner – and to myself also . . ."

"Ah, but that is *just* her manner. You could say that Meg promises much but delivers little! Nowadays, that is. Once it was otherwise. I myself used to enjoy her little kindnesses! Amongst others. But that was before she linked her fortunes with those of the most influential man in the kingdom."

"Was that before she wed John Stewart, or after?"

"Before. That marriage was a nonsense from the start. Done at the King's command, to prevent an open scandal. James has strange notions as to what is scandalous and what is not!"

They were threading all those corridors and galleries during this revealing conversation. "And does not Buckingham object to her ways? Her behaviour with other men? When he is not there."

"Evidently not. You see, Meg is more than just his mistress – she is his listening-post also. Hears all that goes on through her associations with the men she cultivates. And informs him. Oh, Meg is no fool. There is not much that goes on at Whitehall or Windsor or Greenwich or Hampton Court which Meg does not hear of and does not pass on to Buckingham. *He* is no fool either, and ambitious as he is, seeks to be always well-informed. So Meg uses her attractions to find out for him. Very successfully, I think."

"So it is all a mummery, play-acting, her behaviour with other men? You heard how she spoke, even to me, touched me . . ."

"Now it is, yes – although it did not used to be so. I doubt if any get the length of her bed, these days. Save perhaps . . ." Alexander chuckled, "save perhaps his brother!"

"Brother? You mean . . .?"

"John Villiers, yes, the new Viscount Purbeck himself! Of all men. While Buckingham and Charles were away in Spain, I chanced to come across Meg consoling herself with brother John. In Buckingham's quarters here. He and Charles were away for months, you see. I suppose it was over-long for Meg

134

to remain alone of a night! But at least she kept it in the family, as it were!"

"A mercy! And Buckingham – did he learn of it, ever discover it?"

"No, no, that would never have done. Steenie would have been furious. He is a jealous man by nature. No, they kept it very quiet. I stumbled on it by chance. I suppose some of the servants must have known, but no doubt John Villiers paid them to hold their tongues."

"And now? That is all over?"

"I would say so, yes. With Buckingham back, John would never dare offend his powerful brother. After all, everything that is his became so through Steenie's influence with James. And what the King gives, he can take away! No, John will not risk crossing the source of his good fortune. Nor I think, would Meg have it. Anyway, I do not think that it went deeply – if you will forgive my phrasing! Between Meg and John Villiers. I suppose it was scarcely to be wondered at that it happened. He was occupying his brother's apartments here and she was conveniently nearby. And used to frequenting them. And, of course . . . of a warm nature. Those months would seem a long time . . ."

They were back in the ducal chambers now, and Alexander, in saying goodnight, mentioned that if David was indeed going back to Theobalds next day, he might be prepared to carry some papers for him to Lord Middlesex, the Treasurer, connected with requests, pleas and payments, to put before the King. The business of the realm had to go on, deer-hunting or none!

David said that he would be glad to act messenger, and thanked the other for his kindness that night.

It was when lying in his bed thereafter, thinking, that David Gray realised that his visit to Whitehall might well be more profitable than he had ever envisaged. He had acquired some possibly very useful information. If, if he was prepared to use it . . .?

10

Next evening, closeted with Duke Ludovick, David told him of his discussion with the monopoly complainers and of their admittedly very minor offer of one half-penny on the stone of fish, with his suggestion that this might at least be enough to give excuse for a meeting with John Villiers at which some arrangement might be worked out. Ludovick was scarcely optimistic, but agreed that it was worth trying. Anything was worth trying, in this pickle.

That word anything acted as the key to open David's lips on the other matter. He had thought long on this on the ride back to Theobalds Park, in grave doubts as to his course, his behaviour in this matter, the rights and wrongs of it all. He was reluctant to act the extortioner, the threatener. He hoped that he was a reasonably honourable character and not really any oppressor or coercer. Yet, the action he was contemplating was itself calculated to counter greed and harshness. Did that make it the less blameworthy? Absolve him? It was odd, to say the least, that he had been sent south by his uncle to act in very similar fashion, to seek to threaten the King over those letters; and now here again was a guilty secret which could be used to right a wrong.

"My lord, there is something else to tell you," he began carefully. "Which could possibly affect and apply. I learned it at Whitehall, by chance, a matter anent the Lord Purbeck. You will, of course, know the Lady Margaret, formerly Hamilton, since she is wed to your son. Forgive me if this is a delicate subject . . ."

"I am long past feeling delicate about Meg Hamilton, Davie. That marriage was a folly, almost a sin. No true marriage at all. In the sight of God and all honest men, Janet Drummond is John's true wife."

"Yes. Well, I learned that Lady Stewart was the mistress of Buckingham. You will know that also?"

"That is no secret."

"And she seems to be useful to him in other ways. But while he and Prince Charles were away in Spain, she was secretly bedding with his brother John."

"Dear God! No – I cannot credit that!"

"Sir William Alexander it was who told me. He, he came upon them."

"Upon my soul! I trust Will Alexander, yes. This is beyond all. John Villiers and Meg Hamilton!"

"Yes. How would the Marquis look on this, think you, my lord?"

"Steenie – he would be beside himself with anger. Against them both. I do not know what he would do. But something would be done. For he is nothing if not possessive by nature. This would cut him to the quick."

"So I reckoned it. You see what this could mean, my lord? This knowledge. In the matter of my Lord Purbeck."

He did not have to spell it out. Ludovick perceived the possibilities very clearly. "We have him!" he exclaimed. "The young fool! Aye, we have him." Evidently questions did not affect the ducal conscience in the matter. "He will do much to keep this folly quiet. His whole fortunes and advancement rest on Steenie's goodwill. Any rift between them and he could lose all."

"Strange that he did not think of that when he took the lady to bed!"

"Aye, but he is weak. Stubborn but weak. Yet Meg is not. She has a shrewd head on those fair shoulders! *She* cannot have failed to see the dangers. I wonder why she chose Johnnie Villiers, of all who would have had her if they could? She has an eye for men, that one, and could pick and choose if so inclined. Only, she has been careful since she took up with Buckingham. Knowing how he would act. It has been well remarked upon! So, she must have had some purpose in bedding with Purbeck, other than just lust. For he is no great lover, I swear! I wonder whether, whether . . .? Could it be that this was deliberately done? A weapon she could use to hold over John Villiers if the need arose? If her Steenie was to

137

fail her in some fashion? Purbeck is not married. Could this be a means of constraining him, or his brother, one day . . .?"

"Who knows? But, does it signify, for us, my lord? Her intentions. What matters is that we know, and can perhaps use the knowledge to persuade this Purbeck to act less harshly over his monopoly."

"Exactly! You have it, Davie. It is a gift from the gods!"

"You do not think it wrong? A shameful thing to do? To constrain a man, over such weakness . . .?"

"That arrogant pigwidgeon! That insufferable numskull! No, this ought to bring him down a step or two. And make life easier for other folk, not only your complainers."

"Scarcely mine, my lord! But – can you arrange a meeting with the Lord Purbeck, then?"

"I can, and will. And right away. The sooner this is done, the better. James will be in his bedchamber now, with Steenie. Purbeck will be in the Villiers quarters. Let us hope that he is sober enough to know what we are at!"

The Villiers family proved to have an entire wing of the mansion, presided over by the small, shrewish mother, Countess of Buckingham now. David would never have gained access, of course, past family retainers, had he not been with the Duke of Lennox whom none could bar.

They found the new Viscount at dice with a group of his cronies, and less than pleased at being disturbed. But Ludovick showed a different aspect of his character now, playing the duke indeed, and third man in the kingdom, requiring, not requesting, private speech with John Villiers. That individual was not sufficiently sure of himself, despite his grand manner, to reject this demand. He looked doubtfully at David, however, as he rose and led them through to an adjoining apartment. There were no offers of hospitality.

"We are secure here, are we?" Ludovick asked. "None to overhear us? For we have privy matters, for your ear alone."

The other nodded. "What such important matters to warrant this late call, my lord Duke?" It was at David that he looked.

"You will discover! My friend and kinsman here, David Gray, comes today from Whitehall, where he has been

138

speaking with certain Scots lairds who, as you are aware, are much troubled over the charges you are making and imposing in your salmon-fish and lobster monopoly. They complained to the King over this, and now talk of approaching parliament – "

"Let them!" Purbeck interrupted. "They will find that parliament has more to do than to meddle in the affairs of Scotch fish-traders! Besides, the monopolist has the right to set whatever charges he sees fit. I have set mine, and that is an end to it."

"Not quite," the Duke said. "As you shall discover. Do you not wish to hear what the complainers have to say? They have an offer to make." He looked at David.

"My lord, I spoke with them last night. It is this of the import charge that greatly troubles them. The kingdoms are now one, united, and they feel that there ought to be no such charge for Scots fish to enter England, especially when there never before used to be. But they are prepared to go some way to meet your charges. They will pay one half-penny on the stone of fish . . ."

"They will indeed, sirrah – and seven ha'pennies more than that! Four pence on the stone – that is my charge. Nothing less."

"You will not even meet them, my lord? To discuss the matter."

"To what end? I know my rights, if they do not. If they want to sell in England, they will pay. If not, they can sell their fish in Scotland."

"I think that you are being very foolish," Ludovick put in. "Is that your last word in the matter?"

"It is, my lord Duke. A monopoly is a monopoly, and I hold this one, by royal warrant."

"Very well. You have had your chance." He turned and nodded to David.

"My lord," that young man said, far from happily. "This is a painful matter, I fear. It concerns . . . the Lady Stewart of Methven."

Purbeck looked at him sharply.

"I am reliably informed that you and she shared a bed in the Marquis your brother's apartments at Whitehall while he and

139

Prince Charles were in Spain. This, this association, if it came to Lord Buckingham's ears, could, I think, greatly distress him. For he, I understand, thinks highly of the lady."

The effect of those few words was quite remarkable. John Villiers's face seemed almost to crumble before their eyes, all arrogance and confidence abruptly gone. In those moments he seemed to have grown much younger, was almost a boy again, and a frightened, uncertain boy at that, although he was in fact just David's age. His receding chin drooped and his lips quivered, but he found no words.

David was almost sorry for him, then, and hated himself for being the cause of this sorry collapse and spectacle. But there was no turning back now.

"It would be unfortunate to have to destroy your brother's trust and goodwill, my lord. I feel that you cannot let this happen, for both your sakes."

Features working, the other looked away and then all but stumbled over to the window, to stare out at the parkland. For long moments there was silence.

Then Villiers turned, and to the Duke, not David. "You will not let this happen? You will not tell him?" he gulped. "It would be . . . it would ruin all. George is . . ." He was all but in tears. "She, she led me on. It was her doing . . ."

"I congratulate you the less for *that*!" Ludovick jerked.

"There is no need for the Marquis to learn of it," David said. "If you will but see reason in this matter of the monopoly."

"What do you want . . .?"

"Only that you accept the complainers' offer. This of one half-penny. It will still yield you a fair sum." It occurred to David that while he was at it he might achieve a good turn for the English fish-suppliers also – as some salving of his conscience, perhaps. "And reduce your charge on the English salmon and lobster trade also, by one half-penny. That will not ruin you! Do this, and your brother need not be troubled in the matter."

"Yes, yes. But – you swear it? Swear that he will not be told. Can I trust you?"

"You can, and I do. As to my lord Duke . . .?"

"Surely. My concern in the matter is for His Majesty's

peace of mind. Not yours! Nor your brother's. But if this will
settle the monopoly trouble, then yes, you have my word that
Buckingham will hear nothing of it from me."

"Nor, nor the King?"

"No, I shall not tell James how it was. Merely say that you
have accepted an offer by the complainers."

"Yes, that is it. I accept the offer. And must trust you
both."

"Villiers, *my* word is my honour! As I am sure is David
Gray's. We are gentlemen, if you are not!"

The Lord Viscount Purbeck moistened his lips but did not
answer that.

"We bid you a good night, then," the Duke said coldly, and
turned for the door.

"I will inform the complainers that their offer is acceptable," David added. "That should close the matter."

They found their own way out.

On their passage back to the ducal premises, Ludovick
congratulated his companion. "That was skilfully done," he
said. "You have, I think, the makings of an envoy! You
played your part well. And a poor fish he is, to have the fish
monopoly – and to blame all on Meg Hamilton! Aye, but I
wonder, I am still wondering, why she did it? I cannot believe
that she was so short of offers to share her bed. Nor so
overcome by John Villiers's manly attractions! However, that
is another matter. You played your part well."

"I did not enjoy it, my lord. This of seeking to extort mail
by threat is not to my taste."

The other eyed him sidelong. "And yet, Davie Gray, is not
something of the sort what you are ettling to do with your
liege lord the King? Over those letters!"

David bit his lip. "Scarcely that. I seek only to, to discover
the King's will in the matter. For my uncle." Hurriedly he
changed the subject. "What shall we do now? In this of the
monopoly."

"Tomorrow, I would say, you go back to London and
inform the lairds. If all is agreed there, as it ought to be, then
return here and we shall tell James that he need concern
himself no more in the matter. And he will be grateful to you,
I think, which *may* help in the other affair."

141

"Yes. That will be best. I can ride to Whitehall and back in the one day."

"I hope that this may teach James to be more careful in his granting of monopolies . . ."

So next morning early David set off again, alone this time, to reach London by noon if possible. He discovered, however, at this hour, that there was difficulty in finding his quarry, for it seemed that the palace guests did not hang about Whitehall all day but were apt to take a turn about the town. Enquiries at the so-called Scotch Corner elicited the information that many of the visiting Scots tended to frequent a Thames-side tavern styled The Blue Bonnet, run by one of their compatriots, for midday refreshment and amusement. So thither he found his way, to discover quite large premises, where in fact a cock-fight was in progress, amidst much noise and wagering, David's first experience of the sport, the which he did not think much of. He could see no sign of any of his lairds in the vociferous crowd, and was leaving to return to Whitehall when, just outside the door he met Rutherford of that Ilk arriving. That man informed that the Merse group, not being enamoured of cock-fighting either, usually gathered for midday refreshment in an upstairs chamber, whither he was now bound.

He led David round the back to a narrow courtyard and up a flight of steps. In a dark panelled room they found four of the complainer-lairds being served food and drink by a couple of buxom and obliging wenches who, amidst yelps of alleged protest, giggles and slappings of straying masculine hands, managed to maintain disarranged clothing in approximate position. As an alternative to cock-fighting it had David's preference.

Home of Bilsdean was one of the diners. As before, he found a seat for the visitor at his side, and invited him to be his guest, one of the females showing her appreciation of a younger and good-looking customer in suitable fashion – so that the protests now became male ones.

When he decently could, David cleared his throat and announced that he had news for them. He and the Duke of Lennox had seen the Lord Purbeck and persuaded him to

142

agree to reduce the import charge to one half-penny on the stone, their offer. He hoped that this was satisfactory?

There was an astonished silence, and then all five men spoke out at once, all but disbelieving, asking how it had been done, seeking verification, details.

David, assuring that it was fact but, needless to say, not going on to explain how it had been achieved, contented himself with declaring that, under pressure, Purbeck had seen sense; and indicating that the Duke had been very strong in the matter, on the King's behalf.

It was at this stage that two more of the lairds arrived, Paxton and Broomhouse, and these had to be informed. In the ensuing clamour, when David remembered to add that he had got the English charge reduced to a half-penny also, which would save them a further sum, the appreciation reached all but incoherence – to the complete neglect of the formerly protesting and now seemingly disappointed young women.

There were further demands as to how all this had come about, and David was well aware that he did not make his explanations sound entirely convincing, at least in his own ears. He insisted that the credit must go to the Duke, and implied that His Majesty's concern in the matter was important.

"Whatever the pressure you brought to bear, young man, we are all most notably in your debt," Bilsdean announced, at length. "I, for one, am most grateful. And admiring. You have saved us all a great deal, not only of siller but of trouble."

"Then, gentlemen, I – or at least the Duke – can tell King James that all is now well? That you will go back to Scotland content?"

"To be sure. I do not think that any of us will linger here in this London, of which we have had a sufficiency, for more than a day or two now. Eh, my friends? Aye, and look you, David Gray, if there is anything which we, in return, can do for you, in your interests, you have but to ask us."

There were noises of agreement.

"I thank you, but I do not know of anything, sirs." David paused then, as a thought occurred to him. "Save perhaps, in one respect. Are any of you gentlemen close to Home of Primroknowe?"

"He is far-out kin to most of us, I suppose," Paxton said. "But I do not think that any would call him close."

"It is this of the Angus sheriffdom. Like these monopolies, it appears to be in the King's gift, although the Lords Gray have held it for many a year. Now it has been gifted to Home of Primroknowe, and my uncle is much the poorer. Very much so, for it carries with it the collection of the customs and taxation of Dundee town, and all market fees and fines, as well as revenues from other towns and burghs in Angus. I but wondered whether there could be any way by which Primroknowe could be persuaded to seek some other benefit from the King in place of the sheriffdom? Something valuable, to be sure – but different."

The lairds looked at each other doubtfully, but none came up with any suggestion.

"No, I feared not," David said. "It was but a thought. I am my uncle's land-steward, and he would be grateful."

"I suppose that we could speak with him," Bilsdean said. "He has the fishings on the Whiteadder, and will be pleased with what has been gained here. But . . . to give up a rich sheriffdom . . .!"

"No, it is not possible. Think no more of it, sirs. Now I must leave you, for I have to win back to Theobalds this day." He rose.

Amid expressions of gratitude and esteem, Bilsdean escorted him to the door. "This has been a notable day for us, thanks to you, my friend," he said. "Anything to effect that I can do in return, I shall. Even though I have little hopes of this of Primroknowe. And, see you, always you will be welcome at Bilsdean Castle, be assured."

That last declaration and thought sent David on his way northwards with some satisfaction.

There was hunting again next day at Theobalds, but this time David was not singled out to join the select royal group, but just told to attach himself, by the Duke, to the main body of mounted followers, not all of whom seemed notably enthusiastic participants. In the event, he saw little sport, but was

144

none too disappointed over that, quite enjoying the riding about the extensive woodlands of Enfield Chase without having to be involved in the slaughter and butchery. He much preferred his own kind of hunting, stalking stags alone on the heather hills.

However, when the entire hunt assembled again at midday, after much horn-blowing, to partake of refreshment, victuals and wine brought in hampers by a troop of servitors to a wide, grassy and approximately central glade surrounding a marshy pond in the woods where hawking was apparently to take place in the afternoon, he found himself sought out by Ludovick, to be conducted to the group around the monarch. James appeared to be in good spirits, after a successful morning, his clothing satisfactorily blood-stained, sharing a fallen tree-trunk with Buckingham, and lecturing all on the niceties and intricacies of hawking, explaining the superiority of Spanish-trained birds, two of which his beloved Steenie had brought back as a gift from King Philip of Spain. That realm had of course a strong Moorish connection, and the Moors being great falconers, that being their favourite sport in their God-forsaken desert land. David noted that there was no sign of the Prince of Wales in the company; but the Viscount Purbeck was there, looking distinctly apprehensive.

When the King had exhausted his theme to his satisfaction, whatever the interest of his hearers, he beckoned Ludovick and David forward amiably.

"Weel, Davie Gray, my mannie," he welcomed, in his broadest Scots, "I jalouse you winna ken much aboot haaks and haaking, it no' being a science, aye a science mind, much prosecuted whaur you come frae. Eh?"

"No, Your Majesty."

"Aye, weel – maybe you'll learn. But you seem to hae learned some other skills at yon Broughty you come frae, Duke Vicky tells me. Aye, and likewise Johnny the Viscount here. I'm hearing guid things."

David bowed.

"I'm hearing that you won ower thae thrawn Border lairds to see some sense in this o' the salmons and lobsters, and to lessen their wheenging plaints and yammers. A right scunner they've been, wi' it all. Aye, and Johnny here has been right

145

helpful, graciously agreeing to go their way a wee, maist forbearing. So that's that. We commend you, Davie Gray, aye commend." It was not often that James Stewart used the royal we.

David bowed again, even though this was scarcely the version of events he would have put forward.

"We'll hae to see if we canna use your talents some way, laddie, to guid effect. Aye, we'll maybe think on something. For talents are to be used – eh, Steenie? Used and no' buried, the Guid Buik tells us. We'll think o' something. Hech, aye, we are pleased wi' you both." And from the glance at Purbeck it was evident that the regal approval included the wary-looking John Villiers. A wave of the hand indicated that royal encomiums were over.

David caught Purbeck's darting eye as he backed away.

The afternoon's hawking may have been enjoyable for those actually taking part, even exciting on account of the extensive wagering on the performances of individual birds; but for mere onlookers it quickly palled, with very little to be seen. The process was for beaters, with dogs, to put up wildfowl from the reedy verges of the ponds and meres of this low-lying and wet part of the property, mainly mallard, widgeon and other duck, with the occasional heron, and when these were airborne, for the sportsmen to release their falcons, two at a time, these to compete with each other as to which should bring down the quarry, if any, and in the best style, those so inclined, and knowledgeable, laying wagers on performance – although few, save Ludovick, were so unwise as to bet against the King's birds. Since the kills were apt to take place a good distance off, sometimes half a mile and more away, and only those closely involved went riding thitherwards – a horde of horsemen pounding over the ground would have disturbed further game – the onlookers tended to see very little of any interest. When, after an hour or so of this, a number of the latter decided that they had had enough, David was glad to return with them to the mansion.

That evening, when the Duke got back from attendance on his royal cousin, David was urgent to consult him as to his course now. He was already concerned about time, having been longer as it was here at court than either he or his uncle

146

had anticipated. Haste was essential, for the installment of the new sheriff of Angus before the Scots Privy Council could take place at any time, and once that was done, undoing the damage would be difficult if not well nigh impossible. Lord Gray had his friends on that council who might seek to delay it as long as they could, but that could not go on for much longer. Had the King said anything as to his attitude?

"Nothing as to letters, no," Ludovick admitted. "He keeps his own counsel. I would have asked him, but it is difficult now to see him alone. Buckingham is always there – and I do not think it would be wise to involve that young man! But I recognise your problem, Davie. I must try to arrange a private audience. James is pleased with you over this of the monopoly, as you would perceive. To declare his approval before all at the hunt was quite a notable gesture – even though he did include the insufferable Purbeck in his praise. No doubt to please Steenie. However, that does our cause no harm."

"No. What did he mean by saying that he would think of something for me to do? To use me, in some way? Was this in connection with the letters, do you think? It was a strange way of putting it, if it was."

"I do not know. One never knows with James. Although I know him so well, he is often a complete mystery to me. But he must have had something in mind, saying that."

"I hope . . . I hope, my lord, that it does not mean that he has some task for me to do here in London. To delay my return to Scotland. As I say, I have been overlong away already. Do you think . . . do you think that it would be possible to suggest to the King that he might instruct the Privy Council, the Scots one, to delay the institution of Home of Primroknowe meantime? For some reason. While he, the King, considers . . .?"

"But we have no reason to believe that he *is* considering, or reconsidering, this appointment, Davie. All he has cause to consider, at this present, is whether he wishes those Casket Letters to be handed over to him. And whether, in return, he will think kindly of the Lord Gray. That is all. He may guess that you, or your uncle, really seeks to win back the sheriffdom. But that has not been requested – and I would not advise that you did so, either! Not in words."

"No." David shook his head. "It is all so difficult. I wish that my uncle had come here himself to do it. But he could not, he said, in his position . . ."

"You mean he dared not! So he sent you!"

"Something had to be attempted . . ." David paused. "My lord, a thought came to me in that London tavern. This Sir Thomas Home of Primroknowe. If he could be persuaded not to take up the sheriffdom, then all this could perhaps be forgotten, put behind us. It is a rich prize, yes – so there would have to be something offered in its place, something of much value. Or, or . . ."

"Aye – or, Davie Gray?"

"Or Home to be persuaded. Otherwise." That did not sound wholly convincing.

"You mean, more of this coercion? I think that you are like to become something of an extortioner of mail, my young friend!"

Unhappily David shook his head, silent.

"Am I wrong? You came south here if possible to force the King to withdraw his grant of this sheriffdom through your uncle's holding of those letters, with their secrets. Then you learned of Purbeck's indiscreet bedding with Meg Hamilton, and used that knowledge – admittedly, with my help – to coerce him to yield on this of the monopoly. And now, I think, you are wondering whether you could coerce this Primroknowe into yielding up the sheriffdom! Find some guilty secret to hold over *him*? For so youthful and innocent-looking a land-steward, I fear that you are like to become a dangerous young man!"

"No! That is not so. That is not me. I much mislike all this of threats and plaguings. Would to God it was not necessary! But how to right these wrongs otherwise . . .?"

"I agree that your causes are good enough, lad. But it could be a dangerous game, see you. You could make grievous enemies, and in high places. Well, I will try to have James grant you a private interview again. But beware what you say to him . . .!"

In fact it proved less difficult to arrange an audience than

148

Ludovick had feared, for next day the Prince of Wales departed for his own palace of Greenwich, and persuaded Buckingham to escort him thither at least, remain with him if only for the one night away from the King's side. Charles never remained long in his father's company if he could help it, and now to add to their mutual antipathy there had arisen a fierce jealousy over Villiers. James declared that his Steenie was to remain no more than the one night away.

So, although there was no personal contact at the next day's hunt, in the evening the Duke was able to take David to the royal apartments once more, to what seemed almost an exact repetition of the former occasion, James in bed and wearing the same hat – and probably the same bed-wear. The smells were certainly similar. Once the mincing Gentleman of the Bedchamber had been dismissed, the three of them eyed each other in silence for a little.

"Aye, weel," the King said at length. "Davie Gray again! The bonnie lad who speaks mair than the French, and maks folk change their minds! What did you say to Johnnie Villiers, heh? I'm thinking no' a' that changing o' minds cam frae thae Border lairds!"

Distinctly disconcerted by this unexpected opening of the audience, David hesitated. "I, I but urged him to be more, more modest in his demands, Sire. To heed the offer the lairds had made. Since they had moved some way towards him, to move a little towards them. He, my Lord Purbeck, saw . . . reason in that." A thought struck him. "I used this of your Majesty's now united kingdoms. Pointed out that if the kingdoms were indeed one, then there ought surely to be no import charges between one and the other."

" 'Deed, aye! You hae a point there, man – a point. And had his new lordship no' thought on that, eh?"

"Perhaps it had escaped him, Sire. The English in the south, here, being far from Scotland, probably miss the importance of this at times."

"True. I hae noticed the same my ain self!" James turned to the Duke. "This laddie has his wits aboot him, eh Vicky? But the Grays aye had, I discovered – for their ain benefit!"

"Perhaps, Sire. But I see no benefit for David in this matter; only for Purbeck, the lairds – and perhaps our own."

"D'you tell me that! Maybe – or maybe no'! And I'm thinking that Johnnie Villiers would be needing a mite mair than just this Gray's sweet reason, mind, to mak him change his mind. When he wouldna' heed yours."

"The lairds did come some way towards him, Sire. To help a negotiation," David said.

James looked from one to the other. "Aye!" That was eloquent. "So you're seeking your bit reward noo, eh? Frae *me*?

"Reward, Sire? No, nothing of that. I but seek permission to return to Scotland. With your Majesty's instructions for my Lord Gray."

"Ah. So you haste to be awa'? Frae our court."

"Not that, Sire. But I am here only as my lord's messenger. Sent to acquaint you with this of the letters. He will be awaiting an answer. I am but his land-steward."

"I reckon then that you could be mair profitably employed than in land-stewarding, Davie! But that, nae doubt, is why Gray sent you? For profit! Frae *me*! He wants his sheriffdom back – but doesna hae the smeddum to come and ask it himsel'. Guidsakes, I'd been liker to heed the man if he had!"

There was nothing that David could say to that.

"So you're for off, then? But maybe you'll be back? For I might find some use for thae talents o' yours."

David glanced over at the Duke. What could this mean? "My talents are few, Sire, and very modest I fear. I cannot think how such could avail in Your Majesty's service." He carefully sought to get away from that subject, for he had no desire to become a courtier in a humble way, or in any other way. "What am I to tell my Lord Gray, Highness?" he asked.

The King frowned. "As to what?"

"Those letters, Your Majesty. Do you wish them to be handed over to you? This was what I was sent to learn. Your royal wishes."

"Was it, man – was it? I'm thinking it was otherwise."

"Sire, my lord, having found these your royal mother's letters, believed that they might possibly be of value to you. So he offers them, in loyal duty. If Your Majesty felt disposed to show appreciation, that would, I am sure, greatly please my lord. But that is a matter for Your Highness."

"It is, aye. Very much so! I hae thought on this, mind. I want the letters, yes. In especial, one. That consairning the Italian secretary."

David swallowed. It always came back to that.

"Mind you, I could *tak* those letters. Tak them a'. Has Gray no' thought on that? I could hae my officers to call at Broughty and demand them. I ken noo that they are there. Aye, instruct my Sheriff o' Angus to collect them for me!" That came out with a grim chuckle.

There could be no answer.

"You tell your uncle that, Davie Gray. But – aye, since you've done your best, laddie, in nae very honest cause, mind, you could add a wee bittie, see you. You could say that if he sends me any letters referring to yon Rizzio – any and a', mind – I might just possibly consider this matter o' the sheriffdom. Aye, tell him that. It's no' a promise, see you, just a possibility."

David blinked. To have got so far! On the face of it, almost to have attained the object of his mission. And yet, to no effect. For there *was* no Rizzio letter. Or none that he, or his uncle, knew of. The folly of it all!

"You dinna look ower content, my mannie? I'm thinking that you're gey hard to please!"

"No, Sire, no. I greatly esteem what you concede." He racked his brain for something to say. "It is the matter of time, now. Sir Thomas Home could be installed Sheriff of Angus any day now. And then it would be too late, would it not? For Lord Gray."

"I told you, laddie, I'm no' promising anything on this o' the sheriffdom."

"No, Sire. But if you could instruct your Privy Council to delay installing Home of Primroknowe for some small period, then it would give time for . . . decision."

James looked at Ludovick. "Is this no' a right obstinate skellum, Vicky? He'll no' let go. I've clapped folk in the Tower for less!"

"Perhaps determination is another of his talents, James!"

"No' to ken when to stop isna a talent! Forby, to his ain sovereign! But, och – for some peace, and to get rid o' him, I'll better maybe gie him what he seeks, eh?" The King pointed a

151

finger at David. "Aye, weel, Davie Gray, I'll inform my Scots Privy Council to bide a wee ower this o' the Angus sheriffdom – but just a wee, mind. Now, off wi' you, afore I change my mind and send you to the Tower! Awa', laddie, awa' back to Scotland!"

"Yes, Sire. I thank you." Bowing low, David backed away for the door.

"And tell Andra Gray he'd better let me hae yon Rizzio letter right soon, or there'll be trouble!"

"Yes, Sire." He reached the door and got out, closing it behind him thankfully, to the curious stares of the two guards.

David was halfway back to the ducal quarters when Ludovick caught up with him.

"Lord, you are a great risk-taker, Davie," that man declared, shaking his head, only half-humorously. "I cannot recollect anyone else pressing the monarch like that, and getting by with it! I trembled for you there – I did so."

"It was the only way, my lord."

"Was it? Not many would have taken it, that I am sure. I wonder if Andrew Gray knows what he has got as a land-steward? Perhaps he does – that he sent you, instead of coming here himself. So – now you will be off back to Broughty?"

"Tomorrow, yes. And thank you, my lord, for all that you have done to aid me. I could never have won near the King but for you. I well realise that."

"Whether you will continue to thank me hereafter remains to be seen! But I am going to miss you, Davie. Mind you, I have a notion that it may not be so long before I see you again."

On that ominous note, for David, they went to their own bedchambers.

11

One week later, David Gray knew a great sense of satisfaction and relief as his horse trotted over the cobbles of Berwick Bridge across the Tweed and into Scotland. He was thankful to be back. He had not actually feared any recall to London, any interference in his journey north, but he had had a vague feeling of unease all the way up through England; just why he was unsure, some abiding recognition that he had been dabbling in things too high for him. But now back in his own land, somehow that did not seem so serious. And it was only twenty miles to Bilsdean. He should be there in time for an evening meal – after all, its laird had given him an open invitation.

The fact that a thin, warm summer rain greeted him only a short distance north of Berwick failed to dampen his anticipation – for that was Scotland too. Passing Coldingham, he looked eastwards towards St Ebba's Head.

He arrived at Bilsdean Castle to a warm welcome, quietly glowing on Barbara's part and vociferous on Janet's. He had expected their father to be there, but he had not yet returned – and although David had liked the man, he was not unduly disappointed. Presumably the lairds had travelled more slowly than he had, or had found something to detain them in London.

The trio had a cheerfully talkative meal together, with David so busy answering queries that he scarcely knew what he was eating – although he did think to remark as the first course was served, a rich broth, that he was disappointed that it was not lobster soup; which of course led to an extended question-and-answer session on that subject and considerable excitement. There needed to be no secrecy about the monopoly situation, however careful David had to be as to how he got Purbeck to change his mind; also of course on the

153

subject of the Casket Letters. The girls were much impressed. They revealed that their father had been reluctant to go south to petition the King on this matter, but the other Home landowners had persuaded him to go with them, to present a united front. Not that he had not been worried over the new monopoly charges. These could have cost him dear and caused hardship amongst the fisherfolk.

Barbara inevitably asked about the letters situation, and David hated to have to dissemble and hedge. He could only tell her that he had got some way with the King, that there was to be a postponement of the installation of the new Sheriff; but that a full decision was still to be reached. He dared say nothing about the possibility of a Rizzio letter. He did add that he had not had time nor opportunity to mention Fast Castle and the letters to their father.

It was pleasant thereafter to sit by the fire that wet evening with the young women, chatting. They wanted to hear all about London and the court, especially about the King of course, and Prince Charles, the ladies there and how they behaved and what they wore. Janet was particularly searching on this last aspect, suggesting that they were a loose-living lot and that no doubt so well-set-up a young man as David would have had his adventures amongst them. To which he was able truthfully to declare that the only female he had had any association with had been the Lady Stewart of Methven, his cousin's estranged wife, and that had been no enjoyable interlude. They were interested to hear about Sir William Alexander.

Before they retired, Barbara said that she hoped that David was not in such haste to get back to Broughty that he could not spend at least one day with them there? He did not require a deal of pressing, although he admitted that he ought not to delay. But one day . . .

The bedtime hot-water ceremony followed, with Janet offering sundry helpful services, Barbara shaking her head, and David countering by announcing that it was most unsuitable for the ladies to escort a mere male to his bedchamber when it ought to be a man's privilege. He insisted that he was going to conduct Janet down to her room near the kitchen, and then on the way up again say goodnight

154

to Barbara. The water would remain warm enough mean-time . . .

There were some exchanges over this programme but no actual refusals. So leaving Barbara at her door, he went downstairs with her sister, who thereupon announced that she herself liked a good wash in hot water before bed, and he could help her in with what was left in the cauldron from the kitchen. Recognising that he was being out-manoeuvred, David pointed out that so long as it was no more than that he would be glad to oblige, but since Barbara would be waiting he must not delay. On a hoot of laughter, the other asserted that Barbara would not die of waiting – and a little delay would give her time to prepare for bed.

In the great kitchen, where a large iron cauldron hung steaming from its swee above a dying fire, he was given two large pails of hot water to carry through to the former porter's lodge, a vaulted chamber adjoining, the shot-holes of which, now filled in to keep out draughts, had guarded the castle's doorway. This was where Janet slept, and despite its lack of light, she had made an untidily comfortable apartment of it, the walls and curved ceiling whitewashed, sheep-skins on the floor, clothing strewn around.

She stooped to draw out from under the bed a wide shallow tub, into which she instructed him to pour one of the pailfuls. As he was doing this he perceived that the young woman was starting to divest herself of her gown, unbuttoning the already wide-necked bodice. Hastily he set down his pail and turned for the door.

"Sakes, you're no' finished yet!" she exclaimed. "Where's your manners, sir? You've no' so much as kissed me goodnight! Forby, it's no' often I get the chance o' my back being washed."

"Your back is fine and clean, I am sure," he told her. Moving back to her, he put his arms around her now largely bare top half, squeezed all which delectably came to hand, planted a smacking kiss on her upper back, jerked goodnight and bolted for the door, and out.

Her laughter followed him as he climbed the winding turnpike stair.

The door of Barbara's room stood open. He knocked and

she called for him to enter. She was standing by the window, looking out.

"You have not been so long as I feared you might," she said, smiling. "Janet can be very . . . pressing! But there is no ill to her. It is just her way, her way of dealing with her circumstances here. We are, I think, very different."

"I find no ill in you either!" he declared.

"Perhaps, if you knew me better . . .?"

"That would be my wish. Although, after St Ebba's Head, I feel that I know you very well."

"Yes, that was good. However brief."

"I have thought much on it, while I was away. Thought, and been glad. But . . . sad also."

"Why sad, David?"

"Because, because I am but a land-steward. That only," he said, simply.

"Need that sadden you? *I* would not say so." She turned back to the window. "I think that it will be a good day tomorrow. The rain has stopped. And, see, the gulls are flying seawards, and high. A good sign."

"It will be a good day for me, whatever the weather," he assured.

"I hope so. I am happy that you are staying." She turned. "Now, you will be tired, with long riding. I will not keep you from your bed." Frankly she held out her arms to him.

He went to embrace her and their lips met in a long kiss, satisfactory but scarcely satisfying since it left the man at least eager for more, much more, while his hands stroked and fondled. A mind-picture came vividly before his eyes, of the cliff-top at St Ebba's Head, and this happening before. With a determined effort, he restrained himself, and drew away.

"I should not be doing this," he told her.

"No? Even when I let you?"

"Even so. Your kindness but shames *me*! Taking – with nothing to give!"

"I think that you have much to give."

"Not to a laird's daughter." He shook his head. "Down-stairs, now, it might be different!"

She eyed him in the half-light searchingly. "You are a proud man, David Gray. As well you might be. But pride can

156

be a weakness as well as a strength. I know – for I also am accused of pride. Ask Janet! But . . . do not ask her tonight!"

He nodded, clutched her again for a moment, and then hurried for her door also, to all but slam it behind him. No laughter followed him here.

Barbara's prophecy as to the weather was accurate, and they wakened to a bright, warm morning, a sparkling sea and a sun-kissed land. Over breakfast in the kitchen there was a discussion as to how they should spend the day – and it was evident that on this occasion Janet expected not to be left behind. David had been going to suggest going back to St Ebba's Head; but with Janet present he realised that would not be the same. Barbara wondered whether they should go riding into the Lammermuir Hills, then withdrew the proposal on the grounds that David, having ridden all the way up from London, must be saddle-sore by now and better to stretch his legs. That gave Janet her opportunity. David had said that first day that he would be interested in the matter of swimming for the lobsters. He was now, it seemed, much concerned with the lobster trade. And it was a fine warm day for the swimming. Let them show him how it was done. It would stretch his legs fine, too!

Barbara looked at her half-sister levelly, but said nothing.

David responded rather better. He enthused.

Pease Bay was best, with the tide as it was, Janet asserted. Forby, the sands there were good for lying on afterwards, if they felt so inclined. Cove Haven shore might bring them more lobsters, but with the cot-houses of the fisherfolk there, they would probably have to put up with bairns' company. These were the only two areas where there were sandy beaches nearby. She would make up a hamper of food.

So presently they saddled up three horses, with a garron to carry panniers with the fishing gear and for the hoped-for lobsters, leaving David's horse to have a well-deserved day's restful grazing.

As they rode, the girls explained the procedure. Lobster-creels were scattered in various positions along the coast, more or less permanently, really just weighted traps baited with fish-heads and the like. Each had an entrance by a network funnel, along which the lobster could crawl, but once inside could not get out again. These were anchored by stones to the sea-bottom, never very deep, and their position indicated on the surface by pigs' bladders as floats, on cords tied to the creels. To retrieve the lobsters the swimmers had to find the floats, then dive down, see whether there was a catch inside, release the stone weight and swim up to the surface with creel and captive. This was not difficult; they came up readily enough in the buoyancy of the water. Where the skill was required was in extracting the live lobster from the creel, on the surface. This had to be done by using the float as a sort of raft, lying over it for support, to leave the hands free, then holding the creel steady with one hand and inserting the other down the net funnel, to grasp the lobster and draw it out. Needless to say this had to be done with care, catching the creature by the rear end in such a way that its great claws could not reach the hand. Then the catch was put in one of the net bags and carried along by the swimmer, either to the next creel or straight back to the shore and put into a bucket of water, to be kept alive. Even without the water the lobsters stayed alive for quite long periods.

David reserved comment and judgment.

They rode first down to the haven at Cove of Bilsdean to collect scraps of fish and meat from the fisherfolk for bait – apparently quite a normal procedure. With this smelly load in the pony's panniers, they moved on over the wooded hillsides to Pease Dean and Bay.

It all looked very fair this sunny early August forenoon, with the rose-red small cliffs, the green foliage, the golden sands and the blue water. The tide was half-out and ebbing, so it was decided that they would do their swimming from the mid-bay islet. But to avoid any possible difficulty with the horses, they left them tethered on the grassy bank just above the main beach sand. The panniers and gear for their fishing were unloaded, and proved to consist, as well as their food and drink, the fish-heads and scraps, of two canvas buckets and a number of small netting bags. With the bait in one of the buckets and the nets in another, they set off on foot round the eastern side of the bay for the little rocky peninsula which David had already explored.

Out along this they picked their way to its tip facing the islet. There was some three feet's depth of water between. David eyed it, and his companions, uncertainly.

The girls set down their buckets and nets, and in quite businesslike fashion started to take off their clothing. The man, clearing his throat, looked away. Never before had he been in this situation.

It was not long before Janet's voice was raised. "Do you swim with your claes on, in Angus, David? Or are you ower bashful, just?"

"I . . . ah . . . no," he said, still with averted eyes. "No, no."

"He probably finds this strange," Barbara put in. "Undressing before women. A man might. Come, we will take this gear over to the island, and David can follow when he is ready."

That was not exactly the aspect of the situation which was preoccupying David Gray, but he did not contest it. At Janet's skirl of laughter, followed by splashing, he turned, to see two highly attractive, shapely and quite naked feminine back-views wading into the sea, each girl carrying a bucket and nets. He did not look away any more.

Before they were halfway across Janet looked round. "Come on," she called. "Are you feart o' the watter, or what? It'll no' bite you. Nor will we!"

He began to undress, beside the two little heaps of female clothing. There were no burdens for him to carry over.

Part-wading, part-swimming, he splashed across. The water was by no means warm but he had swum in colder, many a time.

On the islet his companions were stooping, laying out the net bags and putting fish-heads or scraps into each. Highly aware of his own nudity as he emerged, and the effect of cold water upon some of it, he could not be other than intrigued, fascinated, for all that, by what he saw before him. Possibly the young women were not so unaware and unconcerned as they looked, but they appeared so entirely natural, in more ways than one, that the occasion became much less awkward than he had feared – in fact, scarcely awkward at all. His male awareness, interest and even judgment quite speedily took over from any embarrassment, and he found himself making comparisons in some measure.

To his uninstructed mind it was surprising how different these two sisters could be seen to be, physically. After all, they had the same bodily appointments, the same basic shape, and both were alluring, their persons in excellent trim and condition. It was in their proportions that they differed. Barbara was slightly the taller anyway, but seen thus her legs were distinctly longer – or was it just that Janet's thighs were more ample without being in any way clumsy or heavy? Barbara was rather more slender altogether and this gave a greater impression of height. Janet's breasts were larger, a little more full, and inevitably therefore less pointed and shaped than her sister's – and possibly for this reason the aureolas around the nipples were noticeably different, Janet's longer, up and down, Barbara's rounder and darker. In keeping with all this, the former was more rounded at the belly than the other, without being thick, and more luxuriantly covered just below. Without consciously cataloguing and assessing all, there and then, the man decided that these differences probably stemmed from the fact that the one had peasant blood in her veins and the other had not. Which made him wonder about his own appearance, for he also was a dairy-maid's son.

Whether his companions were similarly aware and surveying he could not tell, although Janet was eyeing him frankly enough.

"Bonny, bonny!" she declared. "Guid looks arena' all in the face! And I like a man with hair on his chest!"

Barbara forbore to comment, although she smiled warmly, understandingly, at him. "Here is a net, David," she said. "Two baits in it. That will be enough to start with. We will take the pails. Just follow us, and we will show you what to do. You swim well enough, do you?"

"Er . . . yes." That was the first thing that he had actually said for some time.

Barbara led the way over the crest of the little island, which was really only a marram-grassed sand-dune grown on top of a skerry, to the seaward side, David walking behind the pair and admiring the way their hips moved, differing again. He was an observant young man.

160

Barbara pointed in various directions. There were lobster-creels there and there and there. Perhaps he could see one or two of the floats? No? Some were too far off for swimming and would require the boat, but any lobsters caught in these would keep. The first creel they would try was over by that reef where those cormorants were spreading their wings to dry out, in fairly shallow water.

Rather too much aware of all the exciting femininity and pulchritude so close to him to fully take in such directions, the man nodded, wordless.

Leaving the buckets, Barbara waded in and started to swim. Janet gave David a playful slap on the bottom and pushed him after her sister, herself entering the water close behind, David looping his net bag over a shoulder as they had done.

The girls used a strong breast-stroke so David did the same, although he usually used the faster trudgeon. Their first objective was only about two hundreds yards away, and halfway there the cormorants sunning themselves on the reef flew off. David did not see the float, bobbing about on the wavelets, until he was practically on it, a bladder blown up, with a cord attached. Barbara turned on to her back, to paddle gently.

"You can dive down? Then follow me. It is not deep, this one. You will not need to hold your breath for long."

She handed her net bag to Janet and then executed a graceful surface dive, long legs kicking in the air as she plunged. David, more used to diving off rocks, made a more clumsy job of it, but thrust downwards strongly enough. On the surface he had seen nothing below but now he could see perfectly clearly, the cord stretching down and the creel sitting on the rocky, weed-hung bottom. Two things struck him in those active moments: the fact that there *was* a lobster in the basketwork creel but that it was blue-black not red as he had assumed; and the whiteness of Barbara's body under water, her smooth, lovely gliding movements, and the way her hair streamed behind her as though itself alive.

Then they were down at the sea-floor, and the girl was already inserting a hand into the creel, to draw out the stone which weighted it down. This had to be done quickly, before the lobster might attack with those waving claws. Leaving the stone lying, she took the creel by one of its sapling rungs, and pointed upwards. Winnowing her feet, she went up with so much less effort than in the diving down, even with the creel, David following – and only as he broke out into the air again did he realise that what had been somewhat worrying him, holding his breath sufficiently long, had troubled him no whit, in fact he had not thought about it at all, down there.

With Janet there to help, there was no need for Barbara to use the float to buoy her up. She put the creel on it and held it in place, while Janet put her hand down the net funnel, skilfully flicked the lobster round and then grasped it from the rear, but quite well forwards where those menacing-looking claws could not bend backwards to reach her. Drawing the creature out appeared to be less difficult than David had imagined, its various claws and feelers not catching in the netting as they might have done. Barbara, holding the creel steady with one hand, now used the pull of the water to open the mouth of her bag, and into this her sister thrust the lobster. The creature had eaten only part of the bait, so there was no need to renew this. Panting to David that he should not trouble to come down with her this time, as she had only to put the creel in position and the stone back, she handed him the bag and contrived a rather less elegant dive, with the creel to take with her, and disappeared under again.

Eyeing the lobster gingerly, David was informed by a grinning Janet to be careful not to let that bag get under him as he swam lest those claws found something available to nip!

Barbara was soon up once more and asked whether their visitor wanted to climb out on to the skerry for a breather? Since the implication was that *they* would not be doing this, if alone, he said no, he was all right. She pointed out that the next creel was not far away, at another reef round a minor headland. She relieved David of his lobster, and set off forthwith.

At the second float, beside a somewhat larger skerry, it was Janet's turn to dive; and David felt in duty bound to go down with her also. If her actual plunge under water was a little less perfect than her sister's had been, possibly owing to her fuller chest development, thereafter she swam down as rhythmically. Again there was a lobster caught, and she went through the same process as before, extracting the weight-stone and swimming up with the creel. When the catch was transferred to a bag, and a new bait put in, David volunteered to do the replacing in position.

He achieved this without complications, although it was a little deeper down than the first one, and he knew a tightness of the lungs before he resurfaced. Then Barbara suggested that they climb out on to the reef for a little rest. He was glad to agree.

It was pleasant to sit on the weed-hung rock in such company, in the sunshine, as the girls put the two lobsters into the same bag. They would leave this here, weighted down, and pick it up on the way back.

Their next stop was not at a rock or skerry, at least not one reaching the surface, its marker-float stained red to make it obvious some way seaward. Janet said that David should tackle this one on his own, to see how he got on. Nothing loth, at least superficially, he accepted the challenge. There was underwater rock here, he was told. There ought to be no difficulties.

While the girls floated, he plunged under and down.

Before he was halfway down he realised that he had a problem. There was a lobster, but it was not in the body of the creel but apparently stuck in the entrance funnel. This was obviously going to complicate getting the stone weight out. Reaching the thing, he saw that one of the creature's claws had got caught in the netting – and however sharp and strong these might be, they did not seem to be able to cut through the net. The stone lay deeper in, beyond.

Needless to say, he had only moments, with breath held, to decide on what to do. He had not brought a bag down. He could either try to extract the lobster and swim up with it, hoping that it would not bite him in the process, or try to take it, creel, weight and all, to the surface. Could he manage that? His nearly bursting lungs told him that the latter course must be attempted, for getting that lobster out would almost certainly take more time than he had at his disposal. He was not accustomed to carrying things under water.

Grasping a rung of the creel, as Barbara had done, with one hand, and pushing himself off the rocky bottom with knees and feet, he discovered that he went up, even with his burden, with reasonable ease – although ease was hardly a suitable word, with his lungs in the state they were. He did not exactly shoot up, but reached the precious air somehow. He was so busy gasping for breath thereafter that he could only thrust creel and contents at the laughing girls, pointing, wordless.

His companions seemed to have no difficulty in extricating the catch, and while David was still panting and gulping, Barbara dived down with the creel again. When she came up, she asked him whether he had had enough of this?

He had, in fact, but was not going to say so while the others looked so well able to continue with this very odd sport. He waved them onwards without comment, noting with slight alarm that they were still looking further seawards. He hoped that he was not going to drown before this day was out.

They came to two more floats quite quickly, close together, and the young women each went down to one, David volunteering to accompany neither one nor the other, contenting himself with holding the bag with the lobsters. In fact, neither of these creels yielded a catch.

He was quite thankful when Barbara said that was enough for the meantime, and they would head back for the beach, visiting the reef where they had left the first catch, and taking in one outlying position where there were two creels under the one float – why this, was not explained. David was ashamed not to go down with Barbara to one of these, but halfway down he saw that this creel was empty, and since Janet was going down to the other, he was glad to surface again promptly.

When Janet came up with a fourth lobster, all agreed that enough was enough. That beach beckoned.

It was good to wade out on to the warm sand. With all the exercise and energy recently expended David had scarcely thought of the coldness of the water; but now the contrast with the sun's heat was benign and to be relished.

But he was not finished with exercise yet, it seemed. After depositing the lobsters in the water-filled buckets, he discovered that they were now to go running, this being the girls' accustomed routine after the swimming – just why was not clear. He would have thought that they had been sufficiently active already; and his companions gave no impression of being cold and needing heating up. But off they ran along the firm sand of the tideline, calling for David to follow and race them. And, after the initial surprise, this he was glad enough to do – for now at least *he* could do the demonstrating, show them that they did not lead in everything.

They had a start, of course, and not having done any running for some considerable time, he started just a little stiffly. But quickly that wore off and he picked up speed. Soon he was making up on them in great style, and about to pass them with masculine ease – for after all, women were not really built to run so fast as men could, their curvature of body designed for other purposes. Barbara, slightly less burdened in this respect than her sister, was some way ahead. Racing past Janet, with a lofty wave of the hand, David was about to do the same with Barbara when he came to the conclusion that this would not be advisable. It was not, however, gentlemanly courtesy which constrained him so much as more essentially male value-judgment. Passing Janet, he could not but be aware of how her breasts joggled up and down, her buttocks seemed almost to rotate with a rolling motion, even her thighs shook and quivered, all highly attractively. Much better, surely, to run alongside such delectable visions rather than foolishly outpace them? Accordingly, when he reached Barbara he slowed down somewhat, to her pace, eyes not wholly forward-looking, and even began a panted conversation as to why they were doing this, whether it was in fact to warm them up or perhaps to help dry their hair, questions requiring an answer – this merely a device to slow her down so that Janet could catch up. It worked, and before they reached the far end of the bay and turned back, all three were running together – and the man, in the middle, at least appreciative of more than just the scenery.

Back where they had started, at the buckets and gear, with one accord they moved up to the softer, warm sand and threw themselves down on it, panting, the young women heaving delightfully, Barbara on her stomach, Janet on her back.

David Gray was well content.

They lay there in the sun for some considerable time, and

the man would have continued to do so indefinitely, seldom indeed having experienced a more blissful way of passing the time. But after a while Barbara sat up and declared that it was time to eat. David was quite prepared to accept that, but he was less enthusiastic when she went to her clothes and began to dress. Presumably it was improper to eat unclad? Janet, less than eagerly, rose and followed her sister to the food pannier, and the man got the impression that she might be a little more reluctant to dress. But clothe herself she did, and then, strangely, David immediately felt naked in a way he had not done before, and so must go and don his own clothing. It seemed a pity.

Even so, eating together thereafter, in such excellent company, he continued to enjoy his day, so different from anything else he had undergone lately – or indeed ever. Relaxed and at ease, they enjoyed Janet's provision, chatted, watched the gannets from the Craig of Bass diving for fish out in deeper water, and listened to the eiders crooning in competition with the woodpigeons croodling from the trees of Pease Dean behind. David sought to be helpful by spreading the girls' hair carefully over backs and shoulders for it to dry more readily, and in the process achieved a little presumably accidental caressing. There were no complaints voiced.

The afternoon was still young, and discussion arose as to what to do now. Almost, David proposed more swimming, since that would entail undressing again, although he had really had enough of lobster-catching for one day. But he felt that perhaps might seem to be overdoing it, and when Barbara suggested that they might ride over and pay a visit to the Priory of Dunglass, not far away, where there was much of interest to be seen, he agreed, although Janet sounded less keen.

So they packed up, put the lobster-buckets in the panniers with only a little water in each, loaded up the pony and untethered their horses. Looking back, from his saddle, over the yellow sands and the blue-green shallows, David knew that he would not forget Pease Bay, however differently remembered from St Ebba's Head.

They had to return to Bilsdean Castle with the pony and gear, and there Janet declared that, as she had no particular desire for church-going that afternoon, she would stay at home, prepare the evening meal and do some tasks about the house – since *somebody* had to do some work sometimes! That met with no opposition.

It did not take long to ride to Dunglass, which lay a mere mile further up the steep, wooded ravine of the dean, on a sort of shelf where the land began to rise more noticeably towards the Lammermuir Hills. There was a village, or castleton, of the name in the dean itself, with a mill, and above it the ancient priory under the shadow of Dunglass Castle, a much larger and stronger place than Bilsdean.

David was interested in this situation, that the two laird-ships and two castles should be so close together, both Home estates but apparently unconnected. Barbara explained. Dunglass was by far the more ancient. It had been a stronghold of the old family of Pepdie, now more or less extinct, until the end of the fourteenth century, when Sir Thomas Home of that Ilk married the Pepdie heiress and got the property. In the middle of the fifteenth century the then Home of that Ilk was created Lord Home; and the sixth Lord made first Earl of Home in 1605, soon after King James went to London. Actually, the King, on his way south to London in 1603, had stopped for the night at Dunglass, having got this far from Edinburgh – but oddly, seems to have been dissatisfied with his accommodation there and moved off up the hill to Blackcastle, a Hepburn seat near the village of Oldhamstocks. It remained a mystery what had been wrong – but then, as David knew all too well, the King was an odd character. Anyway, it did not prevent him from creating Lord Home an earl two years later. That one died a couple of years ago, and his son James was now the second Earl of Home and Lord Dunglass. The original castle was destroyed by English raiders at the specific command of Henry the Eighth in the middle of last century, and thereafter rebuilt as it was now, large and strong. But the Earl seldom occupied it, living at Home Castle in the Merse and, more often, down at court, for both his wives had been English, leaving it in the care of a steward, a rough and sour character with whom they at Bilsdean had few dealings. Despite his two marriages, the Earl had no son or any child, so the place stood largely empty meantime. Bilsdean had been built less than a century before, really to command the main road south, where it had to cross the steep dean, so that it could close it unless tolls were paid, a custom her father had never pursued, she was glad to say. He was descended from an earlier Lord Home, and his own father had been given Bilsdean, and a parcel of land along the coast, as an inheritance. So they were only fairly remotely related to the present Earl, and the estates now independent. But both lines were buried in the graveyard of the ancient priory, where she was now taking him – although this was not the parish church, that being at the village of Oldhamstocks, a couple of miles further up into the hills.

Avoiding the road up to the castle, Barbara led him by another and clearly little-used track to a very different building, a surprise for David. He had assumed, by the way she spoke, that it would be a fairly small private chapel and family burial-place; but Dunglass Priory was a large and handsome edifice, much finer than any parish kirk he had seen, dignified as to architecture. It was cruciform in plan, with a tall square tower and massive stone-slabbed roof, with the tower placed off-centre above the transepts, to give an unusual effect. There were large and elaborately-traceried windows to east and west, supporting buttresses all around, and a porch which itself was as large as David had thought to see the whole. He expressed his admiration and surprise.

"Before the Reformation this was a collegiate church independent of the parish, under Coldingham Priory, with a provost and six prebendary priests," she told him. "They were all Homes. It served the northern Home lairdships as Coldingham did the southern. But the reformers did away with that, insisting that all worship should be at the parish church, and now this is merely a sort of crypt for the dead. A pity, I think."

Certainly the place looked deserted, last autumn's leaves still lying in corners, some of the window-glass broken. The finely carved oaken door in the porch, however, had a great key in the lock, and gave them entry.

Inside was even more fine than without. The stained-glass of the east and west windows shed a mellow and kindly light. Many carved stone archways, supported on cherub-head corbels, rose to the barrel-vaulted ceiling, this plastered, like the walling, and painted in rich colours, fading now but still eye-catching, Biblical scenes and heraldry. In the chancel was a splendid three-seat sedilia for the priests, a piscina or holy-water basin and a carved aumbry for the reserved sacrament. The dents of the reformers' disapproving hammers were clearly visible on all of this. A feature of the whole was the number of arched recesses in the walling for stone coffins, some covered with recumbent effigies of armoured knights, some empty.

David referred to these. "So many," he said. "Who were they for? Who merited this especial burial in the church? Only the Lords Home?"

"I do not think so. For there are other burial-places outside and a crypt beneath. For the lords, as well as others. No," Barbara told him, "I think that these were for the representatives of the various branches of the clan, only. One for each – that in the choir, there, for the founder of it all, Home of that Ilk. That is, for the northern Homes, for the southern ones are buried at Coldingham, near St Ebba's Head."

"Are there so many? In the north, here?"

"Many, yes. Manderston, Broomhouse, Snuke, Edrom, Whitchester – oh, and many others. Such as Primroknowe, Spott, Tyninghame, Thurston and now, of course, Bilsdean."

"A whole dynasty! I had not known that there were so many, such a host of lairds of the name. Far more than the Grays. Almost like a Highland clan. Are there other Border families so numerous?"

"I would think not. In lairdships, that is. There are probably more folk of the name of Kerr or Scott or Douglas. But not separate landed men, owners of estates. My father called it once 'a pride of Homes!'. He counted over thirty different lairds in the East March. We have been always close-knit, you see, marrying mainly within the name and so keeping our lands in the family, generation after generation. Three-quarters of all the Merse belongs to the Homes. It has been a matter of pride to keep it so, whatever happens in Scotland."

For some reason this all had a depressing effect on the man. He changed the subject. "You mentioned Primroknowe amongst them all," he said. "What do you know of the present laird? Who much interests me, needless to say."

"I do not know him well. I have met him, and cannot say that I liked him. A man of middle years, unwed. Primroknowe lies on the far side of these Lammermuir Hills, not so far away as the birds fly, a mere ten miles probably, but a long way round by roads and tracks. We have no dealings with him. Few Homes have, I think."

"Is that not strange, in your tight-knit clan? Why is that?"

"It was really his father's doing – the Primroknowe before him, George, whom the King made Earl of Dunbar, Lord Treasurer of Scotland, Commissioner to the General Assembly and much else besides. He was one of the King's closest companions, and a clever man. But scarcely lovable. James sent him up as Commissioner, to pacify the Borderland, after the Union of the Crowns. Always, as you will know, the Borderers have been rievers, cattle-raiders, mosstroopers, with their own laws and customs. They did not change all that because the King of Scots suddenly became the King of England also, and proclaimed that there was now no need for a border between his two realms. So George Home, created an earl, was sent up in 1605, I think it was, to bring the Borderers to heel. And he did it most bloodily. He hanged no fewer than one hundred and forty of what he called the worst thieves and robbers of the Border. And they were not all Armstrongs, Maxwells, Turnbulls, Elliots and Kerrs. There were Homes amongst them. So, powerful as he was, he was not loved by the other Home lairds – who were deep in Border rieving and feuding themselves! You will not find *him* buried here, although he too was a northern Home. He lies only in the parish kirk of Dunbar, however magnificent his monument!"

"I see. And this mislike was passed on to his son?"

"Yes. Partly it is that. But also, he is little liked for himself. A difficult man, with few friends, I understand. He keeps himself to himself – save for his strange association with the Earl of Bothwell . . ."

"Bothwell? You mean, the Warlock? Francis Stewart, the King's old enemy. Nephew of Queen Mary's Bothwell?"

"The same. That Earl is dead now, of course. But

170

Primroknowe was close to him for some years before he died, they say."

"But how can that be? Bothwell was banished the realm, both realms, by the King for his witchcraft and plotting. Overseas. To France, then, I heard, to Naples . . ."

"Yes. But once the King went down to London, the Earl used to come back to Scotland, secretly, sometimes. To gain moneys from his lands, no doubt – such as were not forfeited. Came for brief visits. The word was that he stayed with Thomas Home of Primroknowe."

"Sakes! And did James know of this?"

"That I cannot tell you. But surely it seems unlikely. Or would he have given Primroknowe your uncle's shcriffdom?"

"No-o-o. There is some mystery here. James hated and feared Bothwell. The Witch-Master of Scotland! The King has a terror of witchcraft. He has written a book about it. He personally conducted the witch-trials at North Berwick, in which the Earl of Bothwell was involved. I have heard my uncle speak of this often. For we have witches in Angus also. But it is a kind of madness with James. If Primroknowe was close to Bothwell . . .!"

"I do not know, David."

"James is usually well-informed, I learned from Duke Ludovick. He has a host of spies, here in Scotland. There is something very strange in this."

"Perhaps. But is it so important? Now?"

"It could be . . ."

They moved on, to admire the finely carved and coloured coat of arms of the Lords Home over the priests' door to the choir, the paint flaking off now. But it was to the nearby empty niche that the girl pointed.

"There used to be a statue there, to the Virgin Mary, my father says. But the reformers smashed it down. This priory was dedicated to the Virgin. I am no Papist, but I cannot think that it was right to shame and spit upon our Lord's mother. And to deface crucifixes and the like. Can you?"

"No, I can not. That was a kind of madness, too, I believe. The corruption of the old Church was great, to be sure. But Knox and the other reformers went too far, much too far. We lost a lot as well as gaining, from the Reformation."

171

She nodded. "This lovely old church is no longer a place of worship. Only a burial-place for Home lairds. Yet, when I marry – if marry I do – I would wish to be wed here, in this good place."

David swallowed, and said nothing.

They went out, back to the horses, silent.

Instead of riding directly back to Bilsdean, Barbara took him down to the coast again, further west, to see the salt-pans established there. These took the form of shallow iron baths contrived on the rocks of the sea-shore, into which sea-water could be led. Beneath was space for firing, so that the water could be boiled and evaporated as steam, leaving the salt as deposit. The fires would have been best of coals, but since there were no coal-pits nearer than Prestonpans and Tranent, twenty-five miles away, they had to make do with their own wood, less hot and efficient. But the salt was essential. This estate, being a coastal one only, had little arable land and little pasture for cattle. So its income had to be made almost wholly from the sea, and the salted-fish trade was almost as important as the lobsters and salmon.

There was another little fishing-community at Bilsdean Creek nearby, smaller than at Cove Haven, and they went to pass the time of day with the fisherfolk there, by whom Barbara was welcomed and obviously thought much of. She picked up a fine salmon from the stake-nets here, for Janet's kitchen, and they rode back to the castle.

That evening by the hall fire, Janet persuaded her sister to produce her clarsach, a small harp, and play them melodies, Border ballads and traditional songs. Barbara had a tuneful singing voice, and Janet's deeper tones made a pleasing accompaniment. David joined in, presently, in the choruses at least, but was under no illusions that his contribution added greatly to the effect. But it all made a happy and congenial ending to a most rewarding and unusual day.

Or not quite an ending. For when it came to retiring time, hot-water and escorting time, with David, as before, starting with Janet, she this time challenged him.

"You've nae call to be bashful the night, Davie," she declared. "We've a' seen each ither as we are, just. So you'll gie my back a bit wash, where I canna reach mysel'."

"As you will," he said, since that was in the nature of a command – moreover she already had much of her top half bared.

"And dinna mak it sound sik a sair task!"

"No. It is . . . a delight," he admitted, as he applied cloth and water. And that was no lie.

Even so she had a complaint. "You're gey canny as to where you wipe, man!"

"You would not have me trespass on where you yourself can reach?"

"Would I no'? Ah, weel – beggars canna be choosers, as they say! I'll hae to wash my front mysel', it seems." However, she turned round to embrace him, with a warm if damp heartiness.

In these somewhat distracting conditions he kissed her goodnight, and retreated, slightly breathless.

Upstairs, Barbara eyed him quizzically. "You have been a little detained, no? And you look somewhat wet about the clothing, David! Was it . . . trying?"

"Not, not trying, no. But . . . delaying. However kindly meant. For it was here that I wanted to be."

"Yes? Then I am glad. Even though *I* may disappoint. After Janet! You see, she has her difficulties. She is no loose woman, David. But I think that she feels her position keenly sometimes. She is my sister – and yet not really so in the eyes of most. My father's daughter, but a servant. She is not jealous of me, but feels the difference. So she must assert herself, when she can. And she is attractive to men, and knows it. No doubt more so than am I. She can show it this way – when she feels that way. As much to *me*, as to you. Can you understand?"

"I think that I can, yes. Even though I do not agree with you."

"No?"

"In that she could be more attractive than you, Barbara. That is more wrong than you can know. Or that I can tell you!"

"You could try, perhaps?"

"No, lass. For if I did that, I fear that I would go too far, could not control myself. I told you before, I am not a strong

173

man, in many ways. Janet has her problems – and so have I. You must know that, even though you do not show it. Certainly *I* know it! Like her, I am a penniless bastard. A land-steward, a servant of sorts also, even though one with some responsibilities. I have to remind myself of this, always. Especially . . . now!"

"You make too much of all that, David – you *do*."

"Birth matters, as you have just shown."

"Yes. But it is not the most important matter. As you make it sound. What you *are*, in yourself, is what signifies. And you are a fine man, honourable, able – and stronger than you admit. Also, not ill-favoured! But over-proud, in your own way, I say. You are the trusted emissary of the Lord Gray. You are clearly a friend of the Duke of Lennox. And, it seems, trusted by the King himself. Forby, you have served my father, and the other lairds, well over this of the monopoly. Do not undervalue yourself, David."

"None of all that gives me what I need, to start to tell you what I think of you, Barbara – to my sorrow. So, do not tempt me."

She sighed, but held out her arms to him.

That gesture he did not actually reject, at least. But still he restrained himself, holding her close only for moments and kissing her with a quite unsuitable brevity considering the invitation of her open lips.

She did not seek to detain him as he broke away, but shook her head as he made for her door. "Sleep well," she called after him. "And dream without all your restrainings, proud one!"

He did not, could not, answer.

In the morning, both girls accompanied him halfway to North Berwick and the ferry to Fife.

12

Andrew, Lord Gray, stared, glared, at David. "You tell me that all you have gained is a mere stay of the trouble for a month or so! No more than that! God flay you – is that all? After all that we have done."

"Is it so little, my lord? It is a step, is it not? In the right direction. It gives you time . . ."

"What use is that? If there is no further threat to him. *Did* you charge him with this of Rizzio? Make fully plain the threat to him if the proof was to be published?"

"I did not require to. The King himself used the name. More than once referred to Rizzio. Asked whether we had found a letter. He perceived the threat clearly enough . . ."

"Yet he was not sufficiently troubled to, to yield on this of the sheriffdom? Only offered a small delay! That will serve little or nothing. You cannot have pressed him sufficiently, man. Made clear what is at stake."

"How could I, my lord? Had I said more than I did, I could have been in the Tower of London by now! He said that himself, as it was, said that he might put me in the Tower. Openly to threaten the monarch is high treason. Besides, what had I to threaten him with? We do not *have* any letter naming Rizzio as his father. Only the notion that there may be one."

"That notion was sufficient for my father to milk James for years! Why should it be different now?"

"That I know not, my lord. As I say, the King asked if you had such a letter. What could I say? He is not a fool. I could only declare that I did not know – lie as that was. That I was only the messenger. Sent to tell him that you had recovered the Casket Letters. That you were offering them to him, of your loyal duty. And to hint that you would look for some recognition, reward, since they were so important. He

175

perceived the threat behind that, at once. But also knew that the other letters, such as they are, pose no threat to him. They were used at his mother's trial in England, after all – or some of them. In translation. Only a confession by Queen Mary that David Rizzio had been her son's father could endanger the King, make him illegitimate and with no right to the English throne. Without that proof, he is safe. He knows it well. And so demands whether you have it. What could I have told him?"

"He must believe that there *is* such a letter. Or he would not have paid mail to my father. And to others before him. So where is it, of a mercy?"

David spread his hands.

"We need it, and must have it. Why would it not be at Fast, with the others? Why would my father keep it alone, elsewhere? Fast was the most secure hiding-place he knew. Why keep one, the most precious, separate, apart? It must be there still, somewhere."

"We searched the entire castle . . ."

"This underground cistern where you did find the casket. Was there nothing more there? In the hole in the rock?"

David moistened his lips. In fact, he had not probed deeper into that cavity. Once he had felt the casket in its canvas bag, he had drawn it out, so excited that he had not thought of groping further. *Could* there have been more? Another package, behind?

"I felt no other, my lord," was all that he could say.

"But you did not look further, man?"

"There was no looking, only feeling. In the dark. Underground."

"There could have been more. He could have kept it apart, this especial letter. You could have missed it."

There was nothing to say to that.

"You will have to go back," Gray said. "To Fast. To look further."

"But, my lord, how can I? Now? How could I explain without revealing what you look for, and why? Bilsdean himself will be back. It would not be just a matter of returning with the daughter. Her father, if he allowed me to go to Fast again, at all, would be like to come with us. I could not tell him why we wanted it . . ."

"You could say that there was a letter missing. No need to say which, or why. Just that this casket and the letters, all the letters, were to go to the King. So they must all be there. He could not say you nay to that."

"But . . ." David shook his head. "My lord, instead of that, why not send the casket and letters you have down to the King? As gift. It might well serve. He would be glad to have them, that is sure. Be sufficiently grateful to amend this of the sheriffdom, perhaps, without any further pressing. Indeed, why not take them yourself? He asked why you had not come, in the first place. As did Duke Ludovick. That would be much better than for me to take them. Or for more threats . . ."

"Na, na, Davie, that would not serve. If James but took them, said his thanks and did no more, I would be left with nothing. And if I then threatened him with the Rizzio affair, he would have *me* in the Tower, for I could not claim to be any messenger. No, no."

"Not to threaten him, my lord. Just to give him the letters and hope that he would show his gratitude. He is generous enough, it seems; over-generous the Duke says. Gives away too much, to too many. So for the famed Casket Letters he might well show you much kindness."

"No. I will not go to London, man. Begging. Nor will I make him a gift of the letters. Or, not yet. No, you must go back to Fast, and search further. If we can lay hands on that missing letter, we have him! We have got this breathing-space, Home's installation delayed. We must put the time to best use."

"But, my lord, my duties here, as your steward . . .?"

"No buts, Davie. We'll manage fine lacking you for a wee bittie! This is a deal more important. You must go, and forthwith, before James changes his mind."

"I cannot just go back again to Fast and Bilsdean. So soon."

"You can. And will."

"My lord, I cannot see *why* the Master, my grandsire, should keep this one letter apart. If it does exist. More especially in the same hiding-place, but lying separate. Why?"

"I do not know. But, if it was not in the casket, where is it? It may not be only the one letter. There could be others. Where else would he keep them? You searched all else."

"He had other houses. This one. And Fowlis. And Castle Huntly."

"Castle Huntly was cleared of all before it was sold. Such precious paper would not have been left. I have gone over everything here of my father's. And Fowlis is the least secure house he had."

"You have not searched there?"

"No. He little used it. No, if that letter is anywhere, it is still at Fast. Where else could it be?"

A thought occurred to David. "My lord, your sister Mary Gray might have some notion where it might have been hidden, where he might have kept it. Since she was closest to him. Why do not you go and ask her? And I could go to Fowlis and seek there."

"*I* will go to Fowlis. You back to Methven. Mary and I do not always agree. You go ask her. But it will be Fast again for you, Davie, thereafter – that I feel sure."

So next day it was the westwards road to Strathearn once more for David, the thirty-five miles, through the fertile Carse of Gowrie, where the fine summer was allowing the first rigs and fields to be harvested, the crossing of Tay to St John's Town of Perth and on over Tippermuir. At Methven he was, as before, well received by Mary Gray, who accepted from him Duke Ludovick's letter in reply to her own, and was eager to hear all that had gone on at London, especially how her beloved Vicky was, and whether there was any word of him coming north soon? He had not been home since last Yuletide. David relayed the warm messages from the Duke. No doubt he would tell her in his letter what were his hopes of a visit to Methven. But the King was clearly very demanding of his company . . .

"Yes, James is too fond of Vicky for *my* comfort!" she agreed. "There are few that he seems to trust and need so closely. Selfishly, I could wish it otherwise. But – *you*, David? How far did the King trust in you and your mission? I thought much of you, wondering, and wishing you well."

"It was difficult. I was less than happy, I can assure you!

178

But the Duke helped me greatly. Without him I could not have achieved anything."

"You did achieve something?"

"Only the King's agreement to postpone the inauguration of this Sir Thomas Home for a little time. That is all. Do you know anything of this Home of Primroknowe?"

"I fear not. I knew something of his father, the Earl. But not this man. Nor why the King so favours him, in this."

"No. It is strange. For he does not seem to frequent the court. I am told that he was friendly with the Earl of Bothwell. Not the husband of Queen Mary but his nephew. Did you know *him*? He was the King's enemy, was he not?"

"Very much so. Francis Stewart was the son of Mary's third husband's sister. By the Lord John Stewart, Commendator of Coldingham, an illegitimate son of James the Fifth, one of the many such. Thus the Queen's half-brother and King James's uncle. This Francis Stewart, who heired the Bothwell earldom, was therefore James's cousin. But they hated each other. A strange man, he was clever. But evil, or so it is believed."

"Because of this of witchcraft? You say, it is believed? You are not sure of it?"

"I do not know that I believe in witchcraft, David. Oh, there is much that is dark and shameful done in the name of witchcraft. But a deal of it is just mummery, I think, a sort of play-acting. Francis Stewart was deep in it, to be sure. He sought to play the Devil, yes. But it was not what the King made it out to be. All that of creating storms to wreck James's ships, casting spells to harm him, and the like. The King won confessions out of wretched women to that effect, by torture – but the poor creatures would have confessed anything to end their agonies."

"So you think this Earl of Bothwell less black than he was painted? Yet you said evil . . .?"

"Less black in this of witchcraft, it may be. But, that was not all. He did plot against James. I know that, since my father was involved in some degree. He openly invaded the supreme court at Edinburgh and carried off a witness who was to give evidence against him. He attacked the palace of Holyroodhouse, seeking to capture the King and the

Chancellor, but that assault was foiled when the citizens under their Provost came to the rescue. He slew Home of Manderston, he who was known as Davy the Devil, who rivalled him in this folly of playing at Satan, and was excommunicated for it. Oh yes, Francis Stewart was a wild man. You say that this Home of Primroknowe was friendly with him?"

"So I am told. And that is strange, if Bothwell slew Home of Manderston. For was not the Earl of Dunbar, George Home of Primroknowe, father of this one, himself a son of Manderston?"

"So I understand. But that would be twenty-five years ago, at least. Davy the Devil would, I suppose, be your man's uncle, brother to the Earl of Dunbar."

"Bothwell died in Italy, they say. When would that be?"

"I think twelve years ago. Probably 1612. He fled, first to England, then to France. And died at Naples."

"I understand he returned to Scotland sometimes . . ."

"Oh, yes. He came back secretly, many times. It had to be secret, for he was outlawed by the King and if captured he would have been executed. He used to come by sea to Fast Castle, where . . ."

"Fast! That place again!"

"Fast, yes. Where he could land secretly. It was there that my father used to meet him. Where they did their plotting. Robert Logan of Restalrig had inherited Fast, remember, his mother my Aunt Agnes Gray, my father's sister, who had remarried the Lord Home. Bothwell, Logan and my father were close. It is thought that most of the Gowrie Conspiracy was plotted at Fast, in 1600."

"Lord, that hold seems to have been a very viper's nest! And this Thomas Home – could he have been involved there?"

"That I do not know. I never heard my father speak of him. But those Homes were into all kinds of intrigue."

"And yet the King gives him my uncle's sheriffdom!"

"His father, the Earl of Dunbar, was the King's friend and did much of James's ill work for him."

"Aye. Ill work indeed, all round, it seems! What a tangled

180

web of plot and violence. Why? What made it all boil up at that time? So much of hatred, treason and murder?"

"It was largely because of the Reformation, I would say. That, and Henry the Eighth of England's efforts to suborn Scotland, with Mary the Queen being so staunchly Catholic, the land divided and her son James brought to the throne as a babe. All that led to unending intrigue, the taking of sides, violence. Almost, the Catholic religion was re-established. That was behind much of the plotting. With Spain's efforts to aid in that. Spanish gold coming to Scotland, to Fast – the Spanish Blanks. Much of it still there, some say, hidden or lost. My father, Logan and Bothwell in the midst of it all . . ."

"No gold at Fast now, I think! For we searched the place from top to bottom for those letters. And found only the casket. Which brings us back to the missing letter, about Rizzio. If there was one! You have no notion where it might be? Where your father might have hidden it? Since it was not with the others."

"None. Patrick was a man of secrets – only a very few of which he shared with me. It could be anywhere, although I would have expected it to be at Fast. If it ever existed. It all could well have been an invention of his own mind. To frighten James."

"Yes. I told my uncle that. But he will have it that the letter exists. And will have me go to Fast again, to seek further."

"In order to constrain the King? I feared that it would come to that."

David's silence was eloquent.

"Better that there should be no missing letter," she went on. "Tell Andrew that, from me."

That was all, for Lord Gray, from this visit to Methven.

Three days later David was on his way to Bilsdean for the fourth time, in one respect delighted to be going, in another considerably concerned.

One fear, at least, was quickly dispersed on arrival, the quality of his welcome. He had been worried that his so frequent appearances could raise eyebrows, even though the girls' haste-ye-backs had sounded sufficiently genuine. And if the laird was home, that could well not help. However,

Alexander Home, who had indeed returned from London, greeted him warmly, with no hint of reserve; and his daughters showed only gladness.

David made his explanations without delay, of course – he had been considering just how to put it for most of the way from Broughty. Barbara had recounted to her father the quest for the Casket Letters and their finding, so David had not to deal with that, save to indicate that the Lord Gray intended to present them to the King, hoping for some reciprocal gesture anent the Angus sheriffdom, all of which Bilsdean saw as fair and understandable in the circumstances. He apparently had no objections to them having searched at Fast, nor did he make any suggestion that the letters might be *his* property, since they had been hidden in what was now his castle. It was the next part of David's announcement which required the care.

It had been discovered, he went on, that there was probably a letter, or more than one, missing. The King himself, and the Duke of Lennox, had spoken of one which referred to the Italian secretary of Queen Mary, David Rizzio. For some reason, this was important. But there had been none such amongst the papers in the casket, as they had found them. But it was the King's wish to have this. He was surprised that it was not amongst the others. So it must be found, if possible.

"I know why it is considered to be important," Home said, at once. "The man Rizzio was murdered, before the Queen's eyes, only a short time before James's birth. She was greatly distressed. Her husband, Darnley, was one of those who arranged it, and was present – although there were others also. Darnley's dagger was left sticking in the corpse, of a purpose, to show that it was done with his approval. I think that Mary never forgave him. It is said that James's fear of cold steel stems from that deed. The Rizzio murder, some-how, had a great effect on the child to be born, and all his life the King has had nightmares about it, they say. Also, there was the canard some ill-disposed folk put about that Rizzio was in fact his father, however wicked an invention that might be. So any letter of the Queen's referring to Rizzio would most certainly much concern James."

David swallowed. "Yes," he said. "I suppose that is it. But there was no mention of Rizzio in any of the papers we found. Why, do you think, there should be this notion that there *was* such a letter, sir?"

"I do not know that. But perhaps the Queen some time spoke of it? Not to her son himself, for he was only a small child when he last saw his unfortunate mother. But to someone who later told the King. The letters were in the possession of the Earl of Bothwell, written to him, as all know. And were lost, after he fled abroad, and died in Denmark. But somehow they came into the Master of Gray's possession and he seems to have kept them at Fast, for safety – although why he did not hand them over to the King I do not know. But he was very close to the King, at one time, indeed acting Chancellor of this realm, and may well have mentioned this of Rizzio."

"Yes." That was as far as David wanted to take the matter. "That may be it. Anyway, my uncle thinks that the missing letter may still be at Fast. We searched all the castle before we found the casket in that water-cistern. But . . . I did not probe further into that cavity when I found it. There may be more in there – who knows? That is why I am here, sir. May I have your permission to go back and seek again? Lord Gray so requests, of your kindness."

"To be sure, my friend. Certainly you may. It is my leal duty, no less, is it not? To help find it, if the King so wishes to have it. I will, indeed, go with you to look, tomorrow. I have never been down into that water-cistern, never thought to go. It was clever judgment of the two of you to go down into that place."

"It was Barbara who led, sir . . ."

So the thing was agreed thus far at least with the minimum of trouble. They would ride over to Fast in the morning, for Bilsdean was doubtful as to his ability to climb up that rope and shaft from the cave, as required if going by boat.

That evening, in the hall, was different, more formal than heretofore, however pleasant a host was Alexander Home, for Janet was not present. And at bedtime, the goodnight ceremonial was considerably truncated, glances and smiles having to serve – which said something to David, even if he was not sure what.

Next day, the three of them rode off up to Coldingham Muir, over to Dowlaw and on to the cliff-top track to Fast, on a dull morning threatening rain, the sea grey and sullen. In these conditions the castle looked grim and forbidding indeed, perched on its rock-stack above the breakers, proper to its reputation, its halo of screaming sea-birds seeming fit appendage. Fast required sunshine to make it acceptable. Even so, its owner dismounted to lead his horse that last quarter-mile, as I did the others.

At least there was no difficulty as to entrance, for presumably its keeper, Rob Calder, kept a better look-out for visitors than David had thought on that first approach, for the narrow drawbridge began to clank down across the yawning chasm between stack and cliff proper well before they reached it. Leaving the mounts on the little terrace nearby, they crossed the planking as the iron portcullis was raised, laboriously creaking, and the massive gate was dragged open.

The custodian greeted the pair with his master a shade more deferentially than he had done previously.

They wasted no time about preliminaries but, demanding two lanterns, went straight to that trap-door in the flooring of the entrance pend and had Calder raise it open. As before, Barbara went first down the ladder, with one lantern, and when she called, David descended next, then Alexander Home, with the second lantern, very cautiously.

Crouching in that damp dark, with the drip-drip of water the only sound, they peered around.

There was no need for all three to creep round the ledge to that hole. But somehow all had to do it. As before, Barbara went left-about and David right, each with a lantern, the laird gruntingly following his daughter on hands and knees. As he went, David had a mind-picture of his grandfather, the most handsome man in Christendom, reputedly the mirror of fashion and always immaculately attired, crawling round this dismal pit in the rock with his precious, secret hoard.

He reached the cavity first, but waited for Barbara. Pushing the two lanterns in before them, they peered inside.

There *was* something more in that hole, at the back, a small heap of material, probably another canvas bag. They eyed each other, and the laird, crawling up, added his comment.

David, lowering head and shoulders still further – for that cavity was no more that three fcct high and five deep – pushed in, to reach for that bundle. Withdrawing it, he quickly recognised that this, although smaller than that of the casket, was considerably heavier. Backing, he dragged it out.

"Weighty," he said. "Does not feel like papers." There was nothing else in that hole.

Back at the ladder-foot, they opened the stiff folds of the bag. Inside was a rolled-up old shirt, worn and ragged; but with something heavy within. This proved to be another and smaller bag, but of leather. The clink of metal sounded as they lifted it out.

Loosening the damp cord which tied its neck, David sought to look inside. But the lamplight did not penetrate, and he thrust in a hand. It was with a jerked exclamation that he drew it out, clutching a handful. The weight was explained. As he opened his hand in the lanterns' light it was seen to hold nuggets, ingots of metal, gleaming dully.

"Lord!" Bilsdean gasped. "Gold! Gold casts." He picked up one, staring. "So-o-o! That is it – gold ingots! Hidden there . . ."

"But no letters!" David said, groping further. "Just this gold."

They looked from their find to each other, there in the flicker of light and shadow.

Putting the nuggets back in their bag, they climbed out into the daylight.

They took their find to the main square keep of the place, set on the highest point of the pinnacle, and leaving Calder below, went upstairs to the bare, empty hall. On the great table there they opened the bag again and poured out its contents. There were fourteen of the pieces of cast metal, beaten into approximate cubes, all of a size but unstamped.

"The Master of Gray's secret store!" Barbara exclaimed. "More valuable than any letter?"

"That I would not know," David answered. "A letter that a king wanted might be worth more. Who can tell?"

"*I* can tell what this represents, at least," the laird said. "That is part of the Spanish Blanks hoard . . . which must have stuck to your grandsire's fingers, my young friend! You know about the Spanish Blanks?"

"Only a little, sir. By name."

"Aye, well. During the years of what is now called the Counter-Reformation, around 1593, it would be, when it was possible that the Catholic faith would triumph again in Scotland, with many of the lords for it, and Knox and Melville and other notable reformers dead, a letter was captured, or a package of letters. These were blank sheets of paper bearing at the foot of each the signatures of sundry great nobles, with their seals attached – those of Huntly, Angus, Errol and others. Being sent to the King of Spain, enlisting his aid, the details to be filled in by the courier, one Kerr by name, brother of Mark Kerr, Abbot of Newbattle, once he was safely out of the country. Although this appeal never reached Spain, evidently another did, for King Philip responded and sent a great treasure in gold, from the Americas, to aid his fellow-Catholics in their struggle, to buy arms and pay men. It was sent here to Fast, by ship, as a safe and secure place to land it, Logan of Restalrig to hold and distribute it to the lords. Some was distributed, undoubtedly, but it is generally believed that much was not! Since it came in nuggets, unstamped gold, not Spanish coin, so that if found on anyone it would not condemn them, it also got called the Spanish Blanks. The Master of Gray's part in it all is uncertain, for he could play both sides, as all know, and it is doubtful how much religion he had in him! So this, I think, could be the price of his aid, or of his silence – or part of it. The Counter-Reformation failed, of course, God be praised, so the gold never had to be accounted for."

"My grandsire seems to have been no very reputable character!"

"He was a strange mixture, able, clever, excellent company, but lacking scruple. At least, shall we say, his scruples were not those of most men – as were his gifts! With him, the end ever justified the means. And he believed in due reward for his services! If King James had but cherished him, instead of slighting him as he did – for he performed a great deal for James – he would have remained one of the kingdom's most useful servants. For realms *need* such men, I fear. But the

King, although clever also, made this great mistake – and paid for it!"

"Paid, yes. This gold here – is it worth much, think you?"

"Without weighing it carefully I would not know how much. But I should think a deal of pounds Scots." Bilsdean hefted one of the nuggets in his hand. "Hard to tell weights. There could be some eight ounces in these, each of them, I would say. They measure gold in ounces, do they not? How much an ounce I know not, but much money. And there are fourteen here. Fourteen at eight ounces . . .?"

Barbara was better than her father at calculating. "One hundred and twelve ounces," she said.

"Yes. That could be thousands of pounds Scots, I would say. Enough to compensate Lord Gray, in some measure, if he does lose his sheriffdom!"

"But, is this his? It is found on your property, sir."

"It must have been his father's. Hidden there, beside those letters. It would not be Robert Logan's. *He* did not have possession of the letters. No, this gold will belong to your grandsire's heir – that is, the Lord Gray."

"Some proportion should come to you, to be sure."

"And some to *you*, David," Barbara declared. "You found it. Without you, it would never have been discovered. You should get half, I say!"

He shook his head, smiling. "I think not. But, this is not what we came here for. The missing letter. We searched all this castle before, every corner. Is there anywhere else we should have looked, sir?"

"If Barbara does not know of any, *I* do not, I fear."

"I can think of no other," the girl said.

"Then, we must judge there to be no further letters here. If there is one amissing, it is not at Fast Castle."

"Will King James be greatly disappointed?"

"As to that I am unsure," David said carefully. "But my uncle will be, no doubt. Since he believes it to count for much with the King."

"At least, now you have this gold for him," the laird said. "Not the worth of his sheriffdom – but it would help."

On the ride back to Bilsdean, David thought to re-open the

subject of Primroknowe. "I spoke of Sir Thomas Home to you in London, sir," he reminded. "None there seemed to be close to him or to know him well, even though he was distant kin. Barbara says that she had heard that he was friendly with the Earl of Bothwell, the Stewart one. It seems strange, since Bothwell was the King's foe, that James should now be rewarding Primroknowe."

"As I told you, I scarcely know the man. After you had gone, we all spoke of it, in that London tavern, and wondered why James had given Lord Gray's sheriffdom to him. None could make sense of it. He does not frequent the court. And so far as any know, was not close to the King, at any time. But – he must have done some service."

"This of Bothwell? How came they to be friendly, I wonder?"

"That I do not know, either. They must have had something in common. Bothwell heired great lands in Lothian, of course, near to Haddington. And the Earl of Dunbar, Primroknowe's father, owned Spott, which lands border Hailes and the Bothwell Haddingtonshire lands. All these were forfeited, of course, when Bothwell was outlawed and banished. It may be that Primroknowe, who used to live at Spott before his father died, kept an eye on neighbouring Hailes, for Bothwell. May even have collected rents for him, from the tenant-farmers."

"Yes. Such as that could explain much. But not why the King rewards him. Quite the reverse, if it was known." David rode silent for a little. "It was here, at Fast, that Bothwell came, in his secret visits from France and Italy and Spain. So he must either have gone to Primroknowe from Fast, or else Primroknowe came to Fast to meet him. Did you ever hear of that?"

"No. That was in Logan's time. Before we Homes won Fast back again."

"If he did come to Fast, Primroknowe must have also been friendly with Logan and my grandsire? Or at least, on reasonably good terms. Or he would not have gained entry to the castle. So, could he have been linked with their plotting? Was he a Catholic?"

"I never heard of it, if he was. Or is. I suppose that he might have been one of the plotters. I am sorry, lad, that I cannot be of more help to you. But I know so little of the man."

"Why was he knighted? Do you know that?"

"Oh, that was his father's doing. He was Dunbar's only son, although illegitimate. And Dunbar was close to James, and could arrange such matters."

"Could that be why the King favours him now? For his dead father's sake?" Barbara asked.

"Surely not. Dunbar died over ten years past. At Whitehall. Thought to have been poisoned – none ever discovered that mystery. Would James wait ten years so to reward the bastard son?"

David rode on, thoughtful.

A thin rain began before they reached Bilsdean.

That evening, the laird made a suggestion. "Are you in great haste to return to Broughty Castle, young man?" he asked. "If not, and if the rain clears, how would you like to ride over to Primroknowe tomorrow, since you are so interested? Across the hills. You could meet Sir Thomas. Speak with him. He should have some gratitude towards you, over the salmon-fish monopoly. For he has large fishings in the Whiteadder. That would give us excuse for calling upon him."

"That is well thought on. If you would take me, I would be grateful."

"I will go also," Barbara said. "I enjoy riding through the Lammermuirs."

So next morning, much to Janet's disappointment, for she was not asked to accompany her father, the three of them set off again, this time almost due southwards up the Dunglass Water into the foothills. Quite quickly they rose out of the steep, wooded ravine, with all the heather hills beginning to rise before them, crowding all the prospect. Near the village of Oldhamstocks, where was the parish kirk, they forked away left-handed on to the high ground, open grass and bracken now, with heather higher, on to the side of Dod Hill, following a drove-road for cattle. Actually they saw no cattle in these hills, for the Lammermuirs, as their name implied, were the great sheep-rearing terrain of Scotland, with the sheep seeming to cover every hillside, ridge, hollow and moor. Sheep and cattle do not mix well; but their route followed the old cattle-trail, from the low country which flanked the Lothian shoreline, to the markets of Berwick-on-Tweed and north Northumberland.

On across Dunglass Common and Quixmuir they rode, by empty moorlands – empty save for the sheep and the occasional shepherd's cot-house, that is – mile upon mile, where only the curlews' wheepling and the larks' trilling broke the silence, fine free riding country where horsemen could canter on and on without hold-ups or distraction. These hills did not run to lofty peaks and summits, but long rolling contours and great sweeping flanks, far-flung to seeming eternity. As they rode, Home and Barbara pointed out heights and ridges and valleys, Pictish forts, standing-stones and stone-circles, nearly all with names redolent of sheep-rearing – Wedderlaws, Rammerscales, Ewelairs, Tuplaws, Sheeppaths, Lambknowes, Hogsriggs and the like.

After some seven miles of this, while still hilly, the land began to sink towards a major valley system, the vale of the Whiteadder and its tributary waters. Circling a prominent height named Cockburn Law, more pointed than most and crowned by the ramparts of a Pictish fort, they rode past an extraordinary edifice, ruinous but massive still as any castle: a circular, barrel-shaped Pictish broch or refuge-tower, its great walling fully fifteen feet in thickness, built of enormous stones which it might have seemed impossible for men to lift into place, these walls honeycombed with mural chambers and little stairways, rising to four storeys and encircling an open grass-grown central area. This was Edins Hall Broch apparently, named after the same Edin or Aidan, as was Edinburgh. These Lammermuir Hills, it seemed, had been highly populated by the Southern Picts, their forts and settlements everywhere surmounting heights, and refuge-towers such as this dotted here and there for the women and children to flee to from attack by Norse pirates and other seaborne invaders, driving the cattle and sheep into the central enclosures and themselves safe within the chambers of the mighty walling. The Homes knew of no others surviving fairly intact, as this one. David had never seen the like.

Dropping down into the wide valley now, soon after this

they reached, at Cockburn Mill, the fine river of Whiteadder, just a corruption of White Water – with a neighbouring stream called the Blackadder – and turning eastwards along its bank they quite quickly came to the castle, farmery and barony of Primroknowe, a prosperous-looking place set on a fertile terrace above the river's water-meadows, moderate as to size and not particularly strongly placed but all in good order. Bilsdean admitted that he had never actually visited here before, although he had seen the place from across the river.

They rode up to the castle, a fortalice not unlike Bilsdean, L-shaped within its high walled courtyard. The door of the gatehouse stood open, which seemed friendly enough, but there was no sign of life within, no persons nor animals visible. Their rasping of the tirling-pin on the heavy oaken door guarded by gun-loops at first appeared to produce no reaction, and they were about to leave to enquire at the farmery when an old woman came round, apparently from a back door, to eye them, blankly unwelcoming. She said nothing.

"I am Bilsdean, seeking Sir Thomas," Home announced. "Is he here?"

"No." That was flat.

"M'mm. Is he nearby? We have come to speak with him."

"I dinna ken whaur he is, Maister," the crone answered. "He doesna aye tell me whaur he's going."

"Well, is there anyone else at home, whom we could see?"

"No."

"You are alone here?"

"Aye."

"This is surely strange? In so large a house. There is no Lady Home?"

"No."

"You are unhelpful, woman!" the laird exclaimed. "If you cannot give us any help, where can we go to gain information?"

The other pointed out towards the farmery. "You could go speak wi' the steward." That said, she turned and went back whence she had come.

Declaring his annoyance, Home led them out and over to

the adjoining range of stabling and byres, sheep-pens and cot-houses.

A man was shovelling horse-dung for manure into a barrow at a stable door. Him they approached, to ask for the steward.

This individual stared, then pointed over to the largest of the cottages of the castleton, and resumed his shovelling without a word.

"A strange crew at Primroknowe!" Bilsdean commented.

Within the doorway of the larger cottage a younger man was standing, they saw, watching them.

"Are you steward here?" Home asked.

"Aye."

"I am Home of Bilsdean. Seeking Sir Thomas. Do you know where he is?"

"I canna say, sir," the other answered.

"Do you mean that you do not know? Or that you prefer not to say!" That was sharp.

"I dinna ken, sir. The laird's been gone twa-three days."

"And you do not know where? Nor when he will back?"

"No."

"Is there anyone whom we can ask, who does know?"

"I wouldna think it, sir."

Shrugging, Bilsdean reined his horse round. "Come," he jerked to his companions. "There is nothing to be gained here."

"These people are frightened," his daughter averred, as they rode off.

"Frightened? Or but uncivil?"

"The place has a strange air to it," David said.

"Fear," Barbara reiterated. "I can feel it, somehow. Yet it seems a goodly property and well-tended."

"A place of ill manners," her father asserted. "If it is like master, like man, then I can understand why Primroknowe is less than popular!"

They rode westwards now, along the haughs of a quite major tributary of Whiteadder, the Mill Burn, in pleasing meadows flanked by open woodland, Home thinking to go back by Oatleycleuch and Abbey St Bathans and so up over the Lammermuirs again by the Monynut. But after a mile, they came to where another and lesser stream entered the

Mill Burn from the south, amongst wooded bluffs and, in passing, noticed up on the quite steep knoll between the streams, amongst ancient dark yew trees, what appeared to be a church, unlikely a place as this was for such.

"What kirk is this?" Bilsdean wondered. "I do not know it. Preston I know, and Bonkyl beyond. Broomhouse and Cumledge have chapels. But this? Let us have a look . . ."

Dismounting, they tied their horses to the rail of a wooden bridge over the major burn, a bridge which looked as though it was but seldom used, and climbed the slope, to discover a small graveyard at the top surrounded by a broken-down wall. In the centre was a long, low, red-stone chapel, with tiny windows and few of them, obviously ancient but secret-looking, withdrawn, brooding. Those dark trees grew close, with old tombstones leaning drunkenly.

Examining more closely, they found the building simple in the extreme, with no ornamentation, at least externally, no cruciform shape, no spire or even belfry. It looked as though it was stone-vaulted, by its roof, but they could not see within, for its few and narrow windows were shuttered. The only feature to stand out was a wind-vane above a gable, in the shape of a cock. David Gray had seen many weathercocks in his day, but never one like this. Fashioned from iron and painted bright scarlet and black, and freshly so, the lifelike bird was crouching, wings spread and beak open, as though about to mount a hen. The visitors eyed it askance.

Barbara spoke. "I do not like it. That, or any of it here. It is too . . . hidden. Close. For any church. Dark."

The others did not contradict her.

They tried the single door but it was locked, unusual in a church. In the graveyard many of the tombstones were fallen, moss-grown, but some carved with the arms of Home, a silver lion rampant on green. All was gloomy, with that fresh-painted crouching cock seeming to dominate all.

"Let us leave," Barbara said. "There is something wrong here."

The laird, intrigued by those Home gravestones yet not knowing to which branch of the family they referred, changed his mind about their route home and decided to return by Preston, the nearest village, where they might enquire about this chapel. So they turned back down the Mill Burn to its junction with Whiteadder, and proceeded along the bank of this, keeping close to the riverside to avoid Primroknowe itself. They had not gone far when, round a sharp bend in the major river, they came to a salmon-fishers' bothy – clearly that by the nets hanging on poles to dry. Two men sat mending torn netting. Hailed, they rose and answered, cheerfully enough.

"Less churlish here," Bilsdean observed. "Let us speak with them."

They passed the time of day with the pair, who looked like father and son, asking if the fishing was good, to be told that it was only fair, although at this time of year the water was aye low. Yesterday's rain had helped but more was needed.

"Do you belong to Primroknowe?" the laird asked.

"Na, na, sir, we're frae Hutton," the older man said. "We just hae a tack o' the fishing here frae Laird Home. Ithers the same, up and doon."

"He, the laird, does not work these Whiteadder fishings himself?"

"He rents them oot in hauf-miles. I hae this yin, my brither the next doon. Mony ithers. We gie the laird hauf oor catch."

"I see. So he does quite well without having to employ his own fishers."

"Och, aye – fine he does."

"We came to see him, at Primroknowe, about the fishings. King James's monopoly tax. He is from home. None there could, or would, tell us where he is gone."

"Aye." That was laconic.

"They were less than forthcoming."

"They're a soor lot, yonder, sir. Mebbes they hae reason to be. It's an unchancy place, we reckon. They keep themsel's to themsel's."

"It's thae Picts, I'd say, sirs," the younger man put in, "The auld yins. A' these pairts up here were thick wi' the Picts. Stanes and circles a' place. Unyirdly, uncanny folk. Deil-worshippers they say."

"So! And you think the people here are . . . affected by it all?"

"I wouldna like to bide here mysel'!"

"Yet it seems a fair country. And were not the Picts sun-worshippers? The sun, not devils."

The fishermen glanced at each other and shrugged.

David spoke. "That church we passed, above the Mill Burn back there. A strange-like place."

Looking where he pointed, the pair reacted oddly and differently. The older crossed himself, the younger spat, and both turned their backs in that direction. They said nothing.

"You do not like it?" Barbara asked. "I did not either. Why?"

"Yon's no' a proper kirk," the son said. "No' now. Or so they say."

"You mean it is no longer a place of worship?"

There was a pause.

"Depends on whae they worship, Mistress, does it no'?"

"Are you back to your devils again? Pictish devils," her father asked.

"Hud your tongue, Jock!" the older man said. "Best no' to speak o' it. They nivver did us ony hairm. If yon place is bewitched, we'd best hud oor tongues. I've tell't you before. They could spoil the fishing for us."

Bilsdean looked from one to the other. "You believe this? That the place is bewitched? That devil-worship, or witch-craft, goes on there?"

"We dinna ken, Maister. We've nivver seen aught. But – yon's the clash o' the countryside, just. Safer no' to speir. We're just honest fishers frae Hutton, and dinna want oor fishing spoiled."

"But it could be all superstition."

"Sir Thomas Home?" David asked. "Does *he* know of this? Accept it?"

"They say he's the heid man in it," the younger man answered. "It's his kirk, is it no'? But . . ."

"Wheesht, Jock, wheesht!" his father ordered, gripping the other's arm. "Watch your gabbing tongue!"

Bilsdean nodded. "Fear nothing, friends. We will speak no more of it. All foolish talk and auld wives' claivers, no doubt. We'll leave you to your nets. And good fishing to you."

They remounted and moved on.

Out of sight and hearing around another bend, they drew rein and eyed each other.

"So-o-o!" David said. "This was the friend of the Earl of Bothwell! The Witch-Master of Scotland! Witchcraft and devil-worship! That strange church. It could be . . ." He shook his head. "and this Primroknowe is the man that King James, who hates witchcraft, has made Sheriff of Angus!"

"I hated that place," Barbara said. "I felt that it was evil. And I felt fear at the castle."

"Let us not make too much of it," her father told them. "Gossip and superstitious tales. And this of the Picts is a nonsense! Primroknowe may be a strange man but that does not make him a witch-master. Or make that church bedevilled."

"That weathercock . . .!" Barbara said. "And new-painted."

"Aye, well, that could be of no significance. Some fancy." He jerked at his reins. "Come, you . . ."

A thoughtful trio, they rode back northwards, by Preston village and the Drakemyre, where the famous Frenchman, de la Bastie, had been slain by the Homes in James the Fifth's reign, and so over a little pass into the Eye Water valley and on by the western flanks of Coldingham Muir, a longer but less hilly route than they had come by, some fifteen miles.

They arrived at Bilsdean to a surprise, no less than another visitor, in the person of David's cousin, Patrick, present Master of Gray. He had been sent by his father, from Broughty, to inform that a King's courier had come there, with a royal command for David Gray to repair to London forthwith, no reasons given, but James's personal orders.

Astonished and perturbed, David could make neither head nor tail of this. Patrick could give him no enlightenment, although he said that Lord Gray hoped that it was a good sign and the King possibly prepared to come to some sort of agreement on the matters at issue. That might be how it looked from Broughty Castle, but David was less sanguine. However, he had no option but to obey. He would ride south again in the morning, however reluctantly.

So that evening there were two young Grays to be entertained, with Patrick enjoying the company very obviously,

196

and playing the gallant with no lack of flourish, particularly of course towards Barbara – which did not please his cousin – but also towards Janet, in a more familiar fashion such as that young woman appeared to approve. He had all the Gray good looks, even though his features lacked something of the strength of David's. He and Janet seemed to have established quite a relationship in the short while in which he had been awaiting the others' return. All the Homes clearly found him easy to get on with – and this had the effect of making David the more reserved.

The cousins shared David's attic room that night, and Janet did not fail to offer her services in the matter of the hot-water washing, Patrick finding David something of a spoil-sport in it all, and saying so.

David had a lot to think about before he slept – but his last thought was the hope that his cousin would not linger for too long at Bilsdean in the morning, when he himself took the long road to London-town.

13

David stared at the Duke. "France!" he said. "Me?"

"France, yes. Paris. The Louvre, St Germain. The French court."

"But why? Why *me*?"

"James believes that you are just whom he requires. You made your mark with him, David, for better or worse! He considers you reliable, honest and with a good head on your shoulders – even though you are a Gray! Also you speak French. You much impressed him over the business of John Villiers and the monopoly. He thinks that you are just the man for this."

"But . . . I do not understand. Why am *I* needed? When he has hundreds of great ones to call upon?"

"About some matters James is always cautious. This of the French match requires careful handling. Parliament here is very doubtful about it all. They would prefer that Charles married some Protestant bride, some Englishwoman, not this Henrietta Maria. Especially after the Spanish fiasco. But James has high notions about kingship. Only a royal bride will do for his son and heir to the throne. And he is concerned about the succession. He is getting old and no longer a hale man. He wants to see Charles wed, and to a princess, who will produce a royal grandson for him. Forby, he sees himself still as the peacemaker of Christendom, the only monarch who has never gone to war. So there is statecraft in it, also. A French alliance could bring much pressure on Spain, and therefore on the Empire and Austria. Spain and Austria are oppressing the Protestant states, in especial Bohemia and the Palatinate. They have ousted James's son-in-law, the Elector Frederick, from being King of Bohemia and have occupied his Palatinate. James believes that if England, or better, Britain and France were allied, with France already jealous of the Spanish power and wealth, then they might get the Palatinate back for his daughter's husband. He hardly expects to regain Bohemia, but has hopes for the Palatinate. Moreover, because of the Auld Alliance between France and Scotland, he has always favoured a French match. Would much have preferred it to the Spanish one which Buckingham managed to persuade him to . . ."

"Yes, my lord. But what has this to do with me? I know nothing of such matters, a mere Scots land-steward . . ."

"That is partly it, David. You can go with the others, the loftier ones, in a quite humble capacity. Your role, as I see it, will be merely to keep a watchful eye on your betters! James Hay, Doncaster – he has now been created Earl of Carlisle, no less – is to lead the embassage. James trusts him, a good Scot. But he drinks too much and in his cups can do foolish things, like so many another. Also his French is not good. James must send an English lord too, of course, so Henry Rich, Lord Kensington, is to go. He knows the French court well, indeed has had affairs with some of the French ladies there. He is a great ladies' man. Knows the Queen Mother, Marie, well. But that could be a weakness with him also. James likes him, but does not altogether trust him, for he is too close to Buckingham. So your duty will be to keep your eyes and ears open, and keep James Hay informed, especially as to what this Kensington is up to . . ."

"But this is crazy! I cannot influence these great lords . . ."

"You much influenced my lord Viscount Purbeck!"

"That was different. And my French is fair enough for here. But not for France. Why do you not go yourself, my lord? Were you not born in France?"

"I suggested it, although I do not want to go. But James will not have it. He likes always to keep me by him."

"Then Buckingham himself? He went with Prince Charles to Spain. Why not to France?"

Even in his own quarters of Whitehall Palace, Ludovick lowered his voice, however subconsciously. "There is at present some slight trouble in that quarter. About our new duke – for James has made him *Duke* of Buckingham now, so that I am no longer the only duke in the two kingdoms! James still dotes on him, but there are some doubts in the royal mind! Gondomar, the Spanish Ambassador, James's old crony, says that he has proof that Buckingham and Charles were involved in a plot to dethrone him, confine him to Theobalds Park, ostensibly for his own good and comfort, and have Charles raised to the throne forthwith. They both deny it, of course, but it is troubling James. Floods of tears over his faithful Dog Steenie, who may not be so faithful after all! He blames Charles himself rather than his precious Steenie – however daft that is, with Charles completely under Buckingham's thumb."

"You think there is truth in it?"

"The Lord only knows! But Gondomar employs a host of spies and is usually well-informed. And Charles and his father scarcely love each other. If Charles was King, Buckingham, who now sways him in everything, would rule this kingdom – and he is notably ambitious, that young man. James, although he dotes foolishly on Buckingham, does not let him interfere in matters of state. He still has pride enough, and wits enough, to believe in his own divine right to rule. So – Buckingham does not go to France to seek the hand of Henrietta Maria for Charles. And parliament would never agree to that, after the Spanish folly. They are sufficiently against a Catholic match as it is, but they see Spain as the principal enemy and if France can be enlisted against Spain, they see the Protestant cause gaining. It is all very involved, lad. So, James Hay goes to Paris, with Henry Rich – and you!"

David wagged his head helplessly.

"Do not look so glum, man! It is quite an honour, after all. And if you perform well, James will be grateful – and to have a grateful monarch can be no little help in life! Even for a land-steward! And were you not so long past concerned about being thrown into the Tower? Not sent on an embassage to France."

They did not visit James that evening, for apparently he was not sufficiently suspicious towards Buckingham to deny himself the pleasure of that man's company of a night. But they would all be returning to Theobalds Park the next day, and Ludovick would contrive an audience for David there. He did not know how soon the French party would be departing.

Before retiring, David told the Duke something of his visit and findings at Primroknowe, and the suggestions anent witchcraft. Knowing the King's almost obsessive fear and hatred of all such, he was the more mystified that James had seen fit to favour Sir Thomas Home with so important an office as the Angus sheriffdom. Had the Duke any idea why this was done? And if not, could he possibly try to discover? There was something very strange here.

Ludovick had no information on that subject, but promised to try to sound out James on the matter when the moment seemed opportune. He agreed that the witchcraft link was very odd – although it might well be no more than local gossip and tittle-tattle. The Bothwell connection was also interesting.

On the morrow, the royal entourage moved off on the twenty-mile journey north to Theobalds, David with it, riding well to the rear of the long column amongst servants and humble folk. He saw the King, as he took leave of the Duke, and was fairly sure that James saw him, although he gave no sign of it.

David was interested to note that on their passage through the narrow streets and lanes of London the royal party was hooted at and even pelted with ordure, just as he had been on his own. Did this imply unpopularity for the monarch, or was it merely normal behaviour on the part of the citizenry? He could not conceive of it happening in Scotland. The reaction of the guards was almost casual, with little sign of outrage or surprise.

At Theobalds Park Ludovick did not have to arrange an audience, for the King sent for David quite soon after their arrival. This interview, although not conducted from the bed, was held in the privy bedchamber, no one else present save the Duke.

"Aye, weel – you've come, then, my mannie," David was greeted. "No' that expeditious, mind, but timeous, aye, timeous. You'll ken the difference? Uh-huh. Vicky, you've tell't him what's what? As to France?"

"Something of it, Sire. No doubt you will explain your wishes further."

"I will so. You, Davie Gray, are to accompany my envoys to

201

Paris, to negotiate, aye negotiate, the betrothal o' my son Charles to the lassie Henrietta Maria, Louis of France's sister. No' that *you'll* be doing any negotiating! Your task will be to aid Jamie Hay – he's Carlisle, noo, Earl o' Carlisle. You ken him – he was Doncaster before. He's a guid lad, Jamie, and kens what's what. But whiles he loses the heid, see you, when he's drink-taken. So you'll bide close to Jamie Hay, mair particularly when he's at the wine. He doesna hae that much French, the man, and I jalouse he's like to forget what he has, in his cups. So you'll be at his side, just, to gie him a bit hand when he needs it. You hae that?"

"Yes, Sire. But . . . how can I do this? How can I prevail on the likes of Lord Don . . . Lord Carlisle? I am young and of no position. He is not likely to heed such as me . . ."

"Och, he'll heed you, laddie, I'll see to that. I'll *tell* him. I've tell't him a'ready. He likes you, for some reason! He'll be glad enough to hae you by him. Forby, you'll serve to keep an eye on Harry Rich – that's Kensington noo. He's a guid lad tae, or he wouldna be sent. But he's ower weak on the women. And there's going to be a wheen women to deal wi' on this affair. For yon Louis's court is fair dominated, aye dominated, by the women, frae his mither, the Queen Marie de Medici, doon. Plenties o' them. He's no' a strong character, is Louis. I'm feart that Harry Rich may get taigled up wi' some o' them. And they can be clever, thae French women, I'm tell't. When it comes to negotiating the dowry, and what lands the lassie Henrietta's to get here, that could be right expensive!" James jabbed a finger at David. "You're no' weak aboot women your ain sel', are you, man?"

"I, I do not think so, Sire. Not, not that I know of. But – what could *I* do, in such case? I've no . . ."

"You could keep your guid Scots ears open. And eyes, tae. And tell Jamie Hay. You speak the French. You're to be a sort o' watch-dog, you understand. My watch-dog, just. I reckon, after yon of Johnnie Villiers, and a' thae Border lairds, you're just the lad for it."

"But, Sire . . ."

"Nae mair buts! *Yon's* a right weakness o' yours, David Gray. You're aye but this and but that! You watch it, especially to your ain liege lord!"

"Yes, Sire. But . . ." David gulped. "Forgive me, Your Majesty. I am sorry. I will try to remember. But . . ." He stopped, appalled.

Even James had to join in Ludovick's laughter. "Man, you're beyont remeid! Can we trust him, Vicky, no' to go butting awa' in France, and deaving the Frenchies oot o' their wits?"

"I think that we can, James. After all, he'll be listening more than talking, I gather."

"I'ph'mm. Weel – mind it, laddie, mind it. Noo, you canna go to the French court dressed like that! They're right fancy aboot claes there, for some reason. You'll hae to get some better-like claes. Vicky, tak him to yon Ebeneezer Wright, my tailor-man, and get him clad right. Naething ower grand, mind, but just sae he doesna look like he's still got heather atween his taes! And tell the mannie to mak haste, for they sail in twa-three days' time."

David opened his mouth to speak, and wisely thought better of it.

His sovereign was eyeing him from those great, luminous yet shrewd Stewart eyes. "I've no' forgotten the ither matter, mind. That o' the letters. We'll see aboot that – aye, we'll see."

"Yes, Sire. And, meanwhile, the new Sheriff of Angus remains uninstalled?"

"That is so. Meanwhile, as you say! Vicky, afore you go, you'd better go get me a sword. Frae the guard, there."

Surprised, Ludovick hesitated and then, shrugging, went to the chamber door, opened it and passed out.

James was still looking at David, almost calculatingly. "I never thought that I'd be trusting a Gray again, after yon grandsire o' yours, Davie. I hope that I'm no' misjudging?"

"I, I pray not, Sire. I will seek to be, to remain, your loyal and faithful servant."

"Uh-huh. Do you that, lad. Loyal and faithful servants are no' aye sae easy come by, I've discovered! So mind it."

"Yes, Sire. May I ask, in what position do I go? As a servant to my lord Carlisle? Or a secretary, or . . .?"

"You go as a servant, aye – but no' Jamie Hay's. Mine. *My* guid and faithful servant, mind. No, to the ithers you are an extra gentleman o' mine, just, attached. As a servant you couldna go into thae French palaces and the like, wi' my envoys, and speak wi' the Frenchies. You maun hae some standing, see you, or you'll be of nae use."

The Duke came back with a sword, lacking its sheath. "Here you are, James," he said. "That guard was a mite doubtful, loth to give it up. I think he feared that I might be going to use it on *you*!"

The King did not smile. There were some matters which he did not find in the least amusing; and cold steel he had always hated. Almost gingerly he took the proffered hilt.

"Weel, lad, doon wi' you," he jerked, to David.

That young man stared.

"D'you no' hear me? On your knees, Davie Gray." The sword, held in both hands, wavered about distinctly dangerously.

Hastily David sank to the floor, involuntarily jerking back, and head aside, lest the naked steel struck him. In fact it grazed his neck before landing heavily on his left shoulder.

"Aye then, Davie Gray, I dub thee knight," the monarch announced, in something of a gabble. "So – and so!" The recipient had to duck, as the blade came up, and over, less than accurately, to descend on the other shoulder, before slithering off. "Be a guid knight until thy life's end. Uh-huh. Arise, man. Up wi' you, Sir David Gray."

As in a dream David got to his feet, as James thrust the sword back at Ludovick, point first.

"There you are, then, my bonny land-steward! You asked aboot your position – there you hae it. Mind, you dinna rightly deserve to be a knight; it's just that you need a bit lift up if you're to stand beside the ithers in yon French palaces. Sae it's nae virtue on your pairt – or nae much! But, och, I've dubbed worse, many's the time."

The new knight was wordless.

The King went and sat down on the bed, as though suddenly tired. "Noo, off wi' the pair o' you. I'll see you again afore you leave, Davie Gray. Mind aboot the tailor-man and the new claes, Vicky. And if you see Steenie Villiers ootby there, tell him to come in . . ."

Bowing, Duke and knight backed out of the presence.

There was no sign of Buckingham in any of the ante-rooms – not that they looked very heedfully.

"Well, Sir David, how does it feel to be a knight?" Ludovick asked, taking the younger man's arm. "Surprised?"

"I . . . I . . ." David wagged his head. "It is scarce believable. I cannot take it in. Me! This is . . . beyond all."

"Better than the Tower, you'd say?"

"It is too much. None will believe it! Me – a knight. Davie Gray, the bastard!"

"Oh, there have been many knighted bastards. Including my own son, John Stewart, your cousin. And many less suitable, Davie. James is free with his knighthoods. Or – scarcely free! For he usually makes men pay for it, and sweetly! He has made hundreds of knights in his day, most of them less deserving than yourself."

"It is, it is but a device. So that I can go with these others, attend the Lord Carlisle at the French court."

"That, yes. But there is more than that. The fact that James *chose* you to go. He esteems you, trusts you. And James does not trust many, never has done. Perhaps with reason. He was impressed by the way you handled John Villiers and the monopoly trouble. It is not all but a device. Now, we'd better go find James's tailor, this man Wright. For he has not much time to rig you out . . ."

That night, as he lay sleepless, his mind in a turmoil, one thought kept coming to the forefront – Barbara Home. As a knight, he felt suddenly much nearer to Barbara. Was that foolish? He was still a poor man. But, as Sir David Gray, he could hope, perhaps? Hope . . .

14

They sailed down Thames from Gravesend in a fine ship-of-war, the *Buckthorn*, a glittering company, all polished and furbished to impress. David was surprised how large a party they had become – somehow he had thought only of the three names; but in fact there were almost two score of them, over and above servants, all more illustrious-seeming than himself, including a bishop no less. Negotiations, it appeared, would go on at various levels.

That was not the only surprise David experienced. Most encouraging had been his greeting from James Hay, Lord Carlisle, who had received him warmly, clapping him on the back and congratulating him on his knighthood. This was unexpected, for, as the monarch's alleged watch-dog, almost spy, he had anticipated a cool, wary, even perhaps suspicious reaction. But Carlisle, a bluff, hearty character, ugly of mien – old Camel-face, James's daughter Elizabeth had called him – and scarcely the typical ambassador and diplomat, seemed to see him as a useful aide and lieutenant, moreover a fellow-Scot in a shipload of Englishmen. This was a great relief for David.

Lord Kensington, too, showed no hostility, a very different individual, handsome, slender, elegant and witty, rather older than David had imagined, entirely sure of himself, but quite likeable. He reminded David of Sir William Alexander of Menstrie. He paid the new knight no special attention, but was affable enough and gave no impression of bearing any sort of grudge.

As to the others, there were too many for David to identify there and then, save for the Bishop William Laud, of St Davids, a long-faced, slit-mouthed cleric, who was there as the Archbishop of Canterbury's representative, to ensure that the Church of England's interests were not endangered in this proposed Catholic marriage. But there was one fellow-traveller whom David was able to feel some companionship with, partly because they rode down to the port from Whitehall together, but more so because it turned out that he had been specially knighted for the occasion also, a military man newly promoted colonel, young for that rank, and attached to the entourage of the Lord Kensington, Sir George Goring. David wondered whether, in fact, his remit was similar to his own, to act watch on Kensington. He was a pleasant character, somewhat bewildered by the situation in which he found himself and so with a fellow-feeling for David. He indeed had mentioned, as they had ridden past Greenwich, Prince Charles's palace, on their way to Gravesend, that it was strange that the Prince himself should not be going on this errand to France instead of this large company of ambassadors. After all, he had gone with Buckingham to Spain in search of a bride. Why not now, to Paris? David had had no answer to that – save that perhaps the Spanish venture having proved such a fiasco, it was deemed safer to test the water this way?

David, who had never had occasion to do any real seafaring, was interested in all he saw and experienced. The Thames, widening to its long estuary, did not provide many scenic attractions, for its shores were flat and at this range fairly featureless. But it was all much longer than he had realised, as long as the Firth of Forth probably, and both on the Kent and Essex sides there was obviously a large waterside population, with much coastal shipping evident.

Heading eastwards thus, with the prevailing westerly wind behind them, they made good time; but even so it surprised David how long it took to reach the open sea. London, being a great seaport, he had assumed to be much nearer the ocean than it was.

When he was summoned below for a midday meal, it was to find most of the party settled in the crowded, low-decked main cabin, normally the ship's officers' accommodation, drinking, dicing and playing cards. He felt very much a stranger, an outsider, in this company – and almost choked in the thick atmosphere. Automatically choosing a humble place near the door, and not feeling hungry, wondering how soon he could decently escape back up on deck, he heard himself hailed by Carlisle to come and sit at his side. Less than eagerly he went forward.

The Earl was noisily jovial, obviously already considerably drink-taken, pressing wine on David and telling the others that this good-looking young man was the grandson of the famous Patrick, Master of Gray, of whom all must have heard, who had been the handsomest and cleverest man in all Europe, the man who had so largely paved the way for their esteemed monarch to eventually mount Queen Elizabeth's throne. From the expressions of some of those present, David doubted whether this was altogether a commendation. He was thankful when the food arrived and he could seem to concentrate on eating. He would never make a courtier, he well recognised.

Carlisle, drinking steadily, told him that he had known the Master well, and Andrew Gray his son, also David's father; after all, he was a Hay of Errol, the High Constable of Scotland's family, who lived not far down the Carse of Gowrie from Dundee, near to Castle Huntly which had been the Master's main seat. And he knew Mary Gray, at Methven, one of the bonniest creatures he had ever set eyes on. Indeed, nudging David with an elbow, he declared that he would have gone a deal further than just admiring her had she not been so clearly attached to the Duke of Lennox.

The Earl was becoming maudlin before David felt that he could make his excuses and depart for the clean air above. He saw what King James had meant about keeping an eye on the principal ambassador.

He reached deck again just as the *Buckthorn* was passing Sheerness, and emerging from the estuary into the open sea, the vessel now heaving and rolling regularly in a long cross-swell. David had never been seasick and hoped that he was not going to be now – but rather wished that he had not applied himself so assiduously to his food down below. He ensconced himself in a corner up near the bows and assured himself that he was feeling fine, just fine.

He was, in fact, quite glad when Sir George Goring came to join him, and in converse he could forget his stomach. Goring told him that he had been brought into this affair in the position of a courier of sorts, to keep in touch with the King and court at home, and so might well be making this journey back and forth a few times, depending on how long the negotiating took. This rather concerned David, who had not anticipated that the embassage would take more than a week or two, at most; but if Goring's seniors contemplated him making return journeys as courier, then they must be visualising a much longer stay in France. It looked as though Broughty Castle was going to have to do without its land-steward for a considerable while. And, he hoped, Home of Primroknowe remaining meantime only *proposed* Sheriff of Angus.

Goring told something of his background, how he was son of a Sussex squire who had gained the post of Receiver of the Court of Wards, and had bought him a commission as cadet at the age of fourteen, being in the army ever since and reaching the rank of major. He owed his recommendation for this embassage to his betrothed's father, the Earl of Norwich, who was a friend of Lord Kensington. He had been specially promoted colonel, but his knighting had been a great surprise. Presumably it was to facilitate his comings and goings as courier.

Late in the afternoon their vessel changed course from due east to due south, having reached the extreme tip of the Kentish coastline, the North Foreland. One of the ship's officers surprised them by informing that they were now just over halfway to their destination. Scarcely able to credit this, they learned that they had come some forty-five miles from Gravesend, and that from the North Foreland to Boulogne was only another forty sea miles. These would take rather longer to cover, however, for they would not have a following wind. But since they did not want to arrive in port in the middle of the night, that did not signify.

The ship's motion now changed again to more pronounced rolling as they began to cross the mouth of the Channel, and David, lacking any desire for more food, was glad enough to seek his bunk thus early. He had not been sick, but was very aware of his stomach still. Not a few of his fellow-travellers, he noted, had disappeared from the main cabin. But the Earl of Carlisle was still there, fallen asleep over the table amongst empty flagons.

David awoke to the awareness of change, and it took a little while to realise where he was and that the change was cessation of motion. All heaving and rolling had ceased. On deck, he found that they were tied up at a long quay, other shipping all around them, men busy, activity everywhere, in the early morning light. It seemed strange to awake in France – but indubitably it was French which was being spoken and shouted. Fascinated, he watched it all, until his stomach informed him that it was quite recovered – for he wanted his breakfast. He went below, to find Carlisle at his place at table. Whether he had in fact ever been to his bunk was unclear, but he seemed none the worse for his day-long drinking and was eating heartily. He told David that, when he had eaten, he should go ashore and hire horses. They would require many, naturally, some fifty riding animals and as many led-beasts to carry their baggage. And he was not to let the French robbers charge too much for them.

Thus promptly David's responsibilities commenced.

Actually he was able to share the task, for Goring and one or two others were quite eager to set foot on foreign soil for the first time, and accompanied him.

They were quite glad to stretch their legs. Once clear of the extensive dock area, they discovered Boulogne to be no very large city, perhaps the size of Dundee, consisting of a lower and an upper town, the former commercial, all warehouses, stock-yards, fish-curing sheds, breweries and taverns, flanking the River Liane, the latter residential and official, strongly fortified, with a fine cathedral and a town-hall built on the foundations of the early castle of the famous Godfrey de Bouillon; also much handsome housing. They called at the first tavern they came to, to enquire where horses, many horses, might be hired; and, after having to request the innkeeper to speak more slowly, David was glad to discover that his French was sufficiently adequate for the occasion.

They were directed back whence they had come some way, to the cattle-market near the riverside. Here they found that although there were three or four horse-hirers, none was sufficiently large as to be able to supply over one hundred horses. This, although it complicated the business, did strike David as having its advantages, for it meant that he had to interview them all, and so was able to compare the prices asked – and found quite some differential. And this enabled him to play one off against another, to some extent, and beat down the exorbitant – to the admiration of his companions, who made the inevitable remarks about canny Scots. In fact, the prices charged were, according to Goring, less than would have been the case in London, although not in Scotland. So, arranging for the long train of beasts to be led to the quayside berth of the English ship, they were able to ride back in style on the best mounts, selected for themselves.

Meantime, it seemed, Kensington had gone to interview the governor of the city, and come back with a French guide who would accompany them to Paris and aid them on their journey, a young officer who spoke a little English.

There was nothing to detain them at Boulogne, so a start was made before midday on the one-hundred-and-sixty-mile ride to Paris. A party of this size, and with all the pack-horses, could not expect to cover any great mileage daily, especially in a strange land; and their numbers would complicate the problem of nightly accommodation, for they would be too many for wayside inns and hospices. The Church was the great provider of shelter for travellers all over Christendom, but the Catholic Church here might not welcome Protestants, even when they were making for the King of France's court. Moreover, visitors from England might not be popular anyway, for the English had invaded here and occupied this Pas de Calais, in Henry the Eighth's time, for six years; and even seventy years afterwards memories might remain sore. So they reckoned on perhaps thirty miles each day, with nightly halts in sizeable towns if possible.

Proceeding southwards parallel with the coast, through a fairly level and prosperous countryside, they met with no difficulties and reached Étaples before darkening, some fifteen miles, a medium-sized town where, thanks to their guide's efforts, all were installed in various establishments for the night. David found himself in a tavern by the harbour, with Goring and two others, where they need not have worried about their reception, for they were catered for more than adequately, if somewhat fundamentally – indeed to the extent of being offered young women to warm their beds for them. They wondered whether this was normal French hospitality.

Next day they crossed over slightly higher ground to reach the valley of the Somme – although it could hardly be called a valley, a wide, open strath rather, with the country becoming ever more populous. David found it all highly interesting and instructive. He had noted, those months ago now, how different was the English landscape, also the apparent character of the people, from that of the Scots; now he saw the French as still more different. It was not only the scenery and the way the land was used, cultivated and drained, the housing and villages, the canals and the mills, but the folk also. He could only judge superficially here, of course, since the travellers had little real contact with the rural population; but to him the peasantry seemed subdued if not repressed, uninterested in or perhaps fearful of visitors, more like what he would have imagined serfs to be. He noted also the large numbers of manor-houses and châteaux they passed, as well as the prevalence of abbeys and monastic establishments, although few parish or village churches; indeed a fair proportion of their fellow-users of the roads seemed to be clerics travelling in some style.

The second night was passed at Abbeville, quite a large town of millers and weavers, where there was ample entertainment for the visitors, although the Abbot of St Wolfram would provide none. When, the following evening at Amiens, capital of Picardy, with its great cathedral of Nôtre Dame boasting the loftiest spire they had ever seen, over four hundred feet high, the Bishop thereof again refused hospitality, the travellers began to realise the power and pride of the Catholic Church here and its stern disapproval of Protestant England and Scotland. David perceived now that the negotiations for a French royal marriage might well be more difficult and protracted than he had assumed.

From Amiens they moved on to Beauvais, in the valley of the Therain, famous for its tapestries. Now they were only fifty miles from Paris, down the Oise to the Seine. France, they perceived, was a land of great rivers, important for

212

navigation and trade. They crossed the Oise at Pontoise, and remained there overnight – which would allow them to reach their destination in the early afternoon following. Hereafter there would be inevitably a major change in their state and conditions.

Seeking now to look less travel-stained, they came to Paris by St Denis, and were duly impressed by its size, the richness of its palaces and mansions, the multitude of churches, monasteries, convents and the like, its monuments, parks and bridges. It was more open, less huddled together than London, at least where they passed. But it had its poor quarters also, in abundance, its warrens of hovels and tumbledown housing, often cheek by jowl with magnificent edifices and pavilions. And the streets were no less full of beggars, cripples and hucksters, although here they were noticeably more respectful than the Londoners, or perhaps more cowed. There appeared to be a superfluity of clerics again, parading the streets and occupying the crowns of the causeways.

Kensington, who knew it all well, rode ahead with Goring to inform the authorities at the Louvre of their arrival.

David's first sight of that mighty citadel, the ancient and traditional seat of the French monarchy, took his breath away. It was enormous, a fortified town in itself, rearing its lofty, frowning walls and towers and bastions within a wide moat, almost a canal-system, diverted from the Seine. He counted no fewer than sixteen towers, many of them massive, with conical roofs within parapets, other than the innumerable turrets and cupolas. Even from a distance it could be seen that there were courts within courts, a series of curtain walls, gatehouses facing north, east, south and west, and soaring gabled roofing rank upon rank. Gazing, the horsemen fell silent.

They entered this citadel by a daunting succession of three gatehouses, three moats and three drawbridges, but were unchallenged at any of them. In a great central courtyard, large as a city square, they were met by Kensington, with some sort of chamberlain, who conducted them to one of the innumerable wings of the palace, off a lesser courtyard, which was apparently put entirely at their disposal, with its own kitchens, facilities and complement of servants. There was, however, no sign of their hosts.

This situation persisted. Their premises were very fine, palatial indeed, sustenance liberal, service not to be faulted – but apart from the French-speaking servants they might have been still in England. No word came to them from higher authority. They settled in, David sharing a fine room with Goring. Kensington disappeared for the evening – he had his friends here, female, it was understood – but the others waited in vain for any royal summons. They retired to bed around midnight, wondering.

It was mid-forenoon before Kensington turned up again, uncommunicative as to where he had spent the night. He declared that King Louis would give them audience in due course, and meantime they must just wait here. The monarch was apparently away exercising his dogs at St Denis – dogs were his major interest it seemed – and it was not possible for anyone else to see the visitors until they had been duly presented to the King.

So all waited. It was rather like being back on the ship, only in less cramped quarters, playing cards and dice, eating and drinking. David, for one, watched Carlisle imbibing steadily, concerned that he might be in no state for a royal audience when eventually that came about.

He need not have worried, for the entire day and evening passed without any summons. Once again Kensington absented himself, seemingly well content with these conditions; but for the rest of them, they began to feel rather like prisoners, however comfortably immured. They reckoned that they could scarcely sally out into the city meantime in case they were suddenly sent for.

It was the third afternoon before the summons arrived, with a resplendent court usher coming to announce that His Most Christian Majesty would see them forthwith. Something of a scramble ensued, with the usher impatient, Carlisle unsteady on his feet and Kensington absent. Only about a dozen of the party were considered suitable for this interview, including Bishop Laud and Goring and David. Fortunately, a somewhat breathless Kensington joined them, from a different wing of the establishment, before they reached the royal quarters.

214

They were led through a series of splendid salons, halls and galleries, hung with pictures and tapestries and adorned with statuary, some of it eyebrow-raising anatomically. Courtiers were everywhere here, many of whom turned to stare at the newcomers and comment less than flatteringly. If David had thought that the English court habitués were over-elaborately dressed, these put them quite in the shade. He was particularly intrigued as to how many of the women managed to keep the upper parts of their gowns covering any proportion of their bosoms. In one of the galleries, instrumentalists were playing soft music.

When at length they were brought to heavily guarded and ornately decorated doors, their usher left them, to go ahead. The yapping of dogs sounded from within.

It was some time before he returned, to wave them onward past the guards. An inner door opened, releasing a strong smell of dog, and a sudden rush of barking, snapping animals. Shouts from behind added to the din.

Fighting their way through this canine pack, Carlisle all but toppling over as he aimed a kick at one of the creatures, but recovering himself thanks to David's ready hand, they entered the presence-chamber in distinctly ragged order.

It was a large apartment, with more dogs than humans therein. At the far end there was a dais-platform, and on this, under an elaborate canopy of tasselled crimson silk, two throne-like chairs were set. Oddly, the larger one was occupied by the smaller person, the lesser by an enormous woman. Two men and three other females stood behind. All appeared to be shouting at the dogs save for one of the men, a dark, thin, still-faced man, dressed in clerical scarlet.

The envoys had advanced halfway up the apartment when the usher held out a restraining hand and made an elaborate genuflection. They all sought to bow, despite the leaping dogs, moving forward further, for another bow, then a third, Carlisle huffing and puffing disapprovingly. By now they were near the dais-step, and there they were halted.

The occupant of the larger throne was seen to be a young man, probably about David's own age, slightly built, sitting clumsily, dark of complexion, sallow, wearing a sullen expression. There was certainly no smile of welcome from him. The large lady beside him, of middle years and vast frontage, *was* smiling – however, it seemed to be pointedly at only one of them, Kensington.

Raising his voice above the din, the usher announced them. "Your Gracious and Most Christian Majesty, here is the deputation from King James of England, come to your domains to receive your royal decisions on the matter of a royal marriage. They are milords Kensington and Carlisle. And others." This was in French, of course, and Carlisle was pronounced Carleel.

The young monarch merely nodded a surly head. Louis the Thirteenth seemed to be but a disappointing son of the dashing and renowned Henry the Fourth, of Navarre.

Kensington spoke up, in practised French. "We humbly salute Your Majesty. And Your Majesty's royal mother." A deep bow to the large lady, who beamed. "We bring you the greetings of King James of England . . ." A growl from Carlisle resulted in the other's cough. "And of the United Kingdom of Great Britain and Ireland. I am Kensington. And here is my lord Earl of Carlisle. We are sent to seek the hand of your royal sister, the Princess Henrietta Maria, in marriage with Charles, Prince of Wales, son of King James. To the mutual benefit, it is believed, of both realms."

Louis moved a little in his wide chair, cleared his throat, nodded again, and, turning, glanced over his padded shoulder at the red-robed cleric, who made a peculiar sideways inclination of the head, neither nod nor shake.

Nobody spoke – but at least the dogs had exchanged their barking for mere snufflings.

Kensington looked at Carlisle, at something of a loss as to further procedure.

The Earl raised a loud voice, in execrable French, the louder to ensure that his hearers understood. "We are happy to be here. I am a Scot, and we in Scotland value much our Auld Alliance with France." Or words approximately to that effect.

There was still no response from Louis, but the cleric, after a brief pause, said quietly, in fair English, that the ancient relationship with Scotland was approved and cherished by

France. It was unfortunate, however, that there had been no such tie with England.

This did not get them much further, and there was another silence, save for the dogs' noises. Bishop Laud tried.

"I am the Bishop of St Davids," he said, in his clipped tones. "I represent the Archbishop of Canterbury, as well as King James who is head of the Church of England."

That did not seem to impress the hearers, the other cleric in especial looking expressionless.

Kensington sought to exploit the only smile they had received. "Your Majesty," he addressed Marie de Medici, "we bring greetings to you also from our King. And from Prince Charles, whom you received here in Paris some time ago."

"We remember Prince Charles, a shy young man. And Monsieur Buckingham, who was not shy!" That came out with a laugh, welcome indeed. She had a surprisingly high and girlish voice for so large a person.

"The Duke – he is now that, Majesty – would also wish to be remembered, and kindly."

Another pause. Carlisle opened his mouth to speak and then thought better of it.

King Louis adopted a more positive role. Sitting up, he waved a dismissive hand.

The visitors eyed each other questioningly, but their usher bowed low and began a prompt backwards progress for the door, difficult because of those dogs. After a moment's hesitation, Kensington did the same. But Carlisle was for making no such obsequious retreat; indeed he probably could not have achieved a backwards stepping. With the briefest of bows, little more than a nod, he turned doorwards. David, recognising that his hand might be required, did the same, although bowing rather more deeply. The others followed suit, having to watch out for those dogs as well as the genuflecting usher and Kensington. At the resumed movement, the wretched animals had started to bark again.

In little more dignified fashion than on their entry, they won out of the presence-chamber.

The door was barely closed behind them when Carlisle burst out in vehement complaint at their reception. It was

Kensington's turn to lay an urgent hand on the Earl's arm, gesturing towards the usher, who might well report. This had no effect, but fortunately the comments were made in the broadest Scots, and thick-voiced at that, and probably the usher would understand little of it.

They were led back to their quarters in doubtful mood, even Kensington less assured than usual.

There, rid of the Frenchman, and Carlisle calling for wine, they fell to discussion, in indignation, astonishment and foreboding mixed. What was behind that extraordinary reception? Was this sort of thing normal at the French court? Or did it mean that they had come on a fool's errand, that there was to be no royal marriage? And those dogs . . .?

Kensington, to whom all looked for answers, could offer only partial explanations. Louis was difficult always, moody, suspicious. He went in constant fear of assassination, after his father Henry's murder – part of the reason for the dogs probably. He believed that they would protect him, it was said, and openly declared that he could trust only them. He even had a special language which he had invented, to speak with them. He disliked his mother, who had been his regent until comparatively recently. Since coming of age, he had come ever more under the influence of the Bishop of Luçon, now elevated to be Cardinal de Richelieu, that cleric who had stood behind the throne, a clever man, and becoming the real ruler of France, it was feared . . .

But why this hostility, the others demanded? This embassage had been prepared for, the concept of the royal match supposedly accepted by the French, only the details to be worked out, they had thought. Why were they being treated like this?

Kensington did not know. He had seen the Queen Mother privately, and she had not indicated any opposition. But she had no great influence on her son nowadays, superseded by Richelieu, whom she hated. Perhaps that was where the trouble lay.

What now, then? What did they do?

That was not easy of answer. But now that they had been received by the King, however doubtfully, they could move around, not confine themselves here . . .

And the Princess, this Henrietta Maria? Was she here, in the Louvre?

Kensington understood so. He had not seen her. But others spoke as though she was present.

The visitors' disgruntlement was somewhat alleviated in an hour or two, when an elegant, who introduced himself as the Comte de Soissons, arrived from Queen Marie, to invite them all to a ball which she was giving that evening in the Grand Gallery.

So in due course the envoys, duly spruced up to appear at their best, made their way, Kensington leading, by the labyrinth of courts, corridors, and passages, to what proved to be the Louvre's most magnificent apartment, a great gallery built by the late Henry of Navarre at untold cost. They heard the music well before they reached it, joining the throng of gorgeously dressed revellers heading thereto.

To call their destination a gallery was like calling a palace a cottage, only its length relevant. It was a huge salon, its size seemingly doubled and quadrupled by the walls being all but panelled with great mirrors, and honeycombed with alcoves and aisles, some large enough to be described as apartments on their own, many of these presently housing tables laden with wines, meats and delicacies. The flooring was of black and white marble, such walling as was not glass gleaming white and gold, the arched ceiling colourful and eye-catching with painted classical figures, much of it highly erotic, and hung with innumerable glittering crystal chandeliers ablaze with light. The place was crowded, but because of its dimensions did not look it, and dancing was already in progress.

Kensington promptly disappeared about his own business, but the others waited in a group, watching all. They were not left alone for long, however, for quite quickly a positive bevy of ladies approached them, without any introduction or announcement, and began to chatter to them, ogling, even touching them provocatively. Even though much of what they said was unintelligible to their hearers, their welcoming intentions were sufficiently plain. David, oddly enough, found himself to be attracting more attention than most of his companions, certainly more than old Camel-face Carlisle; he

219

did not think of himself as one of the most handsome men in all that gallery – as well as probably the most plainly dressed. Each arm was taken by white-shouldered females, both, he judged, rather older than himself, and he was led off to one of the alcoves, to be plied with wine and sweetmeats, to skirls of laughter at his distinctly stilted converse; admittedly his French was not at its most fluent, he being not a little preoccupied with the bulging breasts which tended to press against his arms and which were presumably intended so to take the male attention since these, like many another he had already noticed, sported red-painted semicircles just where they emerged from silk or satin. He was not so carried away, however, that a fleeting mind-picture of those other bosoms, seen on Pease Dean beach, did not produce a comparison in which he found in favour of the latter, so much less provocative, more natural and to his taste.

Flattered as he might be by these ministrations, David was not unaware of his duties with regard to Carlisle, and presently sought to disengage himself to go back to the Earl. But he was not to detach his ladies easily, and they accompanied him, one on either arm, in his search. However, he gained his freedom soon enough, for when he discerned the bulky form of Carlisle, it was overshadowed by one still bulkier, that of Queen Marie herself, talking with him. When David moved over to stand nearby, in case he might be needed, his two companions reluctantly relinquished his arms and held back.

The Queen Mother was conversing in lively fashion, and by his expression, Carlisle not understanding much of it all. When he saw the younger man, he looked relieved and beckoned him forward.

"Davie," he said, in his own tongue. "I'm no' just getting all this. She's over-quick in the talk, for me. Gie's a hand, lad." Turning back to Marie, he resumed his halting French. "This, Majesty, is Sir David Gray, from Scotland also. My, my assistant."

David bowed, and the large lady smiled on him. "Yes, yes, I saw this young man earlier. I took note of him." Archly she tapped his arm. "An assistant to be valued, I think! Gray is your name, did I hear? I knew another handsome Gray some

220

years ago – Patrick, known as the Master. He became the Lord Gray, I think, later. He visited my husband's court more than once."

"My grandsire, Your Majesty. Although . . . I am a bastard, I fear."

The Queen rippled a laugh, and much of her generous form seemed to ripple with it. "Bastard, yes? How intriguing! I like that, young man. God knows, there must be many bastards in this room, but not all would admit it as you have done! Save those of my dear husband! *They* are proud of it! Yes, I like that."

"What's all that, Davie?" the Earl asked. "I didna catch it all."

"Her Majesty knew the Master of Gray, my lord. I told her that I am his bastard grandson. She is graciously . . . amused."

"Och, well. Ask her, when are we going to see this daughter o' hers, the Princess? Is she here? I've this letter, mind."

"My lord Earl asks, Highness, whether your royal daughter, the Princess Henrietta Maria, is present? He has a letter to present to her, from the Prince of Wales."

"Tcha, tcha, young man, you are in too much haste! Time for that later. She will not be here tonight, no. You will be presented to her on another occasion. Tonight is for entertainment and pleasure. Do you dance in your Scotland? Master Patrick used to dance divinely, I recollect."

David cleared his throat. "We dance, yes. But not as they are dancing here, Majesty. We have our own dances. More . . . lively perhaps. I have not seen this sort," he added, glancing about him. He also looked doubtfully at the Earl. "I do not know whether my lord Carlisle does . . . ?"

"Then you must learn, Bastard David!" she declared. "No doubt there will be not a few prepared to teach you. Now, milord, will you partner me? I am sure that *you* can foot our dances, no?"

Unexpectedly, for David, the Earl not only understood that but seemed happy to oblige, taking a royal hand and encircling some proportion of the royal waist. They moved off on to the dance-floor, leaving David to eye them with some concern lest Carlisle lost his balance – although at least

221

he had a fairly substantial support if needed. The Queen Mother, he noted, danced surprisingly light of foot.

He saw Kensington partnering a surpassingly beautiful, if over-painted and under-dressed, lady, gazing soulfully into each other's eyes – and Queen Marie flicking an admonishing hand to the baronial ear as they passed.

Looking for Goring, David discovered that although one of his attendant ladies had gone off in search of more rewarding company, the other was faithfully awaiting him, and promptly reclaimed his arm. She suggested that they danced, and he had to confess again his ignorance of it all. But as Queen Marie had prophesied, he was at once offered instruction, and all but dragged forward. Resigned, he allowed himself to be guided and propelled, in tune to the lilting music. Nor did he find it either too difficult nor unpleasant, and it certainly seemed to involve a lot of contact with the partner, particularly her bosom, which no man in his senses could object to. He proved, in fact, quite an apt pupil, being far from clumsily built and of lightsome carriage.

In the process, he learned that his instructress was Jeanetta, Comtesse de Charville – and very friendly. Also that the lady whom Kensington was partnering was the Duchesse de Chevreuse, a noted court beauty, with a history.

When that dance was over, David was led back to an alcove and given more refreshment by his Comtesse, who chattered volubly. He glimpsed Goring, and noted that his companion was none other than his former co-partner, and that they both seemed to be co-operating satisfactorily.

Between dances there were entertainments of various types, and a juggling act, remarkably dexterous, was going on when David and the Comtesse were approached, quite purposefully, by still another lady, younger this time, fair, buxom and smiling.

"You are the Scot," she asserted. "I am Anne."

He inclined his head, almost warily. These Frenchwomen were certainly forward, not to say bold.

"I was told that you could not dance. Yet I saw you dancing just now, well enough, Monsieur. So, for an envoy, you need to be watched, no? For you are untruthful! And perhaps untactful as well!"

222

That made David blink. "I was being taught," he said. "It was true. I had never before danced so." This young woman must have overheard his conversation with Queen Marie.

"Jeanetta must be a good teacher, then, sir. You will allow me to give you a further lesson?"

"Well . . ." A little disconcerted by this forthright request, almost a command however smilingly given, he glanced at his Comtesse. That lady had dropped his arm and backed away a pace. Now she bowed, silent.

The newcomer linked arms with him and led him off. The juggling act was finishing and the music resuming. This young female had even more prominent a bust than Jeanetta, was more plump altogether, without being fat, but rather more covered up.

There followed a different type of dance, of more sprightly nature, which David found more easy to adapt to, the footwork not unlike the Scottish steps he was used to, however much it bounced that well-endowed young woman around. She did not seem put out in the least, although becoming quite breathless in her instructions. It occurred to him, however, as the dance progressed, that others were giving them something of a wide berth. Were they being *too* energetic?

When it was over and the young woman had somewhat recovered her breath, she did not seem disposed to hand him back to Jeanetta. She took him instead to the top end of the gallery where there was a raised area, scarcely a dais but a step up from the rest and set with its own tables. Here, offering him more refreshment, she asked him about Scotland, knowledgeable questions, clearly interested and not just making conversation. She even had some English to try out on him.

David was well enough content with this company, and had got the length of offering to teach Anne some of the Scottish dances, if the occasion presented itself, when Queen Marie and Carlisle arrived up at their table, the latter sweating profusely and red in the face. It was David's turn to be red in the face, at least metaphorically, when a few moments later the Queen Mother reproached him with lack of gallantry in choosing to dance with her daughter-in-law Anne rather than

223

with herself. That stated relationship set him staring from one woman to the other, as he caught his breath.

"You, you are . . .?" he got out, in English.

"Why, yes. I told you, did I not? I am Anne. Anne of Austria."

Involuntarily he backed away a little. "The Queen . . .!"

"Did you not know, David the Bastard?" Marie asked.

"No. No, how could I, Your Majesty? Your Majesties!" he amended. "I, I . . ." Words failed him, as he made some sort of a bow to the younger woman.

"Why do you call him bastard?" Anne demanded.

Marie launched into an explanation, holding forth about the beautiful Master of Gray and all his attributes and accomplishments. Which at least gave time for David to recover his wits in some degree. That this Anne, who had seemed so pleasant, such good company, should be the wife of that moody and unfriendly King Louis, seemed scarcely credible, daughter of the King of Spain and therefore sister of the Infanta Prince Charles had tried to wed earlier. And he had been proposing to teach her Scottish dancing, the land-steward from Broughty! David looked guiltily around in case the King himself was there and had seen what went on, but thankfully saw no sign of him.

A lively performance of acrobatics, by what looked like gypsies, was in progress now, and David wondered whether this would give him opportunity to make his escape. But Queen Anne, after a little of it, turned to him and announced that he should now show her how to dance Scottish style. Could he do that without music? Let them try, at least. Her mother-in-law clapping her beringed hands in agreement, David could scarcely refuse. After all, it might be called a royal command.

So, feeling highly conspicuous and not a little foolish, he started by demonstrating the most basic steps, pointing out that these in fact had a French name, *pas-de-bas*, and going on to telling of the circling, the reversing, the arms-linking, of the reels and flings and contre-dance, Anne watching and listening intently. She tried some of the steps herself, necessarily hoisting up her long skirts in fine style, to Marie's amused encouragement. Then she insisted on them attempting

224

a turn or two together; and in trying to get their movements in rhythm. David resorted to humming one of the typical tunes, in the nearest he could get to fiddle-music, meantime Carlisle beating time on the table-top with a slopping wine-flagon and Marie trilling laughter. Anne proved quick at picking up the motion and flourish of it all.

It was when David, raising eyes from their feet, recognised that more people were watching their cantrips than the acrobatics, that, embarrassed, he dropped his queenly partner in less than courtly fashion and stood back, flushing and waving a hand which said plainly that enough was enough. Biting his lip, and without waiting for the royal permission to retire, he bowed briefly, and turning, hurried down into the throng, urgent to get as far away from the scene as possible.

Fortunately, with the acrobatics finishing and the music starting up again for the next dance, the general stir allowed him to pick his way to the other end of the gallery without too much difficulty, although with not a few assessing looks bent on him. There, feeling that departure was advisable before he got into any more entanglements and problems, he was contemplating a return to their own quarters, if he could find the way, and wondering whether he could leave Carlisle thus, when Jeanetta de Charville rejoined him, loud in exclamation and declaring that she was jealous. Was that Scottish dancing he had been showing the Queen? He must teach her, now . . .

Hastily disassociating himself from anything such, he apologised for having deserted her but pointed out that he had little choice. He explained that he was thinking of retiring, but concerned about leaving Lord Carlisle, whose aide he was. But she would have none of that. The night was yet young and there was still much pleasure to be gained from it – she would see to that. Weakly he allowed himself to be led back to an alcove-table and given more wine.

There followed a succession of dances and entertainments, of which David personally had had enough. Jeanetta presently perceived this, for after a while she asked him, if he was set on retiring, whether she might assist him in the matter? He said that he might be glad of her help, for he was uncertain whether he could find his way back to their wing of the citadel unaided, especially with Carlisle to escort. But when he

225

looked for the Earl, he could not see him. It seemed that there were others amissing also, for there was no sign of Goring or Kensington now either. Indeed, now that he looked, he perceived that the numbers in that gallery had distinctly diminished with the passing of time. Concerned for the Earl, he moved up to the dais end again, his Comtesse following. Up there, there was still no sign of Carlisle but Queen Anne was still there, in converse with a middle-aged exquisite. When she saw David waiting to speak with her, she beckoned him forward and introduced him to the Duc de Chevreuse, naming himself as Sir David Gray from Scotland but omitting the bastardy. David saluted the Duke. So this was the beauteous Duchess's husband, lingering here when his wife had departed, presumably with Kensington. The French seemed to abide by a different code than did their partners in the Auld Alliance.

He informed Anne that he was looking for the Earl of Carlisle, to whom he was attached as aide, and who might be requiring his assistance to return to their quarters. She smiled and assured him that the milord was in good hands. When he looked doubtful and asked where he was, she tapped him on the wrist and told him not to fuss, for milord had gone off with the Queen Mother to the privacy of her own apartments. So he would not be requiring Sir David further this night, she imagined.

Somewhat disconcerted, he withdrew, but not before Anne assured him that she would practise the Scots dance-steps he had shown her and would seek the pleasure of his company further, and before long.

Heading back down the gallery, and trying to pick out others of the embassage party, he found that he could spot only two of them. Where were the rest, including George Goring? Were they all being entertained privately by court ladies, he wondered? Was this the high-life equivalent of the bed-warming hospitality they had been offered at inns on their progress through France? A national service towards visitors?

He told Jeanetta that it appeared that he need no longer wait for his Earl, and linking her arm in his, she led him off, without complaint.

As they proceeded, arm-in-arm, along corridors and through halls and arcades, the man recognised that he would never have found his way alone. He also recognised one of his fellow-envoys, amongst many other couples embracing in various degrees of undress, in corners and alcoves, in which statuary also abounded, often explicit enough to engender a suitable mood. But presently he also came to the conclusion that the lady was taking him by a different route from that they had come, for he noted features, stairways, pictures and the like which he had not seen before. When they began to climb one such flight of stairs, and then went on to still another, he expressed his surprise, for on their way to the ball they had come down none of these.

Jeanetta smiled, and told him not to be impatient.

He realised that they must be in one of the many towers of the citadel, and not far from the top of it either. When thereafter his companion opened a door therein and ushered him inside, it was to see that it was a bedchamber, somewhat littered with female clothing. He halted, in something of a quandary.

"Forgive all the untidiness, my David," she said. "I dressed in haste."

He coughed. "No matter," he got out. "I will not be staying."

"Oh, but there is no haste now," she averred. "Come, sit." And she gestured towards the bed, sufficiently large for two, under its canopy.

Confused, for he did not like to offend any lady, especially one being generous, he invented an excuse. "Now that I have escorted you to your room, Comtesse, I must get back to our own apartments. I may be needed."

"Surely not at this hour, David!"

"Lord Carlisle may return . . ."

"You do not go to bed with *him*, do you! That ugly old man! You are not . . .?"

"No, no!" That was sufficiently vehement. "But I have to look after him, in some fashion. When he is drink-taken . . ."

She pulled him to the bed. "Come, a short while, surely."

This was difficult. Short of being unforgivably rude, he

could hardly turn and bolt – or even invent new reasons for being elsewhere.

"Very short, then, yes, I fear . . ." he said, and sat.

Her arms went round him at once, and he could scarcely do other than kiss that eager month. But the kissing immediately conjured up for him a vision of Barbara Home, the last woman he had so kissed – and he knew that he could not allow this embrace to proceed to its accepted conclusion. Only so far . . .

That was more readily decided than achieved, for the lady was far from passive. And without any very evident manipulation the top part of her gown, already so low-cut, slid down, leaving her upper half naked and demandingly accessible. Inevitably he bent to kiss those white shoulders now, a hand cupping one of her breasts.

One thing, of course, led to another, and when Jeanetta leant back from a sitting to a recumbent position, drawing him with her, David recognised that if he let this go on there would be no halting the process – and he would be unable to think of Barbara thereafter without guilt and regret. Why could men and women not enjoy each other's persons and affections without having to go on to the fullest consummation? Surely there was much mutual pleasure and satisfaction to be got from touch, caress, sight and the sense of closeness, appreciation, well short of the ultimate entry?

Firmly he grasped the wrist of her exploring, groping hand. "Not tonight, Jeanetta," he declared. "You are kind – but not tonight. I, I find you attractive, as well as kind. But tonight it must go no further."

"Why, David? Why?" That was almost a wail.

"I have my reasons, my good reasons. I thank you, but, no. Now I must leave you." He hoisted himself up, all manly determination.

She lay there in the dim half-light, staring up at him, on her back and a delectable sight. Feeling strangely guilty in a different fashion, he briefly rearranged his clothing, and stepped back.

"I ask your pardon, Comtesse," he said – and even to himself that sounded priggish and ridiculous. "A good-night to you." And turning, he made for the door.

No answering good-night followed him.

Thereafter, emotions in something of a turmoil, David took a considerable time to find his way to the embassage lodgings, having to ask sundry otherwise occupied couples in the process, enquiries not always well received. When eventually, thankfully, he reached his destination, it was to find few indeed of his companions therein. He had the room he shared with Goring to himself that night.

15

There followed a period of, as it were, marking time, lack of progress. Not inactivity, for the envoys were kept occupied, almost busy, what with one thing and another, but to little advancement of their objective. Social engagements succeeded each other day after day, night after night – play-actings, banquets, masques, horse-races, archery contests, parades, hunts and the like. But no negotiations. At none of these activities did King Louis appear, nor his adviser, the Cardinal Richelieu; and although Carlisle requested another audience or meeting, on a number of occasions, none such resulted.

The visitors, of course, did not fail to enjoy themselves in all this; not to would have been difficult, with both Queen Marie and Queen Anne clearly determined that they should. It was very easy to slip into the rhythm of that pleasure-loving court and accept the lack of progress as inevitable. Kensington seemed well content so to do; but the Earl was more concerned. His representations, however, produced little result. It was fairly evident that the Queens' influence in matters of state was minimal, although Marie had for long ruled, as regent.

David's feared problems over Jeanetta de Charville did not materialise to any extent, partly, probably, because of Queen Anne's very obvious appreciation of his company, so that the Comtesse may have assumed that there was more to it than was a fact, and that she would be wise not to poach on the royal preserves – a situation which David rather shamelessly exploited, although not in his association with Anne herself, needless to say. Jeanetta remained interested, and sought to see much of him, but he was able to keep their association within bounds. He did teach her how to do Scottish dancing, however, just as he did the Queen. The latter ordered a group of court musicians to learn from David two suitable Scots tunes to dance to, he humming them until they got them right. Thereafter, at balls, a Scottish dance was apt to be included – with some curious resultant expositions.

Whether through Carlisle's links with Marie or David's with Anne – for both urged the matter of a meeting with the hoped-for bride for Prince Charles, this was arranged. It seemed that Henrietta Maria was domiciled, with her own attendants, in the Tuileries, another palace not far from the Louvre.

Thither the envoys proceeded one day, to find another enormous establishment, very different in that it was no converted citadel but a range of fine buildings almost quarter of a mile in length, set in gardens reaching down to the Seine. It seemed altogether too extensive and impressive housing for any sixteen-year-old girl. Arriving, they found the two Queens awaiting them, with another woman, tall and middle-aged, dressed as a nun, and introduced as Mère Magdeleine, Prioress of the nearby nunnery of St Jacques, the Princess's tutor, guide and adviser. Thus escorted, they were led through the usual succession of salons to the Orangery, where the girl was waiting.

Henrietta Maria made an immediate impact for so young a creature. Small and slight, like her brother, but very different otherwise, she was dark, pretty, vivacious, curly of hair, round of feature, with lively eyes and a ready smile. She did not seem in the least abashed or overawed by the occasion, and greeted the envoys with frank interest. Marie introduced her as her sixth child and third daughter. She certainly made a striking contrast to her large mother.

Carlisle addressed her first, in his halting French, seeking to say how they had come for to see her, how much all England, and Scotland too, hoped to see her as their future queen, how delighted they were with what they saw now. He then stepped forward and handed to her a letter from Prince Charles.

She accepted this with eagerness, turning it over to examine the seal and superscription, thanking him and declaring satisfaction. She told them that she had met the Prince on his way to Spain, but that he had called himself, on

231

that occasion, Mr Brown! This with laughter. She had thought him attractive. She was quick of speech, and gestured with her hands.

Then it was Kensington's turn. He relieved Goring of a somewhat awkward burden, wrapped in silk, which unwrapped to disclose a framed painting, a portrait of Charles Stewart. Kensington's address was a deal more fluent and flowery.

Taking the picture, Henrietta exclaimed with pleasure. She actually sought to hug it to her slight person. Clearly, if it had been left to her, little difficulty would have attended their mission.

Carlisle then produced another letter, this time from King James, which she took more formally.

These proceedings over, they moved out into the gardens, Henrietta seeming loth to be parted from her picture, which certainly did no injustice to Charles, depicting his undoubted good looks and fine-cut features, so unlike his father's, but omitting the withdrawn and almost secretive expression which so often clouded them. Marie announced that a portrait of her daughter would be produced, to send to Charles in return.

Henrietta then impulsively asked her mother for permission to read the Prince's letter, and laughing, Marie agreed. The girl broke the seal and scanned the spidery writing excitedly, flushing as she read. Twice she went over it, before, without offering it to anyone else, she folded it up and tucked it into the not very capacious bosom of her dress, from which it projected less than conveniently. It was noticeable that she did not seek to read King James's letter there and then.

When, presently, the envoys withdrew, all were much pleased with the proposed bride, and the more enheartened for the success of their embassage – all except Carlisle, that is. The Earl sounded a warning note. The real ruler of France, he understood, was the cleric Richelieu; and *his* lack of welcome and absence from their scene was ominous, he felt. Somehow they must gain a meeting with the Cardinal, and soon.

But how to effect it? Oddly, their contacts and associations here were all with the women, and whatever may have been the case previously, women, however highly placed, seemed to have little influence on the rule of the state at present. Since the Cardinal appeared to be the key figure, some thought that their own Bishop, Laud, was the obvious one to make an approach; but that man declared otherwise. As a Protestant cleric anyone so prominent in the Romish Church probably would refuse to have anything to do with him. Almost anyone else would be better. But through whom? Who could any of them approach, who might be able to reach the Cardinal?

It was David who pointed out that the only religious they had had any dealings with so far was the Prioress-tutor of the Princess Henrietta, the Mère Magdeleine herself. He had had a word or two with her in the Tuileries garden and she had seemed friendly enough, and gave the impression of competence and responsibility. She must be well thought of in higher circles to be given the charge of the Princess. She might well have access to the Cardinal.

Doubts were expressed about this, but Carlisle said that in default of any better suggestion, David should make a trial of it. No harm in that.

So next day David found his way back to the Tuileries, alone, and there sought the Prioress. He was kept waiting for some time but eventually was conducted to the gardens again, where he found Mère Magdeleine in an arbour beside a small pond on which waterfowl swam, at the far side of which Henrietta Maria and another young woman were feeding swans, a pretty scene.

David bowed to the nun, who greeted him kindly enough, asking if he had come with some message for the Princess.

"No, lady," he said, uncertain how to address a nun. "It is yourself that I have come to see. It is our hope that you might be able to help us – that is, the embassage from King James. It is our wish, you see, to have a private meeting with the Cardinal Richelieu. To discuss with him details of the proposed royal marriage."

"But . . . why come to me, young man? This is scarcely my provenance."

"We have not seen the Cardinal since our only audience with King Louis. And we have been in Paris now for almost three weeks. We have no means of approaching him, and

233

believe that if another from the Church, who could gain access to him, were to speak with him, on our behalf . . ."

"But, surely, if His Eminence has anything to say to you, my friend, he would send for you?"

"He has not done so, lady. Yet we understand that he is the King's closest adviser. And therefore must be concerned with the negotiations for this marriage. Some meeting is necessary. And time passes."

"His Eminence must be well aware of this, young man. If there is delay, then there must be reason for it. I do not see what I can do."

"You, Prioress, could gain access to the Cardinal?"

"No doubt. But to what end?"

"This marriage – it is important to both kingdoms. The Princess would in due course become Queen of Great Britain. Details require to be discussed before we can return to King James . . ."

He paused, as Henrietta and her companion came from round the pond, all but at a run.

"It is the handsome Scottish gentleman!" she exclaimed. "The one Anne says . . . the Queen says, has taught her to dance as they do in Scotland. She said that *I* should learn. Will you teach me also, Monsieur?"

David glanced at the Prioress. "I would be honoured, Highness. If it was thought to be . . . suitable."

"To be sure, it is! Is it not, Mère Magdeleine? If I am to be Queen of England, and of Scotland too, one day."

"Yes, yes, my dear. I think that it might be possible. On a suitable occasion, as Sir David has it."

"Why not now, Monsieur?"

"This is *not* the occasion, I think, Henrietta. Sir David has come here with a message for myself. He will be leaving shortly ... ."

Obviously the lady would have him gone, so David bowed, first to the Princess, then to the Prioress.

"Yes. I must go now. With your royal permission, Highness." He paused. "So, lady, you will seek word with the Cardinal, for us? Of your kindness."

Rather doubtfully the Prioress inclined her head as he backed away.

Not very hopeful about this endeavour, David was gratified when, two days later, a young nun arrived at their quarters with a message from the Prioress. His Eminence the Cardinal would see a small deputation of the English envoys the day following, at two hours after noon, in the Louvre's private chapel.

The news heartened them all.

It was decided that five of them would be sufficient for this interview, Carlisle, Kensington, Goring and David, with the Bishop – who doubted whether his presence would assist but was persuaded to accompany them.

So next day the group found their way to the venue, not the main church of the citadel it turned out, which was quite a major and highly decorative edifice, but a small sanctuary in one of the towers, odd, for necessarily it had to be circular, comparatively modest in its features and plenishings. Here a priest received them less than warmly and conducted them to a still smaller room off, in the nature of a sacristy or vestry, and there left them. The impression gained was that Holy Church scarcely approved of them or felt required to pretend to.

They were not kept waiting for long, however. The Cardinal came in, accompanied by another cleric whom he did not introduce, and greeted them with cool formality. It had been agreed that Kensington, with his command of French, should open the proceedings, which he did by declaring that the Earl of Carlisle and himself were joint ambassadors of King James, the Bishop of St Davids represented the Church of England, and Sir George Goring and Sir David Gray were aides. They had sought this interview in order, if possible, to expedite the conclusion of the proposed marriage treaty, for they were beginning to feel that they had burdened King Louis, Queen Marie and all concerned, overlong with their presence, kind as their reception had been.

Richelieu gravely inclined his head. Tall, thin of features and lips, long of nose above moustache and small pointed beard, he had large hooded eyes and an expression of stern and watchful competence, a man of decision unlikely to compromise. David for one did not feel encouraged.

Since the Cardinal did not seem to find comment necessary at this stage, Carlisle put in his blunter and less flowing contribution.

"We feel that it is time that we came to decision, Cardinal, on details of this royal match. It has been agreed in broad principles between the monarchs, before this. Now we have to agree on detailed matters – such as timing, dowry, lands and portion to be allotted, the marriage ceremony, numbers of attendants to come with the Princess to England, and the like. All to be dealt with. King Louis will have his views on all this, and no doubt you will be in a position to assist and advise." He had to refer to David more than once in all that, to find the right wording.

The Cardinal waited until he had finished, and was in no hurry to proceed. When he did, it was in level, clear tones. "Firstly, Messieurs, the agreement to the proposed marriage was made while His Most Christian Majesty was guided by other advisers. The advantages are less evident to His Majesty now."

That was an unpromising start, as it was no doubt meant to be. The envoys looked at each other.

"Secondly, it is not clear that His Holiness at Rome will give the necessary dispensation for the marriage. I have been in communication with him at the Vatican – hence the unavoidable delay. The Princess Henrietta is a devout Catholic, and cannot marry a Protestant without Papal dispensation."

That was received in silence.

"Until this primary matter has been resolved, Messieurs, you will perceive that the details you mention, and others, are scarcely of relevance."

Since no one else appeared to be disposed to raise voice, David was bold enough to speak. "May we ask, Eminence, what are the terms the Pope suggests before he will agree to a dispensation?"

"His Holiness requires that all penal laws against Catholics in England be abolished."

Indrawn breaths greeted that. "Impossible!" Carlisle jerked. "Parliament would never accept that – never!" That was in English.

236

Richelieu raised one red shoulder in the hint of a shrug.

"Cardinal," Kensington put in, in French, "you must understand the position – as surely the Pope must know. King James is head of the Church of England, as Prince Charles will be one day. The laws passed against the public practice of the Roman Catholic faith, by parliament, cannot be abolished by the Crown. Only by the agreement of parliament. And it is certain that the English parliament would never agree to that – nothing more sure. That was made clear from the start, in the preliminary approaches. King James gained parliament's acceptance that the Princess should have entire freedom for herself and her attendants to worship as she would. But by law, the state and monarchy is Protestant. King James could not have the anti-Catholic laws repealed."

"Then, milord, I fear that the proposed marriage may not be permitted."

"But why?" Carlisle demanded. "Why was not this declared before? Why was this embassage allowed to come to France? You have known all along that this was the position. It was never kept secret. Why then, now?"

"His Holiness, milord, so declares."

"Does the Pope rule France, then? Or King Louis!"

Even his companions were somewhat alarmed at the Earl's undiplomatic outburst. There was some clearing of throats.

Richelieu rose. "I do not think that there is anything further to be gained from this meeting, Messieurs," he said coldly. "I will convey your views to King Louis. And also to Rome." He paused for a moment. "And may I remind you that in dealings between monarchs and states all cannot be as plainly and clearly set forth as when buying and selling in a market!"

Bowing slightly, he turned and led his silent companion out.

The envoys returned to their quarters much affronted and dejected.

They discussed the situation thereafter, of course, at considerable length. Carlisle was for packing up almost there and then and returning to London. But Kensington demurred. They could not just give up, at this stage. King James would expect better of them than that. This of the Pope was

237

perhaps just a device to get better terms out of them. That Richelieu was a hard man to deal with; but he was not *France*. If they could but get at the King . . .

Carlisle snorted and said that the only way to impress that young man was to go to him barking like dogs! He clearly had no interest in their presence, and presumably did not care whether or not the marriage took place. That Cardinal was the key to it all, a plague on him, and was clearly against the match.

David hesitated to put in an opinion. But he had just a notion that Richelieu was not quite so adamant as he might seem. After all, he was clearly a shrewd statesman or he would not have risen to his present position. He must have known very well that the anti-Catholic laws in England would not be repealed by parliament. The French Ambassador to King James's court must have told them this. Yet he *had* come to meet them, however belatedly. He need not have done. He could have sent word that no marriage was possible. So he must have had some reason. He might think to bargain.

Kensington nodded, although the others looked doubtful.

A further thought occurred to David. "That parting word he left with us – perhaps that meant something. When he said that about dealings between kings and states not being like buying and selling in a market. I thought at the time that was a strange remark, my lords. And he paused before he said it. Could it mean . . .?"

"It meant, I think, that my lord Carlisle's asking if the Pope ruled France was too . . . rough-hewn!" Kensington suggested.

"It was just, right, deserved, man," the Earl declared.

"But scarcely politic, James! It sent him off in offence."

"But not before he made that comment. About dealings between monarchs," David insisted. "Cannot be . . . how was it he put it? Cannot be as clearly, plainly set forth, as buying and selling. In a market. Could that not mean some agreement might be reached, less than openly. Some understood arrangement, which would get round the difficulty?"

"Och, you are reading ower much into it, Davie," the Earl

238

said. "The man was just trying to put us in our place! These haughty, up-jumped churchmen are the devil . . .!" He glanced over at Bishop Laud. "Umm – nae offence, my lord."

That man, who was more notable for his silence than his eloquence, shrugged, and delivered an opinion, for once.

"I think that I agree with our young friend," he said. "That last remark of the Cardinal's may have been significant. It is worth thinking on, at least. Since we have little else to consider!"

"Consider, perhaps, but what can we *do*?" Goring asked. "We cannot request another meeting, after this."

None could answer that question.

They were invited by Queen Anne to a masque the following evening. It was held in the same Great Gallery where the ball had taken place; but how different it appeared on this occasion. Enormous thought and work must have gone into the preparation, not to mention enormous expense, for the place now represented a clearing in a wood, with a lake in the centre and a mountain at one end – this last of painted canvas, with rocks and cliffs and caves, its trees painted ones although all round the perimeter of the gallery were real trees and shrubs and greenery, in troughs and tubs, even real grass and turfs. The lake, or pond, was represented by more canvas spread on the floor and painted to look like sparkling water, with stuffed swans to add to the effect.

Soft music came from somewhere. The guests mingled amongst the trees. The Comtesse Jeanetta soon found David and attached herself. Wine and sweetmeats were available whilst they waited for the masque to commence.

A great trumpeting introduced the action. First, out of the caves and openings of the canvas mountain issued numbers of characters, male and female, shepherdesses, knights, fauns, hermits, pilgrims, gypsies, dwarfs, fairies and pedlars, in notable variety, save in that all were either masked or had their faces painted black, to hide identity. These came cavorting round the lake, in and out of the trees, in couples and groups, often with lewd gestures and indecent posturings

239

towards the watchers – who endeavoured to put names to individuals. Jeanetta identified one of the shepherdesses, oddly enough, by her massive thighs, frequently revealed.

Then more trumpeting heralded a new development. From behind the mountain appeared half a dozen curious creatures, which most decided were sea-horses mounted by blackamoors, these heaving and diving up and down as though riding the waves of the lake and trailing what seemed to be seaweed. Behind them came another group clad in glistening silvery scales, with large round eyes and waving fishes' tails. These made swimming motions around the sea-horses and riders. Both groups then formed up in two lines, facing each other, on the lake, and there was a third fanfare.

Into view came the *pièce de résistance*, a ship in sail, all white and gold, propelled by completely naked oarsmen, all painted in black. On its stern platform was a great scallop-shell, in which sat five women, four of them supporting a plump creature, diaphanously clad and wearing a white deer's-head mask, her attendants only partially clothed but painted black not only as to faces but halfway up legs and arms, which had the effect of making the rest of their white anatomies seem remarkably immodest. The ship moved down between the ranks of undulating fishes and sea-horses, the deer-headed lady throwing out lines, right and left, baited with oysters which the creatures had to catch and pretend to swallow – all this to music which sought to sound like the rise and fall of tides and breakers.

Past the last of the sea-denizens, the vessel made a rather awkward turn and proceeded back up the avenue. But now the four supporting females left their principal, to cast out netting, this to fall over the fish and sea-horses, which were then gathered up beneath it all as the boat progressed, into a jostling, protesting huddle, amidst much clutching and embracing of persons as the ship was rowed onwards, seeming to draw its netted catch after it, and round out of sight.

Loud and long was the applause, and vehement the declarations of identity, with wagering to back assertions.

Even David could put name to one. "I think the lady with

240

the deer's head was Queen Anne," he suggested. "That seemed to be her . . . build."

"So you are familiar now with the Queen's physique!" he was challenged.

"But who else would it be, sitting there as mistress of all? When it is *her* masque. Did you recognise the Duchesse de Chevreuse exposing herself?"

"Your friend, milord Kensington, would, I swear!"

He shook his head. "And is that all? All that of cost and labour, for so brief a display?"

"There may be other lesser mummery, but that will be the main flourish of the night. How thought you of it, David?"

"I had never seen the like. I thought it most ingenious. But . . . extravagant. Do you ever take part, Comtesse?"

"Sometimes. But tonight I am afflicted with my monthly burden."

"Ah. I, I am sorry." That was untrue, in fact. It might avoid complications later.

Servants brought in more substantial feeding, in great quantity and variety. It was while partaking of this that one of the capering fauns came to him, to announce that Her Majesty would see him now.

Much surprised, David excused himself, Jeanetta declaring less than joyfully that Anne had sharp eyes inside that deer mask. He followed his guide up to and behind the canvas mountain, which proved to have been erected on the dais-area. A doorway off this opened into an ante-room, where he found the Queen awaiting him. She had covered her revealing garb with a silken robe.

When the faun had departed, Anne welcomed him frankly. "So, Sir David, did you like our play-acting?"

"Indeed yes, Highness. It was all most interesting, most entertaining. What did it mean?"

"Mean? It was a masque, a display. Must it *mean* something?"

"Perhaps not. I do not know about these things. I have never before seen a masque. I but thought that there must be some meaning behind it all, the sea-creatures, the ship, and Your Majesty wearing a deer's head. I could not perceive the connection . . ."

She laughed. "My dear Sir David, you are too practical! Too sober. I have heard that the Scots are so, all to be in order, reasonable, for a purpose. This was but fantasy, that is all. A spectacle. I wore that mask merely because it was new-made, and none would know it. Yet *you* knew me, it seems! Is my person so, so outstanding?"

"No, no. Or, well, perhaps, Highness. You are very attractive, I think. Noticeably so!" He blinked as he said that, wondering whether this was going too far?

"I have heard it described otherwise, Sir David! So you can be gallant, as well as practical, and with a seeing eye! And a dancer. I have a pupil for you to teach your Scottish steps. My sister-in-law, Henrietta. She is gone to wash and change her costume. Did you recognise *her*, in your keen looking? She was one of the blackamoors. She will be back when she has washed off the blackness. She has much spirit. Your future Queen."

David agreed, and then thought to take a chance. "Majesty, you think that she *will* be our Queen? Marry Prince Charles?"

"Why not? That is why you are here, is it not?"

"Indeed yes. We are much in favour of it. But we fear that others are less so."

"Who? We understood that only the details are still to be settled. And Henrietta is most pleased. As are we all."

"We had a meeting with the Cardinal Richelieu yesterday, Highness. And he, he was otherwise minded, it seemed."

"Richelieu! I think that you are mistaken, Sir David. The Cardinal is in favour of the match."

"He did not show it, then. He was very . . . dismissive. He said that the Pope would not give dispensation."

"Richelieu said that? And was accepting such refusal?"

"Yes. He said that unless the anti-Catholic laws of England were repealed there could be no marriage. For the Pope would not permit it. And, as the Cardinal must know, there is no possibility of the English parliament accepting repeal. It is too strongly Protestant."

"This is very strange," Anne said, frowning. "Richelieu wants this match, that I am sure. He sees England as necessary to help France curb the power of Spain – my Spain! So it is *I* who should object to it, not him." She gave a brief laugh. "But I do not dabble in statecraft."

"If the Cardinal is in favour of the marriage, Majesty, he has a strange way of showing it!"

"Perhaps that was his way of seeking to get better terms from you? He is a wily one, is Armand Jean du Plessis. It could be but a ruse. His abiding policy is to promote France against Spain, and this marriage is part of that policy. Moreover, he is no friend of this Pope Urban, Cardinal although he be. Indeed he would, I think, not be a Cardinal had Urban become Pope two years sooner! I think that he seeks to play you, like one of my fishes! A device, Sir David."

"Could it be so? He seemed very certain about this of the dispensation. He broke off the meeting very abruptly. But said that such dealings of state were not to be plainly and clearly set forth, as in a market."

"He said that? Not plainly and clearly? Ah, I think that I see it. He means that there might be some less plain understanding, *secret*. That sounds like our Cardinal!"

"You mean . . .?"

"A little quiet bargaining, my friend. Perhaps you are all too much the practical and forthright for that? Your Lord Carlisle is scarcely a subtle schemer, I think! But Henry Kensington now – he should know how to play the game. You will all have to learn, it seems."

"But, what can we do? He broke off the meeting. How can we get him back, to talking? To play any such game. He hides himself away. We never see him about the court. Nor does King Louis see us. How can we bargain with the Cardinal, Highness?"

"You could do as I think *he* does – make a pretence. That is it – pretend that you take him seriously, believe that there is no hope for this marriage, from what he has said. And declare that you are going to leave again for England. I vow that would bring about a meeting sufficiently quickly!"

"You think so? And if it does not? We are then committed to going . . ."

"Be not so timorous, Sir David! In any game of chance one

must risk some stake. I do not think that you would be allowed to leave, like that . . ."

They got no further before the Princess Henrietta arrived, all excitement and exclamation, her face glowing rosily with all the rubbing off of black paint.

As she came, the Queen murmured, "Say nothing of this to her." And then, in her normal voice, "Here, Sir David, is your new pupil. I have a flautist waiting to play for us."

David had some doubts about the practicality of footing Scots dance steps to the music of a flute, especially played by one who had to be taught the tunes first, but he could only do his best.

The musician sent for, an elderly gnome-like character, but lively and eager to please, quite quickly picked up the rhythm and timing and beat of the Scottish tunes from David's humming. Clapping her hands, Anne insisted on demonstrating her own proficiency in the matter first, for her sister-in-law's edification, doing very well after an initial mistake or two, although her loose silken robe, which tended to jerk open with the sprightly movements over the filmy scantiness below, was scarcely the ideal wear for Scottish dancing for a well-endowed young woman, the flouncing and bouncing being especially distracting for her partner. Henrietta squealed with delight.

When it came to the Princess's turn, all enthusiasm, she took to the *pas-de-bas* steps very readily, and was able to go on to some attempt at two or three types of reel. When, a natural dancer, she had got the verve and tempo of this, David suggested that, while eight were required for the full reel, they might try a sort of basic version, in trio. They would do the circling, the linking of arms, the dancing to partners and the reversing. All of this they achieved, by trial and error, amidst much breathless laughter and ebullient femininity. David realised that he was enjoying himself. If Barbara Home could see him now . . .!

Anne, panting, declared presently that they must have more of this hereafter. The flautist must teach some of his fellow-musicians to play the tunes, and she would gather a team of dancers to make up the eight, or even two eights.

These Scottish reels and flings were far more enlivening and exhilarating than their own formal ballroom dancing. Sir David would have them all expert, before he was finished, expert and grateful.

That man, finding his way back to their quarters thereafter, had some difficulty in concentrating his mind on matters of state and diplomacy.

16

At a conference next day, when David recounted the Queen's reaction and advice, he had an attentive audience, all encouraged by what he told them. It was agreed that they should indeed make some gesture about returning home, as though despairing of any success in their mission. Kensington came up with the suggestion that, since Goring had been brought along mainly to act as a courier, to keep King James informed as to progress, and it was high time that he made such journey back, they should put it about that he was being sent to seek royal permission for the embassage to return, empty-handed. This would be more telling than merely saying that they would be going. Also, it would avoid the difficulty of making the consequent delay in their departure seem to cast doubt on their intentions, for they would have to wait for Goring's return with the permission.

This was accepted with acclaim. All were to express their gloom and despondency to their French friends – mainly female, indubitably – and Goring's errand be made much of. Without doubt the Cardinal would be well-informed as to what went on, and would quickly get the message.

David was to keep up his liaison with Queen Anne and the Princess. Who would have thought that Scottish dancing could so aid in diplomatic manoeuvring! Maintain the dancing lessons – but to be careful that this association with the Queen did not reach the stage of causing raised eyebrows at the court, and perhaps causing King Louis to become suspicious. Not that, from all accounts, theirs was any real marriage, but merely a dynastic union, Louis being much more interested in dogs than women.

David was somewhat doubtful about how this carefulness was to be achieved, in the circumstances. He was in no least danger, he assured, of trifling with the young Queen's affections – but she was very friendly and at ease with him. The last thing that he wanted to do was to offend.

So all members of the embassage began to inform their French associates that they would soon be leaving them, unfortunately, for a return to London; and that Sir George Goring would be off in a couple of days to gain the necessary royal acceptance of the situation. It seemed that the looked-forward-to marriage was not to proceed.

It was astonishing how swiftly the news spread through the Louvre. By late afternoon that same day, David received a summons to attend on Queen Anne in her private wing of the palace, at his earliest convenience.

On arrival at her magnificent apartments, he found Anne in no mood to keep him waiting.

"Sir David," she greeted at once, "I hear that your party are indeed proposing to leave Paris. And that one of your number has already gone, or is about to go, in advance. Is this true, or is it you learning to play statecraft games, as I suggested to you?"

"Yes, Highness. This is the result of your kind advice. Sir George Goring *is* going to London, but not yet to ask for leave to return. He came as courier, to report progress, and it is time that he made such a report. We but let it be thought that we deem the mission a failure, thanks to the Cardinal's attitude, and that this is the reason for the move."

The Queen smiled, and patted his arm. "My dear Sir David, you are as apt a pupil as you are a teacher, I swear! This is excellent. I am sure that it will have results. Richelieu will get to hear of it – I shall see that he does, although he may well have heard already. He will be concerned, undoubtedly. Yes, this is a good move. I congratulate you, David." That was the first time that she had dropped the Sir.

"It was not in truth *my* notion, Highness. About Goring going," he disclaimed. "It was Lord Kensington's. I but proposed that we let it be known that we were thinking to return home."

"Yes, I thought that Kensington would see the point. But, alas, I was going to arrange a Scottish dancing-class tomorrow evening for you to instruct. Now, if all are expecting you to be leaving shortly, perhaps that would seem unsuitable?"

"We cannot go so very soon, Majesty, if Goring has to get to London and back with the King's permission. So none could esteem it odd, I think . . ."

"True. Good! Then we shall have our class tomorrow. I will have a small company come, all of the most suitable and lively. And will set the musicians to practising the tunes. Perhaps you could help in that, no? Instruct the players before the dancers?"

"As you will, Highness. But if it is possible, they should play on fiddles, violins, rather than on flutes. Our dances are made for the fiddle."

"Very well, David. I will see to it. Then, tomorrow forenoon perhaps . . .?"

But teaching the instrumentalists Scots tunes was not for David next morning. For a messenger arrived for the envoys, this time from Queen Marie, announcing that the portrait of her daughter Henrietta, to be sent to Prince Charles in exchange for his own to her, was now ready, and the courier they were sending back to England should take it with him. Accordingly, the embassage should wait on her at noon this day, in the throne-room, when the picture would be handed over.

This, needless to say, further encouraged them. It looked as though the Queen Mother, at least, anticipated the match going ahead. Yet, of course, the two Queens might be out of touch with the ultimate authority – the King, advised by Richelieu.

So they went, as summoned, but keeping optimism in check.

A select company was assembled in the gilded throne-room. Marie greeted them amiably, with the Princess herself excited at being the centre of attention. The portrait, covered with a cloth, stood on an easel to the side of the dais.

They had not long to wait before a herald blew a trumpet, and a door behind the dais opened to admit Queen Anne, all bowing. On a ceremonial occasion such as this, the niceties of precedence fell to be observed and the consort of the reigning monarch ranked above her mother-in-law. It must have been quite difficult for them, David thought, with Marie having been for so long Queen-Regent; but they were good friends. There was no sign of King Louis.

Marie, with a bow to Anne, took charge; after all, the

Princess was her daughter. She announced that this was a pleasant occasion, on which they were glad to receive the envoys of the King of England – with a twinkling glance at Carlisle she amended that to the King of Great Britain – whom they hoped were enjoying their company. They had been kind enough to bring from London a portrait of the Prince of Wales, heir to the throne of the United Kingdom, a handsome and, they were assured, a notable likeness. Now it was their turn to reciprocate. King Louis had had a portrait painted of his sister, the Princess Henrietta Maria here, by the accomplished artist Monsieur Honthorst from Utrecht – and she gestured towards a plainly dressed youngish man standing to the side – for presentation to His Royal Highness Prince Charles. It was understood that one of the English envoys was to return to London shortly, and it was hoped that he would take the picture with him.

Goring, thus referred to, was only part paying attention, his eyes elsewhere. He nudged David's arm, and nodded. Behind them, at one side, the scarlet-clad Richelieu had slipped quietly into the listening company.

That alerted the envoys considerably.

Queen Marie moved over, to twitch the cloth from off the portrait, to suitable exclamations from the onlookers. The representation, half-length, was certainly very fine, a fair likeness although making Henrietta seem somewhat older than she was and with rather more figure – but no doubt she would grow into that. Everybody clapped, and the young Princess beamed.

Marie gestured towards the artist, who bowed, embarrassed, and then quietly withdrew. She then signed Carlisle forward and indicated that he was to take the painting.

The Earl's speech of thanks and appreciation was typically brief. He nodded to Kensington, who contributed a much more elaborate flourish, with compliments all round. The portrait was then handed to Goring.

This completed the formal part of the proceedings, and the Queen Mother, Anne and Henrietta moved down to mingle with the company. David found Anne at his elbow.

"You have seen the Cardinal?" she murmured. "*He* did not come to view any painting, I think!"

249

"Do we approach him, Highness? Or wait for him to approach us?"

"Wait. I will be surprised if he does not make a move."

Richelieu was standing alone, none present evidently on easy terms with him. David became afraid that he would turn and leave. Perhaps Queen Marie felt the same, for she went up to him, smiling. After all, it was to her that he owed his advancement, for she it was who had introduced him to court when she was Regent of France and he was only Bishop of Luçon. Now they had, as it were, changed places in their influence on King Louis.

They spoke for a few moments and then the Queen Mother, looking round, beckoned to Carlisle. The Earl went over, while his companions watched heedfully.

Whatever was said was brief, for quite quickly the Cardinal bowed to Marie, merely inclined his head to the Earl and then turned and left the chamber. The Queen Mother linked her arm in Carlisle's and led him off to the refreshment tables. His party was left in some concern, wondering.

Presently Anne, watching all this, went over to join her mother-in-law, and after a little came back to David.

"The Cardinal will meet you all in the library hereafter," she informed. "When you leave here. I think that he will prove more helpful than last time."

So, after they had partaken of the provision, and Marie released Carlisle, they were given a guide to take them to the library, Anne wishing them well, and reminding David that she was arranging the dancing-class that evening.

As well that they had an escort for, despite the length of their stay here, they still had not mastered the lay-out of this vast citadel-palace, and the library seemed to be in a different section altogether.

As splendid an apartment as the rest, but giving the air of being but little used, they were left therein to admire the serried ranks of books, the tables laden with rolls of parchment, the treaties, charters, heraldic achievements and the rest.

When Richelieu arrived, he had with him the same silent attendant of the previous occasion, again not introduced. The envoys were beckoned over to one of the cleared tables, and, with a minimum of talk, sat.

"I have been in consultation with His Majesty, Messieurs. Also discussed the matter with sundry advisers, including the Papal Nuncio, and am empowered to put certain requirements before you, on this of a possible royal wedding," the Cardinal announced, without preamble. "Certain conditions are essential, before His Holiness could agree to give dispensation. This of the anti-Catholic laws in England in especial. But leaving that aside for the moment, there are other points we require to discuss. If you are so prepared?"

They waited, silent.

"There is the question of jointure. What provision is being offered for the Princess's jointure?"

That was easy. Kensington launched into a list of manors, estates, houses and customs-dues, scattered over England, most of which had been the jointure of Anne of Denmark, James's Queen.

Richelieu nodded, without comment. "Then there is the Princess's household, for the sister of the King of France and proposed Princess of Wales. And later, in God's time, as Queen of England. She will require a sufficiency of officers, secretaries, attendants . . . and, to be sure, chaplains. Of Holy Church, naturally."

"That is understood," Kensington said. "No limit is set on the numbers of the Princess's court. Both those she would bring with her from France and such as she would acquire in England."

"And the chaplains?"

"No difficulty there, Your Eminence. She would have clerics, so many as she wished to attend her. French or English."

"And chapels? Places of worship?"

So they were getting back to the vexed question. "As we said before, there would be no restrictions on the Princess's worship – none. In private. So she could have chapels for her own use, and that of her attendants, in her palaces and houses. You understand, Eminence, that there are no Catholic churches now in England. But private chapels are another matter."

"It is this situation which is not acceptable to His Holiness."

Silence. But it occurred to David, at least, that if some

251

compromise was not envisaged, the Cardinal would be unlikely to have gone into these lesser points first.

"On the matter of public worship," Richelieu went on evenly, "there will be occasions when the Prince of Wales will be expected to appear with his wife. In church. This would not be possible in a building heretically dedicated."

"There are differing views on heresy, Cardinal!" Carlisle put in bluntly.

"Perhaps. But Holy Church's view is all that concerns a sister of His Most Christian Majesty."

When nobody seemed to see a way round that, David was emboldened to speak up. "Your Eminence, when, those few years ago, there were proposals for Prince Charles to wed the Infanta of Spain, no such requirements were demanded by the Vatican, I think."

Richelieu eyed him coldly. "At that time there was a different occupant of the papal throne."

"So we understand, sir." David took a breath. "But it does mean, then, that this requirement is *personal*. To the present Pope Urban. Not a matter of vital Catholic doctrine, of unchanging importance?"

Carlisle did not entirely succeed in restraining an incipient chuckle.

The Cardinal frowned. "Young man, I think that you may safely leave vital Catholic doctrine to *me*!" he snapped.

"Yes, Your Eminence. But you will perceive our . . . confusion. In this change of requirements."

"There need be no confusion. His Holiness will not give dispensation unless restrictions on Catholic worship in England are lifted. And papal dispensation is necessary before the Princess can marry a Protestant."

Carlisle pushed back his chair.

"We cannot make any such declaration, Eminence," Kensington said. "You must understand that. It is a decision for parliament. And . . ." He left the rest unsaid.

The impasse seemed to be complete again, with Carlisle heaving his bulk to rise. But David still felt that Richelieu would not be here if there was not a loophole. And he recollected what Queen Anne had said about secrecy, the game of statecraft.

"If we – or my lords here – were to agree as a privy matter, not to be written into any contract or treaty, to make endeavour privately to persuade King James and his advisers to some lessening of the anti-Catholic laws, would that not be of help, Eminence? Treated with secrecy meantime. Would that not enable Your Excellency to inform the Vatican that there would be at least some relaxation?" He realised that the others were staring at him. "I am sure that King James would do his best in the matter. Prince Charles also. And you could inform the Pope that progress was . . . in train. Since France's interests are also involved in this marriage."

No one spoke for a few moments.

When one did, it was the Cardinal, his tone of voice subtly changed. "Some such arrangement might conceivably be helpful," he admitted. And, after a pause. "When do you plan to return to England?"

The envoys looked at each other. "When we have King James's permission," Kensington answered, when no other voice was raised.

"Ah. That will give us a little time, then. You agree?"

All nodded, warily.

"Then I bid you good-day, Messieurs." Richelieu rose, clearly determined to be the first to do so, and took his departure without further word.

The envoys all began to talk at once. The Earl prevailed.

"What's this o' secrets, Davie?" he demanded. "Privy matters? What were you at, there?"

"Little more than a device, my lord. Suggested to me by Queen Anne. It commits us to nothing more than urging King James to seek some lessening of the severe laws against Catholics. Whether he can, or will, is not our concern. But it gives the Cardinal opportunity to tell the Pope that he is making progress, that he is working to have the Vatican's demands fulfilled."

"Will that serve anything? Would a Cardinal so think to deceive a Pope?"

"I think so, yes. Queen Anne says that Richelieu and the present Pope Urban are scarcely friendly. He cannot defy the Vatican. But he himself wishes this marriage and alliance with

253

England to proceed. So he needs an excuse, some token as to his efforts."

The Earl shrugged. "It could be. To be sure, it seemed to reach him, and quickly. And yon bit about no such demand over the Spanish match fair upset him! That was right cunning. I jalouse you've got something of your grandsire in you, laddie! He was a rogue, mind, but a clever one."

"Richelieu said time," Kensington put in. "It would give us a little time, he said. Think you he meant time to inform Rome? At least it had a hopeful sound to it."

All agreed.

That evening the dancing-class proved almost too success-ful, in that instead of the proposed two eights, nearly two score turned up, including the Queen Mother and Carlisle. So David had some assistance in demonstrating the steps and movements, thankful that the Earl seemed approximately sober, and remarkably lightsome on his feet for his weight and age. But he was of no use at the embarrassing business of humming, to teach the instrumentalists the Scots melodies. David had to do that himself, to the amusement and applause of all. At least the orchestra was composed of fiddlers.

Most there picked up the steps and rhythm readily enough, and before the night was out they had three eightsome reels going, after a fashion, with much hilarity, if some confusion. During an interval for breath, David was able to impart to Anne some account of their meeting with the Cardinal. She appeared to be confirmed in her optimism.

They sent off George Goring the next day, with an escort and the portrait, heading for Boulogne. They reckoned that they could expect him back in just over two weeks.

The waiting envoys saw nothing of Cardinal Richelieu in the days that followed, so assumed that he was sending a messenger to the Vatican and was awaiting a reply. They did, however, see King Louis, only their second meeting with the monarch, at a hawking demonstration in the Bois de Boulogne, Anne presenting them during a break. Her husband was scarcely forthcoming, but neither did he display any animosity – nor indeed any concern over the matter of their mission, confirming their impression that he had little interest in being King of France. Indeed it was reported that he had said that he would rather his younger brother had succeeded to the throne, so that *he* would be more likely to be assassinated rather than himself. According to Anne, he was not actually opposed to the English match but would abide by Richelieu's advice.

The royal ladies saw that time did not hang heavily for the visitors thereafter, with a steady succession of entertainments, hunts, displays and balls, the Scottish dancing becoming quite the court rage, however odd some of the interpretations. As a consequence, David became one of the most popular members of the embassage, in some demand for private parties as well as the royally-sponsored ones. The Comtesse Jeanetta became resigned.

It was ten days before they heard from the Cardinal again. He sent requesting a meeting, again in the Louvre's library, Anne suggesting that this was carefully timed before Monsieur Goring got back from London with his instructions.

This time, on arrival they found a number of clerics and secretaries already in the library. The envoys were hardly inside before Richelieu himself entered.

It was hard to say what was different about the man. He was still cold, restrained, watchful, with that dry cough, his greeting no more hearty than heretofore. Yet there was a change. To say that he appeared more purposeful might imply that he had seemed to lack purpose before, and this he never did. But, without being in any way businesslike, this time he appeared to mean business.

Gesturing to a central table, he sat. Almost hurriedly all others took their seats.

"Messieurs," he said, "I am now in a position to inform you as to the principal terms, other than those we have already discussed, on which King Louis is prepared to accede to the marriage of his sister to the Prince of Wales. And on which His Holiness at Rome will grant dispensation therefor." That was announced as a decision rather than any basis for negotiation.

They waited, alert.

"First and foremost, it is understood that it will be conveyed to King James and Prince Charles, secretly if need be, that it is expected that the anti-Catholic laws of England will be repealed at the earliest possible opportunity. This, as was discussed at our last meeting. Only so will the Pope Urban agree to this marriage."

Their nods were less than vehement.

"Secondly, in earnest of the first, it is required that all persons at present held imprisoned for their faith, the true Catholic faith, shall be released forthwith."

Carlisle cleared his throat, but before he could utter Kensington spoke quickly.

"We will so recommend to His Majesty, Eminence. That he should issue a royal pardon. The King, rather than parliament."

"So long as it is effective, and all are released, the authority is immaterial. Thirdly, if the union is hereafter blessed by God with offspring, any such children to be left in the care and nurture of their mother until the age of thirteen years."

"You are saying that they should be reared in the Catholic faith?" Carlisle put to him. "That could not be accepted. One of them would in time become King, or Queen-Regnant, of the United Kingdom, and so head of the Church of England. No professing Catholic could be that."

"I did not say that," Richelieu gave back, smoothly cool. "I said left in the care and nurture of the mother."

"But in hope of the same result!"

"That is in the hand of God. It is agreed?"

Glancing at each other, the envoys either shrugged or nodded.

"Fourthly, the Princess will be accompanied to England with an entourage suitable to her high rank, and all French Catholics. To include one bishop and twenty-eight priests."

"Good God! Twenty-eight! A regiment of priests! Why that number?" That was the Earl.

"His Holiness's requirement."

"The numbers are not important. To us. Although they may seem excessive," Kensington declared.

"Lastly, it is required that chapels or oratories will be provided in every royal palace and establishment, for the use of the Princess and her attendants."

That produced no specific objection.

"Are these terms accepted, Messieurs?"

They looked at each other.

"I say yes," Kensington asserted.

Carlisle rubbed his chin. "We would have to put them before King James. *We* cannot make the decisions."

"That is understood. But, no doubt your recommendations will carry due weight. Since you know the facts. These are the basic requirements. Unless they are accepted there will be no royal marriage." That was flat.

David ventured a word. "But, if they are accepted, Your Eminence, the marriage is agreed?"

"Yes. Together with the other clauses accepted earlier."

Long breaths were drawn.

The Cardinal, who had never once even glanced at his supporting team, pushed back his chair. "I suggest, Messieurs, that the sooner you, or some of you, return to London and gain King James's acceptance, the sooner may this marriage be celebrated." He rose, bowed briefly, and treating them to a last dry cough, turned and left the library.

In some confusion his clerical party gathered up unused paper and pens and straggled out after him.

The envoys were left in possession of the library, not exactly bewildered but certainly bemused. Suddenly, it seemed, their mission was accomplished, for better or for worse.

It was the farewell ball, farewell for those who were returning to London, which included Carlisle and David. Kensington, Bishop Laud and Goring, who had just got back, would remain in Paris and, assuming that King James would agree to the marriage terms as specified, would in due course attend a proxy wedding ceremony for the Princess, with Kensington himself standing in for the bridegroom, before escorting her to England. So in two days, half the mission would depart, after the months of waiting.

It was a brilliant occasion, the two Queens excelling themselves, and Princess Henrietta there and in high spirits. They started with another and more ambitious masque, this time of Biblical theme, and representing Esther coming to the rescue of the oppressed Jews. There were three scenes or

257

tableaux. The first showed Ahasuerus, the High King who reigned from Ethiopia to India, on his throne, and Haman his chief minister persuading him to order the massacre of all Jews in his territories because the Jew Mordecai had refused to bow down before him. The next showed a selection of beautiful young women, virgins allegedly, being paraded before the King for him to select a new wife to replace the disgraced Vashti, who lurked in the background. From these beauties Ahasuerus chose Esther, the youngest – and incidentally the most adequately clothed for the occasion – giving her all the others as hand-maidens. Esther, of course, was the condemned Mordecai's beloved niece, and a Jewess. The very minor part of Queen Vashti was played by Anne of Austria, on this occasion, and that of Esther by young Henrietta Maria herself. The third scene revealed Esther pleading with Ahasuerus for her people, and getting the order for their massacre reversed, convincing the King that he should hang Haman on the very gallows he had had specially made for Mordecai, this hanging ending the masque on a most realistic note, to the singing and dancing of the company.

When, presently, Anne summoned David to her side at the dais end, and asked him what he thought of this masque, he expressed himself as much struck by it all, and was bold enough to wonder whether Her Majesty had in fact taken his previous criticism seriously and introduced a definite theme into the acting rather than just a display? Smiling, the Queen told him not to think so highly of his advice. This Esther story had been indicated from a much loftier source than any mere Scottish knight, however nimble of foot – His Holiness himself. For the Pope had sent a personal letter to Henrietta announcing his agreement to give dispensation for her marriage on the terms agreed, and informing her that she had undoubtedly been chosen by God to be another Esther, to come to the aid of his oppressed chosen people in England, the Catholics, and to raise them from contumely to power in that land.

Suitably impressed by this papal motive for the masque, David was nevertheless somewhat perturbed. What had they, as envoys, started, in these negotiations? Was this French marriage possibly going to have dire effects, in time to come, on Protestant England, not to mention Scotland? Henrietta herself was a delight; but if she did indeed come to see herself as an Esther, when she became the queen of a not notably strong King Charles, might there not be trouble to ensue? Her bishop and twenty-eight priests, her oratories and French Catholic attendants, might not have any major or grievous effect on the English religious scene; but this of her rearing any children of the marriage to the age of thirteen, thereby possibly turning them into dedicated Catholics, *could* eventually have a drastic impact. Had they too easily accepted that clause? Would King James, who was shrewd enough, accept it?

However, this was no time and occasion for such doubts and questions, with the ball and feasting proceeding and his Scottish dancing becoming an especial feature, with notable kindnesses being shown to David by Anne herself, Queen Marie, Henrietta and the Comtesse Jeanetta – to whom he allowed himself to be rather more forthcoming than heretofore, since this was farewell. Not that any of these ladies accepted that they might not see their handsome young Scot again, Anne in especial declaring that, with this new alliance between France and England, as well as the Auld Alliance with Scotland, there were bound to be opportunities for him to return to Paris – and if he did not contrive the same for himself, she would send for him, by royal command.

Much touched, he sought his couch late that night in some emotional turmoil – and was one of the very few of the embassage party to bed down in their own quarters.

Two days later they were on their way to Boulogne, leaving Kensington, Goring and Bishop Laud behind.

17

Their arrival back in England was scarcely triumphant, for King James was ill, apparently seriously, at Theobalds. Not just the gout this time, it seemed, but a more general decline in his health, with vomiting, pains, and a general physical, if not mental, lassitude. He was now in his sixtieth year, and there were fears for him. He had not, apparently, gone hunting for over a month, an unheard-of state of affairs. Goring had told them something of this, but evidently there had been a considerable worsening in the interim.

When David, with Carlisle, reached Theobalds Park, in some alarm at the tidings, Duke Ludovick was at least a little more reassuring. He had known James longer than anyone else, and had great faith in his recuperative powers. He had never been robust, admittedly, and had suffered all his life from sundry aches and pains, some born in him it seemed, some induced by unwise eating, over-drinking, peculiar hygiene and his generally odd life-style. But he had always staged remarkable recoveries. Despite getting on in years, he had a zest for life and was by no means yet relinquishing the reins of government. Indeed he was at present much exercised that Buckingham and Charles were gradually assuming more and more power in the realm, and was determined that this should be halted, much as he doted on his beloved Steenie.

David, who had now been away from home – and from Barbara Home – for two long months, was eager to be off northwards. If the King was ill, he would not be requiring his attendance, would he? Lord Carlisle would inform him of all that had happened in France, or such of it as was relevant, and seek his acceptance of the terms. Could he just quietly depart?

Ludovick said that was not possible, yet. When one was in

the royal service, in however temporary a role, one could not leave court without the royal permission, any more than to attend there. James might indeed have no wish to see him at this juncture, but he could not assume that. He would have to wait until the royal will was ascertained.

The Duke was, of course, anxious to hear an account of the French mission, and questioned David in detail, particularly interested in Richelieu and his predominance with King Louis. If the Cardinal was the man they would have to deal with in future relations with France, it behoved them to know all they could about him. Lord Herbert of Cherbury, the English Ambassador to France, had told them comparatively little, saying only that he was unapproachable and stiff. What was David's opinion?

The younger man agreed that the Cardinal was stiff and unapproachable. But he assessed him as shrewd, able and determined, yet prepared to adapt to circumstances when necessary, a man to watch and treat with care. Louis himself was something of a nonentity, but his adviser certainly was not.

Ludovick knew Queen Marie but not Anne nor, of course, Henrietta, and cross-questioned David, who modestly refrained from indicating just how friendly he had become with the Queen, although he did mention the Scottish dancing. Hearing it all, the Duke announced that he thought that the King also would wish to hear all this, for he doubted whether he would get so much out of Jamie Carlisle – which set David to wondering whether he had been wise in enlarging on the matter, if it was in fact going to delay his return to Scotland.

Before going to bed that night, he asked the other whether he had managed to find out anything as to why the King was favouring Sir Thomas Home of Primroknowe with the Angus sheriffdom – into which he hoped that curious man was not yet installed?

"No, the Scots Privy Council still awaits James's authority to proceed," he assured. "But . . . I have strange tidings for you on this matter, Davie. I asked James more than once, and found him loth indeed to inform me. But one day, when he had a sudden fear that he might be dying, he revealed it. Primroknowe was on the same ill road as your grandsire the

Master, and now your uncle. It is these Casket Letters again. He has been exacting mail from the King for some years now, to buy his silence. Almost certainly over possible confirmation of the suggestion that James was David Rizzio's son, not Darnley's – although James never puts that possibility into words."

David sat forward. "Another one! Lord, that again! This is scarcely credible! How many more?"

"No more, I think. Or James would probably have said it, while he was on the subject of this extortion. He thought to end Home's regular demands by giving him Lord Gray's sheriffdom, with all its revenues – in some kind of poetic justice upon Patrick Gray's son. Which made James the more hot when *you* came here with your uncle's pleas and offers over those letters."

"So that was it! I wonder that he did not commit me to the Tower, there and then! Sakes, little did I know into what a tangled web of intrigue I was being caught! Nor my uncle himself, I swear. But – how could Primroknowe have come to know about these letters and what was in them?"

"That I cannot tell you. Nor does James seem to know . . ."

"A moment, my lord! It has just come to me. Bothwell! The Earl of Bothwell, the last one, not Queen Mary's husband but his nephew, Francis Stewart. He was in league with my grandsire and Logan of Restalrig. At Fast Castle. Where Patrick had the Casket Letters. He was involved in the Spanish Blanks gold plotting, too. He always came to Fast Castle, on his secret returns to Scotland from France and Italy. So *he* might well have known what was in those letters. And Primroknowe was a friend of Bothwell's. They were close. That could be it. Bothwell told Home, and when the Earl died, Home saw his opportunity. And so, my uncle came too late on the scene. By far!"

"That could well be it, Davie. Save us, James will be interested to hear this. Not that it alters the situation. This fear of a Rizzio revelation still threatens all, holds James in dread. Illegitimacy! And that could affect Charles's accession to the throne hereafter, also . . ."

"Bothwell was Witch-Master of Scotland, was he not? That

could account for this possibility of witchcraft at Prim-roknowe."

"Aye, now there is something! James is all but crazedly afraid of witchcraft. His book on demonology says it all. It preys on his mind. If it could be proved that Home of Primroknowe was dabbling in witchcraft . . . ! That is an offence punishable by burning, no less!"

"M'mm. As to that, I do not know. I do not like the sound of burning. But . . ."

They left it at that, meantime.

Next day the Duke was ordered to bring David for audience. As before, it was to the King's bedchamber they went. Although James was again wearing his high hat, and the bed covered with papers and books, David was struck by the change in the royal appearance, the bad colour, the puffiness of feature, the increased dribbling at the mouth. But those fine eyes were as alert as ever, the thick speech as voluble.

"Aye, Davie Gray," he was greeted, "so you're back. I've been hearing aboot you frae Jamie Hay – hearing plenties. You've been gaun your dinger in yon France, heh?"

Not sure how to take that, David bowed again.

"What's this o' Anne o' Austria, eh? You getting far ben wi' the Queen o' France? Up to cantrips wi' your betters, eh?"

"Not, I hope, Sire, out of place. Only teaching Her Majesty Scottish dance steps and the like. She was very gracious . . ."

"Ooh, aye! Gracious is guid! Cavortings and gallivant-ings!"

"Entirely proper and respectful, Sire, I do assure you. And by royal command."

"Uh-huh. Sae you say. Mind, you seem to hae managed some profit oot o' your maist unsuitable birls and bobbings wi' the lassie. For Jamie Hay tells me you learned some gey useful informations as to yon ill limmer Richelieu. Helpful when it cam to dealing wi' him. A right awkward deevil him!"

"Her Majesty was graciously pleased to advise me in some matters yes, Sire. To our benefit."

"As you tripped and flung, eh?"

"Say in pauses for breath, Your Highness."

James skirled a sort of laugh. "Pauses for breath! That's guid – eh, Vicky? This yin has a turn for words, just."

"Sir David seems to have been a notable ambassador for Scotland, James. I think that you were wise to send him."

"Mebbe – aye, mebbe. Jamie Hay says that you fair tripped the Cardinal-man up wi' the fact that the Pope o' Rome wasna withholding dispensation from the *Spanish* match. Aye, and that you it was who got him to admit agreement in the end?"

"Lord Carlisle is too kind, Sire. He was coming round to it, anyway. Once we suggested that some privy matters might be put to your Majesty. And that was Queen Anne's suggestion, not mine."

"Privy matters, aye. You mean this o' the Catholic laws? Jamie Hay was no' right clear on that. *I* canna repeal them, you must ken that."

"No, Sire. We all knew it. But by suggesting that we might put the issue to you, secretly as it were, not written into the terms of the marriage treaty, which parliament must see, we gave the Cardinal the opportunity he required to tell the Pope that he was working towards a solution of that problem – which was the main stumbling-block to an agreement. The Queen said that Richelieu himself was in favour of the marriage but that this new Pope Urban was being difficult. They are scarcely friendly, it seems. So this secrecy talk was but a device. Which appears to have been effective, in some measure. But Lord Carlisle will have told you all this, Sire."

"Jamie's no' sae eloquent as this laddie – eh, Vicky? Is he no' a right born commissary, despite the bad blood he has in him? His mither must hae been a decent-like body, I jalouse! I kent it, mind, or I wouldna hae sent him, and knighted him. Ooh, aye, he'll mebbe be o' some mair use to us, yet, will Sir Davie Gray."

David looked wary at that. "May I be so bold as to ask, Sire, whether you give your royal agreement to the terms Lord Carlisle has brought back?"

"Dinna rush me, lad, dinna rush me. I've no' right decided yet. I'll hae to think on it. But . . . I'm like to be favourable. For we need this French alliance against Spain, need it sairly. And there's no' that many princesses suitable to be wife to our Charlie."

"Davie was speaking of this to me last night, James," the Duke put in. "And seemed a little concerned over the clause which allows the Princess Henrietta to have control over any offspring until they reach thirteen years. Since she is a strong Catholic, this could have the effect of turning her children into Catholics likewise. Which would be . . . awkward."

"Aye. I'm no' daft, Vicky – I ken that. Yon's the worst o' it all. But the bairns would hae a faither, too, mind. And I'll ding it into young Charlie's heid that he's to watch oot for this. He's a guid enough Protestant in his ain way. But we'll no' tell the parliament that."

"That would be wise, I think."

"Aye. Noo, this o' witchcraft, Davie Gray! Vicky tells me there's talk o' vileness and deil-worship at this Primroknowe in the Merse. Is it a fact? Or is it just the havers o' ignorant dolts? Auld wives' clashmaclavers?"

"That I cannot say for sure, Sire. All I know is that there is a very strange air about Primroknowe. And about its nearby church, where there is said to be strange ongoings at times. There is fear about the place. Secrecy. And this talk of witchcraft. We – that is Home of Bilsdean and his daughter and myself – we were aware of this strange air of it all before we were told the witchcraft story. And that was told by salmon-fishers, not auld wives, men who rented Sir Thomas Home's fishings in the Whiteadder, and did not like what went on."

"I need mair than that, man. The fact that twa-three fisher-men dinna like this or that, and talk about witchcraft, is of nae use to me. But, if it could be proved that there's ill work going on there, deil-worship and filthy demonrie – that's different. I could use that – aye, I could! There's laws against the like, mair especially in Scotland. Right potent laws. I ken!"

"Yes, Sire. But I know no more than I have told you. Save that Sir Thomas Home was a close friend of the late Earl of Bothwell. Who *was* involved in witchcraft, I understand."

"Ooh, aye, Francis Stewart was deep in it. That's why I banished him the realm. I could hae had him burned, mind. But he was kin o' mine, and I spared him. I shouldna – but belike he's burning in hell noo, for his sins!" James shook a clenched fist.

There was a silence in the royal bedchamber for a space.

"Aye, weel, I want right proof o' this o' Primroknowe, see you. Proof, no' just talk. Proof I can put before my Scots Privy Council, for them to tak action. No' mysel', but the Privy Council. You understand? My name mustna come into this, or the man Home could say ill things. Publish lies and scandals. There maun be nane o' that. So I need proof. And then the Privy Council to act swiftly. You have it?"

"I understand the need, Sire. But proof may not be easily come by . . ."

"I got proof right enough when I was trying thae damnable North Berwick witches, man."

David had heard about that, and the methods the King had used to extract confessions from those unfortunate women all those years ago.

"What do you wish me to do, Sire?"

"Go you awa' up to the Merse, Davie Gray, and find me proof as to whether there is truth in a' this. You've shown yoursel' to hae quick wits and some judgment. I want the truth. But mind, you're no' to let the advantages to that uncle o' yours, Andra Gray, sway that judgment. I ken fine you'd hae him to keep his sheriffdom, and Primroknowe no' to get it. So you might just think to deceive me – and I'm no' to be deceived, Davie. You could end up in the Tower yet, mind, if you tried that!"

"That I would not do, Sire. But, I do not see how I am to prove this . . ."

"There you are at your buts again! I've tellt you aboot that, laddie. Noo, off wi' you. And bring me the right word in this matter, the truth o' it, ae way or the ither. And mebbe I'll find you a bit reward at the end o' it – mebbe, just. Vicky, you bide a wee. I want a word wi' you . . ."

David backed out, wondering, doubtful. But at least he had permission to go home.

18

All the way north David turned the problem over in his mind – and reached no very helpful conclusion, save that there might be an opportunity here to involve Barbara Home in his investigations. Which was a pleasant thought, at least. Her father too, no doubt, and even Janet. But what could they do, other than make local enquiries, what could anyone do? Proof, the King wanted . . .

These doubts and questionings could not dim David's joy at returning to Scotland, of course, even though it seemed that he was not finished with London yet. He had been away for many months and it was now autumn, the harvests in and the land turning from golden to russet, the heather on the Cheviots and Lammermuirs changing but still colourful, the bracken yellowing. It was good, good to be back, nothing that he had seen in France or England vying with this in colour and scene.

He came to Bilsdean Castle in late afternoon, and heard Janet's skirling laughter coming from the orchard before ever he reached there. Dismounting, he made his way into the high walled garden. At first he could see no sign of life, despite the sounds thereof, only baskets of apples beneath the trees, fish and lobster baskets put to alternative use. Then he noticed more fishing gear, netting, slung from the lowermost branches of one or two of the trees, and even as he looked, apples falling down into the nets. Another peal of laughter came from above amongst the turning foliage.

He went to peer up – and was rewarded with a vision of a large expanse of white legs beneath a hitched-up skirt, Janet's; he was becoming quite expert in such matters. She was throwing small apples over into another tree, presumably at Barbara or someone else, but at the same time dropping usable fruit down into the netting below.

Although quite prepared to watch this indefinitely, David was wondering whether he should go over to inspect that other tree when he was discovered. A yell, a series of yells, came from above, his name squealed amongst them. Janet came down in a tumbling scramble of limbs and clothing to hurl herself bodily upon him. Almost knocked over, he staggered back.

In a deluge of hugs, kisses, shakings, endearments, reproaches and incoherent exclamations, he was danced round, thumped, pummelled, with little opportunity himself to give tongue. As welcome, it could scarcely have been more vehement.

He was still endeavouring to get a word in when he realised that they were no longer alone. Barbara stood there behind them, smiling, eyes glowing. Having almost roughly to free himself, he went to her.

So much more restrained a greeting, but lacking nothing in warm sincerity and gladness. They held each other close for a little, wordless. The words followed, a flood of them from all three.

Janet's voice prevailed. "Whaur have you been? Why so long? All the summer gone. We wondered if you were deid! Or just forgotten us. No word o' you. That London! We jaloused that we werena guid enough for Maister Davie Gray, now!"

"*I* did not," Barbara managed to insert.

"I've been in France."

They stared, even Janet silenced for the moment.

"I could not let you know. King James sent me to France, with an embassage. As an aide to Lord Doncaster, now Earl of Carlisle. Envoys to treat of a marriage between the Prince of Wales and the King of France's sister. It took a long time, much longer than was expected. Much difficulty over religious matters, with the Catholics. I was not important in it, of course . . ."

"But why *you*, David?" Barbara asked.

"Well may you ask. King James said I must go. I can speak some French. And he seemed to think that I might be useful — I am not sure why. I think that Lord Carlisle had recommended me. He also is a Scot. I did not much want to go, but . . ."

268

"The King must think well of you."

"You could have sent us word," Janet accused.

"How could I? From France? Who could have carried a letter? But . . . I thought of you often. Very often." It was at Barbara that he looked, of course.

"Aye." Janet sniffed. "Mebbe. I've heard tell o' thae French women. Shameless hizzies, frae all accounts!"

"I did not go swimming with any of them!" he told her, mildly, and quietened her for the moment.

"We have missed you," Barbara said. "It *has* seemed a long time. Many months. Are you now one of the King's gentlemen? One of his court?"

"No, no. At least, I do not want to be. I still have matters to see to for the King. But I hope that will soon be by with. I do not like the court, nor London."

"Thanks be for that, at least!" Janet said. "You're no' going back to France?"

"Not that I know of. The King is ill, meantime. No, it is up here in Scotland that he wants me to serve him. If I can."

"That is good. You seemed so far away, in London," Barbara said. "Are you on your way back to Broughty?"

"Ye-e-es. I have to go there, first. To inform the Lord Gray. But I think that I shall not be biding there, at present. I have to be elsewhere. Nearer here . . ."

"Good! The nearer the better. Now, we must not keep you talking here. You will be weary, with long riding. Come, you, leave the apples meantime."

The laird, it seemed, was over at Dunglass but would be back for the evening meal.

David found it a pleasure to settle in at Bilsdean again, to be taken to his own room, looked after, and not exactly fussed over but made much of in a distinctly stimulating way, Janet no more backward in her ministrations than in the past. His experiences in France had the effect of making him the more appreciative of it all, and ensured that he was not unduly prudish and proper. It was Barbara rather than himself who sought to keep her half-sister within bounds.

After one of Janet's sallies, their guest produced a counter-parry. "When last I saw you, Janet Home, you seemed to be getting far ben, as King James would say, with my cousin Patrick. You found him to your taste?"

"Och, that one! He's right enough, mind, and guid-looking too. But . . . ower forward!"

Barbara tinkled a laugh at that.

"You, *you* complain of that!"

"I'm no' exactly complaining. But he needs to be kept in his place, yon Maister o' Gray. Like his, and your grandsire, they tell me. If it runs in the family, how come it missed you out?"

"Me? Oh, I know my place, Janet. And so keep it. I'm a land-steward, mind, not heir to a lord of parliament." Again it was at Barbara that he looked.

"You dinna seem to do much land-stewarding these days."

"No-o-o. But the time will come again, I fear . . ."

"You fear?" Barbara put in. "Will you mislike going back to being a steward, David? After all your adventures in the King's service?"

"M'mm. Mislike is not it, so much. But . . . it is scarcely the life that I would choose – not now."

"Now that you have become a kind of courtier?"

"Not that. I told you, I have no liking for the court. Nor yet London. But, being a land-steward is . . . restricting. Not a position to offer any advancement. Where a man can better himself, and so be able to offer anything to another." That was as far as he could go with it.

"I do not think that you will always be a land-steward, David. Even without having to go to London."

"*I* would not object to being thirled to a land-steward!" Janet declared pointedly.

"Perhaps Lord Gray will find you some betterment, after all that you are seeking to do for him," Barbara suggested. "Are you any further forward over the matter of the Angus sheriffdom?"

"The grant has still not been withdrawn from Sir Thomas Home. But nor has he been installed as Sheriff by the Privy Council, on King James's orders. He is waiting. That is part of my task now. To try to discover certain matters about this Home of Primroknowe. It may be difficult indeed . . ."

The clatter of hooves sounding from the courtyard below announced the return of the laird. They all went down, for

David to be presented to him. Alexander Home seemed quite happy to see the visitor, certainly displaying no lack of welcome – a fear apt to come to David on occasion – even if he was somewhat less enthusiastic than were his daughters. Presumably he was still grateful over the monopoly business.

Over the dinner-table that evening, David broached the subject of Primroknowe and the possibility of witchcraft, stressing the King's fear and hatred of such manifestations and his wish to know whether there was any truth behind it all. He was cautious about the way he put this matter in present company, for he was well aware that in a Home castle he might have to go warily about seeking to implicate another Home laird in possible serious trouble and unlawful activities.

His host did not appear to have any resentment, however. "It is all very strange," he declared. "Not only this of possible witchcraft but why the King gave Primroknowe Lord Gray's sheriffdom, in the first place. He was natural son to the King's friend, George, Earl of Dunbar, to be sure, but Dunbar has been dead for a dozen years now, and Primroknowe was never much at court, so far as I know. Why should he be so favoured now?"

David did not want to go into the matter of the blackmail of James, since that could come uncomfortably near home. "Possibly he had some hold over the King," was as far as he thought to go. "But this of possible witchcraft could change all. How am I to discover whether there is any truth in it? Not just idle chatter and hearsay? Proof, the King wants."

"Proof will be hard to find, I would judge, friend. But I have learned that those salmon-netters on the Whiteadder are not the only ones to talk of strange ongoings at Primroknowe. I met Broomhouse – Home of Broomhouse – at Berwick cattle-market one day. His is the nearest lairdship to Primroknowe, his lands lying just across Whiteadder, to the south and east. I asked him what he knew of his neighbour Thomas Home. He said that he knew him but little, a strange man who kept himself very much to himself, the usual story. I said that I had heard unchancy tales about him, and about the kirk near the river, and Broomhouse agreed that he had heard such also – indeed that his folk were scared of the place, and of Primroknowe himself, talking of devil-worship and the

271

like. Mind, Broomhouse has the fishings of the Whiteadder downriver from those fishers we spoke with, so it could be that his netters are but passing on the same tales as the two we saw. All perhaps just ignorant blethers and imaginings."

"It was not all just imaginings at that church," Barbara asserted. "It was evil. I could feel it. And the fear at Primroknowe itself. A goodly place, but something wrong there."

"You are as bad as the fishers, lass!" her father said, but without conviction.

"I can smell fear," she said simply.

"How can I set about changing fear and tales into proof?" David demanded.

The others could not answer that. But they promised to make further detailed enquiries locally in the Merse. Some must know the truth of it all. They would have to be discreet about it, however, or the wrong-doers, if any, might be warned off.

The rest of the evening, at the hall fire, they talked of more pleasant things, David needless to say being questioned at length as to his French experiences. The Scots dancing accounts intrigued most, and presently nothing would do but that he must demonstrate his expertise there and then. Unfortunately only Barbara could provide the necessary music, so that the actual dancing had to be done with Janet – which was of course rewarding, even taxing, but he would have preferred to have been partnering her sister.

With the laird present, the bed-going ceremonial had to be lower-key than sometimes.

In the morning, reluctantly, he took his leave; but it was good to be able to assure that he would be back before long.

It was whilst on his way to North Berwick for the daily ferry over to Fife that something came to David's recollection which might just possibly be of some help in his quest. The first time that he had come this way, en route for Fast Castle, and had called in at Kilspindie Castle at Aberlady, his great-aunt's husband, Patrick Douglas, had expressed himself about the Home clan in no uncertain fashion, as though he knew a deal about them. What were his words, then? That

272

Fast Castle was well-named Faux or False, for the Homes were a false house ever. Something to that effect. That could be mainly Douglas hostility, of course, for the two families had been all but at feud for generations. But possibly there was more to it than that, and that Kilspindie had reasons for his remarks. It might just be worth another visit to Aberlady, perhaps on his way back to Bilsdean hereafter.

However, at North Berwick, David discovered that owing to the state of the tide, the ferry-scow would not be sailing over until the late afternoon – so that he had some five hours to fill in, ample time to ride to Aberlady and back, there and then.

Six miles, and he rounded the great Aberlady Bay and came to Kilspindie Castle. His welcome there was a deal less warm than at Bilsdean, but he had gained a little more confidence and assurance than when last he had called, and made no bones about his errand. Without going into details, he let it be known that he was now, in some measure, in King James's service; and when this was received distinctly doubtfully, he was able to add, in confirmation as it were, that he was now knighted. He had not mentioned this at Bilsdean, feeling that it might seem somehow immodest – for he could not yet think of himself as a genuine knight, in any way deserving of the honour. But here the effect was very noticeable. Clearly he had risen considerably in the Douglas estimation, and they were agog to hear the whys and wherefores of it all.

David cut this short as quickly as he decently could, and came to the object of his visit. "When I was here before, sir, I remember you saying that the Homes were a false house. Not only in regard to Fast Castle, but as a line, a family. I wondered whether you had any reason for saying that?"

"Oh, aye, plenties. False they are, and aye false they have been."

"Not all of them," his wife protested.

"Any I have had dealings with, or heard tell of, woman!"

"I am interested in this, sir, for I have to make enquiries as to one of them . . ."

"You mean that Home of Primroknowe who has been given Gray's sheriffdom?"

273

"Yes. I would learn more about him. He seems to be but little-known."

"*I* know of him, fine – or more than I want to! A false son of a false father!"

"His father was the Earl of Dunbar, was he not? The King's Commissioner."

"Aye. King James has aye found scoundrels to serve him, and to honour!" Douglas sniffed a little and looked pointedly at their visitor, as though hinting that he, who had been honoured with a knighthood for some reason, might well be something of a scoundrel also.

"This Home of Primroknowe, have you any especial reason for naming him false, sir?"

"Aye, Spott!" That was sufficiently succinct.

"Spott . . . ? The estate, you mean? It is also a village and a parish, is it not? I have heard of it . . ."

"Then you'll no' have heard much guid of it, I'll warrant! An unchancy name it has, a place of murders and witchcraft. But a fair enough property, mind . . ."

David drew a quick breath. "Witchcraft? Murder?" he echoed.

"Aye, it has aye been a great haunt of witches and deviltries."

"And this Sir Thomas Home – is he involved in it?"

"Like as not, he is. He owns the place. He's the laird there. He shouldna be, mind, it should be Douglas land."

"How is that, sir?"

"James Douglas, an uncle of mine, married the Home heiress of Spott – and so saved the property from forfeiture. The lassie's father, Home of Spott, was tried and condemned for being art and part in the murder of Darnley. He fled overseas some place. So my uncle got Spott. But later George Home of Primroknowe, him who became Earl of Dunbar, prevailed on King James to forfeit my uncle, claiming that he was in league with the Earl of Bothwell, the last one, to murder the King . . ."

"Bothwell!" David's head rather reeled with all this. "Bothwell again!"

"Aye. It was false, mind. As to my Uncle James. Och, he *knew* Bothwell. We all did. We could scarcely not know him,

274

for he owned much of this part of Lothian, with his seat at Hailes overby. Bothwell may have plotted, right enough. But not James Douglas of Spott. They couldna prove anything against him – but it was enough for George Home to get Spott back, by his friend the King's command."

"So now George Home's son, or Dunbar's, is laird of Spott as well as of Primroknowe? Where is this Spott?"

"No' that far away. About three miles from Dunbar, in the lap o' the Lammermuirs."

"And it is namely for witchcraft you say?"

"Aye has been. Bothwell, to be sure, was the great one for witchcraft. Perhaps he learned the ill trade there. None so far from Hailes."

"Primroknowe also, the present one, was a close friend of Bothwell's."

"Was he? That I did not know. But I'd no' put it past any o' that crew!"

"Witchcraft, I understand, is an offence against the law of Scotland, as well as a sin. A serious offence."

"Oh, aye. We had a witch burned at the Balefire Knowe here – you can see it from here – no' that long ago." Douglas pointed eastwards, to the shore of the bay.

"What had she done? To be burned?"

"The usual. Casting spells, causing neighbours' cows to run dry. Giving bairns the pining sickness . . ."

"But surely, sir, that is but talk and superstitious folly?"

"There was more to it than that, Pate," his wife put in. "They caught her in the kirkyard on All-Hallows' Eve, with a lit candle, peering at the graves. Up to devilish doings. That was three years back."

"Aye, but she was a known witch. For years before that. No doubt she had been practising her deviltries at other All-Hallows, for long enough."

"All-Hallows' Eve?" David asked. "Is that important? Does it mean something special? I have known it for children's ploys, bonfires, apples and nuts, and the like."

"All-Hallows' E'en is ever the great night for witches and warlocks – did you not know that, man? That night they raise the unquiet spirits of the unshriven dead, or so they say. Murdered folk and other lost souls. That is what the bonfires are for – to keep away the evil spirits, the Beltane-fires. It's the witches' night. Decent folk keep to their beds . . ." ̄

"Some do not, sir, it seems – or that poor woman would not have been seen in the kirkyard!"

"Oh, aye, the witch-finders and prickers will sometimes dare the spells and curses, and go looking. They get a reward, mind – but, och, they're welcome to it."

"So All-Hallows is a time when there might be . . . activity?"

"Not here, I swear. If there are any more witches in Aberlady, they will have learned their lesson, I reckon. But otherwhere, yes, no doubt. At Spott, perhaps."

"Or at Primroknowe! And All-Hallows is at the end of this month!"

On his ride back to North Berwick, David did not lack mental exercise.

Lord Gray's reception of his nephew and land-steward was mixed as to quality – demands as to where in the Almighty's name he had been all this time, who did he think he was, why had he sent no word; that and optimism that the fact of Home not having been installed as Sheriff yet was a good sign, satisfaction that at least he was back at last. When his uncle heard that David was returned only for a brief spell, by royal command, he was still more resentful, and that changed to sheer offence when the knighthood was revealed. He had never heard of anything so preposterous, so unsuitable, he declared – his land-steward a knight! Were they all now expected to address him as Sir David? King James must be out of his wits.

David admitted that he had been equally surprised. And the knighting had not been an honour as much as a device to give him some standing for the French embassage, where the King had believed that he might be useful. It need make no least difference, here at Broughty.

As to the sheriffdom situation, David suggested that it was at least more hopeful, not only in the continued delay in installation but in that the King was now prepared to cancel Primroknowe's appointment – if it could be done without danger to himself and his interests. This assertion entailed informing his uncle of the fact that Home had also been blackmailing James over the Casket Letters, and it was in order to put an end to this, to make a final settlement, that the Angus sheriffdom and its revenues and privileges had been taken from that other dead blackmailer's son and given to this one, a strange example of royal justice but typically James Stewart.

Gray received the news, that his would-be supplanter also had been using the Rizzio threat to bring pressure on the King, with something like alarm. Did this mean that *his* position, his effectiveness to constrain the King, was undermined, endangered? How many more knew of these letters? And did *Home* perhaps hold the missing one, the one about Rizzio being James's father?

That thought had not occurred to David, who had assumed that Primroknowe was likewise merely using the possibility of such a letter to threaten making the illegitimacy issue public, as was his uncle. But it could be . . .

He asked Lord Gray what he knew of witches and witchcraft, but got little to aid him. His uncle had had no experience of such matters, and could only repeat the usual tales about sabbats held at midnight, the digging up of dead bodies and distribution of bones, women riding on broomsticks, toads and cats as familiar spirits, and so on. No witch-trials had ever come before him as Sheriff of Angus.

David spent a week at Broughty – and found himself feeling that it was somehow wasted time. Which was strange, presumptuous, for this was his home and where his employment lay. But his thoughts were ever now apt to be elsewhere, at Bilsdean with Barbara, or at Primroknowe in the Merse. And now at this Spott also, although he did not know the place. Was he losing touch with reality? Growing too big for his boots? Sir David Gray, royal retainer! But in fact, land-steward and farmer, and illegitimate at that!

When he spoke with Dod Carnegie, however, in the farmery, he realised that he was by no means irreplaceable here at Broughty. All seemed to be going on perfectly satisfactorily without him, the harvest in and bountiful, the surplus stock marketed, the mills thriving. If this was a little humbling, it was also a relief to him, he decided. It made it seem less inevitable that he should be tied to land-stewarding all his days.

His cousin Patrick, who was now living in Fowlis Castle, on the other side of Dundee, the secondary Gray seat, called at Broughty the fourth day. *He* was not particularly concerned over the King James situation, nor yet in the French visit; but he was very interested in Bilsdean and David's links there. He declared that Janet Home was the choicest piece it had been his good fortune to come across in many a year – which considering that he was aged twenty-two perhaps was less significant than it might sound – and that next time Davie was going to be visiting there it would be a cousinly gesture to take him with him. David avoided making any promises.

So, with All-Hallows' Eve only another week hence, he had his excuse to be off back to the Merse.

Alexander and Barbara Home had not been idle on David's behalf. They had made enquiries, suitably discreetly, in various quarters, as to witchcraft and devil-worshipping, admittedly with no great success. There was, they found, a recognisable wall of silence to surmount about the entire subject in the Merse, as possibly elsewhere, and in all ranks of society. People undoubtedly knew that the shameful practices went on, that there were local manifestations of it, but that it was certainly not to be talked about. Fear undoubtedly was behind this attitude, fear not only of spells, cursings and nameless evils, but of being thought to be in any way linked with such dark doings – for the penalties in law were dire indeed, and once accused, it could be very difficult for anyone to establish innocence. So wise folk did not know and did not want to know. There was therefore great ignorance about it all, this revealed when they did manage to get anyone to speak up, very disparate and contradictory suggestions and stories. One reaction which was fairly general, however, was that All-Hallows' E'en was the most notable occasion for sabbats and sorcery meetings.

So at least the investigators were at one on that.

"You got no link with Sir Thomas Home himself?" David asked. "No fingers pointing at Primroknowe?"

"Not directly, no," the laird admitted. "We avoided going

back too near to that area, lest the word of our enquiries was brought to him. So we did not visit those two salmon-fishers again, although we spoke with others downriver. His name was never mentioned, and we thought it wise not to mention it. But there was one hint we got when asking folk about witchcraft – that it was not only fear of the evil that was holding tongues but fear of someone in power, some authority. As well as being afraid of being thought too interested or knowledgeable about it all, so that the law might be used against them, there was the dread of someone in high position who must not be offended. We sensed this more than once."

"Yes, it was there, especially amongst the salmon-netters," Barbara confirmed. "I put it to one of them – did they feel that devil-worship and sorcery was being led by someone important, someone powerful. And he admitted it, although reluctantly, someone who even had the King's ear, it was said. And his companions nodded at that."

"Sakes, the King's ear! Of all things! How could that have got about? James, who hates and dreads witchcraft. It must have come from some high-sounding source. Primroknowe himself? Who else in the Merse might claim to be in touch with the King? Not even the Earl of Home, I think. Save only the man who has recently been appointed Sheriff of Angus by James's order, the son of the King's late friend, Earl of Dunbar!"

They nodded.

"Or one of his underlings, saying it for him," Barbara suggested.

David told them about Douglas of Kilspindie's remarks anent Spott and witches there, which interested them. It might be worth making enquiries thereabouts. Another deep-hidden Lammermuirs corner. Was there something about these hills . . . ?

More than just enquiries had to be attempted, of course, David declared. He must seek for the proof King James wanted. It seemed that the last day of this month, All-Hallows' Eve, was his likeliest chance. It was possible that there might be some activity or celebration going on that night. But where? This of Spott perhaps complicated the matter. Since Sir Thomas Home was laird of both Spott and

Primroknowe, if he was indeed a witch-master, he could operate at either. Which would be the most likely?

"To do what? What are you purposing, my friend?"

"To go, sir, and watch. Secretly. To go see with my own eyes."

"That could be dangerous."

"Perhaps. But . . . only if I intervened. All I want is to see, to witness, to identify if possible."

"How would you do that? It is Primroknowe you want to identify? You have never seen him. You are going to need assistance in this."

David shrugged.

"You served me, and others, very well over the monopoly. I will go with you, in this, and seek to aid your efforts, lad."

"I do not wish to involve others in possible trouble."

"I will be interested to discover it all. And to help uphold the good name of Home!"

"I also," Barbara said.

"No, no . . ."

"This is no ploy for women, lass," her father asserted. "Leave it to us."

"There will be women there, will there not? Witches are women. I could be useful."

"Dinna be a fool, Barbara," Janet put in, silent until now. "This could be an ill venture. I say none should do it. Tempting the Devil himself. *I* would not go, no' for a fortune!"

"I am going," her sister said quietly.

"It would be foolish for any of us to go without some protection," the laird announced. "I will take two-three of our fishermen with us. Stout lads."

"Would they come? On such an errand?"

"They would, if I told them to."

"But – where to go? Primroknowe or Spott?"

It was decided that some further investigation at both places was advisable, but with them seeking to be as unobtrusive about it as possible. Alexander Home volunteered to go back to Broomhouse, across Whiteadder, where, being on visiting terms with the laird, indeed far-out kin to him, his presence in the area would not be apt to arouse comment; and David, with Barbara who had been to Spott once or twice in the past, would go there.

Next day, then, they all set out, Janet electing to have nothing to do with the entire unchancy proceeding, she at least taking witchcraft seriously. David made no complaints at her decision.

It was about ten miles to Spott, Barbara said, little more than six indeed as the crows flew, all but due west across the hillfoots; but they would have to follow the main road almost to Dunbar, then turn inland at Broxmouth to turn up Spott Dean for another almost three miles – this to avoid difficult territory, steep hills and streams to ford.

It was good to be riding with Barbara again, on a crisp late autumn day, however uncertain their mission – although David was a little concerned at something Janet had let fall, earlier, to the effect that young Sandy Home of Renton had taken to turning up at Bilsdean of late, and not to see the laird or herself! He had no cause to comment on this to his companion now, and Barbara did not mention it, but it rather preyed on David's mind.

The coast road, now so familiar to David, brought them, past Barns Ness, to within sight of Dunbar Castle towering on its rocks, where Queen Mary had had a stormy time with *her* Bothwell and where that wild individual was said to have left the Casket Letters when he fled the country. Here the road crossed the Spott Burn flowing to the nearby sea at Broxmouth, and they turned their horses' heads westwards to follow the stream up, with the hills approaching close and steep.

Over a mile up the winding wooded dean, Barbara pointed out the Doon Hill, at the foot of which the first of the battles of what became the Wars of Independence was fought, when in 1296 Edward of England, who was to become known as the Hammer of the Scots, showed his true colours, his invading army winning the day against the ill-led forces of the disunited Scots nobility, a dire disaster which was to cost the northern kingdom dear. On they rode in the ever-narrowing and enclosed winding valley, into suddenly concealed and secret country, notable after the open coastal plain, apt, they could feel, for a reputation of sorcery and dark doings.

The village of Spott stood strung out along a sort of terrace above the dean, to the south, hidden by the wooded slopes until the last approach, with a small low-browed church, a scatter of cot-houses and hovels. Also a driveway leading to Spott House, unseen, up a side burn, all as masked and withdrawn as the rest.

The visitors were well aware of the difficulties of their task. Two strangers well-clad and well-mounted, riding up to this remote and hidden community, could not fail to draw attention to themselves, the more so if they started to make enquiries. Undoubtedly they would arouse suspicion and learn nothing unless they acted openly and apparently innocently. They decided that the best course was to call first at the church, or at the manse, to seek the parish minister. Barbara could explain that she was a Home and was interested to learn about the Homes of Spott, to which she might well be distantly related. Possibly some of them would be buried in the kirkyard?

Dismounting, they hitched their mounts to the rail at the gate and entered the tree-girt graveyard, to examine the tombstones. One much larger than the others at once drew their attention, erected at the gable of the plain old church, with Home heraldry carved thereon and sundry devices beneath, skulls, bones, angels with wings seemingly sprouting from their ears, and decorative scrollery – but no names inscribed. They were inspecting this when they realised that they were themselves being inspected, by a youngish man in black, standing by the wall which separated kirkyard from the manse garden, obviously the minister. He did not speak.

They went over to him. "I am Sir David Gray and this is Mistress Barbara Home of Bilsdean," David said. "Are you the parish minister? We are interested in the Home family. Who are lairds here, are they not? Distant kin, she thinks."

"I give you good-day," the other answered gravely. "Yes, I am Patrick Simpson, Master, of St Andrews, and I preach God's Word here. I have heard of Bilsdean, but not of any of the name of Gray hereabouts, sir."

"No. I am from Broughty, in Angus, a guest at Bilsdean. We have not yet gone up to Spott House. Is the laird at home?"

"Not so, sir. He is seldom here. He lives down in the Merse. We see him but infrequently."

"He is not likely to be here shortly?" Barbara asked, artlessly. "We could come back."

"I think not, Mistress. His house in the Merse is called Primroknowe, near to Bonkyl. You would find him there."

"Thank you. The Homes have been here for long, have they not?" She gestured towards the large tombstone.

"I do not know how long. I am but a few years here. But that was why the laird's late father took the style of Earl of Dunbar – which as you know is nearby – when he was ennobled by the King. He was a famous man, although a supporter of bishops!" That ended in a sniff.

"Yes. And his son . . . ?"

"Less famous, I think," the other answered carefully.

"We know little of him," David said. "Perhaps a retiring man?"

The Reverend Simpson inclined his head. It looked as though they were not going to get much help here.

"Is there aught else of interest to see here, at Spott?" Barbara wondered. "I seem to have heard there was something . . . ?" That was vague.

The minister frowned a little. "The parish suffers under an ill esteem. Scarcely deserved," he said, rather primly.

They waited hopefully.

"The matter of the murder."

"Murder? Here?"

The other cleared his throat. "It was many years ago. Soon after the Blessed Reformation and the putting down of the idolatrous papacy. The new incumbent here, one John Kello, no doubt a but little reformed papist priest, murdered his wife one Sabbath morning. In the manse, there."

They looked duly shocked.

"And that was not the worst of it," they were further informed. "Thereafter, that disgrace to his cloth and calling proceeded to the church and preached the most eloquent sermon any had heard from him!"

Scarcely knowing how to take this, the visitors glanced at each other.

"How . . . strange," Barbara said, inadequately for her.

"The vilest sin against the Holy Ghost!" their informant snapped out. It was not clear whether he was referring to the murder or the preaching or both.

Suitable comment seemed to be called for. David took a bold decision. "Could this grievous deed, minister, have anything to do with local conditions? Witchcraft, perhaps?"

The change in the other was immediate and pronounced. He stiffened, in person and in features. "That only the sinner's Maker knows, sir," he said flatly.

"No doubt. But there are tales of witchcraft at Spott, are there not? Perhaps foolish ones?"

"Foolish, yes. The ignorant chatter of idle tongues, I esteem it. Not to be believed. Contrived out of nothing. As this of the tree."

"Tree . . . ?"

"The Birley Tree, as they call it. Is it that you heard tell of?"

"Birley Tree?" Barbara repeated. "No, Master Simpson, we have not heard of any such tree. What is this?"

The minister had started to move back towards his manse garden, most clearly disinclined to pursue the matter, or for further discussion. "It is a tree which stands alone. To the west of this village. An ancient ash tree. Nothing strange about it. There are tales of supposed witches. They used to be burned there. No doubt in popish days. But idle talk and folly, as I said. Not to be considered. I bid you good-day." He turned and left them.

"There goes a man who knows more than he allows," David said, as they returned to their horses. "And more than he wants to know."

"I think so, yes. Shall we go see this tree? West of the village, he said . . ."

They rode past the last of the cot-houses and into an open area of cultivated rigs and the stubbles of the oat harvest. Beyond was what appeared to be common grazing, with a few cows and tethered goats, and on a knoll a single tree, gnarled and wind-blown, presumably what they were looking for. They rode up and round it but could see nothing unusual about it save its obvious age, and the fact that there was a large table-like stone beneath it.

284

"An ash, yes. But nothing to be seen here. What did he call it?"

"The Birley Tree. Or Bourlaw. It is a word we have here. Do you not use it in Angus? It means a place where the law is dispensed, locally. Neighbourhood laws. I suppose that it would originally be burgh law. Not that Spott would ever be a burgh, nor even a burgh of barony, as is Dunglass . . ."

"What sort of law would be dispensed here, then? Under a tree? Witch-pricker's law! The burning of poor accused women? How true is this, I wonder?"

"We could ask at one of the cot-houses. If it has a known name, like that, it would not seem strange to ask . . ."

So they halted at the first of the village houses, a mean turf-roofed shack. They did not have to knock at the open door, where a slatternly woman peered out at them and ragged children hid behind her, all evidently fearful of mounted strangers.

Barbara spoke, kindly, reassuringly. "We are interested in that tree, beyond the rigs. The Birley Tree we have heard it called. That is it, amongst the cattle and goats, is it? Can you tell us anything about it?"

A quick shake of the head, and silence.

"Come," David said, encouragingly. "You must at least know if that is it. The right one? This Birley Tree."

"Aye." Even that was reluctant.

"And what does it signify? The word means law-giving, I think. What laws were given there?"

"I dinna ken, Maister. My man would ken, no' me."

"Then ask your man, if you will."

"He's no' here."

"Who is he? And where do we find him?"

"He's the goat-herd. But he's gone. You'll no' get him, the noo. He's awa', ower the hills."

"With goats?"

"Wi' twa-three, just."

"We can try the next house," Barbara suggested. "They may know more there."

Like rabbits into their hole, the women and children disappeared.

They led their horses along to another cottage. Here also

they were being watched, but by a very different sort of female, a big, sonsy young woman with a bold eye and provocative stance. She was assessing the callers frankly, concentrating on David.

"We are asking about the Birley Tree yonder," he said. "We have heard of it. Your neighbour there does not seem to know much, if anything."

"Her! She ought to, for her man's the goat-herd." That came promptly enough.

"So she said. But told us nothing. What has the goat-herd to do with it? This tree?"

"Och, plenties. It's the witches' tree, where they danced."

"Danced. We heard that they were burned there."

"Ooh, aye, they were burned there, tae. Because that is where they danced. It's a gey auld tree."

"Has the goat-herd to do with that?" Barbara asked.

The woman skirled a laugh. "Goats and witches aye gang thegither, do they no'?"

"Do they? We are very ignorant on the matter, I fear."

"As weel to be," the other commented shortly.

"This tree – what is done there?" David persisted.

"Och, you'd better spier at Dod Lillie for that, sir. No' the likes o' me."

"Dod . . . ?"

"Dod Lillie. He's the laird's steward, here."

"Ah. The land-steward. And where do we find him?"

"He bides near the big hoose. But you'll no' get him the day, Maister. He's gone ower the hill."

"Ower the hill? You mean, over the Lammermuirs, there?" And David pointed southwards.

"Aye, just that."

"Like the goat-herd?" Barbara observed.

"Did Aggie say that? Och, well, she should ken. Whit way are you sae interested, then?"

"It was just the tree, the Birley Tree," David said, somewhat hastily. "The name interested us. The minister mentioned it."

"Aye. I'ph'mm."

Barbara touched his arm, and they backed away. "Thank you," she said. "A good-day to you."

286

As they remounted, Barbara murmured. "That one was becoming suspicious, I think. Time that we were away."

"Yes. Did we press over-much?"

"Perhaps. But we learned not a little, did we not?"

"This of over the hills?"

"That, yes. The laird's steward and the goat-herd. Both gone 'ower the hill'. Southwards. At this time. And goats and witches somehow connected!"

"How far over the Lammermuirs from Spott to Prim-roknowe?"

"Not so very far. Let me think – by The Brunt and Elmscleuch and the Monynut to Godscroft and Abbey St Bathans. Then down the Whiteadder. Less than a score of miles. Fifteen, more like . . ."

"With goats – two days' walk, through the empty hills?"

"About that."

"And All-Hallows' Eve three nights from this! I wonder how many more than these two have gone from Spott?"

They eyed each other.

19

Six strong, they rode southwards that last day of October, with mixed feelings, anticipation, hopes and, yes, fears – for this was indeed a venture into the unknown, into the hostile probably, possibly the dangerous. There might be nothing in it in the end, admittedly; but there might equally be more than they bargained for.

They could not hurry, for the three Bilsdean Cove fishermen were by no means expert horsemen, and they were deliberately riding over very rough country, desirous of being seen by as few as possible. Fortunately the Lammermuir Hills were populated mainly by sheep, and even shepherds not thick on the ground, and unlikely to be the sort to hurry off the heather to tell of unusual travellers. But haunts of men were best avoided nevertheless. So they went, keeping well clear of the village of Colbrandspath, over its high common lands to below the steep escarpment of Eweside Hill and so to the Heriot Water, avoiding Fulfordlees. Thereafter, on the lofty moors now, mile upon mile, there was less chance of being observed so long as they kept well away from the travellers' and drovers' shelter of Quixwood.

As the land began to drop towards the great Whiteadder valley, Abbey St Bathans had to be shunned, so they kept well to the east side of the major summit of Cockburn Law, to reach the river where the Otter Burn joined it under the mighty Pictish broch of Edin's Hall. They were now coming into more populous and therefore more dangerous country, although scarcely crowded even so, having come some fifteen round-about and difficult miles, with the Primroknowe area only three miles or so ahead. They had made reasonably good time, all things considered, in windless but chilly weather with a faint mist off the Norse Sea, and the light was failing as they came to the Whiteadder.

There was no lack of questions as to procedure now, timing not the least important. If there was to be, indeed, a sabbat that night, when would it be apt to be held? The notion of midnight came to mind, of course, but that might be nonsense. Presumably it would be in darkness, however, although even that was uncertain as the rest. It would be dark in an hour, anyway.

Then, where? Somehow they assumed that any celebration or rite would be at that chapel on the knoll. But it need not be. It could be held at Primroknowe itself, or otherwise, if at all.

Meantime they must not be seen, six mounted strangers hanging about the vicinity.

It was decided that to avoid the Cockburn Mill vicinity just west of Primroknowe they should work round the south face of this Cockburn Law itself, on the high ground, and so down into the wooded cleft of Oatleycleuch, more than a mile further to the west, where they could hide up meantime. Then, in the late evening, when no one would tend to be about unless on unlawful business, they could move quietly down the Mill Burn to the chapel.

Where to leave their horses, where they would not attract attention, if there was indeed any gathering? They had noticed a track, on that previous visit, leading up the defile of the smaller burn. Where that led to they knew not, but up there, tree-girt as it was, they ought to be able to find a hiding-place for the animals; and thereafter seek to place themselves to observe the church area from cover. They were well aware that all might be quite unprofitable; but they could think of no better plan.

Safely in the Oatleycleuch woods, unnoticed so far as they could judge, they settled, to eat and drink Janet's contribution to the day, ample provision. It was chilly, but they dared not light a fire. The fishermen sat very silent, however much the others sought to talk with them.

Reckoning that they had little more than a mile to go, in the darkness, and leading their mounts along the twisting wooded banks of the Mill Burn, avoiding the roadway which followed its course above flooding level, they set off in the early part of the night. So far as they knew, there were no houses hereabouts, close to these streams, since in winter spates and snow-melt off the hills, they could rise dramatically. So their passage ought not to be seen – unless they were unfortunate enough to be stumbled upon by folk on their way to the possible meeting.

In single file, then, the laird leading, they walked their beasts along the shadowy tree-lined north bank of the Mill Burn, a difficult, stumbling progress in the dark, despite their ever-improving night vision, with trees, growing or fallen, driftwood, entering burnlets, wet patches and earth-slides to negotiate, the bends and turns of the stream in its steep little glen innumerable. Sometimes they were close to the road-way, but in the main a safe distance off. Not that they saw or heard anything of other travellers.

When they reached the junction of the two streams, the road close now, they prospected the ground cautiously. Satisfied that there was nobody about, they turned up the defile of the lesser burn, which rose steeply. One hundred yards or so up this the track levelled off and the land opened out into what seemed to be a sort of hanging valley. Here they found a glade in the trees where they could tether their horses.

They settled to wait, reckoning that it might be a couple of hours to midnight. It was agreed that one should keep watch forward, near the knoll. David volunteered for the first spell.

He moved carefully downhill again, to the foot of the hillock. If people came to it, he was uncertain how they would approach – presumably from the nearby roadway. So if he hid himself at the foot of the knoll at the southern, far, side, he ought to be in no danger of discovery.

Placing himself behind some bushes, less than comfortably, in his riding-cloak, he settled to wait. The silhouette of the trees on the hillock above showed darker against the night sky, even though the chapel itself did not stand out, low-set as it was. He could not but ask himself, now that it had come to this, whether it was all imaginings and wasted effort?

He was still wondering that, after a cold wait, when he heard movement, not ahead but to the side. All alert, he crouched lower – until he heard his name being called, softly. The laird had come to relieve him.

He was answering, when suddenly he stopped. A light,

290

more than one, twinkled up there amongst the trees of the knoll.

Home, creeping forward, saw them also. "There! Folk there!" he whispered. "And who would be there, at this hour, unless . . . ?"

"Aye. I will go get the others," David said.

By the time that he got back with Barbara and the fishermen, not only were there more lights showing up beside the chapel, but there was the flickering glow of what must be a fire.

In hasty consultation, all excited now, they decided to move up the steep bank, amongst the trees. They ought to be able to get reasonably close unobserved. The chances of any newcomers approaching from this side were surely remote?

Up there all was now aglow with lamplight and firelight. As they climbed cautiously up, seeking to make no noise, no cracking of twigs, they realised that such care was probably unnecessary. For they could now hear fiddling and laughter from above. Could it be only some sort of innocent jollification, after all?

That broken-down wall around the graveyard, which they had noted previously, now proved to be a boon. Creeping up to it, they recognised that it would serve to crouch behind, low as it was, and would help to give them added cover. Coming up to this, they peered over.

The scene was spectacular but not particularly exciting nor sinister, at first glance. Over a score of persons, mainly women, were to be seen in the firelight and lamplight, amongst the gravestones, some merely standing around, some cavorting to the fiddle-music being provided by two men sitting on fallen stones. There was laughter and skirling, with all seeming harmless enough – that is, until Barbara pointed over to the right, where a small group were to be seen bending over and working at one of the graves, a young woman holding up a lamp for them. It could scarcely be an interment at this hour.

Faint lights shone out of the high, narrow windows of the church, although the door appeared to be shut.

"No sign of Primroknowe," the laird whispered. "He may be in the kirk."

"What are they doing at that grave?" his daughter wondered.

Even as they looked, the lamplight drew a gleam from what was obviously steel, a knife held by one of the men. As he stopped, they could discern cutting and sawing movements. Then he held up something, as in triumph, and there were shouts and squeals of acclaim. He bent for more cutting.

"Corpses!" Home jerked. "Digging up and dismembering corpses, bodies. I have heard of this."

"Horrible!" Barbara breathed.

Others of the company went over to the opened grave, some of the dancers breaking off, amidst more shouting. Clearly these were handed items, grisly trophies, pieces of bone and decaying flesh, which they then held aloft amidst screams and laughter.

Presumably there were not enough pieces of this corpse to go round, for the busy men with spades and mattocks moved over to another grave and set to work anew.

Presently the fiddling took on a new urgency, and the resumed cavorting likewise, with yells and screeches, the dancing wild, high-kicking and abandoned, with the trophies held high. More than the motion was abandoned as the watchers saw that the women were commencing to tear off their upper clothing, those dancing with men being helped by their partners to do it, women with women aiding each other as they whirled and flung. Soon most of these were bare to the waist, clothing littering the grass, but all clutching their bones and pieces.

David, eyeing them all, could not help but recognise that female nakedness could reveal very different impressions – innocent and a delight, as at the lobster-collecting at Pease Bay; less innocent but still alluring and rousing, as in those Louvre masques in France; and here shameful, abhorrent, the reverse of enticing.

Suddenly, upon this unseemly scene a horn blew, in ululation. Immediately all was changed. The fiddlers stopped playing, the dancing ceased and everybody stood still, turning towards the church.

There the door had been flung open, and two men bearing lanterns hanging from poles topped by skulls, issued forth.

They were followed by two more, these leading goats. Then came another, clad in clerical white alb and dark stole, bearing a large platter covered by a white cloth. Finally came an extraordinary figure, only partially man-like although walking upright. This wore a shaggy, large goat's head, with horns, as mask, realistically fashioned, a black tunic presumably of goat-skin, to the waist, and nothing below, save for an imitation tail with a tufted end, hanging from the back of the tunic. The fiddlers struck up again, this time no jig or reel but a strange, solemn dirge-like march, to which this peculiar procession paced round the graveyard and its central bonfire. All the waiting company got down on knees, to bow heads to the ground.

The watchers behind the wall exchanged wide-eyed glances.

The goat party, its slow circuit completed, turned in to a position near the fire, where a sort of table had been laid resting on two tombstones. On this the priestlike individual laid his platter, the lantern-bearers took up position at either end, the goat-leaders took their charges behind, and a throne-like chair was brought forward for the goat-headed character to sit upon. The music ceased.

After a pause, the clerical figure turned and bowed to the seated and masked master-of-ceremonies, and raising a hand, removed the cloth covering his platter to reveal a gleaming chalice. This he took ceremoniously, to tip over and pour a little of its contents on the table-top, chanting some invocation. The watchers at the wall were too far off to see what was poured out, but they got the impression that it was dark and more thick than wine or water. Then the celebrant took the chalice round to one of the goats and stooped, to put it under the animal's rear and hold it there for a moment or two, before going to the other creature to do likewise. Whether the goats reacted in any way was not apparent.

Returning to his table-altar, the priest bowed again to the seated figure, who rose and waved a hand to the assembled company in a circular motion, commanding, authoritative. All rose from their knees. The fiddlers struck up once more, on this occasion with a repetitive rising and falling rhythm, in fairly slow time.

All the waiting throng now manoeuvred themselves into an odd formation, in a large circle but in couples back-to-back, men with women where there were sufficient of the former, women with women in the majority. In this strange back-to-back position, they commenced to gyrate and circle in a dance of sorts, anti-clockwise, a distinctly difficult process for those going backwards, so that the couples tended to turn sideways, with some inevitable stumbling and little grace.

Round and round they went, the music gradually quickening its curious beat, with much bowing and bending as the dancers passed the goat-figure, the swinging and bouncing of breasts, the tossing of long hair and considerable tripping and floundering.

The fiddling stopped, likewise the dancing, and all the women present formed themselves into a line, clearly in some sort of order for three, seemingly the youngest there, were pushed into the front. Then the priest came over to these, and proceeded to drag down the skirts and petticoats of the three girls, who, already bare as to their upper parts, now stood entirely naked. Taking the first by the hand, a somewhat shrinking creature of perhaps fifteen years, he led her up to the satanic personage on the throne.

That frightening-looking character stood, and turning his back deliberately on them, stooped forward and presented his bare bottom. The priest ordered the girl down on her knees, to kiss the buttocks, holding her face there for some moments. Then the goat-man turned, raised her up, and proceeded to run his hands all over her in obscene, probing fashion. He stooped again, this time to bite one of her breasts, evidently quite hard, for she gave a cry – at which the priest slapped her sharply. Then he took her back to the line, and brought forward the next of the trio.

This was an amply built young woman, far from shrinking. She went through the same performance of kissing the satanic backside, being anatomically searched, and receiving the devil's-mark-bite on one breast. But although she accepted all this without protest, she also received a buffet, for giggling, before being returned to the others.

The third novice, perceiving what was expected of her, went through the procedure without attracting chastisement.

This had all been done in silence. Now the music resumed, if it could be called that, for it was no longer provided by fiddles but by Jews'-harps, in strange, thrumming, twanging tempo. To this accompaniment, the remainder of the long file of women began to move forward, each to go through the kissing and handling process but without the biting, these presumably all being already initiated. With some the prototype Devil took longer and explored more thoroughly than with others.

This took a considerable time. The watchers at the wall were appalled by it all, needless to say, and David greatly concerned that Barbara should be witnessing it. What the fishermen thought they kept to themselves.

The three others held a hurried whispered consultation. Had they seen enough? Should they break in on this devilish business now, and challenge the leaders of it all? Presumably that was Primroknowe himself, with the goat's-head mask. But they could not be certain of it. And was what they were seeing witchcraft? It was foul, filthy and obscene, but was it witchcraft? What, in fact, constituted witchcraft? Were these women witches, the men warlocks or wizards – or just poor deluded folk in search of they knew not what?

They had come to no decision when, the last of the women dealt with, there was a new development. The priest took the centre of the stage again. He spread the cloth, which had covered the platter and chalice, over the table and then, after a brief consultation with the goat-man, went over to the cluster of women, still naked or half-naked despite the chill of a late autumn night, to select the well-rounded young female who had been second of the neophytes. He led her back to his table-altar, and there aided her to climb up and lie along it on her back. This done, he knelt to kiss various parts, making cross-signs, then rose and placed his platter on her bare stomach and put the chalice between her spread legs. He signed to the musicians.

To the twanging of the Jews'-harps and the ragged chanting which began to rise from the company, the priest took pieces of bone and flesh from the platter and made the sign of the cross again, with them, but upside-down, then raised the chalice high, in a dire and dreadful travesty of the mass, with incantations and gestures, using the young woman's body as altar. Then he kissed her all over, and turning, beckoned the goat-headed man to come over, pointing to the girl's private parts.

That was as much as David and Alexander Home could stand. In sheerest anger and disgust, by mutual consent, they rose from behind their wall, hoisted themselves over it into the graveyard, and ran forward. The fishermen duly followed, and Barbara also.

They were not noticed until they were almost into the circle of the firelight, everyone's eyes concentrated on the Satan-figure advancing upon the outstretched girl, his intentions entirely obvious. Into this scene the newcomers burst in shouting fury. David grabbed one of the skull-topped lantern-poles from its astonished bearer, tossing the lamp away, to use the pole like a lance to go lunging at the goat-man. Alexander hurled himself upon the priest.

In moments all was utter pandemonium, men yelling, women screaming. The girl on the altar sat up, staring, then flung herself off it, upsetting the chalice and platter, and fled. The two goats both took fright and bolted. Everywhere people grabbed up clothing and rushed off into the darkness, none either facing up to the assault or lingering to see what transpired. No doubt they had no idea that only six persons were responsible, coming out of the gloom.

At David's charge with the pole the masked man hastily backed away, vulnerable indeed, and in the process stumbled over his own chair and half-fell. Immediately the attacker was upon him, and tossing the pole aside drove his foot against the other's chest to complete his downfall. There he knelt bodily on his victim, first beating at him with his fists then grabbing those goat's horns and using them to wrench and tear off the mask and hood. Beneath, the features of a youngish, square-jawed and fair-haired man stared up at him.

"You . . . evil . . . wretch!" David panted. "Devil, indeed! Now – we have you!"

The others continued to stare and did not struggle.

Alexander Home came to them, leaving the priest to the fishermen. He gazed down. "Primroknowe!" he said. "It *is* you."

"Bilsdean . . . !"

David rose and together they hauled up their prisoner, with one of the fishers coming to help them. One of his companions held the priest and the other had grasped one of the goat-herds. Nobody else, save Barbara, remained visible in that graveyard, although much clothing littered the grass and some lanterns still glowed. Astonishingly all had fled without seeking to aid their principals in wickedness – or not so astonishingly perhaps, when they would not know who and how many had assailed them, but that the penalty for witchcraft was torture and burning at the stake.

"The kirk," David jerked. "Take him there."

Holding their captives secure they led them over to the church, from which a faint light still issued. Inside, a single lantern poorly lit a bare interior, dark stone walls and vaulted ceiling all running with damp. It seemed colder in than out.

They shut the door and posted two fishermen to guard it. There was clothing on two wooden forms. David gestured towards this, and hurriedly their principal captive went to draw on breeches to cover his lower-half nakedness.

"You are Sir Thomas Home of Primroknowe?" David demanded.

The other nodded, unspeaking, glancing from his questioner to Bilsdean and Barbara. He could be seen to be quite good-looking.

"You are taken in the act. Witchcraft and devil-worship. As we are all witness. Foulest blasphemy, also! With this man." And he waved to the cowering priest, still held by a fisherman.

There was no answer.

"We came to discover you. And the poor fools you have cozened and corrupted."

"Who . . . are . . . you?" That came out as a croak.

"I am Sir David Gray. Sent by King James, from London. To uncover your wickedness."

The other drew a long quivering breath at that.

"You know the penalties for what you were doing here?"

Primroknowe bit his lip but did not reply.

David went on. "And it is not only this deviltry here. You have been assailing the King. Threatening him, to gain position and moneys for yourself. Holding James to ransom. Over those letters."

Silence.

"You constrained and persuaded His Majesty to give you the sheriffdom, as the price of not making public something in those Casket Letters. Or so you claimed. The sheriffdom of Angus."

Primroknowe suddenly sat down on the form as though his head swam.

"It was this of Rizzio, was it not? That he was the King's true father?"

The other nodded.

David took the chance. "There was no such letter, was there? No such admission by Queen Mary. It was an invention. Used to coerce James with the stigma of illegitimacy?"

Another nod.

"Speak man! Your life hangs on this."

That had its impact, and perhaps just a gleam of hope with it.

"There may have been such a letter. I do not know. The Master of Gray used the threat of it. He may have had it."

"But *you* have not? Have not seen such a letter?"

"No. Are you of the Master's kin?"

It was David's turn to nod. "But that is no matter. I come from the King. His servant, not his enemy. I told you – Sir David Gray, come from the court."

"What, what do you want?"

And that was it. What *did* he want? Where did one go from here? What was the best course now? If they handed over this wretched man to the law, either to the Sheriff of this Berwickshire, or took him to London and the King, he would die undoubtedly, and horribly. But not only himself. There would inevitably be an inquisition, a rounding up of all suspect participants. Torture, no doubt, to extract confessions, to implicate others. Then more burnings. All those foolish women, those three girls. These two others, here in the church. He could not have that on his conscience – never that.

All this flashed through David's mind. He must contrive it

298

otherwise. "I want your written confession, Sir Thomas Home. *Two* confessions, One, to the fact that you have been unlawfully constraining the King, without cause, that you did not hold any letter referring to David Rizzio, that you promise no further constraints and treasons, and that you resign forthwith the sheriffdom of Angus. Two, that you have been practising witchcraft and devil-worship. This, *I* will keep, not give to the King. For it could mean the death by burning of all who took part with you tonight – these two here and all the other foolish folk. That we would not wish, however much *you* deserve to die. But I will hold such confession secure, lest ever you do the like again, or fail in your written promise. You understand? Two confessions, signed, sealed and witnessed."

The man started to speak, and then stopped.

"You understand?" David repeated forcefully. "Two confessions and your sworn undertaking – or you suffer the penalties for what you have done. Your choice!"

"Yes," Primroknowe got out.

"Very well." David stood back, as though suddenly tired himself. "So be it. We shall go back to your house. You will write and sign the confessions." He turned to the others. "That is best, is it not?"

Alexander Home shrugged. "It may be so. But should this, this miscreant get off so lightly?"

"I am thinking of all these others, sir. If we hand him over to the King or to the Sheriff here, he will be put to the question and forced to name all who have joined with him in all this evil. Many would suffer and die, that is certain. Remember how many burned after the North Berwick witch-trials."

"No," Barbara agreed strongly. "Not that. Better this way."

"As you will. Let us be gone, then. These two – what to do with them?"

"Let them go. We can find them again, if need be. I think that they will have learned their lesson."

Released, the priest and the goat-herd were out of that church and away in less time than it takes to tell, with not a word to say for themselves.

The others ascertained that Primroknowe's horses were tethered nearby. So, held firmly between two fishermen in case he made a bolt for it, their prisoner took them thither. There were two beasts, one with panniers for the gear and costumes used. Leading these, they all retraced their steps to the defile and up it to their own mounts in the glade. There, mounting, they rode for Primroknowe Castle.

They were cautious when they reached the house lest, on his own property, its laird might seek to stage a rescue. But all was dark and silent. If any of his people from here had been involved in the ongoings at the church, they were not in evidence now. Once inside the building, the visitors had its owner lock the door, and leaving two of the fishermen on guard, they mounted to the hall, where the embers of a fire still glowed on the great hearth. Lamps lit, Primroknowe was ordered to find paper, pen and ink.

In his own house, the man was less stricken-seeming and silent, comporting himself even with some dignity, reserved but nowise cringing. At David's dictation he wrote two forms of confession, brief but covering all the essence of it, signed them and produced candle wax to seal them. David, Alexander Home and Barbara added their own signatures as witnesses, and the fisherman with them made his cross. David pocketed the papers.

"We will leave you now, Sir Thomas," he said. "I think that you may consider yourself fortunate. And will in future choose your courses more honestly." He paused. "If I were in your shoes, since other folk might talk, I would think to absent myself out of the country for a space. As your friend the Earl of Bothwell found it expedient to do!"

The other inclined his head silently.

Down at the door, Alexander had a last word. "You have brought shame on the name of Home, man. I am less forgiving than this young man. I say that you should thank him. For your wretched life. For that is what he is giving you."

"I recognise that," the other answered, but he did not say thank you. "A good-night to you."

They mounted and rode off into the night. Bilsdean seemed a long way off. They could not risk the hill-tracks in the darkness, so it was by the roads, by Preston and the Drakemyre and the Eye Water to Coldingham Muir again, all the night-bound miles . . .

For a while they rode in silence, reaction setting in after all the excitement and tension, thinking their own thoughts. It was Barbara who put hers into coherent words first.

"That was all almost beyond belief," she said. "That men and women, ordinary Christian folk, our own neighbours, could behave so. Why? Why? What drove them to it? Those young girls! So many people, lost to all decency, all respect for themselves or others, all faith in God. I would never have believed it if I had not seen it with my own eyes."

"Thomas Home corrupted them," her father asserted. "He learned it all from Francis Stewart, Bothwell, we must believe."

"But why did they respond? What made all these accept such wickedness? Even from the laird. If *you*, Father, were to do the like, which God forbid, would *our* people follow you into such depravity? I think not."

"Only God knows that. Ignorant and superstitious folk are easily led. He may have had some power over them, more than just being laird . . ."

"Do you believe in the Devil?" David asked abruptly. "As a person, I mean, an actual being. I do not think that I did, before tonight. Evil, yes. Evil is always there. But an active Devil, Satan, who can intervene in our affairs? In person. Now, I wonder. I do not mean all that nonsense of goats and foul kissing and the like. But the deliberate and shameful mockery and debasing of the Holy Communion, using the girl's body as altar – that was sheerest evil, hatred of God himself. Where did that come from?"

None could answer that. Pondering, they rode on.

"You were a wonder, David," Barbara went on, presently. "The way that you took charge of all, dealt with that horrible man. It was splendid! And that of the confessions . . ."

"Yes, you did it well," her father agreed. "Acted the part of the King's emissary notably. Even made yourself a knight, for the occasion, I noted! That was clever. All most telling."

"I had to seem to have authority. I am young, you see. But in truth, sir, this of the knight was not just play-acting. I *was* knighted by King James. Before I went to France. Not for my deserts, but so that I might seem more suitable an aide to my lord Earl of Carlisle . . ."

"Lord! So you *are* Sir David Gray, now? And you did not tell us of it!"

"I saw no need. It makes little difference . . ."

"You think not, man? Many will see it otherwise."

"Oh, David!" Barbara exclaimed.

"A device, no more. In my case scarcely an honour. That was the first time, back in that church, that I have had occasion to use the style. Save when in France . . ."

"The King would not have done it had you not deserved it. Oh, I am proud of you! To think that you did not tell us!"

David reverted to Primroknowe. "Do you think that he will do as I suggested and leave the country for some time?"

"He will be a fool if he does not," Alexander said. "Word of this night will be spoken of, that is sure. Think you that King James will be so generous as yourself? When he hears. You will have to tell him of this witchcraft, will you not? Otherwise how to explain how you got the confession to the other matter, the mail over the letters?"

"I will have to tell him some of it, yes. But perhaps I can make it sound less grievous, more folly than wickedness. For the sake of all those others . . ."

"You are kind," Barbara asserted.

"I could not live with myself if I felt responsible for untold suffering and death for them all."

"So now the Lord Gray will sit secure in his sheriffdom, after all! Thanks to his land-steward!" her father said.

"That I cannot be sure of. I hope so. But the King has no love for the Master of Gray's son. He could still think to show him ill will. I will do what I can, but . . ."

"So – you will be off to London again, now?"

"Yes. But first I will go back to Broughty, I think. To see what I can effect there, before I see the King."

"So long as you do not pass by Bilsdean on your comings and goings, Sir David Gray!" Barbara said.

20

Ludovick of Lennox stared. "The Black Mass, as well as all the witchery and deviltry! Is the man mad? That was asking for trouble, indeed. If the Kirk leaders knew of that . . . !"

"They must not learn. Nor, I think, the King. There would be mass burnings. Terror in the Merse. You will not tell the King, my lord?"

"*I* will not, no. But you – you will have to tell him something."

"Yes. But not all. Make it sound as harmless as I can. Mere foolishness rather than evil."

"That might serve. This of the signed confessions was good thinking, Davie. You have him, now. What sort of man is he to do all this? To have sold himself to the Devil."

"I do not know, in truth. He spoke so very little, a closed-up man. Although perhaps he is not always like that. We saw him under very difficult and shameful conditions, for him. He is older than I am, but not yet of middle years, of fair enough appearance . . ."

"Yes, yes, I have seen him. With his father, one time. I meant what makes a man behave so, turn to such wickedness? There is no profit in it, no gain. Women he could have aplenty, without that."

"Power, perhaps, the feeling of power over others? Some need. He was a bastard also, of course . . ."

"Sakes! If all bastards behaved so! Yourself, now. You must assert yourself otherwise!"

"I hope that I do not act as though I was over-much aware of my bastardy, my lord. Perhaps I do, at times . . . ?"

"I might judge you over-modest on occasion, Davie. In words, that is. But scarcely in deeds. But that may be nothing to do with your birth. One must not make too much of illegitimate birth. Some of the best are that. My dear Mary

Gray, your aunt. Our son, John. The King himself maybe . . ."

"You credit that? This of Rizzio?"

"Who knows? Many in Scotland believed it so. But there was never any proof, no admissions of it. Only the Queen and Rizzio himself, and perhaps Darnley, could have told us. And Rizzio was murdered, with Darnley assisting, before James was born. And Darnley himself murdered soon after. Which left only Mary, who of course had to deny it, true or false."

"What a tangle of shame and roguery!"

"Aye, it was a fell and terrible time. Surely even Scotland never had so scoundrelly a crew leading her! Poor Mary – to come back, at nineteen years, from France, to ascend such a throne, a Catholic in a Protestant land. Why she ever wed Darnley, the good Lord only knows. A pretty face, maybe, but that was all. Sickly, weak, vain, effeminate – many doubted whether he *could* have fathered James. It is said that he preferred boys. Indeed, some claimed that he and Rizzio himself had been lovers, and Darnley had him murdered before Mary's eyes mainly out of jealousy that the Italian had transferred his affections to the Queen."

"Dear sakes! What a nest of worms! With all that behind him, it is a wonder that James ever came to the throne, or held it."

"There was no other heir, of the Stewart line. Innumerable bastards of James the Fifth, but no legitimate offspring but Mary. If not her infant James, then the crown would have passed to the Hamiltons, of a far-out link – and few in the land wanted that. And the Protestant lords could control an infant monarch, bring him up a staunch Protestant – as they did. So keep the Catholic cause under. For it was touch and go, then."

"Yes. I knew about the Spanish Blanks, at Fast Castle."

"So James survived all, as monarch. He is a born survivor, is James Stewart. And now, thanks to you, he seems to have survived one more threat. May he live to relish it."

"Live . . . ? Is that in doubt?"

"He is a sick man these days. Seldom leaves his bed."

"Worse than when last I saw him?"

"I would not say worse, but no better. I fear for him. Yet his wits are still sharp. He used to boast that he ruled two kingdoms from the back of a horse. Now he says he does it from his Tibbalds bed! Perhaps once this winter is over, he may do better, and exchange bed for saddle again? Even though Buckingham does not seem to deem it likely!"

"Buckingham . . . ?"

"Aye. Buckingham makes it very clear that he thinks that there will soon be a new monarch! He transfers his allegiance from James to Charles most blatantly. It is indecent, after all the King's affection for him, all that he has done for him. James is deeply hurt by it."

"Those Villiers are a poor crew."

"So I have always recognised – but not James. But that is an old story now."

"When shall I see the King?"

"I shall try to arrange an audience tomorrow. It is too late tonight."

In fact, Ludovick was wrong; it was not too late. For David, weary after long riding, was preparing for bed when the Duke, in a bed-robe himself, came to his door.

"A summons to the royal chamber, Davie," he announced. "James seems to have heard that you are back, and requires our attendance forthwith. He never fails to surprise. I told you that he rules all from his bed. This Theobalds, too. He has folk everywhere to tell him all that goes on, here as elsewhere. So your arrival has not gone unnoticed."

So, hurriedly dressing again, the pair made their way to the royal quarters, David with a parcel under his arm. As on previous occasions, the Duke went into the bedchamber first, leaving his companion outside. He was soon called within.

The room, overheated with an enormous fire, smelt even more strongly than heretofore. The King, wrapped in an untidy heap of bed-clothes, sat up under his handsome canopy, hat askew. In the lamplight, David saw little change in his sovereign's appearance.

"So that's you!" James greeted, pointing an all but accusatory finger. "No' before time." A pause. And then, "Hey, what's yon you've gotten under your oxter, laddie?"

"A gift, Sire," David said, bowing low. "I hope for Your Majesty's gracious acceptance. Brought from Scotland."

305

"A gift, eh? Weel, let's see it, then. Dinna stand there jouking like any doo! Here wi' it."

David advanced with the canvas-covered bundle, laid it on the royal bed and backed away.

James Stewart may have been a sick man, but he gave no evidence of being lacking in interest or energy of a sort. He grabbed the package, had the cord off in a trice, and emptied the contents out of the bag. It gleamed in the lamplight, a silver casket engraved with the arms of the kingdom of France.

"Ha-a-a!" he breathed.

"Sent with my Lord Gray's humble duty and service, Your Majesty."

"Aye. At last! Thae letters! Mine, at last. Are they a' here, man?"

"All that we know of, Sire. All that were in the casket when we found it, at Fast. If there should be a missing one, we do not know of it, have found no trace. We think not."

James sat silent for a little, all but gloating over that casket in his hands. David could not be disappointed over its reception.

"That is not all that Sir David has brought, James," the Duke said.

"Eh? No' all . . . ?"

"No, Sire. I have here some writing which I believe will interest you." He delved into a pocket to produce that paper, signed and sealed at Primroknowe – or one of them – and handed it to the King.

James took it almost gingerly. "What's this? What's this?" he demanded. "A letter? Who scrieves me letters, then? Andra Gray?"

"No, Sire. Another. His seal is attached."

The monarch peered at the embossed wax with the coat of arms, turning it this way and that. "Ha – Home! I ken that device. Lions and popinjays. They gang ill together! No' *Thomas* Home?"

"The same, Sire. Read it." It did not occur to David Gray that such command was scarcely suitable from a subject to his sovereign lord.

Perhaps it did not occur to the King either, just then, for he duly spread out the folds of the paper and scanned it, bending close. "Guid sakes . . . !" he exclaimed, after a few moments. "Save us a'!"

The others watched him, waiting.

Presently, shaking his head and automatically tapping his hat in place more firmly, James spoke, thick-voiced. "How did you get this, Davie Gray?" he demanded.

"I, I persuaded Sir Thomas Home to write it, Sire. After some, some pressing."

"Pressing, aye! But I asked you *how* you did it, man. Answer me."

"It makes a long story, Your Majesty. Scarcely kindly telling."

"Dinna haver at me, laddie. I want it straight." He looked over. "D'you ken what's in this, Vicky?"

"Not in any detail, James. Davie only told me that it is some sort of confession . . ."

"Aye, it's that, right enough. A notable confess. And men dinna scrieve the like lacking persuasion! Here's a man feart! Why?" James turned back to David. "Why?"

"I learned, Sire, that Sir Thomas was behaving strangely. Home of Bilsdean and his daughter had heard of it, and told me. Holding strange gatherings. Festivals of a sort." David had been thinking up how he was to put this, all the way south. "Dancers cavorting of a night, secretly. Common folk, but himself there."

"Ha!"

"I thought it worth the going to see, Sire. At All-Hallows' Eve. That was thought to be a time for such. We went to Primroknowe, Bilsdean and his daughter and some men with me. In case there should be something to see . . ."

"Witchcraft!" the King rapped out. "Witchery, devilment — yon's the time for it. Hallowmass Eve. Was that it?"

"Not truly witchcraft, Sire. At least, we saw none. But lewd dancing in a kirkyard. To a balefire's light. Men and women. Singing and caprioling. And unclothing . . ."

"Witchcraft and devil-worship, I tell you! Thomas Home daeing that! Geordie Home's bastard!"

"We saw no witchcraft nor sorcery, Your Majesty," David

insisted. "Only indecent behaviour. But . . . we knew enough of witches' sabbats and the like to recognise that it was of that sort. Unseemly – in especial for the new Sheriff of Angus!" That he added carefully, in order to explain his further behaviour. "So we broke in on it all, Sire. Grasped Sir Thomas. The others fled. We accused him, yes, of witchcraft. Although we had seen none. Reminded him of the penalties for that. We were hard on him. And so won this admission from him. That he had been shamefully using threats against Your Majesty, for his own gain. Falsely. He wrote this confession, and signed it, so that we might not accuse him of witchcraft. It was no kindly occasion!"

"But it *was* witchcraft, man, was it no'? Yon sounds right like witchcraft and devilment to me!"

"As I say, Sire, we saw nothing which we could declare was witchcraft. No sorcery, no casting of spells, no summoning up of demons. Nothing that we could swear to . . ."

"Och, man, you just didna ken! A' that you saw was just the start o' it, to Satan's business. *I* ken it a'. I've scrieved books on it, Davie. Thomas Home a witch-master!"

"Not truly known or seen to be, Sire. Only behaving lewdly in secret fashion, shameless. But – enough to challenge him, to threaten him with an *accusation* of witchcraft, if he did not confess to seeking to coerce Your Majesty. So – he signed." David could not do better than that. Anxiously he eyed his liege lord.

"Whaur was this?"

"At an old abandoned chapel, near to Primroknowe, in the north of the Merse."

Ludovick came to his rescue. "Does it signify, James? Whether Home would have gone on to real witchcraft or no? He was caught, and will now know better. Or you can take and accuse him at any time. You have the confession. That is what matters, is it not?"

"Ooh, aye. But mind, I'm the Lord's Anointed. It is my God-given duty to stamp oot any devil-worship and witchery and sorcery in my realms. I canna just shut my eyes to this wickedness o' Home's."

"You can keep it as a hold over him, never again to do the like. But, I swear he will have got sufficient fright. The fact

that he wrote that confession to the other matter shows that.
Eh, Davie?"

"Yes, my lord Duke. He was a frightened man, at our
accusation. I think that he will probably leave the country. He
may well be gone, by this."

James looked from one to the other, suspiciously. "I ken
what you twa are up to. You want nae mair o' this. Home to
be let go. Nae outcry. And yon sheriffdom back to Andra
Gray!"

So much for wool-pulling over those lachrymose royal
eyes.

Ludovick actually smiled. "That could be best, James. Best
for all. And you have the confession. And the Casket Letters.
No further danger from any of that. All thanks to this young
man."

"Aye. But there still could be a missing letter, mind."

"Home does not have it, Sire. My uncle does not have it.
Or know of any. Who else could have it?"

"Guid kens! There's a sufficiency o' rogues in Scotland
yet!"

"I will seek to make it my task to try to discover the truth of
it, Sire. From this on."

"You dae that, Davie Gray – dae that. Noo, off wi' you
both. I'm for reading these fool scrievings o' my royal mither,
God forgie her. Leave me tae it."

"Yes, Sire." David bowed, and retreated, Ludovick after
him. At the door they were halted.

"My thanks, mind," the monarch added, almost reluctantly.

"No more than my loyal duty, Sire." David drew a deep
breath. "Can the Lord Gray keep his sheriffdom of Angus,
Your Majesty?"

James Stewart produced an unexpected throaty chuckle. "I
kent you would come to that! Och, aye – meantime. Just
meantime, see you. Sae long as he keeps yon ill Gray hands
clean! You tae! Tell him that. A guid night to you."

Two days of idling at Theobalds, without even hunting to pass
the time, were more than enough for David. He wanted to be
off, back to Scotland; but of course could not leave once more
without the King's express permission. And no word came

from the royal bedchamber. There was a certain gloom about the great establishment, and many fewer courtiers than formerly. Buckingham was at Greenwich Palace with Prince Charles, and most of the Villiers clan and their hangers-on seemed to have gone with him. Carlisle was there, drinking steadily, and the various officers of state. But it was no place for an active young man. Carlisle told him that the French wedding arrangements were proceeding satisfactorily. It was thought that a proxy marriage ceremony would be staged in the late spring, at the cathedral of Nôtre Dame in Paris, and with Kensington deputising for the bridegroom, then bringing Henrietta Maria over to England for the full nuptials. Charles would have gone to France himself, but Buckingham was said to have persuaded him otherwise, for some reason.

So, after two days, David besought the Duke to try to gain him permission to leave. After all, there was nothing more that he could do here, and he had his own life to live. And news to give his uncle.

This appeal had the desired result, an almost immediate summons. This time the King did not see them alone. Lionel, Earl of Middlesex, the Treasurer, was there, with Carlisle, all three using a board on the royal bed as drinking-table, with flagons and beakers. The Duke went to join them, but David stood back.

James eyed him accusingly. "This young man is right anxious to get back to Scotland," he declared, to the others. "I'm wondering why? It canna be that he's a' that keen to be back at his land-stewarding. I jalouse that there's mair than that to it. Twa-three times he's mentioned Home o' Bilsdean having a dochter. I'm wondering if that is it?"

David, embarrassed, bit his lip.

"Are there nae lassies aboot the court here would serve you, whiles? You've got the looks, Davie Gray. If you're that randy?"

"I have been from home overlong, Sire. Much awaits me in Scotland."

"Nae doot, aye. Weel, we'll hae to let you go, then. But, see you, I'm no' that pleasured by a man that I've honoured wi' knighthood going back to be but a land-steward – I am

310

not. And to the likes of Andra Gray. Managing cattle-beasts and the like. It's no' dignified. Are you a' that thirled to yon Broughty in Angus, laddie?"

"It is where I have always lived, Sire."

"I ken that. But maybe you could think to bide some ither place as weel, eh? Maybe even doon in Lothian or the Merse? Nearer to yon Bilsdean, was it? Home's country, eh?"

David swallowed.

"Uh, huh. And frae there you could keep an eye on yon Primroknowe place, and see that there's nae mair ongoings and deviltry there, mind. Or any ither ill ploys those Homes could get up to? How say you to that?"

"I, I would not find that . . . unpleasing, I think, Sire." That was cautious.

"Aye, weel, I've heard tell o' nae offices vacant in the Merse itsel', mind. But the Commissary o' Haddington has died recently – and nae great loss, for he was but a Hepburn, o' the ill Bothwell kin. How say you to being Commissary o' Haddington, Davie Gray?"

Eyes widening, David opened his mouth but no words came.

"It's a responsible position, mind. You'd hae to keep the heid. You're young for it, but you're no' blate, as you've shown. And Haddington's no' that far frae Bilsdean, if I mind aright!"

"Sire, I thank you. Thank you, beyond all telling. But . . . I do not know what it would require of me. Whether I am capable of being anything such. What *is* a Commissary . . . ?"

"There you go, man – buts again! Och, a Commissary's just an official, see you. Under the Sheriff. Ask your Uncle Andra. He'll hae two-three Commissaries, for pairts o' Angus. You'd be working to the High Sheriff o' Lothians. That's Johnnie Maitland, who I made Viscount o' Lauderdale. It used to be yon deevil Bothwell, but we got rid o' him! The Commissaries dae the work, mind, and the Sheriffs cock the snook! They gather in a' tolls and taxes. They enquire into matters to come before the sheriff-courts. They look into complaints aboot boundaries and marches and the like. Och, they're kept busy are the Commissaries – you'll no' be idle. But you'll no' starve either. They get paid for it, their share o'

311

the revenues and fines. And Haddington's the richest pairt o' Lothian. You'll hae a fine bit hoose in that toon. Better than land-stewarding, eh?"

David spread his hands. "Why, Sire? Why all this for me? It is too much. I am not of the, the stature for it. I . . ."

"Wheesht, man, wheesht! Who are you to tell *me* what you are fit for? I ken fine what you are – lacking in judgment in a wheen maitters, and aye butting buts! But passably honest, and wi' some wits. You'll learn. You hae served me weel enough – better than many in higher places than a Commissary. Ask Jamie Hay o' Carlisle. He kens! He's put in a word for you, mind." A royal hand was waved, all but spilling a beaker of wine, in a more or less dismissive gesture. "Sae that's that. Awa' back to Scotland wi' you, Sir Davie Gray, Commissary o' Haddington – since you're so keen. But aye hud yoursel' in readiness to come back here if I need you, see you. I'm maybe no' finished wi' you yet! Vicky, you wait."

"Yes, Sire. But may I be the first to congratulate Sir David?"

"If you must, man. But dinna tak ower lang aboot it . . ."

Somehow David got out of that odoriferous bedchamber, mind in a whirl. For the first time, he forgot to bow.

21

All the long road north, David still failed really to take in the wonder of it, the size and scope of it all, the difference it would make to his life – and of course the possibilities it opened up in more personal affairs. Anxieties, too. Could he, totally untrained for such responsibilities, shoulder the burdens of it? Carry it off? What would the Viscount of Lauderdale say? No doubt he had aimed to put one of his own friends or relatives in as Commissary? Would an ailing monarch down in London be sufficient backing for his support hereafter? If there was highly placed resentment here in Scotland. He had put that to the Duke Ludovick, who had declared that even when James passed on, the new King Charles would have reason to support him, in gratitude for his efforts in the matter of the French marriage. Henrietta Maria would be Queen, and had liked him, according to Carlisle. So he was unlikely to suffer attempts at ousting.

Not that such doubts were his main preoccupation on that long and now familiar journey; much more exciting and pleasurable thoughts tended to engage him – although even then he had his doubts and fears. Barbara. Now he had something to offer her. Now what he had longed for was possible to contemplate. But probable? She obviously liked him and sought his company. But a deal more than that was what he wanted, liking not enough. Unfortunately she had no brother and therefore would be Bilsdean's heiress, a daunting thought. There could be many suitors, especially amongst these clannish Homes – she had once told him how they always sought to keep their lands in the family by selected marriages. So it was not only Barbara herself, it was the laird. He was friendly, yes, but that was not the point. Would the Commissary of Haddington, even knighted, measure up to his requirements for a son-in-law? And a bastard, at that!

David's arrival at Bilsdean, however warm his welcome, set off a new line of questions and fears in his over-doubtful mind. It transpired that he had just missed his cousin Patrick, who had, it seemed, contrived some excuse to come to these parts and had spent a couple of nights at the castle, making excellent company from all accounts. Admittedly, when Pate had spoken about Bilsdean before, it had been Janet he had enthused over in the main. But that could be merely masculine appreciation of attractive and inviting femininity, since it was inconceivable that the Master of Gray could have serious intentions towards such as Janet. But he had come back, and so far as David knew he had had no other links or interests in this part of Scotland, and had stayed for two nights. So could it be Barbara, in fact? The heiress? With Janet as merely a pleasant extra? And *that* might appeal to Alexander Home – his daughter to wed the heir to the lordship of Gray?

This was the sort of state David was in. He cheered up, of course, that evening by the hall fire, with much to tell about the reception by the King of the Primroknowe situation, the Casket Letters delivery and the fact that his uncle would still be Sheriff of Angus – and therefore Patrick presumably succeed to it in due course. With his usual reluctance to seem over-pleased with himself, he delayed telling of the matter of the Haddington commissariat – if that was the word – until the end of his account, and even then mentioned it only seemingly casually.

The reception of this news was anything but casual. Barbara actually clapped her hands, Janet hooted and thumped him on the shoulder, and the laird nodded approvingly, declaring that it was well-deserved and the least that King James could have done in the circumstances. And it could be a stepping-stone to still better things.

David admitted that he had only the vaguest ideas as to his duties in the office. The laird was able to give him some further information, for Home of Houndwood, a distant kinsman, was Commissary of the Coldinghamshire division of the Merse sheriffdom, and Home of Cowdenknowes Commissary of the Swinton division, the Earl of Home being the Sheriff. Which made it all sound the more impressive. The laird also knew the Viscount of Lauderdale, Sheriff of Lothian, who lived at Lethington near Haddington, and he would introduce David to him in due course – which would be a help. Asked whether he thought the Viscount would be upset at no nominee of his own being appointed to the office, Home said that he had no notion; but Lauderdale was a reasonably amiable man and the King's decision in the matter not be to contested.

David retired that night heartened, but still a prey to certain doubts and emotions. He had told his hosts that he would have to go on to Broughty without much delay – which was only fair, for his uncle would be waiting anxiously. But one day, surely, he could stay here? Tomorrow, therefore, would presumably be his testing-time. That was a thought which kept sleep at bay for an hour or two.

In the morning, at least it was a fairly good day for November. David had a new worry – that the laird might have some ploy for them all to engage in. Or even if he had not, that Janet might assume that whatever they did she would go along. Whereas he had different plans envisaged.

Fortunately, he saw Barbara alone for a little before breakfast, and almost abruptly asked her if they could possibly ride again together to St Ebba's Head this day. That previous visit had greatly impressed him, one of the most telling experiences of his life, the memory of which had been with him ever since. Was it possible? He felt that he could hardly add that they should go alone, but hoped that would be implied.

Barbara nodded at once, and said that she had been going to suggest it herself. He tried not to look too elated.

Whether Janet had been warned off or not, she made no suggestion of accompanying them; and the laird was off to Dunglass on his own affairs. So the pair were able to set out in their own time, in mid-forenoon, Janet instructing them not to let their attentions wander, for any reason, lest they fall over those fearsome cliffs.

They rode by Aldcambus up on to the heights of Coldingham Muir, in no hurry now, passing the road to Dowlaw and Fast. It was fitful sun and cloud, but no rain and not cold considering that it would soon be December. Up here the prospects were immense, far-flung indeed, with the moorlands russet, the plain of the sea blue-grey, the cloud-galleons gleaming white or slaty. David's heart sang – save when those wretched doubts assailed him.

Barbara was quiet but by no means withdrawn, and turned to smile at him on occasion, wordlessly. As they passed near to Lumsdaine, where he had heard was a young and cocky Home laird, David was at pains to ask, relevant to their conversation last time they had come this way together, whether there had been any requests for her hand in marriage from such as he? To be told that if so, they had not been made to her – and would not be encouraged if they had been. It did not fail to occur to the enquirer that he could make a kirk or a mill out of that.

After they passed Coldingham village, and turned off to head due eastwards for St Ebba's Head, he too fell silent.

Down into the hidden green valley, around the loch and up the steep ascent beyond, they threaded the little pass until, so abruptly, all infinity seemed to open before them at the cliff-top, the land dropping away beneath them sheerly to the boiling seas those hundreds of feet below. As on the previous visit the horses edged and sidled in alarm.

Dismounting, they hitched their beasts to the old, wind-blown hawthorn tree, and Barbara asked him which of the many individual headlands he would prefer to visit first – the one where they could most likely see seals because of the skerries below, the one most favoured by the puffins, or the sheerest one, underhung beneath, where they could feel as though floating between sea and sky?

"None of these," he told her. "Before, you took me to your 'pulpit' part-way down one of these great chasms, where you listened to your own sermons, you said. I learned something that day there also. And promised myself that sometime, if God was good, I would come back to it."

She looked at him almost searchingly. "And God has been good?"

"So far, very. But whether He still will be . . . ?"

"And you will know here, David?"

"I believe so. For better or for worse."

"Let us go, then, and discover it."

She led the way along the grassy apron where the hardy blackface sheep grazed precariously, to pick their way down that dizzy-making descent where had been sea-pinks and naked rock, amongst the screaming, circling sea-fowl, to that curious cleft in the cliff-face with its ledge on a thrusting spur and the scooped-out hollow with tiny parapet at the end of it. And there they sat, necessarily very close together.

After a moment or two, he spoke huskily. "Here I first put my arm around you."

"I recollect," she said.

He did not repeat that gesture, natural enough as it would have been. Instead he reached over and took one of her hands in his.

"You must guess, Barbara, why I asked you to bring me here this day?"

"To discover whether God was still good to you."

"Yes. And, and I am afraid, lass, desperately afraid."

"As am I," she said simply.

That shook him. "*You* are! Why?"

"Lest God is less than good to me, also!"

"My dear, you fear . . . you fear what I may think to say?"

"Or not to say!"

"You mean . . . ?"

"I mean that you are so proud, David! So high of mind and set in your judgment as to what is meet, proper, fitting . . ."

"Me! Proud?"

"Yes, you are the proudest man I know. In your own way. Not vain, no, but proud. You will never hear of anything, do anything, which does not match what you judge, judge seemly. All must be advisable, befitting. And so, and so . . . I am afraid."

"Afraid of what I will *not* do? Is that what you are saying. Not of what I *will* do?"

"Yes."

He gripped her hand tightly. "That could mean . . . ? That could mean, my dear, that, that *I* need not fear? Any more."

She said nothing.

He went on, urgently now, almost in a gabble. "You know that I love you? Have done from that day, here. At this St Ebba's. Longed for you, ached for you, wanted you, all of

317

you. To make you *mine*. And myself yours. But could never dare to say it. Me, a bastard and but a land-steward. You a laird's daughter, and an heiress forby. It was impossible to think on. Nothing that I could offer you. Nothing to put before your father. But now, now . . ."

"Oh, David, David, you have been torturing us both. All this time. That pride of yours . . . !"

"Not pride. The reverse surely – the opposite of pride! I, I . . ." He stopped and all but shook her. "Barbara, what are you saying? *You* were afraid? You were tortured? And I would not speak? That I would not ask what I longed to ask?"

"Of course, of course! That you would never tell me that you loved me. Feared that it was only myself who loved. That it was all only an empty dream. Oh, I knew that you liked me, but, but . . ."

He tried to find words then, and could not. He could only hold her, and stare into her eyes, shake his head.

She did better. She leant over and her lips sought his.

They had kissed before, of course, but never like this, long, deep, without reserve.

Time, coherent thought, their cramped situation, and all else, ceased to matter.

When words could resume after a fashion, they were anything but connected, well-chosen or adequate, but eloquent enough in their own way, and sufficiently heartfelt.

"Dear God! Love! Oh, wonder, wonder! Barbara, my heart! Barbara!" he got out. "Can it be true? It *is* true – it is! All true, sure, blessed! Here is joy, joy!"

She did not have to seek improvement of all that, for her lips were stopped again. Somehow, despite the constrictions of their physical situation, they came into each other's arms without difficulty or conscious manoeuvre.

When it was that they were able and concerned to express themselves in coherent terms neither could have told. But gradually thoughts sorted themselves and were enunciated in rational speech.

"You will have me? For husband?" he put to her. "Take me, *me*, for always? Wed such as my own self?"

"So soon as I may, David. Need you ask?" She smiled.

"I say that, who have been chiding you for not asking! Oh, I am a fool!"

"I need to ask, yes. For this is the, the most important moment of my life, Barbara. I want you, require you. To hold and love and cherish, all my days. To be my wife, my help-meet, my companion, the heart of my heart. Here and hereafter. Will you be that, all that, Barbara Home?"

"I will," she said, nodding seriously. And then, with another smile. "Herewith I pledge my troth!"

That called for further confirmation by demonstrations.

Then, in a rather different tone, he put it to her. "Your father, lass? What of him? Will *he* accept me? As good-son. His daughter's husband. Me, Davie Gray . . . ?"

"Oh, yes."

"You are sure? This could be no small matter, for him. With no son to succeed him. You, his only lawful offspring. And myself a, a . . ."

She closed his lips with a firm finger. "Do not say it again, Sir David Gray, Commissary of Haddington. Not that that is so important, save in that it has emboldened you to speak up, at last! Yes, he will have you as good-son. We have spoken of it, together. I have made no secret of my love for you. Before your appointment by the King, before your knighthood, he would have accepted you – or lost his daughter's affection!"

"My dear!"

"He asked it more than once. How to overcome your pride. He indeed wondered whether he might be able to find some position that you could hold. In the Home country here. To give you something to make you feel more secure of your standing, to overcome your low opinion of your own place and state . . ."

"He did that?"

"Yes. He admired greatly what you had done over the lobster and salmon monopoly. He is grateful – for you thereby added much to his means and revenues. To others' also. I know that he spoke of it to Dunglass and Ayton, perhaps others, who had benefited. He thought too that the King must reward you, after all you had done for him. Indeed, that I *feared*! That you would be given some position at court, become one of the King's gentlemen down there,

319

and that I would see little more of you! That was another of my dreads . . ."

"Sakes, Barbara! You thought that I would ever agree to that!"

"In my weaker moments, yes. In especial with all that of France. I could have lost you. Even the Primroknowe affair could have caused King James to hold you down there, in his service. So, this of being the Commissary came to my father as relief and satisfaction. To me also, since it gives you more standing in your eyes. For the rest, I care little. Save that Haddington is not far from Bilsdean! Father says that it should bring you in considerable moneys, Haddington one of the best such in the land. So . . ."

"So I can ask for your hand in marriage, now, my dear! And hope that it will be accepted. Glory be!"

"Yes. God has been good to us both, after all!"

"Good indeed. Although I cannot quite believe it all, yet. The wonder of it . . ."

"Wonder, yes. But this is a place for wonder. Remember, you said that yourself, when you were here before. I have thought of that often, when I have come here since. Alone. *I* said, you recollect, that wonder and worship are linked. Or some such word. So I came here, and prayed. As did St Ebba. And St Etheldreda. And others. Not as these holy ones did, of course, but I prayed hard, nevertheless. In this my pulpit . . ."

He rocked her gently in his arms. "I have done some praying too," he admitted.